Beneath The Waves

By

Kristen L. Jackson

Print ISBN: 978-0-578-70465-4
PUBLISHED BY LIGHTNING CREEK PUBLISHING

Publication Date: July 1, 2020
First Edition

SPECIAL THANKS:

I want to thank my husband, Glenn, for selflessly agreeing to change our anniversary trip into a research expedition to Cape Cod in honor of this book. Just one of the many ways you support my writing...as well as giving amazing feedback as my Alpha Reader. Thank you!

To my Beta Readers. Your feedback is priceless, each of you in your own way. I can't thank you enough for volunteering your time and input to my writing:
Leah Ustraszewski, Nancy Bubbenmoyer, John Reinhard, Nancy Zuber, Kelley Dossantos. Thank you Kyle Lechner and Jessica Newsome, my fellow authors who graciously volunteered advice and insight. I'm glad we 'met' as members of the Facebook Writing Group: Fiction Writing.

Thank you Hyannis Whale Watcher Cruises for the boat-ride of our lives, and special thanks to Carol from the Cape Cod Visitors Center in Hyannis for your helpful information about the area.

Beneath the Waves

Chapter 1

*Off the Coast of Chatham, Massachusetts,
Near Monomoy Island*

The great white glided gracefully above her, close enough for her to clearly make out the jagged anchor shaped scar that ran along the massive creature's underbelly. Her heart beat a furious rhythm and she sucked oxygen in quick bursts. Eyes gleaming through the foggy plastic face mask, the corners of her mouth lifted in an awkward smile around her mouthpiece.

Sofiana Marigold Stone concentrated on her underwater breathing.

Breathe in. Breathe out. Breathe in. Breathe out.

Not too fast. Not too slow. Though she had done this possibly hundreds of times, she sometimes forgot to breathe when she became immersed in the moment as she was now.

From her vantage point on the ocean floor her eyes tracked the creature as it moved effortlessly through the swirling waters just below the surface, spotlighted by bursts of sunbeams breaking ethereally through the waves above. Its massive body coasted along as graceful as a ballerina in pirouette. Sofiana felt no fear of the enormous beast, rather the opposite was true. As she continued her vigil, a wave of respect, awe, and even a bone-deep gratitude brought tears to her eyes and fogged her mask.

Planting her flippers as firmly as possible on the sandy ocean floor, she precariously balanced on their tips as she waited and watched, almost forgetting in her fascination to snap the pictures she had come here to take. She peeked at the gauge on her tank and silently calculated how much time she had left. Knowing she would need to surface soon, she blew out a breath. Glancing toward the sunlight still streaking through the surface, she made a decision. *Just a little longer.*

In her opinion, sharks were massively misunderstood by the majority of the public. As if they were murderers searching out the next tasty human to chomp on. Frowning behind her mask, fingers tightening on the camera, her eyes never left the shark.

She had been tracking this particular shark for months now and had playfully named her Baby. Judging by the visible bulge around the beast's belly, she suspected that the 25-foot-long Baby was expecting a litter of her own pups.

Sofiana had given up much to follow this path. In her twelve years as a professional in the field of marine biology, she had yet to find a man who would stick around and wait for her to return from the sea. In this line of business, she spent more time on, or in, the churning ocean waters than on land. And so here she was, 34-years-old, single, and...happy that way. A name fleetingly popped into her head, unwanted.

Grayson.

She quickly pushed the thought, just as she'd

pushed the man, aside.

The ocean and all the miraculous creatures within were her soul mate, her best friend, her lover. She would not give this up for any man, and so she had given up on dating instead. Unbidden, the name invaded once more. *Grayson.* A memory of legs entangled in urgent need flashed through her mind like lightning before she could banish it. Sofiana shook her head. *No. He's not part of my life anymore.*

She mentally snapped herself back to the present, and Baby. The sun gently kissed the dull gray of the fish's skin, lending a deceptively smooth appearance. She knew if she ran her fingers over the dermal scales in the wrong direction, the tiny teeth-like denticles would rub through her own skin creating a brush-burn-like bruise similar to that of a child skinning his knee after falling from his bike onto unforgiving concrete.

Impatiently brushing back her dark brown hair as it floated in front of her camera lens, she watched Baby continue her serene trek through the water. She could stay here all day, if not for the need of oxygen, and would never get bored.

The peacefulness of the moment was shattered in an instant. Her breath was forced out in a surprised *whoosh* when something as solid as a brick wall rammed into her back. In her peripheral vision, an enormous blur disappeared before she could focus through the fog inside her mask. Pain shot up her spine, temporarily blinding her. This second beast, if that's what it was, had knocked her sideways. Her breathing was labored as she began a surprisingly graceful fall through the churning waters into the sand below, kicking up clouds of sand into the water. *What* was *that thing? Another shark?* Since she'd had Baby in her sights at the time of the collision, she knew it wasn't her.

Her camera dropped as if in slow motion to the ocean floor, snapping one final burst of pictures in its descent.

∞∞∞

Sofiana did not panic. Disoriented, she found herself flying horizontally on the ocean floor, hands sinking into the sand as she tried to right herself while simultaneously trying to get her bearings.

The tank weighed heavily on her back in this awkward position as she struggled to her feet. Looking up, she still had Baby in her line of sight, but the shark that had rammed her—or whatever it was—was nowhere in view. Her impulse was to surface as quickly as possible, but she was well versed in the dangers of doing just that.

Breathe in. Breathe out.

She had no wish to suffer decompression sickness—better known as the bends—by ascending too fast while swimming alone with two sharks...possibly more. She had to think quickly. Her eyes focused on the oxygen gauge once more. *Time to go.* She would have to begin surfacing, sharks or no sharks. Pushing off, she kicked upward.

My camera!

The dive would be for nothing if she didn't take those pictures with her. An image of Grayson flashed through her mind, standing with his arm outstretched, that cocky smile of his flashing those dimples. A memory of him handing her the camera adorned with a shiny scarlet bow on their last Christmas together. She quickly pushed the thought aside.

As if in slow motion she awkwardly changed direction, kicking back down toward the cherry-red camera. She would not surface without it.

As Sofiana descended, Baby suddenly darted away in a flash of bubbles. Puzzled, Sofiana looked around to see what might have spooked the massive shark. Spinning in a slow circle, heart racing, she saw nothing. Her breathing came in rapid gulps and her head whipped from side to side. She reached out for the camera, grabbing it as she kicked toward the surface. During the methodically slow ascent, her eyes continuously darted back and forth looking for any sign of movement.

A shiver travelled down her back, her breath quickening to tiny pants. She was known for her fearlessness in the field, and knew her colleagues would be shocked to learn of her sudden agitation in her current near-panic state.

Tossing off the feeling, she continued her agonizingly slow trek to the surface. But she couldn't help the prickles of gooseflesh that rose under her wet suit. As if she were being watched. An icy cold sensation gripped her, making her shake.

That's ridiculous.
Breathe in. Breathe out.
Don't think.
Just Breathe.

Chapter 2

Nauset Beach, Orleans, Massachusetts

Maggie Lee Johnson walked at a leisurely pace, bare feet leaving footprints in their wake on the sand. She loved the feel of the cool, damp sand against her feet, and stopped to push her painted pink toes deeper into the gritty softness. Wiggling them, she reveled in the feel of it. Face raised to the sea breeze the wind tickled her skin and she sighed contentedly. After a few moments, she wandered on. Shielding her eyes, she looked out over the churning waters as a feeling of utter peacefulness washed over her.

There's nowhere else I'd rather be right now.

In the hush of sunrise, her husband of twenty-eight years lay sleeping in the homey cottage they had rented for the week. Maggie had always been an early riser and since this was the last day of their much-anticipated vacation, she did not want to miss a thing. She breathed deep of the salty air and continued on her stroll.

As she ambled along, she once again gazed out across the horizon and watched in pure amazement as a dolphin leaped out of the water. She stopped and clapped her hands, unthinkingly mimicking a child-like reaction that one of her students might have. A giggle escaped her, and she immediately searched for her camera without taking her eyes off the place she had spotted the animal, hands patting and prodding at empty pockets.

Oh no! Forgot my camera. Again.

She sighed and shook her head. She always forgot her camera, and she had left her phone back in the cottage as well. Her husband, Mike, would never believe her without pictures to prove the sighting, or at least that's what he would say. Maggie Lee smiled as she predicted his anticipated teasing.

"Did you see that? A dolphin!" Pointing, Maggie Lee jumped up and down as the words tumbled out of her mouth in excitement. A couple walking hand-in-hand stopped to look out to sea in the direction she had indicated, shading their eyes from the rising sun glinting off the water.

"Are you sure? Sometimes the waves look a lot like sea creatures." The man shrugged, an indulgent smile lifting the corners of his mouth as they continued on their way.

"Wait! Right there...keep watching that spot. They usually travel in pods, so there can't be just one... there!" Maggie Lee clapped again as another fin broke the surface of the water.

She couldn't wait to share this experience with her students back home in Brockton, Massachusetts, after school resumed in...*let's see, exactly 36 days. It will fit perfectly with my unit on mammals.* She loved having summers off, but she was always ready to begin a new school year after a summer away. After so many days off, boredom inevitably set in and she was eager for the challenges that came with a new school year. Maggie Lee was a person of action. Laziness was not in her blood.

Though she was 55-years-old, she did not look forward to retirement as most people her age did. On the contrary, she dreaded it. Maggie Lee was a teacher. Her job defined her. She had not been blessed with children of her own, and she did not know what direction her life would take when she no longer had her students to dedicate her life to.

Snapping herself back to the present, oblivious to how long she stood in that spot, she watched the dolphin pod traveling parallel to the beach until they disappeared from view. Even then she continued to watch the horizon, just in case they decided to return. Once again, she lifted her face to the ocean breeze as it ruffled her shoulder-length, curly, once natural but now dyed-blond hair, and the feel of the sand under her bare feet.

"There you are." Mike's arms wound around her midsection from behind, as he kissed her cheek and rested his head on top of hers, whiskers catching her hair.

A laugh escaped. "You're awake." Her eyes sparkled up at him.

Nodding, he paused to look out and ponder the ocean waves as his wife did. To Maggie, his arms personified his inner strength and his total acceptance of her for who she was, and she sighed and leaned back into him. They didn't always agree, but they could agree to disagree from time to time.

Reaching down to place her arms on top of his, she gave a gentle squeeze. Loving the feel of him against her, she told him about the dolphin pod, blue eyes glowing with excitement as she shared the news. "They were beautiful, Mike. I wish you could have seen them with me."

As she'd known he would, he joked, "Are you sure it wasn't a seagull, or a piece of driftwood floating on the waves? Or even a cardboard box? There's a lot of litter in the ocean these days."

She playfully punched him in the arm. "I know what I saw. It was a pod of dolphins frolicking in the waves."

"Hey, I saw a sign about a Whale and Dolphin Tour at the marina. How about we go book that tour before we leave? Then we'll be sure to see real dolphins today. Maybe some whales, too. The brochure boasts this is one of the best places to view whales in the world." He looked down to wink at her. "What do you think?" Her heart picked up its beat when he smiled, even after all these years.

"I love that idea. I just want to walk a bit farther to see if I can find more seashells for school. Walk with me?"

"Coffee. Need coffee. I'll go back and sit on the balcony with my coffee while you finish your walk, and I'll call the marina to book our tour." Reaching out, he placed her cell phone in her hand. "You forgot this. Enjoy your walk." Giving her another peck on the cheek, he stumbled back in the direction of the rented house.

"I'll meet you there in thirty minutes." She smiled as the sun glinted off Mike's smooth head. For a moment she saw him as he'd been when they had first met, with a full head of curly, strawberry blond hair. Though she'd loved his curls, she thought he was even more handsome now. Like all marriages, theirs had had its ups and downs but they'd always survived life's many challenges together. The biggest test, by far, had been their inability to have children. They had never blamed each other and eventually had accepted that they were just not meant to be parents. Heaven knew she couldn't live without him. She thanked God for bringing Mike into her life every day. If teaching defined her, Mike completed her. He was her true other half. The corners of her mouth lifted.

Hopeless romantic.

Dreamily walking along, she spied a huge slipper shell up ahead. She hoped it was intact. This would be an amazing discovery!

I'll take it to school to show my students, and then I'll take it home. I know just where I can put it...on the end table in the living room, right next to my pottery class vase.

Picking up her pace, she practically jogged to reach the shell. As she bent to remove the shell from the seaweed surrounding it, a flash momentarily blinded her. She held up her hand to shield her eyes from the bright glare of light reflecting off of something to the left of the shell, much the same way a diamond ring sparkled and winked when kissed by the sun. Slipper momentarily forgotten, she picked up the small object in wonder. She ran her thumb over the cool surface in awe, and knew she had stumbled right into some kind of mystery. She had never seen anything like the shiny trinket she now held in the palm of her hand. It looked...otherworldly. She peered around to see if an early morning beach walker like herself had dropped it, but saw no one nearby.

I'll take it back to the cottage and ask around.

Forgetting the slipper shell completely, she turned back the way she'd come and began walking at a brisk pace clutching her discovery in her hand as if she would never let it go.

Chapter 3

Barnstable, Cape Cod, Massachusetts

J ace Calhoun's breath came in short bursts as he ran through the city, shooting aliens. They swarmed the streets, running at him from behind buildings, crashing through windows, even dropping from the sky. He whipped his body from one side to the other, aiming the weapon and pulling the trigger over and over again. His ammunition supply was dwindling. If he didn't think fast, they would surround him in minutes. Every bullet had to count now.

Bang-bang-bang, shoot to kill.

He was a perfect shot, and each creature died with an explosion of green blood and gore that covered everything.

Eyes totally focused on the screen, hands working the controller with an expertise born out of years of practice, Jace pumped his fist in the air as he expertly advanced to the next level of the game, barely noticing the dog's teeth pulling on his pants leg.

As he began the next round, his pup became more insistent, alternating between pulling on Jace's pants leg, laying his head on his master's lap, and whining.

"Just one more round, Crash, and then I promise

I'll take you out."

Crash huffed and flopped himself into a corner, eyes intensely focused on his master for a sign he was finished. Jace tuned him out and once again entered his second home—the world of gaming.

Bang-bang-bang, shoot to kill.

If he could find a way to make it his first home, he would.

At twenty-two, Jace Calhoun was currently employed by the local farmer's market, which just barely paid the rent of his two-room apartment. It was a temporary situation. His goal was to turn his gaming abilities into an income by the time he was twenty-five. If his dream of becoming a professional gamer came to fruition, he would have reached the goal he had set for himself at age twelve, while simultaneously proving everyone in his family wrong.

When the level was complete, Jace reluctantly removed his headset, put down the controller, and stood. Stretching his arms toward the ceiling with a cracking of bones, he groaned. He squinted at the clock, and his red-rimmed eyes widened.

Three hours? Whoa.

He would have guessed he'd been at it for less than one hour.

Time flies when you're saving the world from alien scum.

Jace chuckled under his breath.

At the first sign of movement from his master, Crash immediately jumped to his feet and ran, body wiggling, to the door. He looked back over his shoulder with a canine grin, tail making a thumping sound as it hit the wall repeatedly in his excitement.

Snapping on the leash, no easy feat with the dog in constant motion, they left through the front door and descended the stairs. Crash urgently pulled ahead to reach the small patch of grass located in front of the apartment complex, assuming a squatting position as soon as he arrived.

"You really did need to go. Sorry dude, you know how I lose track of time when I'm playing."

Jace shook his head. *Do all people talk to their dogs?* He wondered but didn't really care. It was just the two of them, after all, and though like most gamers Jace was content with his solitary existence, he was awfully happy to have Crash to talk to.

When Crash finished his 'business', he took off, straining at the leash to pull Jace down the block.

"Okay, okay dude, take it easy. I get it; you want to take a walk. Fine, let's go." Jace rolled his eyes—as if it were up to him. Both human and canine knew who was *really* in charge in this relationship. Besides, it was hard to deny the dog when he was so clearly excited. After all, the poor mutt spent his entire day in the box that was his apartment just waiting on his boy's return home. The reward? Potty breaks to spring him from his confinement and bowls of dry dog food. Jace smiled. Despite that, the animal's happy-go-lucky attitude never faltered, his euphoria raining down on his master with sloppy wet kisses brought on by even the smallest kernel of attention.

Jace knew where Crash was heading. It was the same direction he always went. They lived mere blocks away from the local beach, and his dog loved to swim. He wasn't sure what breed of dog his mutt was. Jace remembered the first time he had seen him at the shelter, all scraggly, hair in knots, and in desperate need of medical attention…and more than that, a friend. Jace filled out the adoption papers on the spot, and they'd been together ever since. These days, though Jace had never been able to afford a groomer, the dog's coat was clean, if unevenly cut by his own amateur hand, and his belly never rumbled with true pangs of hunger. In return, Crash greeted Jace at the door every time he walked in as if he'd won the biggest prize at the summer carnival's water-shooting contest—even if he was gone for mere minutes instead of hours. They were bonded the way some would never understand a human and canine could be. As he plodded along, his sneakers thumping on the sidewalk, his thoughts were interrupted by a voice.

"Excuse me? I'm sorry if this is rude, but I have to ask. Has anyone ever told you that you look like your dog? Or is it that your dog looks like you?" A woman walking past paused to ask with a friendly smile, reaching down to pat Crash on the head.

"Yeah. I get that all the time." He smiled back before his eyes darted down to his Nikes, and continued on.

It was a constant source of merriment when people saw them together. He couldn't deny it. They both had the same shade of black hair, and the cowlick above Jace's forehead made his hair stand up, similar to the way Crash's hair stood out over his eyes. The similarities didn't end there. Jace's long face, combined with his narrow pointed nose was strikingly comparable to Crash's narrow, pointy snout. Jace saw the humor in their matching appearances, and didn't take offense. He smiled to himself. His mutt was extremely handsome, after all.

They continued on their walk. Jace looked down at the taut leash and his outstretched arm as his dog pulled him along.

Walk. He rolled his eyes. *More like drag.*

"Stop pulling, Crash. We're almost there."

Crash looked back over his shoulder with a canine grin, but kept up his pace. If anything, he pulled harder.

"Crazy dog." Jace grumbled.

When they reached the walkway through the dunes, Crash strained at the end of the leash, going up on his hind legs, front legs paddling in the air. His breathing came out with a strangled *H-rrssh, HHH-rr-rsshh, HHH-rrsshh.*

"Crash! Jeez, hold on," Jace's head darted from side to side as he spoke, checking for people. This was a 'Dogs Must Be Leashed' beach, but despite the posted signs, he and Crash often came here for a swim. They hadn't been caught…yet. He undid the leash and rubbed his sore hand.

In a blur of fur and legs, Crash took off in the direction of the water. Jace found a spot in the sand and sat down. It wouldn't take long for his mutt to exhaust himself, he knew. A chuckle escaped as he watched Crash pick up a tangle of seaweed and growl as he shook it back and forth in his mouth, just as he did at home with his toys. A killer instinct that was reduced to decimating stuffed toys, twigs, and rope toys in this domesticated breed of the species. And now, apparently, seaweed.

"Oh no." Jace leaped to his feet when he saw the drenched dog heading in his direction still carrying the tangle of seaweed, which trailed on the ground as he ran. The salty, mildewed smell reached him just before the dog did.

Crash dropped the seaweed at his master's feet, and shook his entire body. The shake seemed to start at his head and travel the length of his body, ending with happy little tremors at the tip of his tail, water spewing in every direction.

"Hey! Stop! D-u-ude!" Holding his splayed hands in front of him, Jace looked down at his wet pants and shook his head. "Crash, that's bad! Bad dog," He mumbled. The dog dropped down into the sand, and rolled onto his back. Tongue hanging sideways, tail twitching, he looked backward at Jace as if to say: 'I'm Sorry'.

"Crazy dog," Jace barked out a reluctant laugh. "I'm still triggered. I should take you back to the pound, that's what I should do." As he reached down to ruffle the soggy, sand-encrusted hair on his dog's head, a glint of light from inside the seaweed forced him to shield his eyes.

"Whoa," he said, moving in to take a closer look. "What's that you got there, buddy?" Jace's eyes widened as he bent to examine Crash's find. The dog, now standing with his chest puffed out and head held high, seemed very proud of his discovery. He leaned closer, his nose twitching before he looked up a Jace, tail whipping a circular pattern in the air.

Jace glanced at him before his eyes were drawn back to the object in the sand.

"Whoa," he repeated. "What *is* this?"

Chapter 4

Yarmouth, Cape Cod, Massachusetts

G rayson Smith leaned precariously back in his old leather desk chair, rubbed his deep-blue eyes, and ran his hands through his short brown hair making it stand on end. The sounds he emitted while yawning were enough to have Rufus' eyes opening to glare at his master before he resumed his canine snoring. He reached for his mug, brow furrowed as he turned it upside down with no recollection of draining it. Breathing a sigh, he stood up and stretched his well-toned arms above his head, leaning from side to side as his back audibly protested in a series of cracks. He turned and reluctantly closed his laptop. His internal gas tank was on 'E', and he glanced at his watch. 3:00 a.m.

Gotta get some sleep.

He had to be at the newspaper at 9:00 a.m. Most of his reporting was done from home, but tomorrow was his check-in day, so he had to make the trip to Boston to meet with his editor.

The news won't write itself.

Pain shot up from his toe when he stubbed it on the chair he'd forgotten to push in.

"Damnit!" He muttered, limping toward the door, and reached around the doorway for the light switch.

After a necessary trip to the bathroom, his body collapsed onto the bed. Reaching down, he pulled the covers up over his head as he did every night. Though his eyes burned for sleep, he tossed and turned in the darkness.

Images of his next chapter immediately fluttered through his brain like butterflies near a field of nectar the moment his eyes closed. One idea formed, and then another flitted to overshadow that one, and so on. The hardest part of writing, for him, was deciding on which path to send his characters, but once the decisions were made the sentences flowed from his fingertips like magical stardust casting words onto the screen.

Should the main character shoot her molester? If she does, how will she escape prosecution? Would self-defense stand? And where did she get the gun? If she doesn't, will she live to regret it later in the book? Or would it be more suspenseful if the gunshot wound isn't fatal? Which would be more shocking to readers?

This always happened when he was in the middle of a novel. It was the beauty, and the curse, of having a writer's brain. 3:15 a.m.

Need sleep.

Another image floated through his sleepy mind. Not one of his characters this time, but the memory of a real woman, flesh and blood.

Sofiana. Sofie.

Why did he think of her in the dead of night? He hadn't seen her in years. Hadn't thought about her lately, either. The hole she'd left in his chest when she'd walked away had taken months to close. Now, lying in bed, he felt the old familiar hurt disguised by anger return as his fists clenched in the covers. A picture flashed in his brain: her tanned hand, fingers unadorned by jewelry or polish, waving out the window as she drove away after telling him it was over. The memory thundered through his brain like a locomotive, as he remembered her pulling away from the curb without so much as a backward glance. *Cold. After all they'd been to each other, how could she be so cold?* He hadn't forgiven her for crushing his heart, but he *had* moved on. That hadn't stopped him from writing her into his next book...and killing her character off. He could be cold, too. It should have given him a twisted writer's kind of closure, but apparently it hadn't.

His body turned on its side, searching for comfort and rest that didn't come. He tossed, legs tangled in the covers, until finally he opened his sleep-deprived eyes. 3:42 a.m.

Just one more chapter. Anything to get his mind off of *her*.

Rufus stirred, glaring at him through one slitted eye as he threw the covers back and slammed his feet on the cold floor. The senior bulldog 'humphed', rolled over with stumpy legs hovering in the air, and resumed his snoring.

Maybe he'd write her into this book, too. An image of her brown hair streaked with natural highlights falling back from her face, head tilted upward, amber eyes filled with passion waiting for his kiss seared through his brain like a poker.

Why can't I just forget?

He felt his body's immediate reaction to the memory of a woman who didn't want him as much as her career. Why, of all people, did it have to be *her* he thought of?

There was no shortage of women around here.

Maybe I'll take Adalina up on her offer tonight... that's just what I need. A little female therapy.

Grayson chuckled to himself as he thought about it. Adalina had been coming on to him for weeks. The contrast of his turquoise eyes with his dark hair was a lethal combination to the opposite sex, and he never lacked female attention.

He hadn't been celibate in the years since Sofiana had walked away. He'd moved on in every sense of the word, or at least in every sense he could control. Purposely pushing her image out of his mind, staring off at nothing, he focused on the words that were already flowing in his mind.

Flopping into his leather chair, his fingers flew over the keyboard as ideas even he hadn't been aware of poured from his brain onto the screen.

He would not think of her again.

Chapter 5

*Research Vessel OA-23, Anchored Off
the Coast of Chatham, Massachusetts*

S ofiana took off her flippers and handed them one at a time to her colleague from her position on the bottom step of the boat's ladder. She could feel the heaviness of the tank weighing down on her with each step up as she emerged in a rush of water. Mouthpiece hanging by her side, facemask on top of her head, red camera clutched in her hand so that her knuckles were white.

"What took you so long, girl? I was gonna come get you myself if you didn't come up for air soon. What'choo thinkin' bout?" Yasmin chided in her fading Jamaican accent. She was dressed in a colorful rainbow tie-dye sarong, with a matching headband holding back her beautiful chocolate speckled with gray dreadlocks. The silver running through her ropes of hair glinted in the sunlight, adding to her grandmotherly appearance.

"I know. I'm sorry. Yaz, I saw her! Baby. She's here, but something rammed me, and then Baby was spooked..."

"Somethin' rammed you? *Rammed you?* Are you alright?"

"Yes, fine. I just wish I knew what it was..." She collapsed onto her back on the deck of the small boat, taking great gulps of air. "Oh, and I think Baby's expecting."

"Well, if that don't beat all. Baby's gonna be a Baby-Mama. That's about the best news I heard all day." She reached down to help Sofiana up. "But next time, you don't go down alone, you hear? And you won't be changin' my mind again. I know better. *You* know better. We are professionals in our field, and still I let you con me into goin' down alone. No more. No. You'll wait until Christian returns so we can double-up." She held up her hand when Sofiana began talking. "No more."

"But you know I can handle myself down there..." At Yasmin's squinty-eyed look, she shrugged her shoulders.

Yaz dramatically crossed her arms. "No. More. You gotta promise me. Or I'm outta here quicker than a toupee in a hurricane."

"Fine. Can you check out the pictures while I dry off? I promise I won't go in the water alone while you're below." Her words dripped with sarcasm as she handed over the camera. Despite her bravado, her hand visibly shook as she began removing the scuba gear.

"Don't be a smart-ass." Yaz growled as she grabbed the camera in a flash of attitude rivaling the vibrant colors she wore and disappeared below-deck.

Sofiana gazed out over the waves. She loved the mesmerizing ebb and flow of the water, the gentle bobbing of a craft under her feet. She'd always thought the ever-changing waves took on a life of their own as they writhed a silent battle and then coalesced in perfect harmony. Like a lover's quarrel and the resulting make-up sex.

Licking the saltwater off her lips, she savored the gentle rocking of the small vessel that carried her along and the soothing feel of the sea breeze on her face. She leaned her arms on the railing, resting her chin on top, and wondered where Baby was now.

Dr. Sofiana M. Stone had dedicated her life to studying marine biology, and was fast on her way to becoming renowned in the field with her studies on the behaviors of great white sharks. The producers of the popular TV show 'Shark Frenzy' had even approached her to film an episode about her work for next year's broadcast. She was considering it. Sofiana did not covet fame, but she did want to share her findings with the world. It was important to the species, and educating the public was essential to their peaceful co-existence.

She had known, even from a young age, that this was her calling. Staring off into the distance, she remembered the long-ago day that had changed her life. The day she'd come upon a beached dolphin while vacationing with her parents. In her mind, she could clearly see the dolphin there in the surf, every movement of its body digging a deeper trap in the sand, as if it were in front of her right now lying helpless. The feeling of urgency to *do* something had overtaken her even at that young age. She could almost feel the tears that had run freely that long-ago day, taste the saltiness on her lips.

"Mom! We have to help her. We have to!"

She recalled the feel of its smooth, rubbery skin under her hands as she had helped her parents pour buckets of cold seawater on the mammal to keep it wet until it could be returned safely to the sea, and the soul-deep connection she'd made with the creature when she'd looked into its too-perceptive eyes. All of that combined with the feelings of both elation and accomplishment as she'd watched in awe when the dolphin finally swam back into the waves, free once again.

She'd been five-years-old. From that moment on, she'd known she would follow in her parent's footsteps in studying marine biology. Sofie had been relentless in pursuing that goal. And she had never looked back.

She was fearless in the water. Wouldn't her colleagues be shocked if they knew she had been spooked so easily by something down there?

What had it been? It had to be another shark. What else could it be?

She mentally ran through a list of possibilities.

Whale? Dolphin? Stingray? Maybe even a grouper or another large fish?

She probably would never know. With a last look out over the endless waves, she took one more deep breath of salty air and went below deck.

"Anything?" She asked Yaz.

"A lot of nothing, but there are a few good shots of Baby. I think you're right about her being pregnant. And this one? There is a good one of her scar." Yaz sat in a small chair, staring at a small monitor as she clicked to view different shots.

"Let me see." She moved in and leaned down for a better view, resting her hands on the back of the chair.

Yaz backed up the pictures. "There." She pointed at the screen, and then zoomed for a close-up.

"Yes! That's the best one yet!" She watched as Yaz advanced to the next shot. "I wish I would have had the video camera. I'm never going on another dive without it." She jumped up to dig her notebook out of the pile on the desk, obliviously scattering random papers in every direction to litter the floor. Later, she would wonder who had ransacked the space. "I need to take notes."

She began furiously writing, as if she would forget if she didn't get it all down right this second. She barely heard Yaz as she whispered.

"What's that?"

"Hmmm."

"Sofiana? What *is* that?"

Sofiana stopped her furious scribbling as she looked up, forehead furrowed, eyes distant. "I don't..." She glanced up toward the screen, eyes going wide. "Can you zoom on Baby's mouth?"

"Zooming."

"There! Stop right there." She leaned closer to the screen.

"She has something in her mouth."

"Yes. It's...shiny. What is that?"

Chapter 6

Maggie Lee fidgeted with the hem of her brand new shirt.

Why did I agree to this interview?

Her eyes searched for Mike, but she couldn't find him. Suddenly, she found her view blocked by a man dressed in a flowing white shirt and sea green skinny jeans with bleach-blonde hair and eye-liner shadowing his eyes, his hand, adorned by no less than three rings, outstretched in invitation. The deep huskiness of his voice had her blinking in surprise. "Hi. I'm Gregory. Gregory Barns. I'll be doing your make-up for the show." She reached out to shake his hand, and blushed when he kissed the back of hers instead.

"N-Nice to meet you, Gregory. Or is it Greg? Sorry, I'm a little nervous. All of my students are watching today. Well, not just my students. I guess everybody around here watches this channel. I know I do, every morning. Mike doesn't enjoy watching the news, he'd rather read the newspaper, but I can't start my day without your show. That's how I stay informed, and I can pass important information on to my students. I just love Kathy Simons! She's so beautiful, and I can't believe I'm going to meet her today. And Drake Cutler. Kathy and Drake in the Morning is the best news show on TV if you ask me. Well, probably if you ask anyone... Oh my goodness, I'm rambling. I talk when I'm nervous. Sorry. I'll stop now. Actually, I don't know why I agreed to this at all."

Gregory held her hand in both of his and waited until she looked at him. "You are going to be fine, Mrs. Johnson. Kathy is a natural, she'll guide you through. It'll be over before you even know it, don't you worry your pretty little head about it."

Maggie Lee giggled as he began applying her make-up.

"Five minutes!" A man called from the doorway.

"Take deep breaths, and remember, you'll be fine. Trust me."

Chapter 7

Robert had retired from the police force with honors fifteen years ago. From his rocking chair, he stared out his window at the parking lot below, lost in memories of his past. For him, the past was a living, breathing thing. It was more real to him than the electronic bed right in front of him, or the roommate snoring in the bed next to his.

A woman entered the room, and he smiled. "Julie?" he whispered. His receding dull gray hair stood on-end, obviously not having seen a brush this morning. Maybe not yesterday, either.

"No, Bob. It's me, Sandy. I'm your nurse. I see you every day, remember?" Sandy pasted a smile she really didn't feel as she approached, knowing what was coming. It was the same every day. 'Playing along' with her elderly patients was just part of the job description around here.

"Where's my Julie? Where's Victoria? Where's my wife?" He demanded.

"Um, she's not here right now, Bob. But I'm here to take good care of you. It's time to go to breakfast. I bet you're really hungry this morning. Pancakes are on the menu. Your favorite." As she spoke she unfolded his walker and placed it in front of his chair, gesturing for him to get up.

"I'm not hungry. Where's Julie?" He said, giving the walker a small shove. It rolled back but remained standing to the left of his chair.

"Oh, Bob, don't be silly. We both know how much you love mealtime. Come on, the others are waiting." She reached for the walker, and placed it gently in front of him again with another forced but assuring smile.

"No. I won't go until I see my Julie." His brow furrowed. "Victoria? Where is she? What have you done with her? Julie! Victoria!" Eyes furiously darting around the room, his breathing erratic, spittle flew as he called, hands gripping the wooden chair until his knuckles turned white and his arms shook.

Sandy sat on the side of the bed facing Bob, and waited patiently until his eyes met hers.

"I'm sorry to have to tell you this, Bob. Julie is gone, remember? Was Victoria her middle name? She passed away peacefully ten years ago. I know you loved her very much. You talk about her every day."

Bob shook his head and closed his eyes. A single tear ran from the corner of his eye and tracked haltingly over the valleys in his wrinkled cheek, catching in the white stubble on his chin.

"No." He quietly whispered that one agonizing word as the memories came flooding back in quick bursts, taking his breath away. "No."

Flash. *Standing by her bedside holding her hand.* Flash. *Watching her fade away.* Flash. *The funeral, and the agonizing weeks after. His children huddled around him.*

Flash. *His driver's license taken away.* Flash. *Selling the house.* Flash. *Moving into this place.* Flash. *Detective Robert Green in an Assisted Living community. Once a decorated hero, now a laughing stock.* Flash. *Alone.*

Bob didn't know which was worse: the confusion that regularly fogged his brain, or regaining the barrage of memories in an instant of time. Sometimes not knowing was easier. He took one long, deep breath, brushed the lone tear track off his face, and nodded.

"Pancake day, you say? I am hungry. Let's go."

His knees cracked when he stood to make the slow trek toward the dining room.

"Mornin'," he nodded to the residents as he shuffled, leaning heavily on the walker, down the short hallway that seemed like an Olympic track to his creaking joints.

Once there, Bob collapsed into his assigned seat and focused on the local news on the television. Some old—funny that he thought she was old since she was clearly younger than he was—schoolteacher was talking to news anchor Kathy Simons about finding something on the beach.

"Ha! They think that's news? In my day, only real news made it onto the television," he grumbled to no one in particular.

On the screen, Maggie Lee Johnson fidgeted with her necklace as she stuttered.

"There were dolphins! A whole pod of them. Oh my goodness, I'll never forget how beautiful they were…"

Kathy Simons interrupted, "What about the silver object? When did you discover that?"

"I-I saw a slipper shell. It was beautiful. I was going to get it to show my students, and then t-take it home. It would

have looked great on my end table..."

"And the object you found...?"

"Yes. Yes, when I reached down to pick up the shell, something shiny caught my attention. I've never seen anything like it before. So I took it back to the cottage we were renting, but no one in the area knew what it was. Someone called the news station, and here I am, talking to you. On T.V. Can I say Hi to my students on summer break? Hi, class!"

"Of course. Maggie, may we see the object you found on the beach that day?"

"Oh. Yes. I have it right here. They told me to bring it with me? So I have it in my purse." Maggie Lee dug around in her purse, face turning red. "I know it's in here. I made sure to put it in my purse before leaving the house." She began emptying her purse onto the circular leather couch. "My husband always says I'd forget my nose if it wasn't attached to my face..."

"I'm sure it's in there. All of us ladies know how easily things get lost in the bottom of a purse." She looked at the camera and chuckled. "Let's pause for a commercial break, and we'll all look forward to seeing the mysterious item that washed up on a local beach when we return..."

"Humph." Bob snorted. "They call that news?"

He savored every bite of the pancakes, and asked for more. Bob no longer cared about maintaining his weight as he once had. In his current reality, the only thing to look forward to anymore was mealtime. And he even forgot about that most of the time...

"Welcome back to Channel 49 News, Kathy and Drake In The Morning. I'm Kathy Simons here with sixth-grade teacher Maggie Lee Johnson, who made a rare discovery a few weeks ago while vacationing at one of our very own beaches. Unfortunately, Maggie Lee seems to have mis-

placed the item."

"I'm so sorry. I know I put it in there...I'm sure it was in my purse when I left the hotel. I can't imagine where it is..." Maggie Lee twisted her necklace in desperation, her *cheeks flaming hot. "I can bring it back another day..."*

"It's okay, Maggie Lee. Can you describe what it looked like?"

"Um. I guess I can. Sure. It is just a little smaller than the size of my palm. And smooth. It's very smooth and cool to the touch, no matter how long you hold it in your hand, it never warms up. And so shiny. That's how I found it, when the sun reflected off of it. And it's round, but not completely. I mean to say that it has rounded edges, but...oh, it's so hard to explain."

"Was it like a coin? Like buried treasure? There are rumors of a pirate ship going down in these waters, you know. People have searched for years to find it, with no luck. Maybe this is a clue."

Maggie Lee *shook her head slowly. "I suppose it could have been some kind of coin, but I don't think so. It's just a feeling..."*

"Well, I guess it'll have to remain a mystery for now. Thank you so much for coming this morning, we'll do some research and see what we can come up with to discover what it was you found on the beach that day. It's been my pleas-ure meeting you." They shook hands, and the picture jumped to the next story.

Bob stared at the screen, mesmerized, as orange juice poured onto his lap and dripped onto the floor from his overturned cup, creating a puddle on the floor. His unseeing eyes looked right through it. Though Bob still sat in his chair, his mind was somewhere else.

Sandy rushed over to help as Bob lurched to his

feet as quickly as somewhere riddled with arthritis can.

His hand shook as he pointed to the television mounted on the wall. "I've seen that before. I've seen it. I have one of those at home. Just as she described it. Where is it now? Where is it?" With each word, Bob's voice rose an octave, color flooding his cheeks.

"Come on, Bob, let's go get you cleaned up, okay?" Sandy guided him toward his room.

"You believe me, right? It's true, I tell you! Ask Julie. She knows. I have one of those things on the television. I do. It's my good luck charm. It's what kept me safe all those years on the force, and before that as a prison guard. I carry it with me every day, I just don't know where it is right now..."

He frantically rummaged through his pockets, turning them inside out.

"Yes, Bob. I'm sure you do. Calm down, it's okay. If you have it in your room, we'll find it. This way, Bob. I'll help you change into something dry. Don't you worry about a thing," Sandy soothed.

They shuffled together down the hall toward his room, Sandy holding Bob's arm in support as he inched his walker along. When they reached his door, she stretched around the doorframe to flip on the lights. "Now, let's get you dry clothes, and we'll see if we can find it."

He turned slowly, his eyes darting back and forth twice, three times, before meeting hers. His pupils dilated and he tilted his head, clutching his walker. "Find what?" Bob looked at Sandy, eyes blank and brows furrowed in confusion. "Who are you? Where's Julie?"

Chapter 8

Boston, Massachusetts

Sitting in the back of a taxi, Maggie Lee swiped at the tears on her cheeks. The pressure of Mike's hand rubbing small circles on her back should have been soothing, but it somehow had the opposite effect. She tried to sigh, but it came out as a sob that ended in a hiccup.

Her hands gestured wildly, her words nearly bursting from her: "Where could it be? I *know* I put it in my purse this morning. You saw me, right?"

Mike nodded. "Yes, I did see you. I watched you put it in your purse with my own two eyes." He pulled her in and wrapped her in his arms. "Are you sure you didn't take it out again after that?"

"Yes. I'm absolutely sure. This is horrifying. Oh, why did I ever agree to this interview? I can't believe I lost it." She buried her head in his chest.

"Well, maybe you didn't lose it." Mike frowned.

She drew back, throwing her hands in the air, gesturing her frustration. "What do you mean? It's gone!"

He gave her arm a gentle squeeze before continuing. "I know this sounds paranoid, but...do you think it's possible that someone took it from your purse?

Everyone there knew you found it, and they would naturally assume you had it in your purse. And Kathy Simons did mention a sunken ship. People lose their heads at the thought of finding treasure. Did you leave your purse at any time while we were in there?"

"Well...yes. A few times, I guess. But who would do something like that? And why? It's just a little thing I found on the beach, it's not like it has magical powers or anything."

"Maybe they thought it was valuable. You're probably right, I'm being paranoid. But then again, where is it? Maybe it fell out of your purse some-where..."

"Impossible. It was in the zipper section. But don't worry, I'm planning to turn the hotel upside down looking for it when we get there. If it's there, I'll find it. We're not going back home until we do."

The taxi driver pulled up at their hotel and stopped the meter. He turned, his long sun-bleached hair fell forward hiding his eyes. The man, probably in his mid-thirties, in a monotone voice asked for pay-ment. "$10.32, please." Those were the only words he'd spoken during this short trip.

Stepping out of the car, Mike twisted to hand him a twenty, "Keep the change." He turned back to reach for Maggie Lee's hand, and noticed the dark blue SUV in an instant as it picked up speed, heading straight toward her. Thinking fast, he called out as he grabbed for her hand intending to pull her toward him out of the way, but it was too late. One minute her hand was reaching out to his, and the next she was ripped away from him and airborne.

The sound of metal colliding with flesh was indescribable as her body flew through the air and landed with a final sickening *thud* on the street as the SUV sped away with a squeal of tires. The picture of a pumpkin purchased last Halloween flashed through Mike's numbed brain. Carrying multiple items from the car, he had placed the pumpkin precariously on the porch table to avoid dropping it. It had fallen anyway, off the edge of the table onto a cement porch where it broke open with a nauseating *crack-thud* that he remembered so clearly now. He thought of this now, as his wife lay motionless in the street. He shook his head once in quick denial. His wife was not the pumpkin. She would be okay. Unlike the orange pumpkin, guts and slimy seeds that had oozed out onto their porch, she would be fine. She couldn't be like the pumpkin. She couldn't be.

The color drained from his face. "No! Maggie! Somebody call 9-1-1!"

Mike felt dread wash over him as his lead-filled feet ran toward his wife's lifeless body.

Chapter 9

Boston, Massachusetts

*N**eed. More. Coffee.*

Grayson refilled his mug for the fifth time that morning. "Aggh!" he cursed as he felt the scalding liquid sear the roof of his mouth.

Scratching at the stubble on his chin, he yawned.

Can't pull all-nighters like I used to. I'm not in my twenties anymore.

He reached for his cell phone when the rock beat of his ringtone sounded. "Smith," he barked, just as his editor stuck his head out of his office and gestured for him to come in.

He held up a finger and mouthed *"A minute,"* while scribbling something on the notebook he always carried with him. "Got it," he said as he stuffed the phone into his back pocket and headed toward the office.

Poking his head in, he said, "What's up?"

His boss gestured toward the cushioned chair in front of his desk. "Come, sit."

"Uh oh. Am I getting fired?" Grayson asked with a crooked grin.

"Don't be a smart-ass, Gray. You know you're

needed here. But you need to get some sleep, man. I can't have you half asleep every day, people are noticing. I'm noticing. Your work is suffering. You have to get your priorities straight. I don't know what you do all night long, and it's none of my business, but it has to stop. I'm saying this as your friend now. I'm worried about you. Is everything okay?"

Grayson ran his hands over his face. "I'm sorry, Dan. You're right. But yes, everything is okay," he paused, then blurted, "I'm writing a novel. I've been up all night writing. It's actually my second book. That's all. I'm not partying, not taking drugs. Not an alcoholic if that's what you're thinking. Just writing. But you're right. I do need to sleep. Even I can tell I'm not functioning. I promise I'll make an effort to get to bed by 10:00 p.m. tonight, okay, Mom?"

"A novel? Why didn't you tell me you're writing a novel? And why didn't I know about the other one?" Dan sat back, relief fluttering across his face.

Grayson sighed. "Well, until I'm the next best-selling, movie-making sensation, it's just a little embarassing. I'm not published yet..."

"As long as you give me a signed copy when its finished, I guess you can keep your job here. I wouldn't want to be the guy who fired the famous author before he was discovered, would I now?" Dan chuckled. "Maybe I'll even get an honorable mention in the dedication: *To my boss and loyal college friend Dan, who gave me a job out of the goodness of his heart, and though he considered it daily, kindly didn't fire me when I was writing this book. I wouldn't be where I am today without him...*"

Grayson barked out a laugh and stood, extending his hand for a shake.

"I'll consider it, but I have to get published first. I'm trying to find an agent to represent me, but so far no success. Hey, at least someone worries about me. Well, besides my Mom anyway. I appreciate your concern, and I'll try not to let it interfere with work. Thanks, Dan."

"How about you go out on a simple lead for a story I just got, and then take the rest of the day to catch up on your Z's?" Dan rummaged through the various papers, eyes lighting when he held one up.

Grayson nodded. "Thanks. I'll take you up on that. What's the story?"

"It's a woman who found some kind of trinket on the beach. But that's not the story. So, she's on the news, right? And she can't find the trinket in her purse on live T.V., *live*, so they just have her describe it. I bet Kathy Simons wanted to punch her, it was so embarrassing. Almost painful to watch." Dan shook his head. "But anyway, the lady gets back to her hotel, and some idiot driver hits her with his car and takes off. She's at the hospital in critical care. Go interview any witnesses and her husband if he's willing to talk. It shouldn't take too long; this is just a filler piece for tonight's run. Do a quick write-up, and then go home. Pleasant dreams, buddy."

"Which hospital?" Grayson scribbled the information, and turned toward the door. "Got it. On my way, boss."

Chapter 10

Research Vessel OA-23

Her eyes burned from staring at the image. Sofiana knew well that she shouldn't be so caught up in something found in a shark's mouth. Sharks would eat just about anything, and all manner of objects were documented as discoveries found in the stomachs of sharks over the years. Tin cans, license plates, bottles, even a suit of armor had at one point been swallowed by ever-hungry and always-curious sharks. A few years back when investigating the mysterious deaths of several sharks in Cape Cod, Sofiana had been present when a diamond ring set, complete with studded wedding band, was pulled out of a tiger shark's gut. It made you wonder if the rings had been attached to a human hand at the time of consumption or if a jilted bride had hurled the jewels into the sea in a fit of rage, only to be swallowed by a predator lurking underneath the churning waters. She shook her head. It hardly mattered now.

Even knowing all of that she still couldn't shake the feeling that this coin, or whatever it was, held some kind of importance she just couldn't grasp. For a week now, she kept returning to the same spot hoping to find

Baby there again.

If only I could get a tag on her…then I could track her from above water.

She zoomed for the hundredth time on the shiny object that seemed to be embedded into the side of Baby's mouth.

Where did she find the thing? Had she tried to eat it, and it got stuck instead?

Sofiana stretched her arms above her head, pulling each bended elbow to the side until her shoulders cracked, and yawned. Her eyes watered as she stood up. She reached for the memory card and ejected it, and shuffled below deck to get some sleep.

As she ran her toothbrush over her teeth, she heard her cell phone beep. Quickly spitting in the sink, she ran to retrieve it from her discarded pants pocket.

"Hello?"

"Sof! Hi baby! I thought we missed you." A familiar voice boomed in her ear.

"Hi, Mom." She stifled yet another yawn as she spoke.

"You sound tired. Sofiana Marigold, are you getting enough sleep?"

"Don't worry about me, Mom. And I've asked you a million times not to call me that."

"Pish! I gave you the name, didn't I? So I can call you that. I named you after my favorite flower, you know. And being off to sea most of the time doesn't allow much time for planting, does it? So you're my flower."

"Yes. Yes, you've told me—a thousand times. I'll text you a picture of marigolds, would that help? You know you wouldn't be happy on land, anyway."

"You know me so well, Sof. It's because you're so much like me." She could *feel* her Mom's sigh through the line.

Oh, here we go, Sofiana thought, remaining silent and bracing for the onslaught.

"I only wish you could find a man like Dad. We thought you had found that with Grayson, but...

"Mom, we've been through this hundreds of times. I don't need a man. That's where we're different."

"Oh, pish, Sof. You can lie to yourself, but you can't lie to your own flesh and blood. You loved that man, but you let him go. I never asked you before, but I guess its safe after all this time. So, what really happened? Did he cheat on you?"

"No, Mom, it wasn't like that. He just...needed more from me than I could give. I don't want to talk about it. It was a long time ago, and I don't even think about him anymore. He's just a distant memory. I've moved on, he's moved on—end of story."

The lie of her words echoed in her own heart. She'd been thinking about him when she'd been diving with Baby just last week. The day she'd been rammed by....something.

Sofiana stifled another yawn, trying to focus on her what her mother was saying. "When two people are in love, they would give anything to be together. Remember that. And don't be afraid to give all of you next time. You've always held yourself back from everything except the sea."

This time, she didn't hold back the yawn. "Was there a reason for your call, Mom? I was just getting ready to go to bed, it's been a long day."

Her mother's voice raised a notch. "Does a

mother need a reason to call her only daughter?"

"No, Mom." Sofie rolled her eyes to the ceiling.

"So tell me. How are you? And how's Yaz? Tell her we miss her. And we miss you." Sofie heard her mother sigh on the other end. "I feel like we haven't seen you in an age. What are you working on right now?"

"I'm tracking a white shark, but we haven't been able to get a tag on her, so it's just a guessing game at this point. I got some good pictures of her last week; she has this awesome scar on her underbelly...very distinctive. I'll text you the pictures in the morning. You'll love her. She's gorgeous."

"I would love to see her! Can you send them now by email? My cell phone's just about dead again. I don't think I can wait now that you've peaked my interest."

Sofiana tilted her head back to stare at the ceiling. She took a deep breath. *Breathe in. Breathe out.* "Give me a minute."

"I'll wait, thanks Sof."

She opened her laptop and inserted the memory card again. Her fingers flew over the keyboard.

"Done. The pictures are on the way." She sank onto the side of the bed to wait.

"Got 'em." She listened to the steady sound of her mother's breathing through the phone and closed her eyes.

"Oh, Sof, she is a beauty! No wonder you've chosen her for your study." She could hear the tapping of her mother pressing buttons on her own computer. "And look at that scar! I wonder what caused that? Maybe a motorboat or something? It looks as if it should have been a fatal injury, doesn't it? Isn't life amazing?"

"I thought that myself, but sometimes scars look worse than they are. It must not have pierced through her thick skin to her internal organs."

"Yes...but I'm sure she must have lost a lot of blood...Oh well, at least we know she's okay. And...oh my, what's that lodged in her mouth?"

"I've been wondering that, too. Any ideas?" Sofie asked.

Her Mom paused. "Well, we both know that sharks are eating machines. It's probably nothing."

"You're right. I know it." She sighed.

"For some reason it seems sort of familiar...I'll think about it, and call you if I remember. Pleasant dreams, sweetie."

"'Night, Mom."

Sofiana heard the click, and flopped back on the bed. Her breathing evened out almost immediately in sleep.

Chapter 11

Massachusetts General Hospital

G rayson spied the parking space and flipped on his turn signal just as a minivan, tires screeching, pulled in right in front of him.

"Damn it!" he stuck his head out the window of his dark charcoal colored Chevy Camaro SS and yelled, "Thanks, Moron!"

He drummed his fingers on the steering wheel, rolled his eyes, and continued his search.

At this rate, I won't make it home any earlier than usual.

This hospital never had a space to spare.

I just want to get this over with and go to sleep. Or, he reasoned with himself, *maybe I can get one chapter in and then go to sleep...*

Grayson shook his head. This happened every time he was in a writing frame of mind. But writing novels wasn't paying the bills, so he had to control the urge to lose himself in his current work in progress, and focus instead on his paying job. He owed it to Dan. They'd been friends since college, and Dan had helped him through some tough times. When he'd made the move to Massachusetts from his home state of Pennsylvania, he'd been thrilled to reconnect with his old friend.

Just then, Gray's eyes zeroed in on a parking spot.

"That one's mine!" He declared to the vacant car, and floored the gas to swing the Camaro into the empty space.

He grabbed his tattered duffel bag out of the passenger seat, and walk-jogged the three blocks to the hospital's main entrance. Flashing his press pass, he walked past the desk toward the stairway. When he arrived, he saw orange cones blocking the way, and a hand-printed sign that read: Stairs Closed For Renovation—Please Use Elevators, with an arrow pointing in that direction.

Great.

He took two purposefully deep breaths, and turned toward the elevator.

No big deal. I can do this.

As he reached for the elevator panel, a slight tremble shook his hand. He continued concentrating on his breathing all the way to the fifth floor, barely noticing his two fellow passengers. When the doors opened, he burst out of the confined space and into the sterile hallway faster than necessary drawing curious glances from his two fellow riders before the doors glided closed taking them ever upward. Wiping his clammy palms on his pants legs, he remained bent over, standing for just a minute with his hands on his knees and his head down, gulping oxygen.

As his pounding heart slowed to a normal pace, he straightened and looked around to see if anyone else had noticed his behavior, face burning. Luckily, no one was paying any attention to the crazy man having a panic attack in the hallway.

Elevators. Like moving metal coffins, just waiting for their next corpse.

He spied the 'Restroom' sign, and his legs began moving in that direction. Once inside, he used his cupped hands to splash cold water on his face, the moisture ran rivulets down his neck and disappeared under his shirt's neckline. He reached for a paper towel and realized there was only an eco-friendly air blower to dry with. Grayson sighed.

I miss the days of paper towels.

He pulled the bottom of his shirt up and used it to wipe the moisture dripping from his face, then looked down at his wet shirt and shrugged.

His still slightly wet hand left a handprint on the door as he pushed out, looking for the direction of room number 504. After spying a sign pointing him in the right direction, he marched off toward it, head up and shoulders squared.

As he approached the room, he spotted a man standing just outside the door, eyes closed in anguish, fingers pinching the bridge of his nose. *This must be the husband.*

"Excuse me, sir?" He waited until the man looked up to continue. When he did, Grayson was taken aback by the misery etched in every line of the man's face. And those eyes, red-rimmed with unshed tears, had Grayson's heart constricting. Though he was a tall man, his demeanor made him appear much smaller than his true height. "Are you Mike Johnson?"

The man cleared his throat and ran his hands over his face. "Yes."

"I'm Grayson Smith. I'm so sorry this happened

to your wife. Can I get anything for you? Coffee? Lunch?"

The man absently shook his head. "No. Thanks. I can't eat right now."

"How is your wife doing? Maggie Lee, right?" Grayson asked.

"Yes, that's her name." Mike fixated on something over Grayson's shoulder, and Grayson turned to see what he was looking at. Just the wall. The man was lost in his own thoughts.

Mike shook his head as if to clear it and continued, "She's hanging in there. She hit her head really hard on the street...they say she has, in their fancy words, traumatic brain injury. It means her brain is swelling. She broke her leg in two places and her right wrist, a few ribs, but it's the brain injury that has me worried. And she hasn't woken up. My Maggie is a strong woman. She's gonna pull through this, I know she is. And we'll go home and everything will be just fine."

Grayson, though he'd just met this man, felt a wave of empathy for Mike so strong that he reached out and placed a comforting hand on his shoulder. He sensed that though they were a generation apart, if they had met under different circumstances they might be friends. "I'm sure you're right, Mike. She's awfully lucky to have someone who cares for her as much as you do. It's written all over your face how much you love her."

Mike's adam's apple bobbed as he swallowed the lump in his throat. "Thanks. She's my life." Those three simple words spoke a lifetime of love. He cleared his throat before continuing. "Are you police? What are you doing to catch the guy who did this to my wife?"

"No, I'm not with the police, but I do want to find out who did this so they can be held accountable for their actions. I'm with the local newspaper, and I'd like to get your story, if you don't mind. I know this is hard for you, and I'm sorry about that, but if we get the description out there fast enough, maybe someone will have a lead to help us catch this bastard."

Mike splayed his hands in front of him, a lost expression on his face. "I want to *do* something. I feel so helpless...I'll tell you anything you need to know to help catch that monster, but I didn't get a good look at him."

"Thanks, Mike. I really do appreciate it. You might know more than you think. Do you want to go to the cafeteria and sit down?"

Mike shook his head. "No, I don't want to leave Maggie. Let's just talk here."

Grayson nodded. "No problem. I understand. Can you walk me through your morning? Sometimes the small details trigger a subconscious memory you didn't know you had."

"Sure. We went to the interview with Kathy Simons this morning at 6:00 a.m. because Maggie was scheduled for her interview at 8:00 a.m. She had to arrive early to prepare, you know? I saw her put the silver trinket into her purse, watched her with my own eyes, and during the interview it was gone. Sometime between leaving the hotel and the interview, someone took that thing out of Maggie's purse. We talked about it on the ride back to the hotel; she was so upset and embarrassed. A dark blue SUV, maybe a Ford Explorer? It came out of nowhere and turned toward her. *Toward her.* This was no accident. I'm telling you he swerved *toward* her on purpose. Why would anyone do this to Maggie?"

"Wait a minute, you're saying someone stole the object from your wife's purse, and then tried to kill her?" Grayson raised his brows and his heart picked up its beat. A tingling began at the base of his neck, as it always did when he was on to a story. This was no filler piece; he could feel there was something deeper. It would not be an early day for him after all.

Mike's voice carried conviction. "Yes. I'm absolutely sure of it."

Grayson's body jerked when a loud beeping came from inside Maggie Lee Johnson's room, and a nurse brushed against him as she rushed past. Mike's face went pale. "No," he whispered, before running into the room. Grayson stood where he was, unsure what to do next. He took a small step toward the room and stopped.

He jumped backward when they rushed out the door, wheeling the bed past him in a rush, the squeak of the wheels echoing in the empty hallway. Grayson waited for Mike to come out. When he didn't, Grayson cautiously entered the room. Mike's face was red and scrunched up as tears streamed rivulets down his cheeks. His chest heaved and voice cracked as he whispered a desperate prayer: "Please God, keep her safe. Be with her, and help her through. She doesn't deserve this; it's not her time. I'll do anything, Father, anything. Please keep my Maggie safe. She needs you now more than ever. I need you. Keep her safe."

His words almost brought Grayson to his knees. He wanted to catch the bastard who had done this.

Taking a step forward, he placed a reassuring hand on Mike's arm. Mike looked up, unseeing. "They're taking her into surgery now. The swelling is too much. She's gonna be okay. She will, right?"

Gray gave Mike's arm a gentle squeeze to emphasize his words. "Yes. She'll be okay. How can she not be with you waiting for her? C'mon. Let's go to the waiting room. I'll sit with you a bit, and then I plan to work on getting the guy who put her here. I promise I won't give up."

Mike's wild eyes glanced back at the empty floor where the bed had been before he let Gray lead him out of the room.

Chapter 12

Caring House Retirement Community

B ob Green mechanically ran the toothbrush back and forth across his teeth as he prepared for bed. When he bent down toward the sink to spit, the ceiling light glinted off the stainless steel faucet, triggering a memory. Something had been nagging at him all week, but he hadn't been able to get a handle on it until right this moment.

"My good luck charm!" He exclaimed as he let his toothbrush drop into the sink and rushed out of the bathroom, toothpaste dripping down his chin. "Where is it?"

Bob tore open the first drawer and pushed his socks around in search of the charm. When that didn't work fast enough, he grabbed handfuls of socks and dropped them on the floor until the drawer was empty. He repeated this with the remaining four drawers, and found nothing. Moving on to the closet, he reached for each jacket, sweater, and pair of pants and methodically searched each item before tossing it aside. The closet was empty except for a few bare hangers that swung, knocking into each other with a clicking sound on the rod like the sound of windchimes clinking together on a windy autumn day.

Don't forget. Don't forget. Don't forget, he repeated like a mantra in his head. *It's too important to forget. I need that good luck charm. It is the answer, I know it. I'll call Kevin. My son will know where it is and he'll help me to...*

He twisted around to rush to the telephone, and tripped over the heaps of clothing on the floor. He saw a flash of white as pain shot into his hip and he heard a 'pop' as it began throbbing like the trumpet-beat in his favorite big band music.

"Help!" He wanted to scream the word, but it came out as a rasp, "Help!"

Bob army-crawled in slow motion, up on his shaky elbows and dragging his left leg, moving tediously across the piles of clothing toward the call button in his room. *If I can just make it over there...*

By the time he reached the button, sweat beaded on his forehead and his heart was pounding a fierce rhythm in his head. His hip was on fire. He weakly reached one arm out and it took all the strength he had left to push the button, and then let his arm drop to his side and lay his cheek on the softly carpeted floor to wait. His eyes fluttered shut and his breathing came in quick bursts.

Within minutes, he heard the knock, followed by the squeak of his door slowly opening.

"Bob? Are you okay? Do you need me?" Sandy called out.

"Yes. Yes, I fell." He weakly replied, his voice little more than a whisper as he closed his eyes again.

Sandy rushed into the room and stopped short of the sock pile on the floor. Her mouth formed an 'oh', and her eyes widened. She put her hands on her hips.

"Bob! What happened, Bob?"

"I fell," his voice was barely a whisper, his eyes closed.

Sandy began rushing to him, but stopped short. "Why is your clothing on the floor?"

"What? Clothing on the floor, you say? Why is my clothing on the floor? It must be washday, and Julie's getting ready to do the laundry. Why am I down here? Help me up."

Chapter 13

Barnstable Farmer's Market, Barnstable, Massachusetts

Jace Calhoun palmed the lettuce placing it on the scale, punched the identifying number on the screen, then put it in the grocery bag next to a bag of carrots. He glanced at the clock and stood up straighter.

Only 45 minutes and I'll be on my way home. Forty-five 'til Crash-time. Ha-ha.

The customer in front of him kept up a steady chatter, but he barely responded. He just kept scanning and bagging, bagging and scanning. Bread, milk, cold medicine, cheese, eggs...

Occasionally, Jace would make eye contact and nod his head, but it was fleeting and his eyes almost immediately darted away. He found it difficult to talk to people he didn't know, so he kept his focus on doing his job and left the socializing to his co-workers. That was just one more reason why gaming was perfect for him. Social skills were not a requirement in the gaming world.

When his shift ended he clocked out and pushed through the front door, his fingers leaving pellucid prints on the glass. Taking one long deep breath, he began walking at a brisk pace, hands in his pockets, head down and shoulders hunched, toward home.

Freedom! This must be what it feels like to get out of jail.

The sun was slowly setting, causing the sky to light up above the trees with a kaleidoscope of colors on the horizon. Crimson bled into purple and fuschia as the wispy clouds drifted majestically above. People in flowered shirts and flip-flops stopped to point and stare, phones held in the air to capture the moment of awe and the beauty of nature unfolding in front of them. They would undoubtedly post the pictures all over social media within moments of the event.

Jace barely noticed. He had one goal: Get home to shoot aliens. Save the figurative world. Though sometimes it felt literal to him. He bounded up the steps to his apartment, and fumbled in his pocket for his key. The sound of scratching and barking greeted him.

"I'm coming, Crash. I'm coming." A small smile lifted his lips. Crash was just as excited at his arrival as Jace, proving that though different species, they had more in common than appearance alone.

When the door opened, he braced himself. Crash jumped up, standing on his hind legs, front paws planted on Jace's midsection while emitting happy little whines. His tongue licked incessantly at his bare arms, and the pup's back legs bounced up and down as if on a spring.

Jace reached down to scratch the dog behind the ears and his smile widened. No one had ever been this excited to see him. Not his mom or step-dad. Not his spoiled-rotten stepbrother. Not his friends. Not the stranger who was his biological dad that had left when he was two-years-old. It was kinda nice to be missed. He reached around the corner to grab the leash hanging on a hook just inside the door, and snapped it onto Crash's collar with a click, leaving the door open.

"Let's go, dude. I'm sure you have to pee."

Crash immediately bounded down the stairs to his tiny patch of grass and squatted, and Jace could have sworn there was a smile on the pooch's face while he urinated.

"Sorry I was gone so long today, Crash-Crash." He sat on the bottom step to wait. The dog sprang out of his squat and ran full throttle toward Jace, his body wiggling as he leaped onto his owner and began licking his face.

Jace laughed and grabbed his dog in a hug, burying his face in the soft fur.

"Dude, you stink. Time for a bath. Not today though, maybe tomorrow." Entering the apartment side by side, he turned to lock the door behind him and leaned his back against the door for just a second. *Home.*

He looked around. Yesterday's dishes were piled in the sink, papers covered the table so that he had to move them out of the way to make space for eating, and the couch pillows were scattered on the floor. None of that bothered him. This was his safe haven.

Crash went to his toy box, picked up something very gently in his mouth, and dropped the shiny object he had found at the beach on Jace's lap. Ever since the day he'd found it, the dog had been almost obsessed with it. He carried it around and even slept with it. Jace picked it up, and reveled in its coolness.

That's probably why Crash likes it so much. It keeps him cool when it's hot outside.

"You really love that thing, don't you Crashy?" The dog tilted his head to one side, then to the other side.

"I have an idea."

Jace pulled open his desk drawer and rummaged through pens, pencils, and random papers. He grabbed a handful of silver paperclips from the bottom, and closed the drawer, not caring that papers now stuck out the top preventing the drawer from closing all the way.

He carefully straightened the paperclip into a semi-straight line, and then repeated it with another one, and another. Twisting the clips together to make one long line, he picked up the shiny metal medallion and wrapped the clips around it on four sides of the circular item creating a square support for it, like a jewel in a crude setting. He then attached it to Crash's collar, so he wore it like a nametag.

"There, now you'll always have it with you."

The dog wagged his tail and jumped onto the couch next to his master, and laid his head on Jace's thigh. The tip of his tail moved in happy little wiggles as his deep brown eyes looked up into his.

"You're welcome, man." He gave his dog one more scratch, and then picked up the game controller. "Now, let's save the world."

Chapter 14

Research Vessel OA-23

T he small research vessel bounced through the water, sunbursts reflecting off the rectangular tinted windows and bright white paint of the tiny cabin and deck. The navy blue underside disappeared into the water, almost blending boat and sea together making it difficult to differentiate where one dark, murky blue bled into the other. Because the boat was on loan from her employer, the white lettering painted on the hull stood out, contrasting the dark and light. No cutesy play on words for this craft. Simply 'OA-23'. *OCEANS ALIVE, vessel number twenty-three.*

Sofiana, along with her team of two, scanned the waters looking for signs of a great white. The rubber seal decoy wiggled along as it was pulled behind the boat, flopping its flat, cutout body in a swimming motion, which mimicked the movement of an actual seal.

Come on, Baby.

Under contract with OCEANS ALIVE—a conservation organization known worldwide—to get footage of a great white breaching, they waited. She'd been in the area where she had spotted Baby for days now, hoping to catch another glimpse of her, and more importantly get a tag on her so they could monitor any movements and follow her. The seal decoy, a.k.a Skeeter, was in the water. The drone was ready for take-off. The tag was prepared, loaded onto the spear. All they needed was the shark to take the bait. Any shark would do, but Sofie was really hoping to spot Baby.

In this pre-dusk time of day, she looked at the water as it lapped against the hull of the small boat and sighed. On T.V., people only saw the awesome sight of great whites breaching, their massive, thick bodies airborne for just a few moments where time seemed to stand still, and it was just you and the shark on this plane of existence. Behind the scenes, not shown to the viewers, was the real-life experience of waiting. Waiting for something to happen. Anything at all. The waiting threatened to take you off your course and make you want to give up if you let it. Watching and waiting, waiting and watching. And if you turn away for just a split second, you could miss the action when it did happen. It was not a glamorous life as most assumed. Nor was it an easy life. But it was her life, and she didn't know how to live it any other way.

"Do you think we should consider moving to a new location? We've been here almost two weeks, and haven't seen any movement on Skeeter." Christian stood, hands on his hips, brows furrowed, his mouth a thin line, sweat pouring from blond hair bleached almost white from the sun. His eyebrows and lashes appeared nearly invisible from so much time spent under the sun's rays.

Sofiana shook her head, handing him a towel, "Not yet. This is where I saw her. I'm not ready to leave this area just yet." Noting his frustration, she placed a gentle hand on his bicep and squeezed. "Give it another day or two, and then we'll move on. Okay?"

"You got it, boss." He forced a smile, and went back to his lookout zone.

Yaz moved to her side, dreads pulled back in a single thick ponytail with a hot pink scarf to match her sundress and sandals. She looked at her over the rim of her sunglasses.

"You know that boy would do anything for you, right? I think he'd follow you just 'bout anywhere. Why don't you do somethin' about that, girl?"

"Not interested. We're just friends, Yaz, you know that. And besides, he's younger than me." Never taking her eyes off the decoy, she continued, "I know she's out there. I can feel it. Just a few more days. She'll come."

"Ha! Don't you change the subject. He's only five years younger. And he's a pretty man, too. Sex would do wonders for your personality." She chuckled at Sofie's sour look. "And you know full well it's possible Baby's moved on. We've been here before, you and me, many times. Why is this time any different? I'm agreeing with Christian on this. I think it's time to move on...but I'll hang on for you a few more days. For you, hear? Don't disappoint me."

Yasmin's eyes lit up when she smiled, like melted chocolate on a warm day. It lit her face from within, shining out through her eyes and into their recipient. She had a way of smiling so you could feel it right into your soul. Her small circle of friends knew she would do anything for them, and Sofie was lucky to be included in that circle. Yaz was like the Godmother she had never had but always wanted. They were family.

Sofie reached out, put her arm around her friend's shoulders, and squeezed.

"I'm so lucky to have you, Yaz. I mean it." She proclaimed when Yaz started chuckling.

"Yes, Sofie, you sure are lucky to have me. And that's the truth." She slapped Sofiana on the back as she spoke, her laughter echoing off the water. "And I'm lucky, too." With one more thump on the back and a peck on the cheek, she ambled away.

Sofiana smiled. She didn't know what she would do without Yaz by her side. She had spent as much time with her as with her own mother during her childhood...

She stared out at the decoy. Still nothing.

Just a few more days.

Chapter 15

Massachusetts General Hospital, Fifth Floor

Grayson ran up the five flights of stairs at the hospital.

Thank God the stairs are open. Good exercise, he thought.

I've been neglecting the gym lately. I need to get back in the habit...

Not that he needed to. With his tall stature and thin frame, he didn't have to work very hard to look good. He just enjoyed the rush he got after a good workout.

At least he didn't have to ride the death trap to the fifth floor this time. He was barely breathing heavy when he pushed through the door into the hallway toward Maggie Lee's room.

He knocked three quick raps on her door before pushing into the room, knowing he would find Mike sitting in the chair next to his wife's bed.

"Hey, Mike. How's our girl doing?"

"No change. I'll take that as good news. The doctors are concerned because she hasn't woken up...but I know Maggie Lee and they don't. She's a strong woman. When we found out we couldn't have children, she was the rock that pulled us both through it. If anyone can survive this, it's her." He stood up and put both hands in the front pockets of his jeans and cleared his throat. "Any news?"

"As a matter of fact, yes I do have some news for you this time, Mike." He leaned on the wall and glanced out the window at the parking lot below. "The police have found an SUV that matches your description. They found it on the side of the road, crashed into a tree, and dug multiple bullets out of the vehicle. Six total. No occupants of the car, so they must have fled the scene. But guess what they found on the backseat floor of the car? You'll never guess..." Grayson smiled.

Mike cocked his head, leaning forward. "I don't know, Grayson. Tell me."

Grayson reached into his pocket and pulled out the silver object Maggie Lee had found on the beach that day.

"You're kidding! I can't believe you found it!" He held his palm out and Grayson dropped it into his hand. It was cool to the touch, just as he remembered. "You know what this means, right?"

"Yes. You were right all along. Someone took this thing out of Maggie Lee's purse, and that same person tried to run her over, and when he fled the scene, he crashed, most likely because someone was shooting at him."

"It just doesn't make any sense. Why? Why would anyone do this over some little bauble that was found on the beach? And who was shooting at him? If it was for this... then why did they leave it in the car for anyone to find? I don't understand any of it." Mike's brows furrowed and his eyes squinted as he looked at Grayson.

"A better question might be, what is this thing? And why is it worth killing for?"

"I wish I knew the answer." He shook his head and looked at his wife. "How did you get it, Gray? Don't the police need it for the investigation?"

"An officer gave it to me to give to you. Officer Gold, I think. He asked me to meet him, and said he thought Maggie should have it back. And that it would somehow help her. I didn't know what that meant, but I have to agree Maggie Lee should have it. Finder's keepers, right?"

Just then, Maggie's fingers twitched. Mike moved to her side and grabbed her hand, giving it a squeeze.

"Have you had dinner yet, Mike?" Grayson inquired.

"No. But you don't have to feed me every day, Grayson. I thank you, but I'm a stranger to you, and still you come here daily like we're family."

"Well, I don't have a lot of family, so I'm happy for the company. It's me who should thank you for spending time with me. And we're not strangers anymore. We've shared a meal on at least five lunch dates to the cafeteria, so I'd say we're ready to progress to the next level in our relationship, don't you think? I guess that sort of makes us family. And I can't wait to meet your Maggie when she wakes up. I feel like I know her already."

Mike barked out the first genuine laugh he'd had since Maggie's accident.

"Okay, but I'm buying this time."

He walked back to the side of the bed, and bent down to whisper, "I'll be back soon, babe. Just gonna catch a bite and I'll be right back. I promise. I love you."

He carefully tucked the covers around his wife's body and kissed her cheek before gently placing the silver disc in her upturned hand, turning to follow Grayson out the door.

Alone in the room, Maggie Lee's heartrate moniter blipped faster, and her fingers closed around the small object she had found just weeks ago on the beach, though no one was there to see it.

Chapter 16

When Bob awoke from the anesthesia, everything was a blur. He couldn't see clearly. *Where am I?* His heart began pounding, and he tried to sit up. Pushing up on his elbows, his vision fogged transforming everything into blurry smudges, he ripped at the wires and tubes on his arm. Blood spurted as he tore the IV from his vein.

A nurse rushed over, "It's okay, Mr...." She glanced at his chart, "Green. You're in the hospital. You had surgery on your hip this morning. You have a brand new one now, and it's going to be much better than your old one. Calm down, now, Mr. Green. My name is Amber, and I'm here to help you. You are in recovery. I'm going to need to replace the IV, and I need to know you won't pull it out again, understand?" She got to work, moving to his other arm.

Bob jerked when she pushed the needle into his vein. "A new hip..." he grumbled. "What was wrong with my old one?" His vision was beginning to clear, and he could see the nurse was very young. Her blue hair was pulled up into a messy topknot on her head, and she chewed gum, cracking it as she talked. A tiny, diamond nose-piercing winked at him when she turned. *She's just a baby,* he thought.

She laughed as she spoke, "Your old one was broken, so we've given you a new one. You just need to rest, now, Mr. Green."

"Mr. Green is my father. Call me Bob."

"Okay, Bob, I think you have some people waiting for you in the Waiting Room. Would you like me to bring them in? Are you ready for visitors?"

"Yes, that would be nice."

"You got it, Bob." She picked up his chart, made some notes, and winked at him before turning and to hustle out the door.

Bob lay his head on the pillow and closed his eyes.

If only I had my good luck charm.

His eyes flew open.

My good luck charm!

Just then Amber returned with his eldest son Kevin, his wife Bianca waddling with pregnancy, and his younger son, Kyle. Bob's smile lit his entire face, and his eyes glowed with love.

"Boys! It's good to see you, boys!" He looked at Amber with pride in his eyes. "These are my sons, Kevin and Kyle. And this is Kevin's beautiful wife..." his eyes took on a blank look as he struggled to recall the name of his daughter-in-law.

She stepped forward and sandwiched his hand in hers. Her beautiful mocha skin contrasted with his paleness, and he squeezed her hand gently. "It's Bianca, Dad. How are you feeling?"

He smiled into her amber eyes. "I'm better now that you're here, Bianca."

"Hi, Dad." Kevin reached out to put a hand on his leg and squeezed. "Glad to see you're awake."

"Thanks, Kev. There's been something I've been meaning to ask you, but I can't remember what it is...it must be the drugs they're giving me."

His sons made eye contact before Kyle stepped up to the other side of the bed and said, "Hi, Dad."

"Kyle! So good to see you! Where's...I can't remember...your wife..."

"I'm divorced now, Dad, remember?"

"Oh no, Kyle! That's just a shame. A real shame. Young people today..."

"It's okay, Dad. It's better this way, and I'm happy. Really."

Bob looked back and forth between his two sons. Kevin favored Julie with his brown hair and green eyes, lean frame, and even his features looked like her. He'd also inherited her easy-going personality. He couldn't help but see his wife when he looked at his eldest son. Quite the opposite, Kyle had always taken after him, blond and blue eyed, with a more stocky build. He'd inherited his father's stubbornness, too.

Bob glowed from the inside-out just thinking about them, here for him when he needed them most. He flashed on a memory of them when they were just boys, Kevin riding his two wheeler bike for the first time, and Kyle crying because he still had training wheels. Julie laughing and running next to the bike. In his mind's eye, he could see it so clearly. More clearly than he saw anything these days. How he longed for those times again...

"When can I go home?" Bob pictured his old house, the one he and Julie had scraped every penny to buy; not the assisted living community he had lived in for the past two years.

"They're going to move you to a room soon, Dad, and you get to spend one glamorous night here at the hospital. Aren't you lucky? And then you'll move to rehab tomorrow. When they say you're well enough, you'll go back home."

"Who's going to take me there?"

"I will, Dad. Don't worry about that," answered Kevin.

"What day is it? Don't you have to go to work?"

"I'm taking a half-day, so I'll be available to take you rehab."

"I could call a taxi, I don't want to be a bother..."

"No way, Dad. It's already done. My boss understands, it's really no problem."

Bob's eyelids were at mid-mast, and his words began to slur as he fought to stay awake.

"You rest now, Dad. We'll see you tomorrow."

"Tomorrow? That's grand. I love to see you." He winked sleepily at Bianca.

"Kevin? Are you here? I wanted to ask you something..."

"Go to sleep, Dad, it can wait until tomorrow."

His eyes, only slits, opened wide, "It's about my lucky charm! Where is it? Do you know?"

"Sure Dad. You sleep now, we can talk about it tomorrow."

"Who's going to take me home?"

"I am, Dad. Shhh. Now go to sleep."

Bob's final thought before his eyes drifted closed in slumber was: *I have to remember...*

Chapter 17

Barnstable, Massachusetts

"C'mon, Crash. Stop pulling. Can't you ever just walk?" Jace moaned as he was dragged along, arm outstretched in front of him, feet thumping on the sidewalk in a half-run to keep up.

Crash paid no attention to his master's words. He had one goal: Go swimming. His tongue hung sideways out of his mouth and his collar dug into his neck, but he just kept pulling to reach his final destination. The shiny trinket swung from side to side on his collar, glinting in the glow of the moon.

The closer they came to the beach, the harder the leash dug into the skin around Jace's wrist, causing lines of indentations that would remain long after the leash was removed.

When his feet sank into the sand, Jace pulled back on the leash to free the pup. It was night time, so no one was around to report him for bringing his dog to a public, leashed-dogs-only beach. Once unhooked from the restraint, Crash took off at a run toward the water, barking happy little yips all the way there. Jace ambled along behind.

The moon was full tonight, lending just enough

light to see clearly. Normally, Jace didn't notice the beauty of nature, usually lost deep inside his inner musings and oblivious to his surroundings, but tonight even he had to admit it looked like a picture postcard with the moon mirrored off the water giving it an otherworldly look, as if our planet had two moons. Of course, that led to thinking about aliens, and his game...

"Okay, Crash, time to go." The dog ignored his words, and kept romping in the surf. Jace huffed and put his hands on his hips, leaning to one side. "You have five more minutes."

As if he's smart enough to know how long five minutes is.

He sighed and looked out over the water with its double-moon glow.

Sensing the end of his friend's patience, Crash loped up to Jace and sat down; looking up into his eyes, tail leaving an angel's wing in the sand as it flew back and forth.

"Good boy! All done? Okay, let's go home." When he reached an arm out and grasped the collar to hook on the leash, he was distracted by the sound of people talking, their voices drifting on the breeze. Soon the talking turned to shouting. He couldn't make out what they were saying, but the tone was clear enough. Crash tilted his head, let out one quick bark, and took off running toward the sound just before the lead attached.

"Crash!" Jace ran after him, feet leaving prints in the sand. His foot caught on a piece of driftwood that was invisible in the dark, and he fell, hands automatically coming up to stop the descent, stopping just short of face-planting in the sand. He cursed and pushed himself up just as the sound of Crash whimpering traveled to him on the wind. It was a sound unlike he had ever heard his dog make, and gooseflesh sprung down the back of his neck, spreading to cover his entire body. The frantic cries gew louder, but what was even more alarming was the abrupt silence that followed.

"Crash?" His heart tripped as he ran in the direction from which he'd heard the terrifying sound. "Crash!"

He listened through the symphony of surf, and heard one small whine as he came upon his dog lying in the sand. A man stood by holding a knife up in the air as he took one backward step, and another man ran in the other direction. The moon reflected off the knife, its macabre jagged-edged point highlighted even more by the glow.

"What did you do?" He croaked to the man as he fell to his knees next to his best friend, hands flying over the prone body of his dog. His hand shook as it came away wet. He gathered Crash in his arms as tears ran like rain down his face.

"Your d-dog attacked me, man! He ran right up, I-I didn't know if he was going to hurt me, its dark..."

Jace didn't even hear the man, his entire focus on the limp body of Crash. Crash, who had been frolicking and running just minutes before, now lay still as death. "I have to get help. It's okay, Crash, I'm gonna get you help and you're gonna be okay." He started walking, his feet digging deeper into the sand with the added weight of his dog bearing down on him, but he kept moving as quickly as he could. "You're okay, little dude. You're gonna be okay."

His mind was racing through his desperation,

and he could barely see through the tears leaking from his eyes, but he kept moving, without a clear destination in mind.

The vet is closed at this time of night. Where can I go? Who can help us? What should I do?

He dug with one hand in the back pocket of his baggy jeans, the other hand supporting Crash, and weaved in the sand as he tried to keep moving. He stopped just for a second to focus on his contact list, blinking through the salty tears, and dialed the veterinarian's number, then resumed his staggering pace.

"*You've reached the offices of Dr. Lee, Veterinary Services at Cape Critter Hospital. Our offices are closed right now. If you have a true medical emergency, please dial...*"

Jace ended the call, and punched in the numbers. After five rings, a woman answered.

"This is Dr. Lee's answering service, do you have an emergency?"

"Yes! Yes, my dog's been stabbed. There's a lot of blood, I don't know...I-I'm at the beach and I d-don't know where to go."

"Stabbed? Hold on while I contact the doctor." After a short pause, she returned. "Dr. Lee will meet you at his office in ten minutes. He says put pressure on the wound."

"Thanks. Thank you. I'll get there as soon as I can." He closed his eyes and took a deep breath, sliding his phone into his back pocket.

He took off running, and when he hit the street, his legs picked up speed slapping the sidewalk, hugging his dog close to his body, using his hand to push on the wound.

"It's okay, Crash. Dr. Lee is going to help you. He

will. You're going to be fine."

The words came out in a litany as he ran. His brain rejected the fact that his dog's chest had stopped moving, and his head hung limply at his side.

Chapter 18

Research Vessel OA-23

Maybe we *should* move to a new location, Sofie thought as she continued her vigil, staring blindly at Skeeter as the fake seal was dragged yet again behind the boat.

Skeeter's the only one that's happy to be seeing no action.

And they'd had zero action. Literally. Not one shark had attacked the decoy. Not even an exploratory nibble.

Maybe Christian and Yaz are right. I should trust my team and move on.

It was just so hard to give up on Baby. At this point, getting a tag on any shark would be a win. She just couldn't shake the feeling that this was the right place.

"Okay, guys, one more hour and then we move."

Yaz looked skyward, clapping her hands together as if in prayer. "Thank God, girl! I'm 'bout ready to push one of you two into the sea to get me some action 'round here. This place is driving me batty-crazy."

"Agreed." Christian barked his first real laugh in twenty-four hours. "We're not making any progress here."

"Anything is progress in science. Remember that. We know that we saw Baby here, but she was spooked by something, so maybe you're right, she's moved on. But why did she move on, that's the question. This area is usually crawling with sharks, so I wonder why we've had no luck. We know it's not Skeeter's design. He's been tested and proven to attract sharks…" Her eyes squinted and she tilted her head in thought.

"Oh, no. There's no changing your mind now, girl. I can see your wheels turning. One hour. No more." Yaz rolled her eyes.

"Okay, okay. If there's nothing in the next thirty minutes, I'm going down one more time to check out the situation below."

"That's fine. I'll come with you, and then when we surface if there's still nothing, we go." Yasmin spoke in her mother's 'no argument' voice. Though she had no children of her own, she had always thought of Sofie as her daughter by circumstance. She'd raised Sofiana as much as her parents had.

"Deal."

The boat moved along, Skeeter happily flopping along behind, occasionally jumping out of the water over a wave, as if taunting the seemingly absent sharks below.

Sofiana, hairband between her teeth, reached up behind her head to gather her medium-length, sun-kissed brown hair into a ponytail. Sweat dampened the hair underneath at the base of her neck causing it to curl into tiny ringlets. One drip ran a sporadic path down her back, under her snug black tank top to disappear between her shoulder blades. She sighed as the sea breeze cooled the dampness, and took a moment to just hold the hair off her neck in bliss, completely oblivious to Christian's desire-filled eyes following her every move. He quickly turned his head when she glanced his direction.

Just as she was preparing to wrap the band around her hair, a shark launched itself out of the water at full speed, Skeeter clasped in its mouth, before belly flopping back into the sea.

The hairband dropped from her fingers and rolled across the deck, hair falling loosely around her shoulders. Sofie didn't miss a beat as she jumped into action. "Was the camera rolling?"

The camera was attached to the boat's stern, pointing out to sea and keeping track of every move Skeeter made. The blinking light on top of the camera had her smiling.

We got it!

Christian was already preparing the drone for launch, and Yaz was hooting from her position, camera in one hand, spear loaded with a special tracking device in the other. Sofie threw a large hook pierced with a chunk of tuna over board, as close as she could to the area the shark had attacked.

"Was it Baby?" Christian asked.

"I'm not sure. It was so fast. I don't think so. It seemed too small to be her."

To the left of a now shredded Skeeter, the bait floated and bounced on the choppy water, leaving a trail of blood. Sharks could sense small amounts of blood from great distances, so any shark below would smell a potential meal from a mile away.

The drone, now hovering above the bait, wobbled in the sea breeze, but stayed airborne. Christian maintained control with a remote, while monitoring the image on his iPad.

"He's circling! Whoa, he's interested, all right. Ten O'Clock! Pull it closer, that's it. Slowly...slowly."

A gray fin broke the surface and then re-submerged, disappearing again, invisible to the crew on the boat. The camera recorded its every move from the air as Christian continued to monitor the live video feed.

"He went deep. I don't see him...there! He's definitely interested!" He hooted from his position on deck.

Sofie continued slowly pulling the baited hook closer to the small boat, luring their quarry closer. Her unblinking amber eyes never leaving the water, she reached for the tracker-carrying spear that Yaz held out to her, ready to dispense its tiny homing device if the shark came close enough to reach.

"Here he comes!" Christian shouted. "Get ready..."

She let go of the bait line just in time to save her hands from rope burn, as the medium-sized white shark attacked the tuna, eyes going white, teeth extending forward to gouge its prey. It shook the tuna back and forth in a wild frenzy, and then ripped off a chunk of meat and disappeared under the water once again. Sofie pulled the bait in closer to the boat, until it was right up against the hull.

"Definitely not Baby. He's a looker, though. Hold steady. He'll be back for a second course." Sofie ordered.

Yaz's hands gripped a third hand-held camera, recording the entire scene from the deck. She sucked in a gulp of air when she realized she had been holding her breath, and checked yet again for the blinking red light to make sure she was recording.

Sof will kill me if I don't get this, she chuckled to herself, *and so would her Mama.*

"Anything, Christian?" She whispered, her voice shaking.

"No...no. Not yet."

One minute stretched into two, three, four...

The small crew of three began fidgeting. They could feel every passing second pounding in their heads like a drumbeat.

Sofiana leaned her body precariously over the railing above the bait, hair hanging down and blocking her view. Reaching up to push her hair out of her eyes, she slipped on the deck and fell to her knees when the shark surfaced three feet away from her face, its gray eyes boring into hers before they went white as he went for the bait again, body colliding with the side of the boat. She sucked in her breath, oblivious to the blood dripping from her knees, her heart pounding against her ribcage, and then remembered what she was here to do. She grabbed for the spear, and took aim toward the great white. The tracking device needed to be placed at the base of the dorsal fin in exactly the right spot to be effective. The perfect shot was in front of her.

Now!

Her arm went back over her head, and in one quick move she thrust the pole forward. At that exact moment, the shark jerked its body and turned toward her, creating a U-shape with its body, which caused the spear to glance off the fin. The tracker released from the pole, bounced off the shark's back, and into the churning waters below, disappearing from sight.

"Oh no! The tracker! We lost the tracker!"

"Shit!"

"What happened?" Yaz placed her hand on Sofie's shoulder and squeezed. "Its okay, girl. You invented that tracker, you can make another."

"I have two! Quick, grab the other one from the cabin!"

Yaz ran the short distance to the cabin, stumbled through the door, and flung her arms out grabbing onto the captain's chair to keep from falling. Recovering quickly, she grabbed the yellow plastic case that housed the second tracker, and raced back.

"Got it!" She held it out to Sofie.

"Quickly!" Tearing the tracker out of the box, she re-loaded the spear, and looked back at the bait, feet braced apart and arm back, ready to launch.

They watched and waited. *He'll come back, now that's he's got a taste for the bait.* Sofiana lowered her arm a fraction of an inch as it began to shake.

"I see him! Get ready!" Christian shouted.

The shark appeared seconds later, attacking the tuna once again. Sofie threw her arm forward, catching the shark in the perfect spot, at the base of the dorsal fin.

"Yes!"

"Got 'im!"

"Woo-hoo! I'm calling him Romeo. He loves us so much, he keeps coming back even though he knows he shouldn't." Christian chortled. "Break out the bubbly, we're partying tonight, ladies!"

Sofie smiled. After all the waiting, they'd tagged their shark, and captured great video of it breaching. OCEANS ALIVE would be happy for the report. Their mission was a success. *Romeo.* She shook her head, still smiling.

I wonder if Baby's nearby. She stared out over the waves without seeing them.

"I only had two trackers with me. I need that other tracker." She mumbled.

"We'll go back, you can make some more, and return to this area. No big deal-io, Sofie." Yaz crashed down from her high at the look on Sof's face. She recognized that look.

"But I need it now. What if we find Baby?" She stared out to sea, brows furrowed and eyes squinting in deep thought. "I knew there might be a problem when I traded a mini-camera for buoyancy. It should be on the ocean floor just below us. I designed it to sink straight down." She tapped her foot, and made a decision, "I'm going down."

"No, Sofiana Marigold Stone, you are not. I will not permit it." Yaz scolded. Her worried eyes followed Sofie as she moved around the deck preparing to dive. "You can't go down now. We've been baiting. And your knees are bleeding. You'll be baiting them with your own blood if you go down. There could be a whole party of sharks down there. Wait. Wait until tomorrow. We'll come back tomorrow and retrieve it. Not now."

"I've been in the water with whites before. I'll wrap my knees so tight they won't sense the blood. C'mon, Yaz. I know how to handle myself down there. You know that better than most. It'll be a quick dive. Retrieve the tracker and get out. Bam, bam." She clapped for emphasis.

"I know that. I do. But, Sof, I have a bad feeling 'bout this. Don't you go. Please." She pleaded; her chocolate eyes blurred by unshed tears.

Sofiana hesitated for just a beat, and then shook her head. "I'm sorry, Yaz. I really am. But I have to do this. Christian, lower the anchor and track the tracker. See if its recording and we can get an idea where it landed. I'm going down."

Chapter 19

Room 504, Massachusetts General Hospital

Maggie Lee Johnson's eyelids felt like they were held shut with bricks. She willed them to open, concentrating so hard on that one thing, that one simple desire her sole focus, until sweat beaded her unmoving brow with the effort. Inside her mind she could see it happen, the flow of light that would at first blind her until she adjusted to the onslaught of brightness invading her brain. But no matter how much she wanted it to be, no matter how hard she tried, the lids refused to budge. In fact, if anyone were to enter the room at that moment, they would see no change in her immobile body as it lay prone on the bed as it had since the accident. Though her brain was waking, her body remained in slumber. The first fingers of panic began to take hold inside her, evidenced by her heart rate monitor blipping like a heavy metal song. Maggie Lee lay alone in her hospital room with no one to notice the bead of sweat trickling sideways past her temple or the increased pace of her heartbeat.

Internally, she desperately experimented with moving her head just an inch, but still her body refused to listen to her silent command. She ceased her attempts to claw out of the darkness when pain shot like a lightning strike into her skull, ending with a wave of fog clouding her already misty brain. She squeezed her eyelids more tightly shut and whimpered. Her consciousness ebbed and surged, as if passing through a tunnel attached to a seesaw, increasing and decreasing its intensity as it moved up and down, up and down on an endless pivot.

As the pain waned just a bit Maggie Lee was able to resist it, instead choosing to focus all her energy on one thing—a beacon in the darkness. The glorious heat radiated into her body from one origin point: her right hand. She could not hold a coherent thought in her battered brain, but the wondrous warmth spread outward from her palm, moved up her arm and into her heart as it pumped its light through her arteries. It continued traveling throughout her body and into her mangled brain where it began its real work.

Maggie Lee sighed and embraced the tiny tender glow, before entering into the void once again. The corners of her mouth turned up just slightly and her brows smoothed as she gave in to the total blackness and surrendered herself over completely to the languid feel of heat. *Warmth.* The panic receded and her heart rate returned to its usual steady rhythm.

In her hand, her fingers clutched around it, the small silver trinket she had found on the beach glowed a luminous red.

Chapter 20

Cape Cod Rehabilitation Center

B ob sipped ice water from a straw, letting the chill travel down his throat and into his body, causing the hair on his arms to stand on end as goose bumps appeared.

What I would give for a cup of coffee. Strong black coffee.

He flopped back onto the lumpy bed pillow and pulled the thin, white, standard-issue covers up to his shoulders as a shiver took hold of his body. Looking up, he stared at the same jagged crack that began in the corner of the ceiling, his eyes tracking the zig-zag pattern it made all the way to the other side of the room, ending at the cobweb that blew sporadically each time the air conditioning vent kicked on. He huffed out a breath. It was the same crack he'd been staring at for days, and he had memorized its path. It reminded him of a lightning bolt snaking its way across the sky in one quick flash of light. Unlike other people who feared storms, he liked to go outside and sit on his porch just to watch the wonder of nature unfolding before his eyes— at least he used to. He longed for those days.

The throbbing of his hip, followed by a now

familiar shooting pain had him reaching for the call button. He stared through blurred eyes at the hospital standard round clock on the wall, its black hands contrasting with the white background, taking him back to his school days staring at the hands of the clock and willing them to move faster. He'd been impatient then, and he was even more so now. Another hour passed. A million more to go.

Bob was ready. Ready to leave this earth. He felt as though he had lived an eternity, and the seconds, minutes, and hours all ran together in his confused brain into a wall of nothingness. In moments of semi-clarity, he spoke to God, asking him to take him home. *I'm tired. So tired, Lord. I'm ready to meet you. What is left for me here? I've been here so long. Too long. I want to be with the people I love. All the people I lost. So many of them...and so many mistakes I've made. I don't want to make any more. I'm ready, Lord.*

He lay there on his back and closed his eyes, willing his old heart to stop beating. His eyes flew open at the sound of the door moving forward on it squeaky hinges, followed by the soft squeak of sneakers on the tile floor.

"Hi, Dad." Kyle smiled at him, walking toward the bed. He reached for his father's bony hand. "How're you feelin' today?"

"Where am I?" Bob barked.

"You're in Rehab, Dad. You fell and broke your hip, and they gave you a brand new one. You're here until you can go back home."

"Home? To the house?"

"No, Dad. We sold the house a few years after Mom died, remember? You'll go back to Caring House

Retirement Community when you're back on your feet, remember it there? You share a nice room with Arthur Caroll."

"I don't like him. I don't want to go back there. They aren't nice to me. I want to go home."

"Oh, Dad, that's not true. Sandy, your nurse? She takes good care of you, you know that. And Arthur's so nice. You'll remember when you get back home."

Bob snorted, and looked up at his son's face, not even noticing the stubble that grew on his chin, or the smudges under Kevin's blue eyes that spoke of sleepless nights. "You don't care, anyway. No one cares about me. I might as well die. I want to die."

"Dad, that's ridiculous. You know we love you, and we come as often as we can. I hurts me to hear you say that."

Bob turned away from his youngest son, and stared up at the crack in the ceiling, following its path to the cobweb and back again, dismissing him. Kyle dragged a chair across the room and flopped down into it. He straightened his leg in front of him, pushed his hand deep into his pocket and held up a deck of cards for his father to see.

"I brought cards, Dad. Remember we used to stay up late and play? Do you want to play now? I'll bring the tray over, and we can..."

"No."

"Please, Dad? I'd really like to play cards with you."

"No. I don't want to play cards. Where am I?"

Kyle sighed and ran his hand over his face. "You're in rehab, Dad. You broke your hip, remember? They gave you a brand new one, and you're only here temporarily until you feel up to going home."

"Home? To the house?"

"No, Dad. To your new home at Caring House. Remember? You share a room with that nice man Arthur."

"I want to go home and see Julie. I need my good luck charm. Who are you? Where's Victoria?"

Kyle sucked in a breath, and his eyes burned with unshed tears. His father had forgotten lots of things in recent years, but he had always remembered his sons. Until now. "Its Kyle, Dad. Your son? Remember? Kevin and Kyle, your boys?"

"Where's Victoria? You're not my son. My son is Adam. Where's Adam? Does Adam have my good luck charm?"

Kyle slowly stood up, gulping deep breaths. Two tears escaped, one from the corner of each eye, snaking paths over his cheeks as he rushed from the room.

Upon leaving the room Kyle immediately pulled out his cell phone, looked up his contact list, and tapped the green call button on the screen when he saw Kevin's picture. After three rings, his brother answered.

"Hey."

"Kev. It's Kyle. I'm with Dad."

"Is he okay? What's wrong, Kyle?" Kevin's voice was sharp. He sensed sorrow in those six words, even through the receiver.

Kyle sighed. "He doesn't remember me. He said I'm not his son, he said Adam is his son. Who is Adam?

And he asked for someone named Victoria. He didn't say mom, he said Victoria. Who the hell is Victoria?" He paused to take a deep, jagged breath, his hand shaking as it held the phone. "Kev, do you think dad had an affair? Could we have a step-brother we don't even know about?"

"No way. I'm not going there, Kyle. You know Dad loved Mom. You know it. Remember them together? I won't believe that. He doesn't know what he's talking about. We knew this day would come eventually. Though it doesn't really make it any easier."

"I don't know, Kev. It's weird. You didn't see his face. I just don't know..."

"He has Dementia. We've been lucky that he's remembered us this long. I'm coming in. You know how he goes in and out. Let's see if we can jog his memory together."

"Okay. I'll wait for you. Oh, and Kevin, he also mentioned that good luck charm he used to carry with him. Remember it? It was a silver stone of some sort that he thought kept him safe. Did we get rid of that when we cleaned out the house? I think he'd like to have it if we can find it. Maybe it would calm him."

"I'm not sure what happened to it. We can look for it. If either of us have it, it might be in those boxes we put in storage. Let's check it out tomorrow. Are you free?"

"I can be there early, if that works for you."

"I'll talk to my boss and see if I can go in late, and let you know. See you in thirty." Kyle pushed the button to end the call, and shoved his phone into his back pocket. Wishing he had someone to call while he waited for Kevin to arrive, he covered his face with his hands and his shoulders shook with the force of holding back the tears he ached to shed.

He stood up and paced the narrow hallway, and could not summon the strength he needed to re-enter his father's room alone. He fell back onto the bench in the hallway to wait for reinforcements.

Chapter 21

Cape Critters Veterinary Hospital

J ace used his back to push through the front door, his arms and legs shaking with numbness and the exertion of running ten blocks with Crash in his arms, his wheezing breaths coming in bursts. If not for Jace's strong determination to help his dog, he would have likely fallen to the ground in exhaustion blocks ago.

Dr. Lee met him there, a glum look in his eyes as he scanned Crash's body.

"I don't think he's breathing!" Jace's frantic voice broke as he carefully lay Crash on the examining table, and then wrapped his arms around himself to still the tremors. "And he lost a lot of blood."

"I see that." Dr. Lee's kind brown eyes looked up over the rim of his glasses, and traveled over Jace's bloodstained shirt and he began his examination. "Why don't you sit down? You look like you're about to fall over. I can't take care of both of you." The doctor listened to Crash's chest with a stethoscope. "He's still with us. There's a heartbeat. It's faint...but a heartbeat nonetheless."

"I'm not leaving, I'll just sit on the floor over here. In case you need me for anything." Jace put his back against the wall, and slid until he was sitting on the checkered linoleum floor and focused on calming his breathing. He rested his elbows on his bended knees, and lay his head down in his forearms wishing he had his inhaler with him. As his breathing became less sporadic, his tears made a barely audible plopping sound in the eerie quiet of the examining room as they fell to the floor. He stared at the drips, focused all his attention on them, until he couldn't see or hear anything else except that one salty, moist, drip. As shock began setting in, his mind did not register what the liquid was or why he was here. He simply escaped into the wet, worn, black and white checkered linoleum as if nothing else mattered. The sound of metal dropping onto metal snapped him out of his trance and his head jerked up.

So much blood...

"Let's take off his collar..."

"No!" He wiped his nose with the back of his hand, and then swiped at the tears on his cheeks.

"But I'll be able to work a lot easier if this isn't in the way. I promise I'll put it on as soon as the surgery is done."

"No. I'm sorry, but Crash loves that thing. I want it to be with him."

"Suit yourself." The doctor had just set up an IV drip, and now he placed an oxygen mask over Crash's face. Jace kept his head down. It hurt to see his friend in this condition.

"It's a clean cut, but with all that blood—I want to be straight with you. I think he has about a 25% chance of survival. Maybe. How old did you say he was?"

Only a 25% chance? Oh, Crash.

"Um. I think he's two? Or three? They weren't sure how old he was at the shelter."

"Good, he's young, that raises his chances a bit. He might just pull through. As long as he hasn't lost too much blood, and I have no way of knowing how much he's lost. Can you come here and hold this over the wound while I go get what I need? I have the bleeding contained. Wash your hands over there first." He jerked his head in the direction of the sink.

Jace struggled to his feet and walked on shaky legs to the sink. The sight of blood running off his hands and turning the water crimson broke through the impending shock, and he quickly dried and moved to the table. He reached a hand out to hold the gauze and the doctor rushed to the cabinet. With his free hand, Jace stroked his pet's blood-soaked fur, and leaned down to whisper in his ear. "Did you hear that? The doc says you're gonna be fine. Just hang in there." His hand stroked the hair on top of his mutt's head down to his neck, where he scratched under his collar knowing that was Crash's favorite place to be scratched.

A red light reflected onto his arm, and Jace's brows drew together as he searched for the source. It was coming from the collar. Or, more specifically, from the little metal medallion Crash had found in the seaweed that day. He parted the dog's wiry hair, and cupped the smooth, rounded object in his palm. His eyebrows shot up when his hand touched it. Unlike its usual cold temperature, the metal, if that's what it was, now felt warm to the touch. Not hot, just...pleasantly warm. A reddish-orange pulsing glowed from within. When it was no longer against the dog's body, the glow began to fade, and the coolness returned within seconds of losing contact.

"What the…?"

"Is something wrong?" The doctor called from the other room.

Is something wrong? Yes! Everything is wrong! Jace wanted to shout. But instead he said, "No. Nothing."

He heard the *shuffle-scrape* of the doctor's footsteps on the floor, and though he didn't understand why, he parted the hair at his base of the dog's neck on the underside where it wouldn't be seen, and placed the silver medallion directly on his skin before getting out of the way. The medallion was completely hidden from the doctor's view in its position underneath Crash's body. Jace walked backward until his back came in contact with the wall a second time, and he once again slid down to a sitting position, wide eyes never leaving the table.

Chapter 22

Research Vessel OA-23

"If I become a shark's supper, its gonna be your fault." Yaz complained as she strapped on the oxygen tank, pulling the cords to tighten them.

Sofie sat on the deck and pushed one foot and then the other into her lime-green flippers, then reached up to put her matching facemask on, leaving it on her forehead, "Don't come with me. I'd rather do this alone, anyway."

"You know I can't do that, girl. You *know* I can't."

"Then that's your choice, Yaz. Don't get upset because I'm making mine."

Christian cleared his throat, "Um, excuse me, but I'm here too? Did either of you ever consider that maybe I'd like to go down? Why do I have to stay with the boat?"

"Seniority, buddy. Seniority."

"That just sucks."

"Yes, it does. And some day you'll be in charge. But that's not today." Sofie patted him on the back to take the sting out of her words, then glanced at Yaz, "You ready?"

"'Bout as ready as a green banana. Are you sure, Sof?"

In answer, Sofie fell backward into the water and kicked her legs to stay afloat. Reaching up, she pulled off her facemask and spit into it. Rubbing the saliva around with her fingers to prevent the mask from fogging, she placed it over her eyes and nose and tasted the rubber of the mouthpiece as she wiggled it into her mouth. Christian handed the empty spear over the railing, and she grasped it in her left hand. Biting down on the mouthpiece, she took three experimental breaths, and submerged in a trail of tiny bubbles.

"That girl gonna be the death of me." Yaz mumbled just before she let go and fell into the water on her back, repeating the process.

Sofie, eyes wide and alert, moved cautiously, turning in slow circles as she descended. No sharks were visible, at least none close enough to see. A flurry of bubbles from above had her spinning around and holding her breath, until she realized that it was Yaz entering the water. *Breathe in. Breathe out. Breathe in. Breathe out.* She carefully continued her descent.

She reached the bottom moments before Yaz did, and when the tips of her flippers touched the sandy ocean floor they kicked up a flume of sand into the water. When Yasmin joined her, they stood back-to-back, eyes alert and scanning the area. Though they had pulled Skeeter and the baited hook out of the water before diving, little fragments of blood and bits of tuna meat still swirled where they had been, fogging the waters around the boat.

It wasn't long before she tapped Yaz on the sleeve, pointing when her friend made eye contact. Her head swiveled up. Romeo had returned, looking for another bite to eat. He circled the area, clearly confused that his dinner had mysteriously disappeared. Yaz gave a nod and kept watch, her eyes tracking the shark at the surface. Sof saw her unzip her pouch to retrieve the long jagged switchblade she always carried with her on a dive. She held it with a death-grip by her side. Though she was a skilled diver, as she'd gotten older she preferred to do most of her work above the water. Unlike Sofiana.

Sofie began searching the ocean floor for the small tracking device. It wouldn't be easy to spot in the murky waters. She could only hope it hadn't gotten buried in the sand. She moved until she was directly below the cloudy waters next to the boat, and began searching below. Wishing she had the time and equipment to set up a grid search, she instead drew the lines in her mind. It was the best she could do.

She heard Yaz make a muffled sound through her mouthpiece creating large bubbles that raced to the surface just before she tapped Sofie's leg and pointed. Romeo was still near the boat, but another shark appeared to the left and began slowly circling. *Too small to be Baby.* Knowing more could be on the way, she frantically continued her search.

A tiny blinking light caught her eye, lying to the right of the anchor, and she took a deep pull of oxygen on a sigh.

There it is!

Legs kicking up and down, flippers propelling her through the water, she reached out to grasp the tracker in her gloved hand.

She replaced the device onto the end of the spear,

tapped Yaz on the shoulder, and pointed upward. At Yaz's nod, they began their slow ascent while keeping the sharks in their sight. Both white sharks above circled the boat, not even noticing the two humans beneath them, their only concern the bloody flesh and death they smelled with their keen senses.

I should have brought the camera.

As they stopped about halfway to the boat, directly under the circling sharks, a third shark appeared from the right as if in slow motion. This creature was huge, dwarfing them in size, and the other two sensed its dominance immediately and darted off in a flurry of undulating tailfins and bubbles.

Baby? Could it be?

As Sofie's feet began moving slowly back and forth propelling her toward both the surface and the beast, Yaz reached a hand out to grab her arm, detaining her. Looking down to meet her friends eyes through her mask, she saw Yaz furiously shake her head side to side, trying to speak through her mouthpiece, spewing a flurry of bubbles that raced desperately upward.

With one decisive headshake, she yanked her arm free and kicked up quickly, stopping just as the enormous great white swam above her, blocking the sun's rays and creating a giant shadow where Sofie now floated. Her eyes widened and she drew in a sharp breath. The jagged, anchor shaped scar was clearly visible on the shark's underbelly.

Hello, Baby!

Sofie's eyes burned with tears, and as she instinctively reached up to swipe at them her hand bumped the mask. She chuckled to herself and blinked her eyes in rapid succession. As she looked down to check on Yaz, her eyes caught the reflection of the spear in her own hand.

I can tag Baby. I can do it under water. Its risky, but...

As she prepared to kick upward, she felt the pressure of a hand wrapping around her ankle from below. *Yaz!* Sofie kicked free and swam closer to the shark.

Chapter 23

Yarmouth, Cape Cod, Massachusetts

Grayson flopped down into the faux leather desk chair in front of Dan's desk, slapped his hands on his knees and leaned forward. The long drive from his home in the heart of Cape Cod to Boston had him wired.

"It's shaping up to be quite a story, but I told you, it's not ready yet. I have more questions than answers at this point."

"I want to print the story ASAP, Gray. You know stories lose their spark if you don't jump right on them. If we don't, someone else will, I guarantee it."

"No one else is looking into it. I need more time, Dan."

His boss drummed his fingers on top of his desk, making a repetitive tap-tap-tap-tapping sound that seemed to echo off the walls in the small office as he stared out the window lost in thought. A minute ticked by. He blew out a breath.

"Fine. I'll give you more time. But I can't promise how long." He emphasized his words by pointing a finger. "If I get even a whiff that our competition is investigating this, we print what we have."

"Thanks, Dan. You won't regret this. I promise."
As Grayson reached out for a handshake, his cell phone
vibrated.

"I better not, Gray. Now go, get busy."

Distractedly nodding, Grayson dug into his
pocket and pulled out his phone as he walked out of the
office, glancing at the display. He frowned at the blank
screen. Tapping 'Accept', he barked, "Smith."

"Is this Grayson Smith?"

"Yes, the one and only. And you are?"

"Mr. Smith, it's Detective Gold. I thought you
might like a tip on that story you've been working on?"

Gray's body froze. "A tip? What kind of tip? Have
you found the guy that hit Maggie Lee Johnson?"

Detective Gold's voice was smooth as he evaded
the question. "Mr. Smith, did you give the stone to Ms.
Johnson?"

Grayson frowned. "The metal stone? You mean
her trinket? Yes. Yes, she has it."

"Good, good. A body has been found, washed up
in the bay. You might be interested."

"What body? Who is it?" Grayson's frantic questions went unanswered. The line went dead. Knowing
it was most likely futile, he pressed re-dial and waited.

*"We're sorry, your call cannot be completed as dialed.
Please try again."*

He punched in the numbers manually, and got
the same response. Staring at the screen, he frowned.
He grabbed his bag, jogged to his Camaro, and sped off
toward the bay.

Why would the officer call me?

Around every bend, he uncovered more and
more questions, but still no answers.

None of this makes any sense.

Brows lowered, he pushed his phone's menu button.

"How can I help you?"

"Siri, please search for a body in Cape Cod Bay."

"Searching for A Body in Cape Cod Bay...Got it. A body was found this morning. Would you like to display the results?"

"Yes. Male or female?"

"Unknown."

"Siri, dial the Barnstable Police Department."

"Dialing."

"Barnstable Police Department, is this an emergency?"

"No, I'd like to speak to Detective Gold."

"I'm sorry, we don't have a Detective Gold here. Can another Detective help you?"

"Wait, I just talked to him. Maybe he's with another department?"

"I can run him through the system. Please hold."

He listened to the static silence. "I'm sorry, sir. None of the departments in the Cape Cod or surrounding areas have a detective by that name."

Grayson slowly lowered his phone and placed it in the cup holder.

What is going on? And why did he call me about a body?

His hands tapped on the steering wheel and then abruptly stopped.

Unless it's someone I know. Someone who works in the water...

Oh my God.

Sofiana.

His foot pressed harder on the gas as he sped toward the bay.

Chapter 24

Massachusetts General Hospital, Fifth Floor

Maggie Lee forced her eyelids apart and squinted through the nighttime light in her hospital room. She moved her eyes to the side, and spotted Mike asleep in the visitor's chair.

"Mike?" Her voice was barely a rasp, and he didn't stir.

Experimentally moving her head to the side, she tried again, "Mike?"

"Hmm?" His eyes slowly came into focus, and landed right on his wife.

"Maggie? Maggie?" He jumped from his chair and staggered to the side of the bed, "Is this a dream? Are you really awake?"

"Not a dream. Thirsty. I'm so thirsty." She squeezed his hand with a surprisingly strong grip.

"Thank God! I'll get you water in a minute." Mike whispered as he climbed into the bed next to her, cradling her body against his. "You scared me. I can't live without you, Maggie. I love you so much. Don't ever do that to me again." Tears streamed down his cheeks as he kissed her face.

"What happened? The last thing I remember is...

the interview. Oh, no, the interview!"

"Forget about that, babe. We can talk about all of that later. You rest, now. I'll go get you some water. Be right back." He winked as he strode out of the room.

While she waited for Mike to return, Maggie's eyes traveled the room. Everything seemed so clearly in focus, and she couldn't immediately understand why that might be strange...

I'm in a hospital. But why?

She closed her eyes and concentrated on her memories.

They came back in a flood. Leaving the interview, the taxi ride, a dark-blue SUV, her own body flying through the air...

But more importantly, she could see the face of the man who'd hit her as clear as glass in her mind.

"Mike! Mike! I remember him! I remember everything!"

Mike ran into the room, followed closely by a nurse.

"Hello, Mrs. Johnson. It's nice to finally meet you. My name is Marie and I'm your nurse for the night shift. You've been out for some time. I've contacted the doctor and he's on the way. May I check your vitals?"

"Yes, but...Mike, I remember! I remember the man who hit me."

"I'll call the police and let them know. But right now, you need to focus on getting better." He patted her hand.

She sat up straighter. "I feel good."

"Maggie, you've been in a coma since the accident..."

She shook her head. "It wasn't an accident, Mike.

That man *tried* to hit me."

"I know, babe. But you need to heal now. Let's just concentrate on that."

"But, Mike? I feel like I'm fine. I don't feel like I need to be here."

"Babe, your brain has been swelling inside your head, the doctors are going to need to run tests..."

"I'm telling you, Mike. I feel better than I did before the accident."

"That can't be true, sweetheart. Let me get your glasses. I have them right here."

Maggie looked once more around the room. She took in Mike's worried wrinkles on his forehead, the fine detail of the heart-shaped tattoo on her nurse's neck just below the ear, the spiderweb in front of the window; all in crystal clear focus...and suddenly realized why all of that was strange.

Mike held her glasses out to her, and she shook her head.

"I don't need those anymore. I can see just fine." She looked down at her hands, turning them over to do a thorough study, and inhaled in surprise. "And look! You know those scars I got when I was ten and fell into the barbed wire fence at the farm? They're faded. You can just barely see them now. I've had them nearly all my life...why would they change now? That's strange, isn't it?"

Mike swallowed past a lump that had suddenly formed in his throat, and nodded.

Chapter 25

Hyannis, Massachusetts

Kyle's Jeep screeched to a stop in front of the large garage-type door, stones flying in every direction. Leaping down, he slammed the door with an echoing *Bang*. A flock of starlings that had been foraging in the gravel scattered, chattering as they landed on the roof of the storage unit. Kyle paced outside the rented storage unit and shook his head. When they'd moved Dad out of the house, he had wanted to go through everything then, but Kevin hadn't been up to it. So instead, they boxed everything up and split a small fortune each month to store it here at U-Store-It. He couldn't help thinking that if they'd done it then, he wouldn't have to be here now. A frustrated sigh escaped as he shoved his hands into the pockets of his faded jeans.

Turning toward the sound of stones crunching as tires rolled over them, he spotted Kevin's red Sierra pick-up truck ambling along the path as it slowly approached. A derisive smile turned up one corner of his mouth. Their driving styles matched their personalities.

Lifting a hand to wave, he reached into his pocket

for the key, and began opening the door to the storage unit.

He called over his shoulder, "Hey."

"Hey. You ready for this?" Kevin jumped down, slammed the door, and ambled, much as his truck had, over to stand next to his brother.

"No, but it needs to be done. Kev, I really think we need to go through everything. After what dad said about that woman and his son, I've been on edge."

"Agreed. I only have a few hours today, but we'll get done what we can. You're right, this is long overdue." He paused. "But Kyle, I don't think there are any 'clues' to find. Dad is dad. We *know* him. We have to admit that he is no longer with us. Not really. The dementia has taken most of him from us already. It's only going to get worse. You can't listen to his ramblings. He doesn't know what he's saying." He reached out to grab his brother's shoulder, giving it a gentle squeeze.

"I know. I do know that. But you weren't there when he said he had a son named Adam. You didn't see his face, Kev, when he talked about that Victoria, whoever she is. I did, and let me tell you, I just can't shake this crazy feeling that we don't know dad as well as we think we do."

"Well, let's go in there and get started. You'll see when we don't find anything unusual."

"Do you think, even if we find that stupid 'lucky charm,' Dad will even remember asking for it?" Kyle shook his head.

Kevin shrugged in answer. "I don't know, Kyle. I really don't. But we have to try. It's the one thing we can do for him right now. Let's get started."

Kyle raised the garage-type door, and they both

took a deep breath as they stepped forward. Their whole childhood was boxed up in here along with the entirety of their parent's lives, and they hadn't even looked inside some of the boxes when they'd brought them here for storage. Boxes were stacked on top of each other, eight high in some places, and they just stood and stared for a moment, unsure where to begin.

Kevin stepped forward, and chose the box closest to him.

"I guess this is as good a place as any." Kyle nodded.

Kevin looked inside and found pictures. Stacks of pictures as well as scattered photos, all thrown into the box. Reaching his hand inside, he picked up the photo on top. It was a picture of when he was an infant, cradled in his mother's arms as she sat on the old brown plaid sofa. He grabbed another, and in it he was ten, then another and he was fifteen. There seemed to be no order to the way the pictures were placed in the box, so he just reached in and grabbed a stack. His eyes burned as he held up a picture of his mom and dad standing in front of their Christmas tree. Rapidly blinking, he placed the picture back in the box and closed the lid, clearing his throat past the sudden lump that had taken root there. "I'm gonna put this in the truck and look at it at home, if that's okay with you. If I start looking through these now, we won't get anything else done. There's another box of pictures over there. How about you take that one?"

Kyle absently glanced in his brother's direction as he pawed through a box of kitchen utensils. "That's fine. This is going to take forever, anyway. Why did we keep all this stuff?" He held up an ancient rolling pin, and shook his head when a memory flashed so clear it seared his brain. His mother making piecrusts, flour on the floor, in her hair, smeared on her cheek. Laughing as she showed him how to use the roller. The sound of her laughter echoed in the confined space as if she were standing right next to him. Slowly, he lowered the rolling pin and replaced it in the box.

This is going to be harder than I thought. Even after all this time.

He stood, took a deep breath, and grabbed another box. This one was full of old clothing. He grabbed a trash bag, and began stuffing clothing into the bag to donate.

"Don't forget to look through the pockets. There might be money or something stashed in them."

"Oh, right. I didn't think of that." Kyle sighed as he began removing the clothing from the bag he had just filled to check the pockets. He pulled out countless crumpled tissues, an ancient and dried-up Chapstick, fifty-three cents, and an old grocery list in his mother's flowery handwriting. Though it was nothing but a meaningless list of food items that no longer had any meaning, the sight of her writing was suddenly so important it took his breath away. It was like looking at a piece of her, and he couldn't bring himself to throw it into the trashbag. He shoved the grocery list into his pocket and kept going, glancing at his watch. Kyle's eyes widened. "We've been at it for ninety minutes, and we haven't even made a dent!" He moaned, hands on his hips.

"We are making progress. I still have another hour. One box at a time. We'll do what we can and come back on Saturday, if that works for you."

Kyle threw his hands into the air. "This is going to take a month of Saturdays!"

"One day at a time, little bro." He punched Kyle in the arm as he spoke.

Kyle retaliated by punching him back, and found himself in a headlock. Some things would never change, no matter how old they were. And being in this place, surrounded by memories, sure did bring back their childhood. It was as if seeing all of these momentos somehow reverted them right back to the antics of the teenaged brothers they had been, erasing the years of adulthood one box of memories at a time.

"Okay, okay. You win. Let's get back to it." Once released, Kyle reached for another box. More clothing. Sighing, he opened the lid. "Look, Kev. It's Dad's uniform. Should we give it back to the police department?"

Kevin shrugged. "Maybe. We can't donate that. We don't want just any ol' lunatic walking the streets wearing a police officer's uniform. Put it aside, and let's decide later. We can contact the department and see if they're interested in having it."

Kyle placed it on top of another box and turned to continue, then stopped and turned back. After fumbling through all the outer pockets and finding nothing, he paused, wiping the sweat off his forehead with his sleeve. Something was creating a barely noticeable bulge in the front that couldn't be reached from the outer pockets. He felt around the pockets again, sure that he had missed whatever was in there the first time, but once again, he could not find the source. Turning the jacket inside out, he ran his hands over the inner liner of the jacket, and felt a small zipper sewn into the satin. He moved the zipper and reached his hand into the hidden pocket and felt something smooth and round, like a polished rock. When he pulled it out, the shine made him squint, so intense it was despite the darkness of the room.

"Uh, Kev. I think I found it. Dad's Good Luck Charm. This is it, right?"

He held up the glowing, silver object for his brother's inspection.

"Yes. That's it. Can you take it to him tonight, now that he's back at Caring House? He'll be so happy. Well, at least I think he will..." Kevin shook his head.

"It's so cold...Why is it so cold when it's so hot in here?"

"Who cares, as long as he has it? Maybe it will give him some piece of mind just having it with him."

"Maybe." Kyle shoved it into the front pocket of his aged jeans, and reached for another box.

Chapter 26

Cape Critter's Veterinary Hospital

J ace felt the earthquake. His body rumbled and shook, and he heard his name being called from far off in the distance. No, not his name. His father's name. Mr. Calhoun.

"Mr. Calhoun? Mr. Calhoun, you fell asleep on the floor. Wake up now, son." Dr. Lee's voice vibrated through the mist in his head as he continued to gently shake Jace's shoulder. Not an earthquake, just a wake-up attempt.

He forced one eye open, and then snapped it closed as the bright fluorescent light dilated his pupil. A groan escaped from deep in his throat. A dull, throbbing ache began to break through the fog of his brain. It originated in three places. His back, his neck, and his butt.

What the...

Forcing both eyes open, Jace blinked up at the veterinarian from his position on the floor and scowled as the memories flooded back in a flash. Crash was in trouble.

How could I sleep at a time like this? His eyes widened as he struggled to push himself to a standing position. His legs felt as if needles were poking and prodding him, and he shook each one in an attempt to shake off the lethargy.

"Crash?" He croaked, as he impatiently reached up to brush back his hair, the cowlick making it stand on end.

"He made it through the surgery. I wasn't sure he would, so that's a good sign. He's all right for now. You need to rest. Why don't you go home, and you can come back first thing in the morning. I'll sleep here on the cot tonight. He won't be alone. I promise."

Jace gave a brisk nod, "Can I see him?"

"I don't see why not. He's still sedated, but the sound of your voice might just soothe him. You can help me move him to a crate."

As Jace approached the table where his dog lay, the sight of his chest steadily rising and falling gave him hope, and he picked up his pace until he was right next to the table. He gently laid a hand on his best friend's soft fur, and rubbed lightly.

"You're doing great, dude. What a good boy. Dr. Lee says you're gonna be just fine. I knew you would be. I just knew it," he rasped, wiping his nose with the back of his bare arm. Jace inhaled sharply when the tip of Crash's tail moved.

"Look, his tail's wagging! He can hear me! That's it, Crash. Good boy!"

"It's probably just a reflex. He's still under sedation." The doctor cautioned.

"What do you think, dude? Was it a reflex, or can you hear me?"

The dog's tail moved up and down twice.

"Yes! I knew it! He can hear me!" Jace reached

around to scratch under Crash's collar, and his tail wiggled back and forth excitedly.

The doctor approached the table, eyes narrowed. "It is odd...usually there is no response at a time like this. Talk to him again."

"That's it, boy. You're the best dog in the world, you know that Crash-Crash?"

Once again, the tail began moving back and forth. Jace carefully laid his head on top of his dog's shoulder and continued his scratching.

"I'm going home now, Crash. But I'll be back in the morning."

A low whine echoed through the quiet room as the dog seemed to moan in protestation.

"I promise I'll be back first thing, dude."

Another melancholy whimper broke the silence, and Jace's eyes flew up to meet the doctor's. "He wants me to stay."

"More likely, his anesthesia is wearing off. Even if he were coming out of it, he wouldn't understand your words. Just like people, anesthesia affects animals in different ways. It's normal, and nothing to worry about. You go on home now, get some rest."

"I want to stay." At his words, Crash's tail began incessantly wagging. He pointed at his dog's tail, "How do you explain that. He wants me to stay."

"As I said, it's probably the after-effects of the sedation. Nothing more." He pushed his glasses up to rub at his eyes. "Have it your way. You can sleep in the waiting room if you're so inclined. I'm tired, and I'm going to lay down now. I don't have the energy to argue."

"No need to move him to a crate. I'll be right

here with him. I can pull up two chairs right next to the table. I can sleep anywhere." He hesitated, looking up to meet the vet's eyes. "And doctor? Thank you. For everything."

"You're welcome, son." He smiled. "I believe that you could sleep anywhere after witnessing you asleep sitting up on my linoleum floor. That's fine. Wake me if there's a change. G'night." He reached up to cover his yawn as he shuffled through the doorway.

"I'm right here, dude. I won't leave. I promise, Crash-Crash."

Looking back over his shoulder to make sure he was alone, he reached under the dog's head, around the underside of his neck, and pulled out the silver medallion. He cupped it in the palm of his hand, entranced by the red glow and low heat that seemed to emanate from within. The moment it lost contact with Crash's skin, it instantly began cooling off, and the red glow faded. For the second time that night, though he had no good reason for it, he placed it back against the dog's neck, right up against his skin and hidden underneath him.

Though Crash's eyes remained closed, his tail whipped back and forth so forcefully it made a rhythmic thumping sound as it hit the table.

Jace curled his lanky body up on the two chairs, laying his head down on the armrest. Within minutes, his breathing slowed as he lost consciousness.

Chapter 27

Below Research Vessel OA-23

Sofie barely moved her legs as she gently kicked upward. Her mind was in overdrive as she calculated the best way to get the tracker onto Baby without either one of them getting hurt. It needed to be attached to the base of the dorsal fin, which posed the biggest problem from her position underneath the beast.

I need to get above her, but how?

The situation was not ideal, but she was not willing to let this opportunity slip away without at least trying to tag her. She gave another slight kick and closed the distance between her and the shark by another few inches. This would be her first experience with administering a tracker while underwater, though some of her colleagues preferred this method.

Pausing to check the spear and tracker one more time, she glanced down at Yaz. Her friend's eyes were huge inside her mask, the whites glowing in contrast with her dark skin through the plastic, giving her an odd otherworldly appearance. Her medusa-like dreadlocks floated mysteriously around her head. Sofiana wanted to reassure her friend, but that was impossible at the moment. She gulped a deep breath of oxygen on a sigh. And this was too important for her to give up on.

I'll just have to make it up to her later.

She gave one decisive nod, and turned to focus all of her attention on Baby once again.

The enormous great white swam in lazy circles around the boat. Its tailfin languidly propelled it through the water with what appeared to be little effort. The gracefulness of this gigantic beast contradicted every myth that existed about these amazing creatures.

I wish the public could see how peaceful sharks really are. Not the barbaric killing machines people think they are.

Glancing down at Yaz once more, she pointed to the right and began moving in the direction she'd indicated, gradually swimming parallel to the boat.

I could get back in the boat and try to tag her from there...

Her mind racing, she stopped once again.

But I'd run the risk of scaring her away. No, I'll try to tag her from down here, and if that doesn't work, I'll get back in the boat and try again from up top.

Decision made, her legs scissored as she continued swimming parallel to both the boat and the shark.

Chapter 28

Nauset Beach, Orleans, Massachusetts

G rayson parked the Camaro sideways, slammed the car door, and jogged across the dunes and right up to the yellow crime scene tape, heart pounding and chest heaving as his breath came in short bursts. Wet circles were forming under his armpits, and though sweat beaded his brow his face remained pale as an eggshell.

Sofie.

His mind was filled with nothing but her image. Her amber eyes, crinkling as she laughed up at him, her shoulder-length brown hair streaked with natural sun highlights pulled back in a messy ponytail, curly tendrils framing her heart-shaped face. Her hand reaching out to take his as she looked up at him.

If anything happened to her...

An officer ran toward him as he lifted a foot to step over the tape. "Stop! You may not cross the police line. This is an active investigation."

Grayson put his foot back down on the sand. Relief flooded his body in a wave of numbness as his breathe quickened. He recognized the man. "Sorry. Mark? It's Grayson Smith. I'm with the Boston Sentinel now, but we went to college together, I think? How are you doing? How's your wife? Liz, right?"

"Oh." Mark frowned, nodding. "Hi, Grayson. Been a while. Liz is fine. Expecting a baby in a few months."

"A baby? That's great. Congratulations to both of you. Listen, I need to know who that is." He pointed in the direction of the body.

"You know I can't tell you that. This is an active investigation. Anything you report at this point in the investigation could mess it up. You should know that." He shook his head. "How did you even know about this already?"

"I got an anonymous tip. Please, I know you probably don't know the identity of that body over there yet, but I need to know one thing. I'm begging you, for old times sake. I won't release it until I have the okay from your department, you have my word." He paused, his words coming out in a rush. "Is the body male or female?" Something in Grayson's desperate eyes must have broken through the officer's rough exterior.

"Male. That's all I can tell you, Grayson. Good to see you." He turned and took a step toward the crime scene.

"Oh, Wait!" Gray called.

"I don't have time for this," Mark mumbled, frowning.

Gray held up his hands in a gesture of surrender. "One more thing. Please? Do you know an Officer Gold?"

He turned his head and called over his shoulder, "Sorry. I don't know anyone by that name, officer or not."

"Mark! Just one more question. I swear. Best

guess. Did the victim die by drowning?"

"Definitely not. He probably died from the multiple bullet wounds we found on his body. That's all I'm telling you, Grayson. I don't even know why I told you that much. I better not see it on the evening news. I'll deny it," the officer called over his shoulder as he walked away.

Grayson stood, arms hanging at his sides, and looked up at the clouds blowing lazily across the blue sky. The sun beat down on his face, its warmth misleadingly jubilant under the circumstances, considering the corpse that had washed up just yards away. Someone had died today, and yet the sense of relief that enveloped him made him dizzy. He breathed slowly and purposefully as his heart rate returned to a normal pace—just as he'd been trained to do when confronted with a panic attack. Prior to this, he'd only had a problem with elevators. It seemed his fear now extended to murder as well. He hoped there were no other additions to his list of things that triggered this blasted anxiety. He couldn't hold back the sigh as Sofie's face once again flashed across his vision.

It's not her. Thank God.

He closed his eyes for just a few seconds, and her image was as clear as if she were standing in front of him. The possibility of her lying dead on the beach had left him weak at the knees, and quite shaken.

Why do I care so much?

He shook his head, deciding he would have to think more about that later. Right now, he had bigger questions to answer.

First, who was that lying dead on the other side of the crime scene tape?

Second, why did someone pose as a police officer to tip me off about it?

And third, what does all of this have to do with Maggie Lee and her trinket?

Chapter 29

Massachusetts General Hospital

Maggie Lee slid out of the hospital bed to face the doctor, chin raised.

"Dr. Ficke, I want to go home. You said it yourself, I've recovered faster than anyone could have imagined. I don't need to be here. I'm leaving."

The doctor pursed his lips. "Please. We don't understand why you've recovered at such an alarming rate. We want to run more tests so we can better understand..."

"I'm leaving, doctor." She moved to pick up her handbag, and he blocked her way. "Kindly move out of my way. I don't want to be rude, but I'm leaving, with or without discharge papers. Excuse me."

"You could have a relapse..." Dr. Ficke splayed his hands in front of him.

"If that happens, I'll be back here faster than you can blink. Trust me." Maggie Lee sighed, the air coming out of her like a deflated balloon. "Let me ask you this. Is my brain still swelled?"

He took a long slow breath before mumbling: "No, your brain looks completely healthy."

"Do I have any remaining broken bones? Or

sprains?" She cocked her head, a small smile lifting the corners of her mouth.

He slowly, grudgingly, shook his head. "No. Your bones have healed, almost completely."

Maggie's twinkling laughter filled the small room. "I'm healthier than you are, doctor. And I feel great. I have you to thank for that. So thank you." She reached a hand out for his and smiled into his eyes. He reluctantly grasped her hand in his, giving one quick shake before breaking contact.

"Now, I'm leaving." She turned toward her husband. "Mike?"

Mike's eyes roamed over his wife, not missing a detail. Her cheeks bloomed with a healthy pink glow; her eyes—sans glasses—were crystal clear. Even her hair appeared more vibrant. Was it possible some of the gray had vanished? She looked ten years younger than two weeks ago. He chewed on his bottom lip; brow furrowed, and took one long breath.

As long as she's okay.

He wouldn't question the miracle that had brought her back to him.

"I'm here, babe." He reached for her hand and gave it a gentle squeeze. "Let's go home." Lord knew he'd give her anything she wanted right now. All she had to do was snap her fingers, and he'd do whatever it took to keep her safe and healthy.

They walked side-by-side, hands clasped, toward the elevators. When she stopped to push the button, he leaned over and kissed the top of her head.

Maggie reached into her purse, feeling for the pocket that housed her trinket. She clasped the zipper and pulled, then cupped the small silver object in the palm of her hand, sighing. A slight smile flashed—different than the one she'd bestowed upon the doctor just minutes before—into a grin that did not reach her eyes.

Mike shivered, pretending not to notice the gleam that lit her pupils. He gave her hand a gentle squeeze, sure he must have mistaken the possessiveness he thought he'd seen there for just an instant.

Since waking, Maggie Lee hadn't let the trinket out of her sight for more than a few minutes, and had even taken it with her to the bathroom when she needed to go. As they continued walking, her eyes darted back and forth, searching for anyone worthy of suspicion, someone who might want what was hers. It had happened before right under her nose, at the news station, when she had been naïve. It wouldn't happen again. Someone was after her trinket, and she wouldn't let them take it from her again.

Ever.

Chapter 30

Caring House Retirement Community

Since his return to the assisted living community he grudgingly called home, Bob had been in a surly mood. His roommate, Arthur, hadn't stopped his incessant chattering since he'd walked through the door yesterday morning. He reached up to rub circles at his temples, trying to ease the pressure building there.

How can I get him to stop talking?

"I'm gonna take a nap," Bob growled while rolling over. A gasp tore from his throat and he clutched a hand over his hip as the pain shot upward and the deep throbbing began. He'd forgotten all about the injury, and in fact couldn't even remember how he'd been hurt in the first place.

"I'm calling for help. You need your pain medication. They'll be here in a minute." Arthur sighed. "Or twenty." He spoke while pushing the red button next to his bed.

"I just want to sleep," Bob mumbled.

Arthur nodded. "That's fine, you'll sleep better after Sandy comes with the pain killer."

"I don't need a pain killer. I'm fine," Bob argued.

He inhaled sharply and pushed his head back into the pillow, closing his eyes as yet another breath-stealing pain shot up from his hip.

Arthur sighed again. "It's good to have you back, Bob. It was too quiet in this room when you were gone."

"Humph." Bob turned his head away.

Gone? I didn't go anywhere. What's he talking about? Can't he just leave me alone? Can't everyone just leave me alone?

He kept his eyes closed when he heard the door opening, feigning sleep at the sound of Sandy's voice.

"Bob? Are you okay?" Her sneakers squeaked on the linoleum flooring as she approached the bed. "Bob?"

Arthur's voice broke the silence from across the room. "He's awake. Just grumpy. He needs his painkillers. He was clutching his hip."

Sandy's voice was closer this time. "Bob? I have your pain pills here. You need to swallow them and you'll feel better."

Bob grumbled without moving his head or opening his eyes, "Go away."

"But Bob, you'll feel better if you take these. Don't you want the pain to go away?" Sandy asked.

"No."

"Please, Bob. You've had surgery. You need to take the pills."

A now-familiar look of confusion crossed Bob's face. "Who are you? I just want you to go away. Bring me Julie. Why doesn't she come?"

"Fine." A cool weight appeared on his hip. "If you won't take the pills, then here's an icepack to hold on your hip. It will help," Sandy cajoled, the sweetness in words seeming forced.

Bob could feel the cold pack seeping through his clothing and bedsheets. Though it made the throbbing lessen almost immediately, he grabbed the icepack and threw it across the room in a fit of rage. It slammed against the window, and ice flew out of the bag to scatter on the floor.

"Just go away. I want Julie." He turned his head once more, eyes squeezed tightly shut.

Sandy's long, drawn-out sigh reached his ears, and she conceded, "Okay, Bob. Have it your way."

The sound of her retreating feet made the corners of his mouth lift just slightly, as if in victory. A small win but nonetheless a point in his column, despite the aching of his hip or the fact that the combination of ice and medicine would surely have helped him.

"Julie, I'm ready," he whispered. "I'm ready to come to you."

When Sandy left the room, she headed straight for the nurse's station. She took out the white three ring binder labeled 'Patient Emergency Information', and with her finger holding the place, dialed the first number on the list when she reached Bob's name.

After three rings, a male voice answered, "Hey."

"Mr. Green? Is this Mr. Kevin Green?"

"Yes."

"It's Sandy from Caring House Retirement Community? I'm the nurse assigned to your father."

"Yes, I remember. Hi Sandy. Is everything okay?"

"Yes and no. Your father seems to have fallen into a depression. He won't take his medications or interact with me or his roommate, Arthur. It's probably nothing, I'm sure he'll be back to his normal self when he feels better, but I wanted you to be aware of his condition. He's always forgetful and can get surly, but it's unusual for him to be violent."

"Okay, thanks Sandy. I'll see if I can fit in a visit tonight. Do you know if my brother visited last night? I know my wife brought him there from rehab yesterday morning, but did anyone else come in last night?"

"As far as I know, he didn't have any visitors yesterday after he arrived from rehab."

"Okay, thanks. I think my brother has something that might cheer Dad up. He was supposed to bring it to him last night, but...let me give him a call, and I'll see if we can both come in tonight. Thanks for the update."

Chapter 31

Cape Critters Veterinary Hospital

J ace's eyes widened as he stared at the bill in his hand. Four digits. He flexed his hand involuntarily, crumpling the edge of the paper. The pounding in his head began at his temple, galloped down his neck continuing over his shoulders and into his back. He hadn't felt this way since middle school, when he'd unknowingly walked into class with his zipper down, electric blue bikini briefs on display for the world, and Miss Thomas, to see. From then on, Brendan Flannigan, captain of the basketball team and worshipped by all, had bestowed upon him the nickname 'Blue'. To his horror, the moniker had stuck with him until graduation. His face heated now similar to the way it did every time he heard the color blue spoken out loud.

I could work double shifts for two years straight, and I still wouldn't be able to pay this off.

"Uh." He cleared his throat, "Can I pay something toward it each month?"

"I'm sorry, sir. The balance needs to be paid in full at the time of service. We do accept credit cards. And we offer a special card that you can apply for today. It's universally accepted by most veterinarians and medical doctors, so even if you go somewhere else, you can use it. Would you like to apply?" the receptionist asked.

Clutching the paper so hard it crumpled even more, Jace answered. "Um. Yeah, I guess."

Don't really have a choice, do I?

Sweat beaded on his forehead and he hunched his shoulders even more than usual.

Jace filled out the paperwork, and as he was handing the clipboard back over the counter, Dr. Lee carried Crash out to the waiting room.

"He's doing great, Jace. Better than expected. Give him his medication twice a day, and call me tomorrow to let me know how he's doing, okay?"

"I will. Thanks. For everything." Crash's tail wagged incessantly when he saw his boy. Jace reached out and took Crash into his arms, his dog's rough tongue licking his chin repeatedly as if he couldn't get enough. Jace took a moment to bury his head in the mutt's fur, taking a deep breath. A strange combination of salt, dog, and the medicinal odor of the vet's office filled his nostrils, and he savored the scent as tears burned behind his eyes. He could feel the strong beating of Crash's heart against his chest, and reveled in it, tears springing to his eyes that he blinked back. *Thought I'd never feel that again.*

The receptionist stood up, interrupting the reunion, "I'm sorry, sir? You've been declined for the credit card. Do you have another way to pay?"

Jace's heart pounded erratically as he shook his head from side to side, heat creeping up his neck. "No."

Dr. Lee stepped forward, laying a hand on his shoulder. The veterinarian's eyes met those of the receptionist, and he said in a gentle voice, "It's okay, Sarah. Set up the payment plan. It was an emergency, after all, and my pleasure to help Crash. Get it done."

"Okay, Dr. Lee." Sarah rolled her eyes as she pounded the keyboard, her eyes darting back and forth between the doctor and Jace. She mumbled to herself as she prepared the bill, a frown accentuating the creases between her eyes.

Jace forced his eyes to meet the doctor's. He whispered, "Thank you."

Dr. Lee squeezed his shoulder, "As I said, my pleasure, son. Take good care of Crash."

When the taxi pulled up at the curb, Crash leapt off Jace's lap to push his head against the window, tongue smashed against the glass.

"Take it easy, dude. You're hurt." Jace reached for the dog with no luck. He paid the taxi driver, and gathered the wiggling dog into his arms. When Crash saw his patch of grass, his body trembled. Jace bent down and gently placed him on the grass.

"Gotta go, huh?" He smiled down and Crash met his eyes, smiling his goofy canine grin back up at him.

"Hurry, dude. You're supposed to be resting."

Crash finished his 'business,' and trotted up the steps to the door. Jace shook his head.

How am I supposed to convince a dog to rest?

He reached up to run his hand through his hair, and opened the door.

"Go to bed, Crash. The doc says you need to rest."

Crash looked back over his shoulder at Jace as if contemplating his words, and trotted in, stopping to sniff at his toy basket. He gently nudged stuffies, rope toys, and balls aside with his nose, finally settling on an old stuffed teddy bear all the way at the bottom of the pile. He had long ago chewed off one ear, the bow, one leg, and removed the squeaker, but it remained a favorite. His soulful brown eyes met Jace's, and he walked to the couch and jumped up as if he'd never been injured, turning in one circle and then flopping down to lay his head on the teddy bear. His eyelids were heavy as he kept watch of his master.

"If I wasn't there, I wouldn't even believe you were hurt." He held up the circular dog cone. "And don't mess with your bandage, or you'll have to wear this."

But he *had* seen it. He shook his head as a flash of blood flowing and his pup's limp body seared through his brain. In his mind he saw an image of the macabre knife pointing skyward and his knees went weak. So much blood.

I'll never forget it. I wish I could find the man who did this...

"I'm getting a shower." Walking over, he reached down to scratch the dog behind the ears, his hand reaching under the collar just as Crash liked. A glimmer of sunlight reflected off the medallion that still hung around his dog's neck, flashing its satiny silver glow into the shadowy corner of the room. He gently rubbed a thumb over its smooth surface, and then let it drop as he turned toward the bathroom.

He pulled his blood-soaked t-shirt over his head and stopped to stuff it into the already-full trash on his way by. When he looked back over his shoulder, Crash was snoring.

Chapter 32

Below Research Vessel OA-23

Each kick of her flippers brought her closer to Baby. She angled her body so that she was swimming behind the great white and around the other side of the boat, hoping to get above the massive creature to attach the tracker.

When the shark glided around the other side, she paddled her legs in quick succession, propelling herself into position. She was still below and to the left of the boat, now looking down on the area she calculated Baby should come back around if she continued the swimming pattern she had been following since arriving there. She checked the tracker once more and waited in place, arm poised to release. Sofie could only hope that the great white had not grown bored and decided to move on.

C'mon, Baby. I'm not gonna hurt you. Where are you, beautiful?

Eyes wide and alert, afraid to blink, she scanned the area she expected to see the shark appear, taking in every minute detail. Tiny bubbles sent into motion by the current raced toward the sunlight. A lone sea robin, with its remarkable wide mouth and peculiarly large and spiny pectoral fins darted by; spooked by either her presence or that of the shark she sought. Tiny comb jellies floated as if one with the movement of the tide, oblivious to the scene playing out around them.

The water was churning, making distance visibility difficult from her position near the surface, and she lost sight of Yaz below her. Her heart beat a fierce drumbeat, in both anticipation and concern for her friend.

Breathe in. Breathe out. Breathe in. Breathe out.

Where is Baby? It's been too long. Damn it! She's moved on...

Yaz did not take her eyes off Sofiana. She knew she should be scanning the area for threats, but could not make herself look away. The girl had balls. It was both a blessing and a curse, and what made her excel in her field. It was also one of the reasons Yasmin admired and loved her so much.

She audibly growled into her mouthpiece, creating a muted sound in the surrounding waters, and admitted to herself that she would have done the same thing thirty years ago. It was only in recent months that her mortality had become real to her, and she'd started having bouts of anxiety while diving, though she'd kept that information to herself.

The irony was not lost on her. Two months ago, she'd learned of the rapidly spreading cancer that was even now slowly eating away at her own body. It had begun in her bladder, and moved on so that now her internal organs were overrun by disease. A little blood in her urine, and one doctor appointment later her lifeline was shorter than she'd ever anticipated. After seeing one more doctor and confirming the diagnosis with a second opinion, Yaz decided to live her life as normally as possible. She'd kept that to herself as well. Sofiana would insist she try the experimental treatments offered by the specialists she'd been referred to, but Yasmin wanted to live the rest of her life on her own terms—cancer be damned. And if today was her day, here in the depths of the sea, then she should be thankful that the cancer had not won. But it was not Sofie's time, of this she was sure. So she would fight for her girl.

From her position below, she could clearly see what Sofie could not. Baby was slowly circling back. Within minutes, she would be in the perfect position to dispense the tracker. If everything went according to plan, it would be done momentarily. At this stage in her life; however, she'd learned that it was rare for anything to go according to plan. Life, she mused, was a curious thing. And so was death.

Yaz realized she was holding her breath. A dangerous thing to do in the depths of the ocean. Forcing herself to breathe, she continued her vigil, unsure what she would do if something went wrong. She clutched the blade in her right hand until her knuckles hurt. Her legs kicked of their own accord, bringing her slightly closer to Sofie, but she immediately stopped the movement. It was best if she stayed out of the way.

The muted sound of her own scream was swallowed into the water as she saw the shark above suddenly pick up speed, change direction, and make a path directly toward Sofiana. She kicked her legs, knowing that she could never get there in time, and wondered what she could do even if she did.

Chapter 33

Brockton, MA

F lying on Route 6, fingers drumming on the steering wheel, Gray sped down the tree-lined road, the patchy pitch pines mixing with oaks in a shaded green blur in his peripheral vision. The towering, white metal of the majestic windmills spun in slow circles as he left the Cape, on his way further inland. The rotation of the blades made him smile, bringing to mind one of his favorite literary tales: *Don Quixote of the Mancha* by Miguel de Cervantes. The yellowed pages of his copy of the novel were jagged from so many reads. He clearly remembered his mother—a decendant of Spain who had immigrated to the United States as a young girl—handing him the novel with pride for his fifteenth birthday, dark eyes crinkling. She had recounted the story to him regularly as a child with emphatic hand gestures and almost comical voice inflections, and he'd fallen in love with Don Quixote and his clumsy horse, Rocinante, as any child would with Yesenia Fernandez Smith narrating the tale. She'd given him the book along with almost prophetic words written inside: *To remember me and your heritage when I'm gone.* Two weeks later, he'd lost her in a fatal car crash.

He squinted at the ever-spinning windmills shrinking in his rearview mirror. From this distance and at this angle, he could almost see how the propeller's moving arms might be mistaken for a monster's attack. Maybe Don Quixote hadn't been as mad as everyone thought.

Parking the Camaro at the curb, Grayson did not take the key out of the ignition when he reached his destination. He glanced around the quaint middle-class street, admiring the graying wood siding typical of houses built in the classic weathered style of the area. Trees lined each side of the road, forming a canopy of leaves and providing welcoming shade. The shuttered houses were well tended; walkways lined with blooming hibiscus, scattered sprinklers watering lawns so that they almost glowed green, and not a weed in sight. Even the streets were swept clean.

So, this is where the Johnsons live. It fits them.

Three words immediately popped to mind: *Cozy. Welcoming. Home.*

He palmed the key, stepped out, and twisted his body to one side and then the other, then reached up to squeeze the muscles that had bunched at his neck with his head bent back. Reaching into his back pocket, he withdrew his phone and brought up his contact list. Without thinking his fingers scrolled down, stopping at one name. Just three letters. How could three letters cause such a stir in his blood?

Sof.

His thumb hovered over the call button for just a second before he shoved the phone back into his pocket. He hung his head and huffed out a breath.

She doesn't want you, man. She made that crystal clear when she walked away without a backward glance.

Running his hand through his already tousled hair, he slammed the car door and stomped up the stone pathway. There were more important things to worry about right now than Sofiana Stone.

When he reached the porch, he rapped three times on the red wooden door, and glanced around. The brown wicker sofa and matching chair were adorned with burgundy seat cushions, and the ceramic pots containing plants that added bursts of green to every corner were painted in the same hues. Petunias in a mix of various vibrant colors were scattered along the front of the house, and a seagull wind chime, probably purchased while vacationing in the Cape, tinkled soothingly in the breeze. The house screamed of coziness and care.

After a minute with no answer, Grayson leaned forward and rang the doorbell, then stood back to wait again. He took out his cell phone and scanned his email, and leaned on the railing.

"Grayson!" Mike came around from the side of the house, and reached a hand out as he climbed the steps. He was wearing an apron that read 'Grill Master'.

"Hey. Thanks for inviting me." Grayson smiled.

"Glad you could make it! Come, come. We're around back."

Grayson pumped his hand once, then followed Mike around the back of the house, past hydrangea bushes, black-eyed susans, and more splashes of light pink and violet colored petunias planted and perfectly spaced in the mulched beds alongside the house.

In all of his adult years, there had been only one woman who had made him want this kind of life. He shook his head and gritted his teeth. *Why do I keep thinking about her? I don't even care anymore. At least, I didn't think I did....* Forcing himself back to the present he slapped Mike on the back, mentally shaking himself. Between memories of his mother and thoughts of Sofiana, an air of melancholy seemed to hover just overhead.

Rounding his shoulders, Gray nodded, pushing his inner musings aside. "Thanks for having me, Mike. How's Maggie Lee doing?"

"Gray, you won't believe it. I'm not going to say anything. I want you to see for yourself."

Grayson tilted his head. "Okay. As I mentioned on the phone, there's something else I want to talk to both of you about, after dinner. It's important."

"Sure, Gray."

They came around the corner and found the woman in question standing with her back to them, holding out a hose to feed even more flowers under the oak tree. Her hair was pulled into a messy ponytail that stuck out the back of her navy blue baseball cap creating a poof of curls, and she turned when they approached. A smile bloomed across her face, and she dropped the hose and hurried to where Grayson had stopped in place upon seeing her for the first time since he'd seen her in the hospital.

If he hadn't witnessed the change for himself, he would never have believed it. The first thing he noticed was the wrinkles. Or more accurately, the lack of them. During all the days he had stood with Mike in her hospital room while she had been in the coma, he had inevitably noticed the laugh lines around her eyes, creased forehead, and the slight sag of skin at her neck. Gone now. At present, she had tight, smooth skin replacing the old. Her hands had a youthful glow, too. No more loose skin surrounding her knuckles. For the first time in as long as he could remember, Gray was speechless. It was the same woman—only it wasn't.

"Uh..."

"Grayson! I'm so glad you came!" She stopped within a foot of him, grasped his forearms in both of hers, and went up on tiptoe to peck his cheek. Taking a step back, she continued, "I want to thank you. Mike told me how much you helped him when I couldn't. I don't know how to thank you."

Gray struggled for words. "Um. Well, I *am* writing a story about everything. He told you that part, right?"

"Yes. But you did more than research. You were a friend when Mike needed one. I don't believe for one minute it was just for a story. Now, what can I get you? A soda? Water? Beer?"

"I'll have a beer. Please." He watched as she bounced away disappearing into the kitchen, and then looked at Mike. "What the hell?"

"I know. I wanted you to see for yourself, to make sure I'm not crazy. She looks like she did when we were in our thirties. I'm a cradle-robber. A woman in the grocery store asked if she was my daughter yesterday."

"I don't understand. How is this possible? She was so sick in the hospital, she should still be recovering. Instead she's thriving..."

"I know. I know, and I'm so thankful. Truth is, it scares me, too. The doctors are baffled at her fast recovery, and so am I. But apart from her looks, she is the same Maggie as ever. Well, except..."

"Don't stop now. Except what?"

Face pinkening, Mike blurted, "Well, except in

the bedroom, if you know what I mean. I can't keep up. And..."

Gray chuckled. "And?"

"She keeps that silly trinket with her everywhere she goes. Even sleeps with it. It's starting to concern me."

"Does she have it with her now?" Grayson frowned.

He nodded, "In her pocket. I'm telling you, she *always* has it." Mike cleared his throat and continued, "You're gonna think I'm crazy, but I wonder if that thing has anything to do with her recovery."

Gray's eyes widened. "That thing? What? You mean the trinket?"

"Yes, the blasted trinket! I'm beginning to dislike that thing."

"Mike, how could a small trinket have anything to do with her recovery? It's an inanimate object."

"Logically, I know it doesn't. I know. But *think* about it. She started getting better after you brought the trinket back, remember?"

"Just a coincidence, I'm sure." He tilted his head, his teeth absently nibbling his bottom lip.

Maggie Lee returned with two beer cans and a soda, and handed one to Grayson and one to Mike. "Cheers!" She held her can up to clink against theirs.

After a sip, she said, "What are you guys so serious about all of a sudden? What did I miss?"

The two men made eye contact, and Mike nodded. "We were talking about you, babe."

"Oh? Good things, I hope?" Her laugh cut-off when she caught their somber expressions. "What's going on, guys?"

Grayson cleared his throat, "I was surprised at how different you look. You've had a very fast recovery. Do you know how hurt you were just a week ago?"

"Yes, it's a miracle, isn't it? I'm one lucky woman." She smiled.

Mike chimed in, "Mag, we were also talking about your appearance. You look younger than you did when you went into the hospital. Haven't you noticed?"

She shrugged, hands splayed in front of her. "Well, I feel younger, too. So?"

"Don't you think that's odd?" Mike asked.

"Odd? No, not odd. Just lucky." Maggie smiled. "Every girl's dream is to look younger than she is."

Mike's voice cracked. "I'm the lucky one, babe. I almost lost you. I don't know what I would've done..."

Maggie Lee reached for Mike's hand, and rubbed her thumb over his palm, her eyes welling with unshed tears. "I'm here, babe. I'm here. Always."

Grayson cleared his throat. "Maggie?"

Her head turned, looking from her husband to him. "Yes?"

"Do you think it's possible that the trinket helped you heal quicker?"

"My trinket? Helped me heal? No. That's ridiculous."

Mike interrupted. "Your health only started improving when I put that trinket in your hand."

"Coincidence? How can a trinket heal someone?" She frowned.

"Good question. I don't have the answer. Maybe we could try an experiment?"

"What kind of experiment?"

"Let's see if it works for someone else." Gray

reached into his pocket and took out his key ring. His multi-purpose knife was on a keychain on the ring, and he pulled up the pocketknife and sliced into his finger. A bloom of red appeared almost immediately forming a line of crimson. "May I hold your trinket? Let's see if it has healing powers."

She looked from one man to the other, shook her head, and took the trinket out of her pocket. Holding onto it for longer than was necessary, she hesitantly held her hand out to him, a frown creasing her forehead.

Grayson took the trinket and placed it directly on his fresh wound.

And they waited.

Chasing windmills, Gray thought, though he couldn't seem to stop his heart from picking up its beat in anticipation.

Chapter 34

Caring House Retirement Community

"**S**orry, Dad. I was going to bring this to you yesterday, but I got called in to work to cover the late shift. We found your good luck charm."

Bob inhaled sharply, "My good luck charm? You found it?"

"Yes, I have it right here." Kyle pulled the charm out of his pocket and gently placed it in his father's outstretched hand. The look of awe on his face had Kyle's lips turning up. Dementia sometimes elicited extraordinarily youthful reactions.

It's like we've switched roles. He's the child and Kev and I are the parents now.

Kevin placed a hand on his father's shoulder, and nodded at Kyle.

Bob couldn't wait for his sons to leave. He clutched his long absent good luck charm to his heart. Oh, how he had missed the small keepsake. Though he couldn't explain it, he felt whole again for the first time in years.

"What do you have there, Bob?" Called Arthur in his too-loud voice from his side of the room.

Like fingernails on a chalkboard, Bob flinched. "Nothing. It's none of your concern."

"It looks shiny. Is it a necklace? I didn't take you for the jewelry type."

"No. It's nothing." Bob grumbled as he rolled onto his good side, hugging the smooth object to his chest. He closed his eyes, and his face relaxed into the first true smile he'd had in a long time. He drifted off to sleep feeling...hopeful.

Within minutes, the good luck charm became warm against his palm, taking on a red tint that reflected off the white sheets onto his skin. The welcoming heat began traveling through his body, warming him from the inside out.

He sighed in his sleep, still smiling.

Chapter 35

Barnstable, Massachusetts

W hen the alarm blared its siren sound, Jace jerked awake with his heart pounding. He moaned and squinted at the clock, trying to make sense of the blurry numbers. Five o'clock. Time for dinner. His stomach rumbled in anticipation, and he became aware of a tremendous pressure in his bladder. He stretched, yawned, and looked toward the window. There was only a faint muted glow coming through the gray curtains. *Why is it so dark this early in the evening?*

He remembered showering upon his return home with Crash; the blood washing off his body in a mesmerizing crimson swirl as it circled the drain. He'd eaten a peanut butter sandwich, and had fallen into bed to let the physical and mental exhaustion take over his body. He squinted again at the clock. Five-oh-two.

Wait. Is it 5:02...AM? Morning? Have I been asleep for...fifteen hours? Oh no! Crash!

Throwing back the covers, he leaped out of bed and stumbled toward the other room calling, "Crash?" The dog met him halfway, tail wagging, a happy grin on his face.

"Are you okay, dude? I'm sorry I slept so long. Why didn't you wake me up?" Bending to scratch the dog under the collar, Crash sat and reached up to place his paw on Jace's bicep. The movement caused the silver medallion to brush against the skin of his bare arm, its metallic smoothness cool to the touch. Goosebumps formed and traveled upward, causing a shiver.

Strange. What is this thing? It was warm at the vet's office, and now it's cold again...

Jace shook his head and stood up, bee-lining for the bathroom. Nothing really mattered except that Crash was healthy and home with him once again.

When he entered the second room in his apartment, which consisted of a combination kitchen/living room, his feet stopped moving and his eyes widened. All of the toys from Crash's toy basket were lined up in a neat row on the couch, and the television was turned on to the Children's Network. A football, a rope toy, the teddy bear, a stuffed bunny, a marrowbone.

I don't remember turning the TV on...Crash must have bumped the remote.

Satisfied, he moved further into the room.

Chuckling under his breath, he reached for Crash's lead, snapped it on, and lumbered out the front door to let the pup relieve himself. While he waited, he pulled his phone from his pocket, scrolled, and hit the call button.

"Hi, Brock? It's Jace Calhoun. I might be just a bit late for work today, if that's okay. I'm supposed to start at 5:30 today."

"How late?" His boss's brisk voice barked.

"Maybe 30 minutes? My dog was stabbed, and he

had emergency surgery. He's back home, but I overslept and I don't want him to be alone for long. I want to talk to my neighbor before I leave and see if she'll check in on him today, if that's okay."

"What? Did you say stabbed? By who?" Jace held the phone away as Brock's booming voice bellowed through the airways.

"I-I don't know. It was some guy on the beach."

"So the guy just got away with it? That's awful. You should call the cops, too. Take an extra hour; we're not busy this early anyway. Or take the day off. It's your choice. Your dog's okay?"

"Yes. I'll be in. I-I need the money to pay for the surgery. And I'll volunteer f-for any overtime you have coming up. Thanks." Jace pressed the end button, and stuffed his phone back into his pocket, blowing out a breath.

Guess I'll have to put gaming on hold for a while.

When his head came up, he saw that Crash had finished and was staring up at him with his head cocked. Upon making eye contact, the dog stood up and pulled on the leash, but instead of heading toward his own door, he veered to the left and sat down in front of the neighbor's door. Looking up once again, he wagged his tail, then turned back to stare at the door.

"Why are you...?" Jace's eyebrows shot up. "Did you hear me on the phone?"

The dog's tongue hung out of his mouth sideways as he panted.

Jace laughed out loud. "That's crazy. Of course you can't understand me. You're a dog. A recovering dog. You must be confused from the surgery." Shaking his head, he knocked on the door.

Shoulders slumped a little lower; his breathing came in quick spurts...much like his dog. He twisted the leash around his fingers until it wound around several times and the tips of his fingers began to turn red. He barely noticed.

Jace did not make a habit of socializing with his neighbors. In fact, he had never actually spoken to the girl who lived next door, and wasn't even sure of her name. *Candy? Sandy?* It was no use wishing now that he had.

The downfall of an introvert.

While disentangling his fingers from the lead, the door jerked open.

"I don't want to buy anything." She declared. Her short bushy hair was a tangle of hot pink with black roots sticking out from her face, and her slightly slanted sea green eyes—unadorned by make-up—squinted sleepily at him.

Jace's eyes darted immediately downward as he whispered, "Um...no. I'm not..."

"What do you want, then?"

"Uh. I wondered if..."

"Spit it out, I don't have all day." She leaned on the doorframe. "Hello? I'm up here." She said as she pointed with two fingers at her eyes.

Jace forced his eyes up and struggled not to look away. *Just ask, moron!* He took one more deep breath, hastily blurting, "Can you check on my dog today? I have to work, and he just had surgery. I'm worried he'll hurt himself again. I live right there." He punctuated by pointing toward his door.

"Well, why didn't you just say that in the first place?" She squatted and addressed Crash, "What happened, sweetie? Did you get neutered?" Rubbing his sides, she looked up at Jace. "So? What did happen? Are you gonna tell me or is the dog?"

His face pinkened. "He was stabbed."

"What? Oh, poor baby, did someone stab this cute little baby? How could anyone do that to someone as handsome as...?" Eyebrow raised, she cocked her head.

"Crash. His name's Crash."

"Crash? How could anyone do that to poor Crashy-crash-crash?"

The dog's tail thumped excitedly on the doormat, and he looked at his new friend with adoring eyes.

"Fine. But he'll need to stay with me in my apartment. I work nights, you know? So I need to sleep. Bring over some food and stuff, and I'll watch him today. Just leave it out here. But don't get used to it, okay?" She took the leash from Jace's hands, and pulled the more-than-willing Crash into her apartment. The dog looked back over his shoulder with an enthusiastic canine grin as the door slammed in Jace's face.

He shook his head. Taking a deep breath, Jace took the few steps to reach his own door. As he turned the knob, his head snapped up.

I still don't know her name.

Chapter 36

Below Research Vessel OA-23

Baby came speeding out of the murk, violently brushing against Sofie's midsection and sending her deeper into the water before darting away. She was now once again below the shark, which swam in a frenzied circle around her and the boat. Clutching the spear in her fist, her head swiveled left and right as she tried to get her bearings. She thought she heard a far-off muffled scream, and tried to locate the source, a nearly impossible feat while caged in by bubbles. It was hard to know which way was up while trapped beneath the waves.

The bubbles! Which way are they moving? That way!
She kicked her legs to follow the bubbles.
Yaz! Where is she? And where is Baby now?
The first sliver of fear burst through her in an explosion of numbness that traveled down her limbs. She remained in control. Sofiana scanned the murky water, eyes sharp and spear at the ready. When Baby shot toward her this time, she was prepared. Or at least thought she was. The blinding white abyss of the great white's gaping mouth, surrounded by those nightmarish jagged teeth, was heading straight for her. Her legs

scissored in bursts, but she knew that no amount of kicking could be fast enough to escape the jaws of the enormous animal down here in the water. Her heart racing, she held her breath and braced for the attack, her hand fisting in the split second before impact. She would not go quietly.

∞∞∞

Yaz watched from below, raw panic taking root in every pore of her body. Eyes wild, she kicked her legs toward the scene unfolding above her. Helplessness was her lone companion as she kicked futilely toward Sofie. *No! Not Sofie! Not my baby girl!* The intense under-water silence was shattered by her muffled scream, the sound swallowed into the depths of the yawning sea.

She watched with horror-filled eyes as Baby took Sofie's midsection into her mouth and continued swimming, carrying her girl along.

Why? Why Sofie? Why not me? I'm already a dead woman. Sofie has so much to live for...

Just then, in her peripheral vision, a movement caught her attention, and she tore her eyes away from the place where Sofie and the shark had disappeared. Her breathing ceased as her wide eyes beheld the crea-ture rising from the murk before her. Yaz froze in place, not daring to blink. When the enormous beast began swimming in the direction where her girl had disap-peared, her legs began moving. She frantically kicked toward the light, surfacing next to the boat. Tearing her mouthpiece out, she screamed hysterically, "Call the Coast Guard! Christian, go! Get on the radio now!

The shark has Sofiana! And there's something else down there! They went that way. Pull the anchor. Go, go, go!"

Pushed by adrenaline, Yaz nearly leaped into the boat, shedding her gear faster than seemed possible, and took the wheel. "She had the tracker. We can track them. Let's find her!"

Pushing the boat to full throttle, she followed the red blinking light on the screen as if it was her lifeline, recurrently muttering a desperate prayer for help. Her frantic mind warred with her rational side, arguing against what she knew must be true.

Sofie is not dead. She's gon' be fine, dat girl. I jus' know it.

Chapter 37

Brockton, Massachusetts

Grayson, Maggie Lee, and Mike leaned forward in unison, three pairs of eyes focused solely on Gray's hand. The seconds ticked by in silence, each lost in their own thoughts.

"I don't think anything is happening. It just feels cold," Grayson whispered, as if any noise might interrupt the healing process.

Mike responded, "Maybe it takes more time, Gray."

On a nervous giggle, Maggie Lee wheezed, "Or maybe it's just a trinket." She looked up, eyes darting between both men, "We must be crazy, thinking this thing has the power to heal. Can you imagine?"

"Well, in any case, I don't think it requires all of us staring at it. Go ahead and prepare dinner. I'll keep holding it a while longer, in case." Gray gestured toward the grill.

"Oh! My ribs!" Mike rushed over to check on his specialty. They had been cooking on low for hours now, and he didn't want to them ruined because of a distraction.

"Mike makes the best ribs in Massachusetts,

Grayson. You're in for a treat." Maggie winked.

"Can't wait. I usually just eat toast or cereal. Or take-out. It's easier."

"That sounds awful, Grayson! We're going to start having you for dinner more often. And you're not going home without leftovers to heat up. You're family now," Maggie Lee exclaimed.

Grayson swallowed back the lump that had formed in his throat. "That's...Thank you. I don't know what to say. I don't have much family left. I...appreciate it."

When dinner was ready, they sat around the circular glass table edged with cast iron filigree on the brick patio as the sun sank lower in the west creating a picturesque fuchsia-tinted sky above. They talked about mundane things—the weather, the food, work. All the while, Grayson clutched the little metal-like trinket against his wound.

Gray pushed his plate back, sighing in pleasure. "That's the best meal I've had in a very long time. Thank you."

"You're very welcome, Grayson. And I meant what I said. You are welcome in our house anytime, son." The irony of the youthful woman in front of him calling him son had the corners of his mouth lifting. And yet, the warmth of her personality did remind him of his own mother. Yesenia Smith would get along fabulously with Maggie Lee. His smile grew.

Right now, she looks more like she could be my sister, not my mother.

His smile faded as he remembered what he'd come here to tell them. "I wanted to talk to you both about something." He met their eyes for emphasis. "It's important. A body was found, washed up on Nauset beach. It hasn't been identified, but the male victim died of multiple gunshot wounds."

"That's such a shame! That poor man!" Maggie's eyes filled.

"That's not all. Remember, the car that hit Maggie Lee was found with bullet holes in it." Gray paused to let his words sink in. "I think the two things might be related."

Mike inhaled sharply, "You think the dead man is the one who hit my Maggie?"

Grayson nodded. "I think it's a strong possibility. And another thing, Detective Gold called to tip me off about the body. *Before* anyone else was tipped off about it. But when I tried to call him back, no one could find him. The police in the area don't know of any Detective Gold."

"So, what you're saying is..." Maggie Lee's eyes widened, "Detective Gold isn't an officer? Well. Then who is he? And why did he give you the trinket to give to me? And for that matter, where on Earth did he get it in the first place?"

"Those are very good questions, Maggie. I don't know the answers." Grayson shrugged.

Maggie and Mike looked at each other. "What does this mean?"

Grayson paused, his brow furrowed. "I'm not sure. I just know that you could be in danger. Is this Gold, if that's even his real name, a friend or a foe? He seems to want to help us, but I suspect he may have been the one to get rid of our hit and run driver, so that means he's capable of murder. I want you both to be careful, and be aware of your surroundings. Don't trust anyone. Maybe don't do anything that puts you in a position of being alone..."

"This is crazy. Why would anyone want to hurt us?" Maggie asked.

"It is crazy. All of it. The fact remains, someone *did* hurt you, Maggie Lee. None of it makes sense, but it happened. And you said yourself, it wasn't an accident," said Grayson.

She got up to pace, shaking her head as she worked it out. "Okay, so the first thing we need to do is get permission to look at the body. I remember what he looked like. I can identify him if he's the one who hit me. Then we'll know for sure."

"Maggie, do you think that's a good idea? If he's been in the water a long time, he may be...unrecognizable." Mike stood and placed a hand on her arm to soften his words.

"I think I have to. There's really no choice here."

"I think it's a good idea. At the very least it's a good starting point." As Grayson pushed his chair back, he realized he was still clutching the trinket in his hand. He held his hand in the air. Three pairs of eyes focused intently on his finger at once.

He carefully reached over to clasp the trinket in his other hand, and pulled it away from his injured finger. The cut was unchanged, a perfect line of red still sliced across his finger.

Nervous laughter filled the yard, "Well, at least we know that the trinket is just a trinket. Not a superhero healing machine. Although if it did have the power to heal, it would have explained why people are willing to kill for it."

Chapter 38

Caring House Retirement Community

Bob sat in the rocking chair in his room, back ram-rod straight, slowly rocking as he faced the window. The chair squeaked a *crick-crack* sound each time he rocked back and forth. It was soothing in its monotony, and Bob's legs continued pushing off the floor of their own accord. The pale glow of the newly risen moon cast an unearthly glow on his face, the corners of his mouth turned down.

Though by all outward appearances he seemed to be staring at the view of the painted evening sky laid out in front of him, in reality he looked with un-seeing eyes at the breath-taking sight. He was living in a world of his own creation, re-living his entire life in his mind's eye. Through a tunnel, he saw only the past. The beautiful, heartbreaking past. His breath hitched on a sigh.

Bits and pieces of bygone memories were coming back to him, like parts of a puzzle suddenly fitting into place. Though he did not have all the pieces yet, hour by hour, minute by minute, even second by second, more pieces became clear to him, as they hadn't been in so long. The blurry edges began creeping away, leaving behind moments of semi-clarity. The memories took on a sequence and a meaning, as they hadn't before in his tattered mind, and now linked together in a way that began to make sense to him.

Glancing across the room, he nodded. His roommate had given up on conversation hours ago, though sometimes he did enjoy talking to himself. The quiet, it seemed, was too much for Arthur. Right now, he was snoring in his bed, loud enough that the people in the room next door could likely hear him.

Bob glanced down at his fisted hand, a faint rosy glow escaping the cracks turned the surrounding skin pink. The good luck charm.

My good luck charm.

It was both a blessing, and a curse. His feelings were so jumbled he wasn't sure how to feel. Maybe living in the dark place he'd been was better than the knowing. Maybe, he should toss the good luck charm in the trashcan and let the fog consume him once again.

Instead, he clutched the small good luck piece tighter in his fist. Rising, he clumsily made his way to the bed and fell into it, sending a jarring pain through his injured hip. And still, he struggled to adjust the covers over his prone body with sweat beading on his forehead and under his arms. He *needed* to pull the covers up, despite the warmth emanating from his body.

I don't want anyone to see my good luck charm. Best to hide it under the blanket.

Bob closed his eyes, and sank into the abyss of memories that snuck in through the windows of his timeworn brain.

He slept. And while he slept, his charm continued its arduous work.

Chapter 39

Barnstable Farmer's Market

J ace shook his head, baffled by the show of support.
We're only co-workers, and they've all gone out of their way to help. He stared at his scuffed sneakers. *Would I have done the same for them?*

He swallowed the knot that had formed in his throat, whispering, "Thank you. Really. Just...thanks."

There was a small gathering in the break room, all of them coming together to help him. To help Crash. His face a blotchy crimson, the direct result of all the attention, his breath hitched when his boss pounded on his back.

"When you told me what happened, I knew I had to do something. Setting up a Go Fund Me account was easy. All of us have decided to make a small contribution to get it started. I'll just have to talk to you about how much you need, and we'll finalize it. And we're going to take up a collection at the registers, too. Working overtime is great, but that could take forever to pay off the vet bill," Brock slapped Jace's back once more.

"Thanks. Thanks. I'm...thanks," Jace whispered. Red hives traveled down his neck.

Brock continued, "I think we should call the

media, too. This will be perfect advertisement for the store. Oh, and as a side benefit maybe you'll catch the guy who did this."

"Uh, I don't know..." Jace mumbled.

"This is the kind of story people love, Jace. I can see it now," Brock said, clapping his hands together with one echoing *crack*. "We'll put a picture of your mutt with the collection box. People will eat that up."

"Um..."

"Do you have a picture of...what's your dog's name? We'll put that on the sign, makes it more personal," Brock cocked his head, waiting.

"C-Crash."

Brock grinned. "Ha! Love it! Do you have a picture of Crash?"

"Um. Just on my phone," Jace said.

"That'll do. Send it to me, okay? I'll take care of everything." Brock walked into his office and closed the door.

Jace stood and stared at the closed, paint-chipped door. He focused on the part at the bottom, where you could see the old blue paint bleeding through the white, and in some parts even bare wood showed through. Little black smudges were scattered at foot level, left from whatever had rubbed against it in the past. For a minute, he didn't move. Just stared.

What just happened? He slowly shook his head side to side. *I hope he doesn't think I'm going on the news. I can't do that. I won't.*

A tremor started in his legs and traveled up through his body. A thumping took root in his brain, and continued its incessant pounding through his entire shift. His hand shook as he mindlessly pushed produce over the scanner, counting down the minutes until he could get out of there.

I'd rather work to pay the vet bill for the rest of my life than be interviewed on TV.

At the end of his workday, he clocked out, more than ready to escape the attention he was receiving from everyone around him. Brock stopped him on his way out the door, and he looked back over his shoulder with one hand frozen on the door.

"Hey, Jace! Send me that picture, okay?" He called across the aisle.

Jace shook his head, took out his phone, scrolled, clicked, and hit the 'send' button.

"Got it! Thanks!" He barked out a laugh. "Hey, did anyone ever tell you that your dog looks like you?" His laughter faded as he turned and walked toward the back of the store.

Hunching his shoulders, he pushed out the door and stuffed his hands deep into his pockets.

Home.

Taking a deep breath of salty air, he hustled all the way there, as if something dark was at his heels. He thrust the key in the lock, opened the door, and when he was met with only quiet, remembered Crash was next door. Sighing, he turned to rap on the door adjacent to his.

More socializing. I just want to shut the door in my apartment and never open it again...

The door was yanked open. "Oh. Hi." She turned to look over her shoulder and called, "Crash! Daddy's home!"

The dog bounded out the door and jumped up, placing his paws on Jace's midsection, his tail whipping side to side. When Jace bent down, Crash licked his face with happy flicks of his tongue, and then he jumped down and ran to the girl—he still didn't know her name —repeating the same with her.

Traitor.

"Come on, Crash." He forced his eyes to meet hers. "Thanks."

"No problem." She said. "He was good. Doesn't really seem like he's injured though, you know? He's a happy guy. If you want to bring him over sometimes to visit…you know, I wouldn't mind. I can't afford a dog of my own, so I could maybe borrow him?" The girl talked faster than a hurricane.

"Sure. He likes you." Once again, Jace's face filled with color.

"Well, okay. Great! I'll watch him while you're at work, then? We'll be like a divorced mom and dad sharing the kid." She smiled, and his heart stuttered.

"Um…every day?" Jace asked, eyes wide.

"Why not? Bye! See ya tomorrow, Crash-kins." She threw the dog a kiss and slammed the door in his master's face.

Jace took one involuntary step back, reaching up to scratch his head.

A divorced mom and dad? What is she talking about?

For the third time in the same day, Jace was left staring at a closed door.

Will this day ever end? How is all this happening?

All at once, his life seemed to be spiraling out of his control. Decisions were being made that affected him and his solitary existence, and he seemed to have no say in the matter. The people around him were taking over his life. A moan escaped.

He and his dog entered their own apartment, and when he closed the door, he latched both locks, shoulders rising on a long sigh. Here, at least, he had control.

Looking at Crash, he said, "Well? Do *you* know her name?"

Crash's head nodded as if to say 'Yes'.

He laughed out loud for the first time all day, wheezing, "At least one of us does."

Heading toward the kitchen, he got out a bowl and poured cereal into it. As he was spooning cereal into his mouth, he caught Crash in his peripheral vision moving back and forth in a frenzy. Taking the bowl to the sink, he walked into the living room, really just the other side of the room, and put his hands on his hips.

"Dude, what'cha doing?"

The dog ignored him, continuing his task with frenzied movements. Urgency had gripped the animal, and Jace stood back to watch. He had his bone, rope toy, a pencil, and the remote, all placed on the floor in perfect perpendicular adjoining lines. When he finished he looked up at Jace and yipped, tail wagging across the floor as he sat, almost regally.

"What, dude? What did you do here? Pretty proud of yourself, aren't you?" Jace laughed.

"Yip." The dog answered.

"Okay, you want something from me. What is it? Do you have to pee?"

"Grr." Crash lay down and covered his eyes with his front paws, then jumped up again. He placed a paw on top of his creation, and yipped again.

"Okay. Let me see." Jace walked closer, staring at the floor. The objects Crash had arranged on the floor looked familiar. They were placed in the shape of a perfect letter 'T'.

"T?"

Crash leaped onto Jace and licked his face, his body wiggling in triumph.

"Wait. It's a T? You made the letter T?"

OMG. He chuckled to himself. *That's impossible. Dogs don't know the alphabet. It's been a long day.*

He shook his head and went to change out of work clothes. When he emerged, more objects were placed on the floor.

"What the...?" He whispered.

Holy shit.

Chapter 40

*Deep in the Ocean, Somewhere Off the
Coast of Chatham, Massachusetts*

Numbness.

Sofie felt no pain. She let her body go limp, knowing that if she struggled now, she would only help the razor-sharp teeth take deeper purchase in her flesh. Baby was swimming at a brisk pace. So fast, she had to close her eyes to stop the disorienting nausea that bloomed in her gut.

I'm dying. I can't feel anything. This must be the end.

She considered for a moment removing her mouthpiece to speed the process.

Better to drown than be ripped apart and eaten alive in the middle of the ocean.

Though she was a steadfast marine-life conservationist, she was also a realist and knew that once blood infiltrated the water, all manner of predators would arrive to partake of an easy meal. Even if Baby left her alive, and that was a big 'if,' something else would come along to finish the job. Her scientist's brain could manufacture a regrettably realistic picture of what would happen.

I don't want to die. Her eyes snapped open. *What*

are my choices? Think!

When the shark had first taken her, she'd tried everything she knew to do. Pummeling at the eyes, using the spear. No result except the feel of daggers slicing into her midsection.

Why is Baby swimming so fast? This is not typical great white behavior. She hasn't eaten me...yet. This is no exploratory bite. It's like she wants to take me somewhere.

Her frantic inner dialogue continued. *That's ridiculous, Sofiana! Sharks aren't that smart! You've probably lost too much blood to think rationally...*

Just then, the shark picked up speed, its mouth tightening just a fraction as it held her almost gently in its jaws. Sofie bit into her mouthpiece as the pressure increased, her eyes going wide before she squeezed them closed again as she braced for the fatal bite. She saw the glint of silver in the mouth of the shark just before her eyes closed. Tiny points of light danced behind her lids.

Ironically, her last thought before the blackness claimed her was of him.

Grayson! I'm sorry. I wish I could see you just one more time to tell you...

Chapter 41

Cape Cod Morgue

"**A**re you sure about this, Maggie Lee?" Grayson asked one more time.

"Yes. I'm sure. I was sure the first time you asked me, and all the times in between. I need to do this." She gently squeezed his arm as she looked at him sideways from the passenger seat. Turning to gaze out the window, she whispered, "I can see his face as clearly as I can see yours. It haunts my days...and nights. I know this is a very non-Christian thing to say, but I'll be glad if he's no longer on this Earth."

Gray stared at her. *Is it possible she looks even younger than the last time I saw her?*

Mike sat with his arms crossed in the back seat and grumbled, "Well, I'm not. I still don't think it's a good idea, Mag."

"I know that too, Babe, and I'm sorry. But I have to do this."

The subsequent silence that filled the car was broken only by the *click-click-click* of the turn signal as Grayson turned into the small deserted parking lot.

"I called in a favor to set this up. I hope it's the right decision," he said, looking her in the eye. "The medical examiner thinks you're searching for your lost son, and that you want to look at the body to make sure it isn't him."

"No problem. It's like we're undercover cops." She stopped short when she took in their somber expressions, chiding, "Will you two stop worrying about me? I'll be fine. You'd think I was some weakling or something. I'm tough. I work with children. Believe me, I've seen it all." With that, she flung open her car door and stomped into the street, shoulders squared.

Grayson's brows furrowed as his eyes found Mike's, before unfolding his own body out of the car and following in her shadow toward the door.

"Let me go first. He knows me. This is not generally the way they do this kind of thing around here. He's doing me a favor."

Stepping inside, his eyes scanned the small, barren office, taking in the metal folding chairs and the hand-me-down desk. A light blinked on the desk phone, and unfiled folders were stacked unevenly next to it. The radiant afternoon light bursting through the uncovered windows seemed an oxymoron in its cheeriness.

"Hello? Zeke?" Grayson called down the narrow hallway.

A short, blocky man ambled into the room, wiping his hands on a paper towel. "Grayson? Is that you?" His glasses rested on top of his head, covering the sparse wisps of white hair that remained. "Time got away from me."

"Hi, Zeke. Thanks for doing this for me." He held his hand out for a shake.

"Well, I do want to help anyone who has to go

through the pain of a missing family member." His eyes cut to the Johnsons. "I'm Zeke Barns. My son went missing thirty years ago. Believe me, I know your pain." He cleared his throat. "I hope you get some answers today."

Maggie Lee's eyes welled with genuine tears, her voice cracking as she answered, "Thank you. I'm Maggie Lee, and this is my husband Mike. May I ask what happened with your son? Did you find him?"

Zeke stilled, giving a barely perceptible negative shake of his head. "Still missing. Follow me, this way."

Maggie's eyes dropped, and the color drained from her face. "I'm so sorry."

He turned and began walking, not acknowledging her response.

They followed him down a sterile hallway, and Grayson breathed through his mouth as the smell of formaldehyde mixing with a variety of other chemicals burned his nostrils. From the corner of his eye, he saw Maggie Lee reach up to cover her nose.

Stopping at a metal door, Zeke turned. "The man in this room was in the water for probably a day or two at most. Even so, the water takes its toll. I did my best to make him...presentable. You ready?" He said as he turned the doorknob. "I'll be just down the hall. Take as long as you want."

"Yes," Maggie murmured, straightening her back before stepping into the room. "I'm ready."

Gray watched as Mike wrapped his arm around his wife. In response, she leaned slightly into him. Then his eyes traveled to the body on the table in front of him. The ocean had not been kind to this man.

The pale face was waterlogged and puffy, devoid of any expression. Grayson might have believed they were standing in a wax museum admiring the sculptor's work had he not known what was in front of them had been a living, breathing, man mere days before. Whatever emotion this man had felt in his last moment of life was forever erased from his now-sagging face. The tip of his nose was missing, nibbled off by all manner of tiny sea predators no doubt, and though Zeke had done his best to cover it with make-up, Gray's imagination could readily supply the details. The body was covered by an olive green army-style blanket from the neck down.

I wonder what other parts of him are missing?

His morbid thoughts were interrupted when Maggie Lee whispered, "It's him." She turned to leave the room and everyone followed.

"How can you be sure, Babe? He...doesn't look good."

"I remember everything about that man. I can see him clearly. I can't explain it, but I remember every last detail of that man's face," she replied as she stared unseeing at the ocean mural picture on the wall. "Odd, since I only saw him for a second before he hit me. I can see him in my mind as clearly as I can see you."

She continued, "The three wrinkles on his brow, the mole on his chin, his widow's peak hairline, the shape of his eyebrows..." She turned to meet each of their eyes.

"It's him. I'm absolutely positive."

Chapter 42

Caring House Retirement Community

"Hi, I'd like to speak to Kevin Green please?" Sandy twisted her hair around and around her finger. The tapping of her foot seemed to echo in the small office.

"Speaking."

"Hi Mr. Green, this is Sandy from Caring House Retirement Community? Your father's nurse?"

"Yes, hi Sandy. Please, call me Kevin. Is everything okay?"

"I'm afraid not, Kevin. Would it be possible for you to come in for a visit today?"

"Um...yes. Yes, I think I can make that happen. What's wrong?"

"Your father wants to leave."

Kevin's sigh followed by a light-hearted chuckle could be heard through the phone line. "That's nothing new. He always wants to leave."

"No. This is different. *He* seems different. And he even *looks* different. I know this doesn't make any sense at all, but if you'll just come in you can see for yourself."

There was a pause before Kevin replied, "Would after work be okay? You wouldn't classify this is an emergency, would you? Is his health in danger in any way?"

"Well...no. I guess not. But the sooner the better, if you want my opinion. I know this sounds crazy, but your father needs you."

"Give me a few minutes. I'll call my brother, talk to my boss, and see how early I can get out of here. You're sure he's not in any medical trouble?"

"I'm sure. He seems healthier than he did on the day he moved in with us."

Kevin frowned, a bit annoyed at having to re-arrange his busy day for nothing. He was sure this would be a wasted trip.

Chapter 43

Barnstable, Massachusetts

J ace plopped onto the sofa, placed his elbows on his knees and leaned forward. His unblinking eyes stared at the floor, and his mouth hung slightly ajar.

"You made another letter? T and now A? T-A? Ta?" He jumped up and began pacing, muttering to himself, clearly shook, "This isn't real. It's loco, that's what it is."

He slowly turned his head toward the objects on the floor, and his logical brain couldn't deny that his dog had placed random things on the floor in the definite shape of the letters T and A. Shaking his head, he resumed pacing. "What the...? This is freakin' crazy. It must be a coincidence. That's all."

He looked up as Crash returned from the bedroom with his mouth stuffed full of...things. Mesmerized as his mutt frantically began placing Jace's toothbrush, the toothpaste, a hairbrush, a pack of batteries, and his inhaler into yet another shape in line with the other letters.

"Oh, snap." Jace rubbed his eyes as he began his monotonous patrolling once again. "I'm not seeing this. It isn't real."

Crash finished his work and sat in front of it. "Yip." He raised a paw in the air toward Jace.

"Okay. N?"

"Yip!" The dog bounded across the room and jumped up, placing his front paws on his master's midsection, jumping happily as if trying to take flight.

Jace walked closer, muttering, "T-A-N? Tan? What does that mean to you? Oh, jeez, I'm talking to a dog and waiting for him to answer me."

Crash once again disappeared, this time he returned walking backward, pulling a pack of twelve toilet paper rolls into the living room/kitchen area. Jace walked to the letters, bent and picked up his inhaler. Taking two quick puffs, he then carefully placed it on the floor in the exact position it had been. He turned and flopped onto the sofa again, and sat back with his eyes never leaving Crash.

"I'm not even gonna yell at you for this mess. That's how crazy this is." He crossed his arms as the pup gently broke the plastic wrap and one by one took each roll into his mouth and placed it on the floor.

The process repeated until six letters were placed on the floor in an almost perfect parallel line. One word.

"T-A-N-D-I-E? Tandie? What's that supposed to mean? That's not even a word." A nervous laugh escaped. "Here I was thinking you were, like, the smartest dog in the world, and you spell TANDIE?" He shook his head. "C'mon, dude. Let's clean this up. And you know you owe me a new toothbrush, right? I'm not using that one now that it's been in your mouth."

Rap-rap-rap. Both heads jerked toward the door.

"What now?" Jace mumbled as he headed for the

door. Looking through the peephole, he recognized the pink hair immediately, sighed and opened the door.

Crash leaped through the doorway and the girl reflexively caught him, staggering back a step.

"Aww. Isn't that sweet? He missed his Mama." She smiled as the dog licked her chin in happy little bursts. "Okay, Okay, Crashy-poo, I have to go to work soon. No messing with the make-up." She bent to place Crash on the floor. "Wow, your place is a mess. You should really put all that stuff back where it belongs. Especially since you have a recovering patient here." She scratched behind his ears as she talked, looking up at Jace.

"Uh. Crash did a little re-decorating when we got home." He glanced over his shoulder at the mess. From this angle, the objects appeared to be randomly placed.

"Well, I hope he doesn't think he's doing that at my place. All he did all day was watch children's shows on TV. Oh, here's his ball. I forgot to give it to you. And I realized I don't know your name. So, what is it?"

"Jace. I'm Jace Calhoun."

"Nice to meet you, Jace Calhoun. I'm Tandie. Tandie Ohiro." She rolled her eyes and continued, "And yes, I'm half Japanese. If you have to know, the other half is Irish. And no, I've never been to either place. I grew up in New York. Well, I'm off. Have a great night, Crashy-washy! I'll pick him up on my way back home so you don't have to wake me up at the crack of dawn." *Never mind that she would wake him in the middle of the night.* "Oh, and here's my cell number in case you need to talk to me about Crash." She took out her phone, "What's yours?" After giving her the number, she shoved her phone into her small handbag and turned to go.

Blowing a kiss over her shoulder at the dog, Jace stood speechless as she flounced away. Crash sat regally staring up at him, a smug canine smile lighting up his face. A *huff-huff-huff*-ing sound escaped from his open mouth.

"Are you...laughing at me?"
He didn't shut the door until she drove off in her dented white Sonoma pick-up truck.

Chapter 44

Research Vessel OA-23

C hristian manned the boat, his eyes completely focused on the red blip on the screen. It was a strong signal, but he couldn't help but wonder what they would find when they finally caught up to it. A tightness settled in his neck, and his stomach muscles clenched.

Is there still even a possibility of Sofie surviving this?

He shook his head, and glanced at his watch. With each passing minute, the chances of her coming out of the water alive were dwindling. If they even found her. Or any part of her.

Turning to look over his shoulder, he observed Yaz. She stood gripping the railing, her eyes darting back and forth over the water. She would not give up, he knew. Never leave this area of deep water until they found her girl. One way or the other.

His eyes focused once again on the red blip. Dr. Sofiana Stone had invented this special brand of tracker, and it was soon-to-be the best on the market. There was no need for this device to break the surface to send a ping. It could be tracked under water as well. How deep was still a question. It was currently in the testing phase, but he was sure that her invention would revolutionize sea life studies for years to come. Her tracker wouldn't fail. The woman didn't know how to fail. Questions that had been asked for hundreds of years would finally be answered. And he would be a part of that history.

Will she be here to see it?

His eyes clouded.

Don't think about it. Just follow.

The crackling of the radio interrupted his rumination.

"This is the Coast Guard. Please cut your engine and prepare to be boarded."

He picked up the receiver on the VHF marine radio system, and responded, "Coast Guard, this is OCEANS ALIVE Research Vessel number two-three. Two on board and one missing. We have a woman lost in the water, and we are tracking her location. Repeat, this is OA-23, and our crew leader is missing, taken by a great white shark. We need to start a rescue mission ASAP."

A commanding voice came through the speaker, "I repeat. Cut your engine and prepare to be boarded. ASAP."

"We radioed for help. A woman is missing. Please."

"Cut your engine, or we will be forced to do it for you."

His squinting eyes met Yasmin's furious ones. She retrieved the binoculars and focused on the quickly approaching boat.

"If that's the Coast Guard, why aren't they using a Coast Guard vessel? And why are they aiming their weapons at us?"

Christian reached for the binoculars and looked for himself. The unmarked pristine white yacht was at least triple in size compared to their own, and two men onboard looked back with their own binoculars, both casually aiming weapons in their direction.

"Cut the engine. I have a bad feeling about this. And Mama always said to trust your gut," Yaz said, her frown deepening.

Christian nodded, turning the key. The eeriness of the proceeding quiet sent a shiver down his spine, and he felt compelled to raise his hands in the air as the larger craft approached, sidling up alongside them.

Definitely not Coast Guard as they claimed.

Chapter 45

Cape Cod Morgue

"Okay, so we know that the man who tried to kill you is dead. We know that he was murdered, and the murder weapon was a gun. Who did it? Gold? For what reason? And what does this tell us? I'm not sure what our next step should be. None of this makes any sense." Grayson's knuckles whitened as they clutched the steering wheel.

"Well, I know I'm going to sleep better tonight knowing that the man who hit me is not around to finish the job." Maggie Lee leaned her head back on the headrest and closed her eyes. She took a deep breath and continued, "I don't think we need to do anything. It's over. The man got what he deserved, and now we're safe."

Mike sat forward in the back seat, gripping the back of the passenger's seat. He retorted, "Maggie Lee, you know that's not true. Think about it. Someone killed that man. Murdered him. His murderer is still out there somewhere. And he could come after you next."

She shook her head. "No, I don't think so. For whatever reason, it seems as if that person was trying to protect me. Like a guardian angel or something."

"Maggie..." Mike huffed.

"That's a dangerous way to think. If someone is capable of cold-blooded murder, then he, or she, can't be trusted. Even if this person was on our side, we could never trust him." Grayson stopped at a red light and stared out the side window. "Whatever our side is."

Deafening silence filled the Camaro, each of the three occupants lost in their own thoughts. Minutes ticked by, and Gray reached for the button on the radio, flipping it to his favorite country station. His fingers unconsciously tapped the steering wheel, keeping rhythm with the twangy music, but his brow remained furrowed as he followed the now-familiar roads toward the Johnsons' home.

"I think we're being followed." Grayson's eyes darted back and forth between the rearview mirror and the road.

Maggie's head whipped around to look out the back window. "Where?"

"Two cars back. It's the black Dodge Charger."

She nodded. "I see it. Are you sure?"

Gray shook his head. "No. But it's been there a while. And it makes every turn we make. Shit, it could just be paranoia. I don't know. I never would have been looking for a tail two weeks ago. This whole thing is crazy."

"Maggie, turn around. If someone is following us, we don't want to let them know that we are aware of them," Mike said.

"What difference does it make if they know? I don't really think it matters one way or the other." But she turned to face front anyway.

"Do you two have anywhere safe to hide out for a while? I'm not sure it's safe for you to go home," Grayson asked.

Maggie shook her head, curls bouncing. "I'm not hiding, Grayson. We're going home. It's our place, and it's where we belong."

"I didn't mean permanently. Just for a while, until this gets straightened out." Grayson sighed.

"How long will that take? Days? Weeks? Months? And how would we even know when it's over? We don't even know *how* to straighten it out. No. Take us home, please."

Grayson ran his hand through his hair. His blue eyes squinted, and he whispered, "I'm worried about you. Both of you."

Mike leaned forward to place a hand on Gray's shoulder. "We'll take care of each other, Gray. Don't worry, I won't let anything happen to Maggie Lee."

Gray inclined his head. "I think I have an idea. My boss has been pressuring me to write Maggie's story. Maybe I should. If it's out in the open, then whoever this person is will know that everyone's aware of...whatever is happening. He'll know that he's not the only one watching you, and maybe he'll leave you alone."

"What will you write, Grayson?"

"The truth. How about I let you read it before I hand it in. I promise I won't print anything without your approval. Despite what the world thinks, the media has its positive uses."

Maggie Lee turned around to search Mike's face. At his nod she replied, "I trust you, Grayson. Go ahead and write your story."

"I'll get started tonight."

∞∞∞∞

The man known only as 'Gold' turned off just before the street the Johnson's lived on. He pulled over at the curb, and spoke into his secure cell phone.

"She's safe. They've arrived at home, without a tail."

He listened, and then responded, "Yes, they know he's dead. Yes. I'll make sure that doesn't happen. No one was following them except me...No."

After listening to more instructions, he hit the 'end' button, and shoved the phone back into his pocket. Pulling out, he continued to patrol the area until he saw the Camaro on its way back home. Turning his car around, he followed Grayson at a discreet distance.

He'd been listening to the conversation between him and the Johnsons through one of the bugs he had placed in both cars while Mrs. Johnson had still been in the hospital. He knew all of their plans as soon as they did.

Grayson Smith would not print a story about what was happening. Gold, and the organization he worked for, couldn't let that happen. He shook his head.

Such a shame. I actually kinda like the guy.

∞∞∞∞

This time, Grayson knew beyond a shadow of a doubt that he was being followed. At one point, he drove around the block and back again just to test his theory, and sure enough the Charger did the same.

So, they're after me, not the Johnsons.

That was better anyway. He could lure them away and the Johnsons would be safe.

Unless there are more of them.

He continued driving and dialed Mike.

"I'm being followed again. Whoever it is must have been waiting for me to leave. Now that he's with me, you and Maggie should pack up and go. Somewhere. Anywhere. You're not safe."

"Gray, it sounds like you're the one who's not safe. I've changed my mind. Come back and get us, and we'll all go together. I don't like this. Any of it," Mike pleaded.

"Me neither, but I'm not coming back. I don't want this guy anywhere near you."

Mike's voice took on a hard edge. "Call the police. If you don't, I will."

"And say what? Someone's following me? Don't you think they get false calls like that all the time? No, I'm gonna try to lose them. I think I have an idea," Gray replied.

"It doesn't matter if you lose them, Gray. They probably know where you live. If they want you, they'll just wait for you at home. Lose them, then come back to get us. We'll pack some things and wait for you."

"I'll try. If you don't hear from me in thirty

minutes, I want you two to leave and go somewhere safe. Somewhere that they can't trace back to you in any way. And don't use credit cards. Do you have cash on hand?" Grayson asked.

"Yes. We have a stash in the safe for emergencies. I guess this qualifies. Grayson? Be safe, okay?" Mike said.

"I'll do my best. Same to you both." Gray ended the call, glancing once more in the rearview mirror. The black car still followed. Shivers raced up his arms and his heart hammered in his chest. He pushed harder on the accelerator.

Chapter 46

Caring House Retirement Community

Kyle paced up and down the steps leading to the front door of Caring House Retirement Community as he checked his watch one more time. He couldn't understand how his brother could always be late. He himself was punctual to a fault. Opposites. They'd always been opposites.

On a deep breath, he made a decision. *If he's not here by the time I reach the top step, I'm going in without him. I don't know why he wanted me to wait in the first place.*

Just as he reached for the door handle his eyes caught a reflection in the glass of the red truck pulling into the parking lot, and his hand dropped to his side. He turned and nodded in brief greeting as he saw his brother and sister-in-law step down from the truck.

"Hey. 'Bout time," he called.

Kevin chuckled. "You probably got here, what? Like, twenty minutes early, right?"

A reluctant smile tugged at the corners of his mouth. "No. Only fifteen. And you're just as late. Hi Bianca. Beautiful as always." He leaned down to give her a kiss on the cheek.

"It's your brother's fault we're late, not mine. It only takes me five minutes to get ready."

"I know it. He's always been slow." Kyle winked, then turned to his brother. "So, what do you think is up with Dad?"

Kevin shrugged. "Sandy only said he wants to leave."

"That's nothing new. I don't know why we all had to drop everything and run out here for that. Isn't it their job to calm him when he wants to leave?" Kyle grumbled.

"Well, let's just go in and see what we can do, okay?" Kevin walked ahead.

The inimitable odor of geriatrics combined with a touch of disinfectant flared his nostrils the moment he entered. He turned his head to the side as they hastened down the hallway, following Bianca's always-brisk pace even now during the eighth month of her pregnancy. They sped past the first wing, barely noticing the holiday decorations adorning each doorway and shelf, or the black and white throwback pictures that decorated every ledge.

Klop-klop, klop- klop. Klop-klop. Their footsteps echoed on the Berber carpeting with each step. The hallways were deserted. Kyle held his breath, not wanting to be the one to break the never-ending silence. The quiet sent a chill from the base of his skull down his neck.

Odd. There are usually patrons scattered throughout the hallway.

Kyle tilted his head, noticing for the first time that all the room doors were closed. On an ordinary afternoon, residents could be found sitting on the benches placed invitingly in the hall, or on the cushioned rocking chairs strategically placed in the corners of each wing.

His head swiveled toward Kevin, whose eyes were focused on his phone as he walked, his thumb scrolling down the screen. Clearly oblivious to the stress now all but emanating from his brother's pores.

As they approached the great room, Kyle sighed as the sound of an old movie blared through the speakers on the television. The chuckle escaped before he started breathing again.

That's why no one's around. Everyone's watching a movie. Movie night. Way to freak out, man!

When the trio reached the doorway to the community room, they stopped in their tracks.

"Where is everyone?" Kyle stepped further into the room, his eyes scanning each and every empty sofa, chair, and window seat.

Kevin replied, "I don't know. What's going on?" He blinked, shoving his phone into his back pocket.

Bianca placed a hand on her husband's arm. "I'm sure there's a logical explanation. Maybe they are playing Bingo or something?"

"Don't they usually do that kind of thing in here?"

"I don't know."

Goosebumps rose on Kyle's arm as he turned to race down the hallway toward his father's room. He could hear the pounding of his own feet on the carpeted floor as he ran. A shiver ran down his spine as he reached the door, and he paused.

The door was ajar.

All of the doors were closed. Except Dad's?

Kyle frowned, calling out, "Dad?" He stepped into the room.

Empty.

"Dad? Where are you, Dad?"

He turned back toward the hallway, colliding with his brother.

"Where could he be?"

"I don't know, and I don't like this."

"Me neither. It doesn't feel right. Let's go to the office and get some answers."

Bianca stood between them, her arms wrapped around both men.

"Calm down, guys. I'm sure there's a perfectly logical reason for this. Maybe it's a fire drill? Or something like that. I'm sure Dad's fine. Let go find him."

Chapter 47

Barnstable Farmer's Market

J ace's leg bounced nervously as he sat in a chair in the staff room, his eyes on his worn sneakers as he spoke, "I can't do this."

Brock pounded him on the back. "Sure you can. You want to find the guy who stabbed your mutt, don't you? If it was me, I never had a dog, but you know if I did I would move heaven and Earth to find out who hurt my pet. And it'll be good for business. Don't forget, I've raised almost the full amount of cash for you to pay off your vet bill. You can do this one small thing for me."

"But…" Jace stammered.

"The camera crew will be here any minute. Go to the bathroom and get ahold of yourself. It's just a few questions. Nothing to get all hot and bothered about."

"I…" His last protest was interrupted by the phone.

His boss put the receiver to his ear and listened. He responded, "Great! Tell them we'll be right down." Hanging up, his eyes found Jace. "They're here. Meet me downstairs in five."

Jace fumbled in his pocket for his inhaler. He breathed in two quick puffs, and gulped in oxygen at an alarming rate. Sweat broke out on his brow, and his face flushed.

I can't do this. I can't do this. I can't do this.

The impending panic attack threatened to erupt any second, and he was powerless to control it.

What should I do? What should I do? I don't know what to do.

His hands shook as he entered the bathroom. Splashing water on his face did nothing to hide his red cheeks or calm the storm brewing inside him.

I can't. I won't.

He nodded and pushed out of the bathroom. The moment he emerged, Brock was on him.

"There he is! This is Jace. You look awful, man." He looked at the reporter and whispered, "He's just so broken up about his dog. You know?"

"Understandable." The woman, face painted heavily, held out her hand and Jace wiped his palms on his pants before taking her extended one in his trembling grip. "I'm Beth. I'll be covering your story. I'd like to interview you here, and then get some footage of the dog, if that's okay."

"Uh. Crash isn't here," Jace whispered.

"Wait, the dog's not here? We really need the dog for this piece, ya know? Can you get him here?" asked Beth.

"Um..." Jace stuttered.

Brock intervened. "Sure. Sure he can. Right Jace?"

"Um..."

Brock's eyes bored into his. "Didn't you say your neighbor is watching him? Why don't you call your neighbor and see if he can bring him here."

"She," Jace whispered.

"What? Your dog's a she? All this time I thought it was a boy dog. Ha-ha-ha," Brock's high-pitched cackle made his temples throb.

Jace shook his head. "No. My neighbor's a girl. The dog's a boy."

"Ah, gotcha. Well, then call this girl and see if she'll bring Crash. Chicks love T.V. She'll come if she thinks there's any possibility of getting on the news," Brock winked.

Jace stood rooted to the spot, wiping his clammy hands on his pants. "I don't know..."

"Make the call, Jace." Brock's eyes narrowed until he turned back to the reporter, and then he was all smiles once again.

Jace turned his back to them, and stared down at the phone in his hand. He had no idea how Tandie would respond to his request. Taking a deep breath, he pushed the 'call' button, and waited.

She answered on the third ring, "Hiya."

"Um...Tandie?"

"Yes, this is Tandie. You called my number, didn't you? Who's this?"

"It's Jace."

"Oh, hi Jace. Crashy's fine, if that's why you're calling. You want to talk to him? Here, Crash, Daddy's on the phone!"

His eyes rolled as he heard rustling and then panting. "Uh, Hi Crash."

Three loud barks made his ear ring, and he held the phone away from his face until he heard her laughter.

"He's very excited to talk to Daddy! Good boy! G'boy, Crash-kins!" There was a pause, and then, "Well, if that's all..."

"Wait!" Panic laced Jace's voice.

"What?" she answered.

"Um. Can you bring Crash down to the market?"

Tandie hesitated before responding. "What? Why?"

"There's a reporter here. To talk about his injury. They want to see him."

"A reporter? Why would a reporter care? I bet dogs get injured all the time."

Jace shuffled his feet. "My boss? He's raising money for his vet bill?"

"Oh. Well...okay, I guess I can bring him. He could probably use a walk. But I'm not getting on camera. I don't want to be on the evening news."

"Me neither."

"That makes no sense at all. Then why are you doing it?" she asked.

"It's out of my control."

"Nothing is ever out of your control. Okay, I'll be there in 30 minutes."

"Thanks." Jace's hand shook as he shoved his phone into his back pocket.

Chapter 48

Research Vessel OA-23

C hristian's eyes met Yasmin's as two men leaped onto their tiny boat, faces devoid of expression. She hissed, "What's going on here? We are here on official research for OCEANS ALIVE. Why are we being detained?"

"We need to search your vessel. Step back." The first man held a machine gun on them while the other—clearly the leader—headed toward the cabin.

Yaz spread her hands in front of her. "I don't understand. We aren't breaking any maritime laws that I know of. We have the proper ID, if you'll let me show you."

"Just shut up. If you want to keep this civil, shut up," he hissed.

Christian gave an imperceptible negative head-shake, and remained standing with his hands in the air. He whispered, "Just let them do whatever they need to and be on their way."

The man holding the weapon on them agreed, "Good advice. My partner does not tolerate insubordination. From anyone, least of all a nosey Jamaican *Quashie* who can't shut up."

Yaz sputtered, "Insubordination? Who are you people? You're obviously not the Coast Guard as you claim to be. How stupid do you think we are? You have no reason to detain us. We have done no'ting wrong. Who do you work for?"

The man flipped his weapon around and butted it into her cheek. She stumbled back three quick steps, hand covering the instant bruise seeping blood that ran along her cheekbone.

Christian grabbed her arm. "Stop it. Just stop. Do you want to get yourself killed?"

He stared into her eyes, willing her compliance. She slowly stepped back, giving him a small nod as she took a deep, calming breath.

The other man emerged from the cabin—he had the look of a regular 'Joe' with his semi-attractive dark looks—returned with arms loaded. At a glance, he looked like the kind of neighbor you'd ask for help mowing the lawn, and he would selflessly lend a hand with a smile. His trust-evoking face might have you giving him the key to your house so he could 'take care of things' while you were away...while unbeknownst to you he'd be secretly pilfering the reserve of cash hidden in your cookie jar. The only thing that belied his charming appearance was the slightly menacing L-shaped scar that ran along his temple to his cheekbone. Another clue to his true personality, that most people missed, was the greedy gleam in his eyes when he smiled.

That calculating smile lit his face now. In his arms he had all of Sofie's notes, files, and memory cards. Her computer. Cell phone. Even the empty case that had housed the trackers. All of her research was about to be taken off the boat.

Yaz drew in an enraged breath. *Stolen. Stolen off the boat. By these pirates.*

"Is that what this is about? Her research? You're no better than a bottom feeder. The dregs of the ocean. Why don't you do your own research, instead of stealing someone else's?" she screamed.

Christian grabbed her arm when she took a step forward. "Don't…"

"Let go!" Yaz yanked her arm away. "I can't let them take her life's work!"

"Yaz…just let them go. Please, let it go. We have to find Sofie," Christian pleaded.

Her eyes filled with tears. She squared her shoulders and gave a slight nod. "You find her. Promise me you'll find her, Christian."

He nodded imperceptibly. "Yes. I'll find her."

"Good. The oxygen tank behind you is not empty," she breathed below a whisper. "There's no way they are letting both of us out of this alive. I can sense these things. Be safe, and tell my girl I love her. There's no other choice. Go!"

Yaz ran and leaped onto the man holding Sofie's things. She pulled his hair and bit his neck, drawing blood. The man who had hit her turned and aimed his weapon, knowing he couldn't fire without hitting his colleague. He dropped the weapon so it hung over his shoulder by the strap, and reached for the woman.

While both men were distracted, Christian inched toward the side of the boat, where the oxygen tank and equipment that Yaz had recently abandoned still lay. He grasped the tank along with mask and mouthpiece, and in one quick leap, jumped overboard and began swimming toward the ocean floor hugging the tank to his chest. When his lungs felt as if they might explode, he stuffed the mouthpiece into his mouth and breathed deep as from above a volley of gunfire broke through the surface of the water. The bullets slowed as they entered the water, giving the appearance of fireflies sporadically flying above him in an aquatic mating dance.

Just then something larger entered the water, creating a storm of bubbles surrounding it. When the water cleared, it went burgundy as bullets continued to pelt the water and the body hovering above jerked with each hit as it slowly sank downward toward him. Her dreadlocks fanned out around her.

Yaz! Oh, no. Yaz. Should I have stayed with you? Then we'd both be dead.

He looked around, and began swimming away from the two boats, having no idea which direction he was heading. His eyes landed on the oxygen gauge.

Shit. I'm in trouble. Keep moving.

Trying to even out his heavy breathing to conserve the little oxygen he had left, he continued moving through the water with no plan in mind except to survive.

Chapter 49

On the Road Between Brockton and Yarmouth

Grayson clutched the steering wheel until his fingers turned white. His heart tripped an erratic rhythm as he put more miles between the man behind him and the Johnsons. In the short time he had known Mike and Maggie Lee, they had become family. It was funny how some people just seemed to fit into your life like missing puzzle pieces, Grayson mused. There was no way this guy was going to get close to them. Not as long as he had oxygen in his lungs and a heart beating in his chest.

Despite the air conditioning blowing directly on him, sweat trickled down the side of his face as he eased up on the gas, eyes darting to the rearview mirror. The guy was still back there. Two cars back. He'd been secretly hoping that the black Charger behind him would turn off and prove that he was only paranoid, after all. No such luck. No matter how many turns he made, the car was not far behind. Could this be the end of the line for him? Goosebumps traveled up his arms.

On impulse, he grabbed his phone from the cup holder, and his thumb found the call button.

Ring. Ring. Ring. Ring.

The sound of her voice punched him in the gut, and he had a desperate desire to talk to her. A *need* for her. Right now. There were so many things to say...

His hand shook as he listened to her brisk message. So like her to get straight to the point.

"Sorry, can't take your call. Leave a message, I'll get back to you when I can."

Grayson's words poured out of him as he drove, "Sofiana. Sof. It's me, Grayson. I just...I-I don't know. I needed to talk to you. Something weird is happening, and I-I've been thinking about you lately. Thinking about us, and what went wrong...anyway, I just wanted to talk to you. Just talk. If I make it through this night, I'm going to the place we went to escape for Christmas. Do you remember where it is? That's where I'll be, with friends. Their names are Mike and Maggie Lee Johnson, from Brockton. Maggie found something that came from the ocean. You're gonna want to see it. It seems to have...power of some sort. If something happens to me, you can trust them. That's all I can say for now. Call me."

He slowly returned the phone to the cup holder, took a deep breath, and scanned the road. Just hearing her recorded voice had been enough to boost his morale. He *would* get back to her. His eyes scanned the road. Nowhere to lose the tail here. Fortunately, there was always plenty of traffic at this time of day, so he thought he was safe. At least for now.

Think. Think, man! There must be a way to get out of this alive.

But the goose bumps remained, and the feeling of doom that accompanied them. *There are two clear choices. One, keep driving and hope to lose the bastard. Or two, stop and confront the guy.* The choices were not in his favor. He debated, and agonized over what to do. Stopping would be ignorant. He had no weapon to defend with, no combat training to speak of. *I'm a writer, for God's sake! I'm in shape, but not prepared for a fight.* Although, he'd had his share of fistfights in school...but that was years ago. *Wait; maybe it doesn't have to come to that. I'm a writer. There's power in words. Maybe if I talk to him...*

Grayson's fingers drummed the steering wheel. He swiped at the sweat over his brow, a frown marring his handsome visage. Thankful, this one time, for the evening traffic that always plagued this area, he inched forward and braked, inched forward and braked. And thought, or more accurately agonized, over his choices. Stop or keep driving. Keep driving or stop. Playing through every possible conclusion his writer's brain could concoct. None of the outcomes were desirable.

So he kept driving. For now.

Chapter 50

Caring House Retirement Community

The trio jogged toward the office located at the back of Caring House Retirement Community. Bianca kept up, hands cradling her baby bulge, as she shuffled along. Down another long corridor that veered to the left. When they rounded the corner, they could see that the dining room's double doors, usually always open, were closed. The sound of muffled voices escaped into the hallway.

Kevin breathed a deep sigh. "The dining room. It must be dinner time." He chuckled as he reached for the handle.

The dining room was packed full of people. The dull, supposed-to-be-cheery yellow paint covering the cinder block walls was devoid of decoration, creating a barren look, exactly opposite of the intent. Some of the residents sat in chairs, others leaned against walls; still others sat on their walkers with built-in seats. But no one was eating.

The staff was scattered throughout the gathering, offering support to whoever needed it. Kevin's eyes were drawn by an officer in full uniform standing off to the side talking to a man just before Sandy stood and walked toward him.

"Mr...I mean Kevin. I'm glad you're here." She glanced in his brother's direction and nodded. "Both of you. I'm afraid something terrible has happened."

"Dad? Where's my dad? Is he okay?"

"We don't know. He got out of the building, somehow. And he hurt his roommate in the process. It's why we've gathered everyone here, in case he comes back and gets violent again..."

Kevin interrupted, "Arthur? What do you mean? My Dad hurt him?"

Kyle stepped forward, his harsh voice filling the quiet room, "Where is my father? What do you mean you don't know? I don't believe he intentionally hurt anyone. You're delusional if you think my father would hurt someone. He's a highly decorated retired police officer."

Kevin put his hand on his brother's forearm, whispering, "Kyle, let's hear them out. Maybe he wasn't in his right mind. You know he hasn't really been... Dad." He looked back at Sandy and then made eye contact with the now approaching officer. "Can you start at the beginning, and please tell us what happened?" The tall, lean, middle-aged officer with speckled gray throughout his brown hair whose nametag read Officer Schultz nodded at Sandy, and spoke in a deep voice, "I'd like to hear your version of what happened, too. You're his nurse, right?"

"Yes. Yes. I-I...last checked on him at noon, and then I didn't go to his room again until I went to get him for dinner..." Her breath hitched as she inhaled, and she looked down at her fidgeting hands. "W-when I got to the room, Bob wasn't there. He was a-already gone. I don't know how long he's been out there. I just don't know." Her head dropped into her hands, and a sob escaped. "Arthur was on the floor by Bob's bed. He'd obviously fallen, and there was blood drying around a wound on his temple. He was unconscious, or at least that's what I thought. I got down on the floor to check for a pulse, and he opened his eyes. He whispered a few words to me before he lost consciousness again."

"Yes? What did he say? Anything about Dad?" Kyle prompted.

"Y-yes. Yes he did. H-he said 'Bob hit me'," she mumbled before rubbing her face with her palms.

"Bullshit! My Dad wouldn't hit anyone. You're lying. Why are you lying?" Kyle burst out, taking a step toward Sandy.

Both the officer and Kevin grabbed for his arm. Kevin got there first. "Whoa, Kyle. Calm down. We aren't helping Dad by making accusations. Why would Sandy lie about this?" He took a deep breath before continuing, "How is Arthur now? Is he awake? Can we talk to him?"

"Yes. He's awake, but resting. I'll ask him if he's up to talking to you. Stay here," Sandy replied as she ambled away toward the far corner of the room where a cot was set up. As Kevin watched, Sandy spoke in hushed tones to Arthur, and he raised his head and made eye contact. Kevin nodded, and Arthur looked back at Sandy and nodded.

She gestured them over, and they walked together, Kevin holding Bianca's hand, Kyle, and Officer Schultz at the rear, to Arthur's bedside. Kevin felt the blood rush to his face as he took in the lump jutting out from the older man's forehead.

Did Dad really do this? And where is he?

Pushing the unanswered questions aside, he spoke directly to Arthur, "I'm so sorry this happened. Are you okay?"

"I'll be right as rain in a few days. Just a bit dizzy, is all."

"Good. Good. If you don't mind, can you tell us what happened? We need to understand what state of mind Dad is in. We'd appreciate your insight."

"Sure, sure. Bob's been acting very strange the past few days. He's been hiding something under his bed sheets. I just wanted to see what he had there, that's all. I wasn't gonna take it, I was curious. That's all. I swear it."

Kevin laid his hand gently on Art's arm. "Of course not. Can you continue?"

"Well, I saw a glowing light under his sheets, and I was worried about him. And, like I said, I was curious. So I went to the side of the bed and I lifted the covers to see the thing. And Bob? Well, he was furious. He cursed and yelled at me, and he jumped out of bed and hit me with the small metal thing. He hit me more than once. And I fell. That's all I remember." He stared off at the yellow wall. "I never did get a good look at the thing." Shaking his head, he lay back and closed his eyes. "I'm real tired, now."

"Thanks Arthur. I'm sorry Dad hurt you. I'm sure he didn't mean to. It's the dementia. Not to make excuses, but…" he trailed off as Arthur laid back, closing his eyes.

Feeling Bianca's hand squeeze his, he raised his eyes to Kyle's.

"Where's Dad?"

Chapter 51

Barnstable Farmer's Market

Will this ever end?

The reporter, Beth, kept firing off questions. Jace's saliva had long ago dried up, and his tongue felt swollen to the roof of his mouth. Swallowing, he answered yet another question, "It was two men. On the beach. They were arguing."

"And then what happened?" Beth tilted her head toward the camera.

"Uh. Crash got off his leash. And he ran toward them. He wouldn't hurt them. He was just curious." Jace's voice trembled as he recounted the events of that night.

"Has he ever attacked anyone before?" she asked.

He shook his head. "No! H-he isn't mean. Crash loves everyone."

"So, what did the men do when Crash arrived?" she continued.

"Um. It was dark. I heard Crash cry. And the man was holding up a knife. There was blood..."

"So, the man stabbed him with the knife?"

"Yes, he said Crash ran toward him, and he didn't know if he was friendly..."

"Where was the other man?" she pressed.

"He was running down the beach. Away," Jace added.

Beth flipped her hair. "What did you do?"

"I checked on Crash, and I called the vet," he answered.

"Did you call the police?"

Another head-shake. "No. I-I was only worried about Crash."

"So, this man got away with it?" Beth's voice rose on the question.

"Y-yes," Jace stammered.

"Did you get a good look at him?" she asked.

"No. I-It was dark." Jace took a deep breath. *Please let this be over soon.*

The reporter turned toward the camera and began a dialogue.

"If anyone has any knowledge of the two men on the beach, please contact us at the number on your screen. We'd like to help catch the man who did this. The store has raised most of the money to pay for Crash's vet bills, but we'd like to bring this man to justice as well. If you'd like to donate to Crash's Go-Fund-Me account, the information is on our website."

Jace breathed a sigh and started inching backward out of camera range just as Tandie entered the store, arm outstretched, with Crash pulling the lead in front of her. When Crash spotted Jace, he broke free and ran in a wiggling beeline for his master. Jace squatted down to catch him as his dog rained kisses all over his face, and looked up and made eye contact with Beth. She motioned for the cameraman to follow, and walked toward him.

"So, this is the guy, huh?" She bent slightly at the knees and patted Crash on the head, then immediately stood, brushing imaginary hair off her skirt, clearly not a dog-lover. "That's funny."

"Huh?"

"Well, your dog seems fine. He doesn't act hurt at all. Do you mind showing me his wound?"

"Uh. The vet said to keep it covered. I haven't removed the gauze since the surgery."

"Please? It will help with my descriptions. Just a quick peek, and then we'll put it right back. Pinky swear." She held her finger up in the air and tilted her head.

Jace sighed. *Might as well let her get what she needs. Maybe she'll leave.* He nodded his head and reached for the bandage.

Crash looked backward over his shoulder, tongue hanging sideways, and seemed to roll his eyes at Jace.

Tandie leaned down and whispered, "Are you sure you want to do that? Don't let her bully you." She stood and glared toward the reporter.

"It's okay," he replied, pulling the gauze off slowly and rocking back on his heels.

Beth leaned down, and gasped. "Where's the injury? You said he was stabbed, right? So, where is it?" She took a step back, her eyes practically glowing. "Oh, I get it. You're a fraud. You've wasted my time here. And for what? Money? You've conned all these innocent people into giving you money for your dog, when you really only wanted it for yourself. You wanted a little fame, did you? Well, you're going to be famous all right. Just not the way you wanted to. We're going live. Now." She straightened her hair and motioned for the camera to roll.

"No. No. I mean…"

"You've said enough. 3-2-1, and this is Beth Ramos reporting live from a small Barnstable Corner Market, where we've uncovered one man's scheme to con people out of their hard-earned money. Should charges be brought up against him? That's for you to decide…"

Brock grabbed his arm and yanked him toward the office. His feet stumbled along as he was dragged. "Brock, I swear…"

"Shut it. You've done enough. I can't believe you would do this to me. To all of us. Nothing you can say would change my mind. I'm disgusted. And worse than that, you've made me a laughingstock. You're fired. And you can't have any of the money that was raised for your healthy dog."

"Brock, please. It's the truth…"

"Get your things and get out of here. You're a disgrace."

His boss, or ex-boss, stormed out of the room, leaving Jace to stare once again at the closed door.

What just happened?

Heat crept up his cheeks as he skulked out of the room. Tandie was on him as soon as he emerged. She waited, hands on hips, until he met her eyes.

"What's going on? Did Crash really get hurt?" she asked quietly.

"Yes. Yes. I wouldn't lie about it." He looked at the floor, eyes burning.

She nodded. "Okay. I believe you. Let's go."

His head snapped up. "You…believe me?"

"Of course I do. I can always tell when someone is

lying to me. It's all in the eyes."

"Th-thanks. I just got fired."

"Let's get out of here. We'll get lunch. My treat."

Crash jumped onto his leg and scratched three times. When he looked down at his dog, he could have sworn there was an apologetic look on his face.

Chapter 52

Deep in the Ocean, Somewhere Off the
Coast of Chatham, Massachusetts

C hristian hugged the ocean floor and concentrated on regulating his breathing. Without flippers and weights, every bit of ground he gained was a struggle. It was like swimming through jello, each stroke moving in slow motion. He kicked off his shoes and continued along.

Where can I go?

He stared at the gauge with a look of panic.

I'm going to die down here. With Yaz. And Sofiana. This is not how I thought it would end. For any of us.

His progression stopped as he momentarily lost himself in self-pity and acceptance of his doom. *It's over. There's nothing I can do about it. What have I done with my life? Do I have anything to be truly proud of?*

His head snapped up.

What am I doing? I have to at least try.

He continued his arduous trek along the ocean bottom, startling an octopus from its resting spot, perfectly camouflaged until his arrival. It rose like a hot air balloon from beneath, and using its arms as a propellent, darted off to find a new hunting ground, a myriad of glowing colors pulsing through its body.

Can't go to the boat. I'm in the middle of the ocean, with dwindling oxygen. Think. Think!

Eyes darting back and forth, he continued on. What else could he do? Not knowing in which direction he traveled, he kept moving.

Don't look at the gauge. Just think of a plan.

But his eyes disobeyed his inner voice, and of their own volition, found the small needle indicating he had only minutes before it was over.

Okay. I'll just have to surface and hope I've gone far enough away from those men.

Continuing his struggle through the water, he spied a school of mackerel darting past him, spooked by his presence. He inhaled in gasps as the oxygen came in sporadic bursts.

Not even minutes. I'm not gonna make it to the surface.

Despite acknowledging the truth, his efforts doubled. Instinct kicked in, and the need to survive overcame him.

I don't want to die here.

His vision blurred, and his head pounded, but still he continued on. His lungs were on fire. He tried to focus on what was in front of him, and thought he saw something moving toward him through the murk.

Shark! I'm not going to drown; I'm going to be eaten. He had no time to decide which was worse, before something clasped his arm and ripped the mouthpiece that contained the remainder of his pitiful supply of oxygen out of his mouth. His head swung side-to-side, bubbles carrying the remainder of the air in his lungs up and away. Now holding his breath, his legs kicked while his arms frantically searched for whatever was in front of him. The first inhale of water would be the start of the end, he knew. He struggled with the puny strength he had left, holding the last of the precious air in his lungs for as long as he could, before something was forcefully shoved into his mouth. Instinct kicked in and he fought it, head thrashing.

He involuntarily took a deep breath, preparing for the burning sensation of water as it entered his lungs. It never came. Precious oxygen instead pumped into him, his lungs rejoicing as the sustaining air filled him. He reached both hands up to hug the mouthpiece closer as he breathed. His vision began to clear, and his lungs sang the song of renewed life.

Oxygen. But how?

His head shot up, eyes locking with a man in scuba gear. He did not recognize him. The man nodded, and pointed for Christian to follow him. He nodded in reply.

Must be one of the men from the boat. But what choice do I have? I'll follow and find a way to escape later. Live to die another day. Ha-ha.

He swam along, side-by-side with his savior.

Chapter 53

On the Road Between Brockton and Yarmouth

Grayson's foot eased onto the brake. He swiped at the sweat covering his brow with the back of his arm, and made a decision.

Let's do this.

He couldn't see any other way. Slamming his foot down on the gas, he pulled the Camaro off the road and jumped out of the car, turning to confront his follower, arms flexed for battle. A hundred drivers served as witnesses to the anticipated confrontation.

See if he tries to harm me in front of all these curious eyes.

The Charger eased onto the side of the road, blocking his exit.

Maybe not my best idea...but too late to go back now.

The man slowly unfolded his tall frame from the sedan, the receding sun glinting off the mirrored sunglasses he wore, his smooth brown hair gelled back and shiny. Grayson recognized him immediately as the man who had returned Maggie Lee's trinket while she was still in the hospital. The same man who had called him posing as an officer to alert him of the body on the beach.

He spoke in an exasperated whisper, "Gold? Why are you following me?"

"Mr. Smith. Nice to see you again."

"Wish I could say the same. Answer my question. Why are you following me?"

"You don't want to know the answer to that question, Mr. Smith."

Grayson's face paled. "But, why? What did I do to you?"

"You've done nothing to me. I have orders. And you've become a threat to the company I work for. Don't make this harder than it has to be. It's not personal."

Running his hands through his hair, he barked, "I'm a threat? I'm probably the least threatening person you'll ever meet. Tell me who I'm bothering, and I'll stop. Hell, I'll even apologize if you'll just tell me what it is I've done."

"It's not what you've done, Mr. Smith. It's what you plan to do."

"What I...that doesn't make any sense. How do you, or your company, know what I plan to do?"

"We know everything."

"Great. You know everything, and I know nothing. That doesn't help me. Why did you help Maggie Lee Johnson? You *have* been helping her, right? And now suddenly, you want me gone? It doesn't make any sense. Maggie Lee likes me. She wouldn't be happy if you hurt me."

"Oh, I'll make sure it doesn't hurt too much. I'll make it as quick as I can. I like you, too."

"Am I supposed to thank you? Maybe turn around and walk into the woods to make it easier for you?

Well, that's not going to happen, and there are a hundred pairs of eyes watching everything you do, so I don't think it's in your best interest, either. Talk to me. Please. How can I fix this?"

"You can't. You'll lie to get out of this alive, so there's no way I can trust you. Plus, I'd be in trouble with my organization if I disobey my orders. I'm known for following all orders to the letter. To the letter, Mr. Smith. I may not be able to complete my mission here, but you can't hide behind witnesses forever."

"Maybe I can help you. We could work together. If you tell me what to do, and what I shouldn't do, it doesn't have to come to that." Grayson could feel the sweat beading on his brow.

Gold blew out a long, slow breath. "How do I know I can trust you?"

"Because I love the Johnsons. It seems to be your mission to keep them safe. Well, I want the same thing. Give me a chance. Tell me what it is I was going to do that puts your organization in jeopardy. Please. If I like your mission, I may become *part* of your organization."

Gold stared off into the overlapping pitch pines, then shook his head before speaking, "This is against my better judgement. But I *do* like you." His eyes swung back to stare intently into Grayson's. He sighed. "If I hear even a whisper that you're working against me, I'll carry out my orders. And it won't be quick. I swear it."

"Understood." Gray nodded.

"Don't print a story on Maggie Lee and her ocean find. It needs to remain secret from the public."

Grayson's eyes widened. "Her silver trinket? I should have known that's what this is about. What *is* that thing? Sorry. Don't answer that. Okay. I-I can promise that I won't print it. I can even sabotage the notes tomorrow in my office. But I can't guarantee that my boss won't assign someone else to the story. He's anxious to go to print. But you have my word that I'll do everything I can to make this story disappear."

Grayson held out his hand, and Gold grasped it in one brisk shake.

"Don't disappoint me." Gold turned and walked away.

Gray flopped into his car, leaned his head back, and closed his eyes. After several deep breaths, he started the car and eased back onto the road.

I'll go in tomorrow, take care of the loose ends, and get the Johnsons to safety. Just as he had said in his message to Sofie, he already knew where to take them.

Chapter 54

K yle sat next to his brother in the police station. Chills were starting to spread throughout his body, contradicting the sweat that beaded on his brow.

This can't be happening. Dad, where are you?

"This is ridiculous! My dad has dementia, and you haven't found him yet? That's just crazy. I can't believe this. Any of it. Where could he be? He's been gone for hours now." Kyle's arms gestured in front of him as he spoke.

He jumped up and started pacing the cardboard box they called an office. The gray cinderblock walls were cold, and the thrift store painting that was an attempt to brighten the place hung sideways in utter failure. The compressed wood desk had a book underneath one leg and was piled high with scattered papers. This place looked like it hadn't had a good cleaning in years.

How can I trust someone who is so blatantly disorganized to find my missing father?

"We're doing what we can, son. We have two patrolman out looking in the area of the retirement community. He can't be far. We are searching for him, especially since he may be armed and dangerous."

"Armed and dangerous?" Kyle snorted. "That's crazy! He has a small silver rock-thing. Not a weapon."

The officer asked in an infuriatingly calm voice: "He did use that small rock as a weapon once today, though, correct?"

"I don't believe that for one minute! Art said that. It's his word against Dad's. We don't really know what happened." Kyle's face flushed and spittle formed at the sides of his mouth.

The officer sighed. "True. But the man was obviously hit with something. *Someone* hit him—he has the bruises to show for it. And he was unconscious on the floor of his room for possibly hours, was he not?"

"I don't know. I wasn't there. And neither were you. I just want to find my father. He's out there somewhere…alone." Kyle flopped back down into the metal folding chair like a deflated balloon.

He felt Kevin's hand on his arm and shook it off. He heard his brother say, "We just want to make sure Dad is safe. We're worried about him. I think I'll go drive around to look for Dad, too. You have our cell numbers if you get any news."

Kyle jumped up, "I'm coming with you. Let's find Dad. It's more than *they* are doing."

They drove in silence, each lost in their own kind

of torture. Kevin imagined all manner of scenarios in which his father was in need of assistance; lost, confused, helpless. While normally he held a positive outlook on any situation, he was finding it hard to find the bright side in any of this. Dad's condition had been getting worse. He'd never find his way on his own.

He navigated the tree-lined streets for the dozenth time, unsure where else to search. An unseen weight rested on his shoulders, and pain traveled up his neck and into his pounding head. Eyes burning with unshed tears, he drove on.

His body jerked when his cell phone signaled an incoming call. Since his phone was synced with his truck, he put the call on the interior speakers so his wife and brother could hear.

"Yes?"

"Mr. Green? This is detective Wentz."

"Did you find our father?"

"No. No, I'm sorry, we haven't had any luck in locating your father. But we do have a report of a stolen car in the vicinity of the retirement community. I'm sorry to ask you this, but do you think your father would know how to hot-wire a car?"

Kyle's voice boomed over his own, "You guys are useless! This is a waste of our time! My dad has dementia...he doesn't know where the cafeteria is, and he goes there three times a day. How would he know how to hot-wire a car? And my dad is not a thief! This is unbelievable!"

"Kyle. Shut up, and let the officers do their job. I'm sorry, Officer Wentz. We're under a lot of stress. Please forgive my brother." He shot a warning look at Kyle, and for once his brother stayed quiet. Sometimes his outbursts were so embarrassing. "To answer your question, yes. Dad would most likely know how to hot-wire a car. He is a retired police officer, and before that a prison guard. Would you know how to hot-wire a car, sir?"

"Yes. Yes I would."

"Then most likely, at some point in his past career, he may have learned that skill. But as my brother mentioned, Dad has dementia, which has been getting worse lately. I doubt he would remember how to do something like that, even if he once knew how. You can verify that with his doctor. I'll sign off my permission as his power of attorney if you need me to. It is my opinion that he would not be able to steal a car."

"Okay. Thanks, Mr. Green. I'll be in touch."

He pressed the end button, glanced at his brother who was slumped in the passenger seat and glaring out the window, and continued to drive.

What else can we do?

He felt the comforting touch of his wife's hand on his arm from the back seat, and reached up to squeeze her hand.

Dad, where are you?

Chapter 55

Barnstable, Massachusetts

J ace slumped as low as his lanky body would allow in the metal scrollwork chair at the small round matching table outside the eatery, Crash lying on his feet. A riot of limelight hydrangeas surrounded them with their cone-shaped white flowers happily blowing in the breeze. The sun filtered through the dense foliage, which lined the street creating a cozy atmosphere that was lost on Jace.

His head fell into his hands, elbows propped on the table. "I need a job. What am I going to do?"

Tandie's voice was firm. "Well, stop feeling sorry for yourself, for one thing. We can start filling out applications on the way home, okay? It'll be fine. You know what they say. When one door closes..."

"Another door slams in your face. Been staring at lots of closed doors lately," Jace mumbled.

She blew air through her teeth. "Oh man, you're a downer. Look at this as your chance to do something. Something you've been putting off. Something you've always wanted to do. We all have something. So, what is it? Your 'something'?"

He looked up and met her eyes, then spoke in a

rush, "I want to be a gamer. Like, a professional one."

"I didn't know that was even possible. Okay, so what are the steps to make that happen?"

He shrugged. "I'm...not entirely sure. I need to enter some competitions, I guess."

Tandie nodded. "Okay, we'll go back to my place and research it. Are you any good?"

The corners of his mouth lifted as he spoke, more confidently this time, "Yeah. Yes, I'm good."

"Well, that's the first real smile I've seen from you, so I'm going to help you make this happen. I can see it's important to you." She winked.

"Tandie..." Jace looked down at Crash.

"What?"

His cheeks went crimson. "Thanks. I mean, for everything. You know?"

Tandie smiled. "Oh, you're gonna make me blush. No problem, we do share a 'kid' after all, so I'm glad to help." She chuckled while gathering their trash, and tossed it into the trashcan on the way by.

When Jace stood, he caught a flash of the flat screen television inside the restaurant, and saw that reporter, Beth, and pictures of himself and Crash flashed across the screen. His body froze. He didn't need to hear what she was saying to know this wasn't good.

Tandie sidled up next to him. "Put the gaming thing on hold for a minute. I have an idea. Which veterinarian did the surgery on Crash?"

"Dr. Lee at Cape Critters," he answered.

"Let's go pay him a visit. He can put all of these claims to rest, and you'll be vindicated. Before this gets out of hand. Do you have his number?"

"Yes." Jace scrolled down his screen, and hit the

send button.

Why didn't I think of this? I'll talk to Dr. Lee, and he'll talk to that stupid reporter, and this will all be over. Maybe I'll even get my job back...

He stood up taller and breathed for the first time since they'd left the market.

Chapter 56

*Deep in the Ocean, Somewhere Off the
Coast of Chatham, Massachusetts*

C hristian followed along behind the man in the
water. Flipper-less, he struggled to keep up. The
burning sensation in his arms and legs did not
subside as his aching muscles hauled him through the
seawater.

*Now that I have oxygen, maybe I should try to get
away...*

His eyes darted left and right, and he shook his
head. Nowhere to go. And it would be a temporary freedom only. *And* the man would be on him within seconds.

*Following is my best chance, at least down here. Once
we're back on the boat, it will be a different story.*

Yes, that's what I'll do.

*Bide my time and find another way to escape. Just
stay alive in this moment. Then the next, and the next...one
moment at a time.*

His feet kicked double-time compared to his
captor's.

Flippers. I'll never take them for granted again.

The man stopped every few feet to look back

over his shoulder, making sure his prisoner was obeying his hand-signal command to follow. Christian studied his face, frowning.

Definitely not one of the men who'd shot Yaz...maybe from onboard the boat posing as the Coast Guard? Guess I'll find out soon enough...

Christian's eyes scanned his surroundings, and he spotted a silvery glint on the ocean bottom up ahead. Squinting, he swam the remaining few feet down to the ocean floor, trying to pinpoint the source of the light he had seen in his peripheral vision.

The man ahead turned, and began gesturing wildly for him to follow. He looked back and forth between his captor and the sandy floor, held up his finger in a signal to wait, and continued his search.

His feet kicked up clouds of sand in a four-foot radius, creating a swirling sand tornado all around him, and he turned back to follow, barely able to make out his captor through the murk, as the glint again flashed in his side vision. Changing directions, he reached into the sand below, scaring a flounder from his hiding place as it darted away. His hand groped through the sand until it bumped something. Grasping the cylindrical shaped item, he smiled as he pulled it free of the sand.

Raising it up to his face, he groaned through his mouthpiece, reading the words on the can.

Damn it! Diet Coke. On the bottom of the ocean. Some asshole probably threw it off a boat...

He felt for his diving bag, remembered that he wasn't suited up, and stuffed it into the waistband of his shorts. Looking up, he could see the man more clearly as the sand settled around him. On eye contact, the man began gesturing.

Christian nodded, and kicked his legs to follow.

Who are these people? Where are we going? The boat can't be that far.

But his burning arms kept pushing through the water, and his legs scissored along. Christian didn't know how long they swam before he checked his gauge.

Not much time. What is he thinking? He must be almost out of oxygen, too. If he's taking me somewhere to kill me, why did he save me at all?

His heart pounded and he gulped air in bursts. He wanted to tap the man on his tank to get his attention, but could not get close enough. Eyes squinting, his head jerked when he spied a movement below him. He stopped. Swam closer without any regard to the possible danger.

What the...? The sand is moving.

Eyes widening, he identified the creatures moving along the ocean bottom below him. Horseshoe crabs. Hundreds of them. Maybe thousands. Bodies moving. Swarming.

I've never seen anything like this. What are they doing here?

Their armor-plated bodies piled on top of each other as their spider-like legs squirmed underneath. The undulating heaps all converged on one area of the sea floor, creating a mountainous hoard below him.

Feeding? Mating? How strange.... And history making. Wait until Sofie hears...

His breathing stopped for a second as he realized Sofiana would never know.

Christian's arms moved back and forth as he stayed in one place, hovering above the mass of bodies below him.

Chapter 57

Yarmouth, Cape Cod, Massachusetts

Well, being unemployed will give me lots of time to finish my book...

Well, being unemployed will give me lots of time to finish my book...
Grayson replayed the earlier conversation in his condo as he packed a bag with all the things he thought he might need for the next few days. Maybe weeks...

The shredding machine whirred as he put the last page in. When it was done, he walked to Dan's office and flopped into the chair.

"Dan, I'm not printing the story."

"The hell you're not! What are you talking about, Gray? You've been working on this for weeks."

"I can't explain it to you, but I can't do it. I like the Johnsons, and I don't want to hurt them, or draw attention to them. It's done. I've destroyed all my notes, deleted my files...it's finished."

"What the...? Why would you do something like that, Gray? Are you trying to ruin your career? Did you really destroy everything?" Dan demanded.

"Yes. Every last note," Grayson replied, emphasizing each syllable.

"Well, you've gone and done it. You know you've left

me no choice. After all we've been through, I can't believe you'd do this to me." He stopped to run his hands over his shaved head. "You're fired, Gray. I can't make excuses for you anymore. Your decision makes me look bad. I'm done covering for you. Effective immediately. Get your stuff, and head out. Unless I can persuade you to change your mind..."

"No. I told you. It's done. Thanks. For everything, Dan. I wish you the best." He stuck out his hand, and Dan reached across his desk to grasp it, and then sat back down, dismissing him as he began typing.

Gray shook his head as he stuffed another pair of jeans into his duffel bag. His whole life was spiraling out of his control, and he didn't even know why.

"Come on, Rufus," he called as he pulled the drawstring to close the bag, flinging it over his shoulder. Grabbing a nearly empty bag of dog food and the dog's favorite rope toy, he turned around to look for the dog himself. He found him feigning sleep, curled into a fat ball in the corner of the sofa, giving him the side-eye through slitted lids. Bulldogs were known for their stubbornness, but now that he was up in years, this particular canine took it to the next level. Rufus opened one eye, squinting up at him, then pushed his head into the crack between the pillows and 'humphed.' His breathing came in wheezing huffs as he ignored Grayson.

"We don't have time for this. Come on, boy. We're going on a trip." He grasped his collar and pulled, but Rufus pulled back.

"Wanna go for a walk?" He grasped the collar and pulled harder. The dog didn't budge.

"You're too heavy to carry. You have to get up."

The dog made a grumbling sound. Not a growl,

exactly. Just enough to let his master know he didn't appreciate having his nap interrupted.

"Hey, I'm in charge, remember? You're supposed to follow me," he shook the bag of dog food as he spoke.

Rufus lifted his head and raised his ears, then lay his head on top of his paws, droopy eyes alert. But he still did not make a move to get up.

Grayson put down the duffel and dog food, and pulled with both hands on the collar. The dog's response was to roll over onto his back, head cocked sideways, stumpy legs dangling in the air.

"Fine. I'm leaving without you." He looked back over his shoulder as he walked out the door. Damn dog was curling up into a ball again.

He loaded the car and returned.

"Have it your way." He pushed both arms under the dog, lifting all 65 pounds of his overweight pooch and cradling him like a baby. A very fat baby. The dog looked him in the eye as if to say 'Seriously, Bro?'

"Your choice. All you had to do was get up and walk the short distance to the car."

Stopping to glance around the room, he pushed the door closed with a backward kick and walked to the car with his load.

Once Rufus was settled into the back seat of the Camaro to resume his nap, Grayson headed to the farmer's market. He would need a few things before the trip they were about to take.

He pulled into the parking lot, leaving the car running and air conditioner on full-blast for Rufus, and hurried into the store. He grabbed dog food, lunchmeat and non-perishables, a few other essentials, and headed for the checkout. As he stood in line, feet shifting, he scanned his email. The cashier was involved in an intense discussion with the customer in front of him, obviously someone he knew. Grayson glanced up and saw him holding up a collection jar with a picture on it.

"Yeah, can you believe it? He worked here for two years, and I never woulda thought he'd scam all of us. But that's what he did. He said his dog was stabbed on the beach and almost died. My boss put out these jars, set up a Go-Fund-Me account, and he even set up an interview right here at the store. But when the reporter removed the bandage, the dog wasn't even injured."

"Tsk, tsk. I remember him. Never made eye contact. You can always tell by the eyes," The elderly woman shook her head as she spoke.

Grayson narrowed his eyes. "Excuse me, but can I look at the picture?"

"Sure. But we're not collecting anymore. It was all a scam."

"No problem. Just want to see the dog." He reached out and took the collection jar, wondering why he was so intrigued by the image. "Cute dog. Wonder what breed he is?"

As he reached out to hand the jar back, he caught sight of the dog's neck, and pulled it closer again.

Grayson pointed. "Uh, what's that hanging around the dog's neck? That's a weird dog-tag."

"I have no idea. Why do you care?" The cashier cocked his head.

"No reason. Do you mind me asking what the guy's name is?" Gray asked.

"Uh...I guess not. I mean, the story's all over the news, so I think everyone knows by now. And he doesn't work here anymore. He got fired. His name is Jace Calhoun."

"Thanks." Gray scanned his credit card, grabbed his bags, and took off at a jog for the car.

Pushing buttons on his phone, he called Mike. "Hey. I'm gonna be a little late. Something came up; I'll fill you in when I get there. Thanks."

He leaned his car seat back, and made one more call, to a source in the records department of public housing.

"Hey, Jack. It's Grayson Smith. Yeah. I'm good. Can you look up an address for me?" He listened, and then pleaded, "I know, I know. But remember how I helped you last year when..." He paused to listen.

"Great! Thanks, Jack. His name is Jace Calhoun. I know where he works, if that helps." His fingers tapped the steering wheel as he waited.

"Hold on, I need a pen. Thanks, Jack. Now I owe *you* one."

Chapter 58

Leaving Sandwich, Massachusetts

B ob was not confused. Not in the least. His mind was sharper now than it had been in his youth. He remembered everything. Even things that would be better if left lost in the dark segments of his brain.

He drove the stolen car around the block a third time.

I need to go somewhere that I can get on the internet to research. I must find that woman.

The problem was that he didn't have any money. Not really. Oh, there was plenty of cash in his bank account, but he no longer had any of the information he needed to get it. His son, Kevin, took care of all of that for him now. No phone. No wallet. Not even identification. He had nothing. Except the twenty-dollar bill plus a handful of change he'd found in the glove compartment.

I can't explain this to Kevin. He wouldn't understand. And he's way too practical to believe any of it, anyway. He would convince himself it was the dementia talking.

Even though I don't have dementia anymore.

Think! Where can I go?

Oh, there were plenty of places with free wi-fi. But he needed a computer, too. He drove on in circles, thinking as he hadn't thought in years, all thought lines following a clear path, but still not coming up with a solution.

His eyes landed on a blue sign on the side of the road, the white picture of an open book with an arrow pointing right.

Of course!

He followed the signs until he came to the library parking lot, and tucked his stolen car in the furthest spot from the door.

Walking boldly up to the counter, he spoke to the librarian, "Excuse me, but can I use the computer? I want to shop for my wife's anniversary gift, and she's always right there.... I just want to surprise her. It's our 55th wedding anniversary next week, you know."

"Aww, how sweet. Congratulations. Sure. All you need is your library card."

"Can I sign up for one?"

"Yes. I'll just need to see your photo ID."

"Oh, right here..." he patted his pocket. "I seem to have left my wallet at home. Is there any way I could get the card now, and bring it in tomorrow?" He winked and smiled at her, leaning his elbows on the counter. "If I don't order the gift soon, it won't be here in time."

She giggled, and her cheeks pinkened. She looked over her shoulder. "Well, I'm not supposed to...but I guess it wouldn't hurt anything for you to use the computer."

Brand-new library card in hand, he sat in front of the computer. It had been a long time since he had used one, and things looked different than what he was used to. He squinted at the screen, and began clicking.

After playing around for a while, he typed a name in the search bar, and a slow smile spread across his face as he saw the address appear on the screen; complete with a picture of the one he searched for. He hit the print button, and walked over to the printer to retrieve his prize.

Chapter 59

Cape Critters Veterinary Hospital

J ace's leg bobbled up and down, causing the chair to squeak as he sat in the empty waiting room at Dr. Lee's office. All the emotions from that disastrous night were alive in this room, and a drop of cold sweat zigzagged a path down his back causing a shiver. He reached down to rub Crash's neck; the feel of the soft fur between his fingers reassurance that his dog was going to be okay. The black and white checkered tiles seemed to jump off the sub-floor, and he could feel the coldness that had spread throughout his body when he'd been sitting on it that not-so-long-ago night. Could see the blood as it had dripped onto the patterned floor in a splash. *Drip. Drip.* A shudder rippled up his frame.

The dog leaned up against him, sensing his discomfort. He lay his head on Jace's leg and stared up at his face. He wrapped his arms around the dog, burying his face in his fur. The smell of dog filled his nostrils, and his mouth turned up slightly. Tandie sat in the chair next to Jace, on the other side of Crash, flipping through a canine-themed magazine.

Jace avoided looking toward the secretary, who kept cracking her gum and leering at him over the rim of her glasses; long, manicured nails clicking furiously over the keyboard. The doctor had agreed to see him after his last appointment, and she had made it clear that she would not stay one minute past quitting time.

Minutes ticked by in double-digits. Finally, Dr. Lee appeared in the doorway to the waiting room. Crash leaped to his feet and bounced to him; body shaking, tail whipping. Jace stood, feet planted in place.

"Dr. Lee. Uh, thanks for seeing us."

Tandie went to stand in front of him in three long strides, sticking her hand out; she spoke in a rushed voice, "Hi Dr. Lee. I'm Tandie. I'm Jace's friend, and Crash stays with me during the day when Jace is at work. Well, he did before he got fired, anyway. It's nice to meet you." She pumped his hand up and down through the entire speech, and he looked on with a half-smile.

"Well, it's very nice to meet you, too. Now, let me see our boy." Dr. Lee bent to look at the wound site, and his eyes flew up to meet Jace's. "What's this? He's nearly healed. I've never..." He ran a gentle hand over the shaved spot. There was a thin line of scar tissue, but no other evidence that the dog had been mortally injured mere days ago.

The doctor raised his eyes slowly. "This is incredible. If I hadn't performed the surgery myself, I'd never believe it." He rubbed his eyes and got down on his knees next to Crash to look again, as if this time he might see something that he hadn't seen before. "In all my years in veterinary medicine, I've never seen a dog heal so quickly. It's nothing short of a miracle." He jumped up, calling over his shoulder as he rushed out of the room, "I've got to document this!"

Dr. Lee returned with a camera, a medical measuring stick, and a notebook. "Oh, I wish I had pictures after the surgery to compare! No one will believe me..."

Tandie interrupted, "Yes, that's the problem. Jace is in trouble because his co-workers took up a collection at work to pay the vet bill, and a reporter came and everything, but she took off the bandage and now she's saying Jace lied to try to get the money. She said he made up the whole thing. He got fired. We were hoping you'd talk to the reporter..."

"Well, sure. I'll talk to her. I performed the surgery. I'll tell her all about his injury." He looked at Jace. "Everything will be alright, son. Don't worry. What's her name, and what station does she work for?"

As Jace relayed the information, Crash jumped up, placing his front paws on the counter. The receptionist squealed, and shot up out of her seat, the wheeled chair flying into the wall behind her with a *thud*.

Crash took the phone into his mouth, and ran back to sit in front of Dr. Lee, tail flying.

"Give that back!" she screeched. "Oh, that mutt broke my nail. I just had a manicure yesterday!"

"I'll take care of this, Sarah. You can go now." Dr. Lee intervened.

In a huff, she grabbed her purse and flounced to the door, pausing to say, "Check your messages. There's one from that reporter." With that, she disappeared through the door without another backward glance.

"I know what you're thinking. But she's good at her job." He sighed. "The paper part, anyway." He reached out for the phone and Crash gently placed it in his hand. "Isn't that funny...it's almost like he understood what we were saying. Ha-ha!" He stood and walked behind the desk to rifle through the stack of papers. "Here it is."

Crash's brown eyes met Jace's, and the dog's shoulders shook as he made a *he-he-he* sound. Jace barked out a quick laugh in response.

Tandie was right. Everything's going to be okay.

He looked over to where she was standing and saw that she was studying him. A slow smile spread across her face when his eyes met hers, and she winked at him and blew him a kiss. His heart fluttered in his chest.

Chapter 60

Deep in the Atlantic Ocean, Somewhere
Off the Coast of Chatham, Massachusetts

C hristian swam an arm's length away from the horseshoe crab mob. He reached out, gliding his fingers across the smooth shell of several of the arthropods as they passed below. The small arachnid-like creatures remained oblivious to his presence while they continued their frantic crusade. His biologist's brain kicked into overdrive.

Has to be a mating ritual. Wish I had a camera...

He'd almost forgotten about his abductor when he was suddenly yanked back by a hand on his arm. When Christian's eyes swung around, the man tapped on his tank and pointed ahead. Nodding, he began swimming again, this time side by side with his captor.

Glancing back one more time to observe the horde behind him, he lamented that he couldn't stay and study the behavior.

Maybe someday I can come back...If I live through this.

As he moved through the water away from the activity, he kept a keen eye on the ocean floor, and spied the occasional lone horseshoe crab creeping along, heading toward the mass now behind him. Well, most of them anyway. There was one heading in the opposite direction, away from the rest, something seemed to be caught on its back. He caught a shiny flash of light as it moved.

Probably another soda can. People are so ignorant.

Looking up, he swam on. He had been so distracted by the crabs that he'd missed what was right in front of him, and his eyes widened as his body lurched to a stop. His sharp intake of oxygen caused him to cough awkwardly into his mouthpiece. He squeezed his eyes shut, then opened until they bulged.

What the...?

The man preceded him, furiously gesturing to follow, but Christian was frozen in place as he raised both his hands, palms up, in silent question. His wide eyes spoke volumes as he took in the scene before him, his brain rejecting the image even as his pupils dilated in recognition.

In front of him grew an expansive coral reef. But that wasn't what had his heart beating in triple time. No, it was what lay hidden underneath the coral that had frozen Christian's body in place.

A metal rectangular building rose up from the sea floor on elevated legs jutting out of the sand, with circular windows perfectly spaced along the side. The entire structure was perfectly concealed beneath the reef itself. If the man had not led him here, he would never have found it himself. In fact, in the event he survived and returned to this place, would most likely find it nearly impossible to locate it again.

I guess that's the idea. The perfect hideout.
Shit.

No one will ever find me here.
Who are these people?
And what do they want with me?

Chapter 61

Barnstable, Massachusetts

P arking the Camaro at the curb a few cars away from the apartment building, Grayson opened the windows for a sleeping Rufus, and headed toward the door of apartment 1B. Glancing at the paper with the address scribbled across it one more time, he raised his hand and rapped swiftly on the door.

Nothing. He knocked again, and placed his ear on the door, but heard nothing but silence from inside.

Don't have time to wait. I have to get to the Johnsons...

Undecided, he looked around, checked the time, and sank onto the top step stretching his long legs out in front of him.

Twenty minutes. If he's not home in twenty, I'm leaving. It's just a hunch anyway.

Jace pulled onto his street and into the resident's

parking lot. Crash jumped out of the car as soon as the door opened, and bee-lined toward his patch of grass, then froze. His hair stood on end as he crouched low to the ground when the silence was interrupted with a deep "R-r-ruff-ruff-ruff."

He watched Tandie squat down to stroke Crash's head and croon to him, "It's okay, Crash-Crash, it's just another doggie." She focused her attention on the bull-dog hanging halfway out of an open car window. "Well, you're a funny guy, aren't you? No need for barking, we come in peace." She held both hands in the air as if in surrender, a smile spreading.

Drool hung like shoelaces from each of the bull-dog's jowls, and he closed his mouth and cocked his head, all the while balancing precariously half-in and half-out of the car. When he barked, one drool-string fell to the ground. The other dripped onto the car door, leaving a jelly-like spit line down the side.

Jace turned when a man sauntered over to the Camaro, "Rufus, are you trying to kill yourself?" He turned to them. "Sorry. He was sleeping, so I left the windows open for him so the car wouldn't get too hot. I'm Grayson, and this guy is Rufus." He held out his hand, and gave them each a quick shake.

"No problem. I'm Tandie, and this is Crash and Jace. Crash is the furry one. I know it's hard to tell them apart. They're like human-canine twins or something. Maybe soul mates. I don't know. Well, it was nice to meet you, Grayson and Rufus. Have a good day."

She turned to leave, and Jace lowered his eyes to walk past when he heard Grayson's response.

"Wait. I actually came here to talk to you. Jace Calhoun, right?"

Jace's eyes darted up at the man. "W-why?"

Tandie interrupted, "You're not, like, a reporter or anything, are you? We've had enough of reporters today, thanks." She laughed.

"Actually, I was a reporter until a few hours ago when I got fired. But I'm not here as a reporter."

"Then, why?" Jace murmured.

"Yeah, Jace and Crash have been through enough today. If you're here to cause any more problems, you and your pal Rufus can just go back where you came from." Tandie stood tall as she delivered her speech, and Jace's face reddened.

No one has ever stood up for me before. Not even his mother, who had clearly chosen his step-dad's side in every situation, fair or not. Funny that now, this almost-stranger was the one who would rise up to defend him. He couldn't take his eyes from Tandie's set expression, her body rigid, hands on her hips. She was actually angry on his behalf. Jace shook his head in disbelief.

Grayson opened the car door to let Rufus out, and the two dogs ran in circles around each other, sniffing, bowing, and barking happy little yips at each other.

"Seems like these two are going to get along." He raised his eyes to look at Jace. "I know this is going to sound crazy, but hell, I'm kinda desperate so I have to make this quick." He took a deep breath and continued, "I'm here because I know a woman who found a small, round, metal-like object on the beach. She was wounded pretty badly by a hit-and-run driver, and when she held the object; she calls it a trinket, anyway, when she held the object in her hand, she healed. Much quicker than doctors had predicted. And I went to the market and saw a picture of your dog wearing something that looks an awful lot like the object my friend has, and I heard this story about how your dog healed very quickly. So...I came here to check it out."

"Um..."

Tandie burst out, "That's the most ridiculous thing I've ever heard! A dog tag healing a stab wound? No offense, Mr. Grayson, but I think you should go now. Come on Crash." She took two steps, looking back over her shoulder. "Jace?"

Jace stood rooted in place, staring with his mouth ajar at Grayson. Keeping eye contact much longer than was his norm, he sized up the man in front of him, and made a split second decision.

"Wait," the word came out as a croak.

Tandie spun to look at him. "What do you mean, wait? This man is talking crazy. Let's go."

"No. Wait." He swung his head around to face her, staring deep into her eyes as he never did. "There are some things you don't know." He looked up and down the street and continued, "Let's all go inside. I'll tell you everything."

Chapter 62

Sandwich Library, Cape Cod, Massachusetts

Bob clutched the scrap of paper to his chest while hurrying out the library door. He looked back over his shoulder once, and then folded himself into the car. Taking a deep breath, he reached for the open wires to re-start the ignition.

I can't drive this car much longer, but what else can I do?

He glanced around the parking lot, eyes landing on each vehicle. Jeep Grand Cherokee. Toyota Camry. Ford Explorer.

He shook his head side to side.

No.

These people did not deserve to come out of the public library and have their lives turned upside down just so he could get where he wanted to go.

He sighed.

But I can't get caught. They'll lock me up in the mental ward. They'll never believe I recovered from dementia.

He reached over and rummaged through the glove compartment, hand landing on a small, rectangular plastic case.

This will do!

His hand closed around the compact screw-driver, and his eyes darted around the lot, scoping plates. Two teenagers pushed out the door, laughing and talking in loud voices, just as he was reaching for the door handle. His hand fluttered to his lap.

Need to find a more secluded parking lot.

He put the car in reverse, and eased out of his space. As he merged back into traffic, he racked his mind for a place to go.

After driving aimlessly for twenty minutes lost in thought, he found himself in an all-too-familiar place.

Must have driven here without thinking...

His eyes filled, and he blinked to clear his vision. He pulled up to the curb in front of the small Cape Cod-style house he knew so well. Though the shutters were painted crimson instead of the familiar black, and new hydrangea bushes sprouted where the rose bushes used to be, he saw it as it had been...and remembered.

Home.

This is where I married my high school sweet-heart.

God, how I miss her.

They'd born their first-born son here. Right up there in that very bedroom.

And lost him here as well.

I can't...

His breath hitched as it all flooded back. Every emotion, deep and rich, came to him now in an over-whelming rush, and his head fell to his hands, re-living every heart-wrenching moment of the loss as if it had happened moments ago instead of years.

His stomach heaved, and he fell out of the car

onto the front lawn, heaves racking his body, until he could retch no more. A cold sweat broke out on his brow, and he sat there on a stranger's property, leaned back and tilted his head up to the sun. Eyes closed, he concentrated on his breathing. A voice jerked him out of his reverie.

"Are you okay?"

He peeked through squinted eyes. A woman, probably in her mid-forties, short crop of red hair in a curly mop on her head, approached him, a frown marring her pixie-like beauty.

Bob cleared his throat. "Yes. Yes, I'm fine. I'm sorry..." He indicated the mess on the lawn.

"Don't you worry about that. Rain's comin', and that'll take care of that. But are you okay?" She reached a hand down, grasping his wrist to pull him up.

"Yes, ma'am. Thank you. You know...I used to live here. A very long time ago. Have you been here long?"

"I've lived in this house for over twenty-two years. I didn't know the previous owners. Wait until I tell Rick! Do you want a tour?"

"Oh, thanks so much, but I couldn't ask you to..."

"Nonsense. Come on, it'll be fun. I'm Alana, by the way. You can tell me everything I don't know about my house. Or should I call it *our* house?" She laughed out loud, the noise resounding down the block. "And I'm sure you could use a drink of water. C'mon."

"Thanks. I could use a drink." He followed her up the stone walkway.

"When I lived here, there were rosebushes. My wife sure did love those rosebushes. I used to pick them when I got home from work, and bring them in to her.

She always had vases filled with roses. And if she ran out of vases, she used cups, buckets, whatever she could find. In every room of the house." He stopped, his eyes going blank as for the moment he lived in another time.

"What a lovely memory. You'll have to bring her back sometime! How long have you been married?"

"Oh, she passed away several years ago." Bob looked at his shoes.

"Oh, I'm so sorry." She grasped his forearm, giving a gentle squeeze. "Well, come inside and I'll get you that water."

His eyes scanned the cozy living room; tropical plants scattered throughout, seashell décor adorning every table and wall. The red, white, and blue plaid sofa and the knitted, tattered throw hanging along the back, the fireplace now showcased a homey mantle that hadn't been there in his days. A cat, disturbed from its slumber, glanced at him and darted up the stairs.

The steps to the second floor had been re-finished and stained, the fronts painted a cheery white, and the railing had been replaced. He stood mesmerized by the staircase, caught up in a long-ago scene that replayed in his mind. Shaking his head, he turned back toward Alana. Despite the memory, the space had an air of homecoming, and a slow smile turned up the corners of his mouth.

"I like what you've done with the place," he said.

"Thanks. That means a lot to me," she answered as she handed him a glass filled with water.

"May I see the backyard?" Bob pointed to the back of the house.

"You got it. Right this way," she laughed out the words, eyes sparkling. "I guess you know the way."

He nodded. "That I do. But you lead anyway. Is the garage still there?"

"You bet. I don't know what Rick would do without it. It's his man-cave." Alana held the back door open for him to follow.

Coming to a halt on the back patio, he gazed down at the patterned bricks he had laid with his two hands, brick-by-brick so long ago. The color was faded pink, and moss grew rampantly in between the chipped edges, only adding to the feeling of coziness.

Bob's head slowly lifted to the garage in the back corner of the yard. The bare bones of it were the same, but everything else had been updated. It was painted a cheery white, and the red shutters matched the house. Bushes had been planted around it, giving it the appearance of a home of its own. He almost expected a gnome to come out and greet them, maybe offer them coffee, it gave off such a fanciful vibe.

"When you planted the bushes...did you come across anything buried? An old metal box?"

Her brows furrowed, as she answered, "No. At least, not that I'm aware of. I think Rick would have told me something like that...let me text him at work."

As her thumbs furiously tapped her phone, Bob walked closer to the garage.

"He says no, he didn't find anything. Did you bury something back there?" she asked.

"Yes. A long time ago."

"Do you remember where you buried it?"

He nodded. "Oh, absolutely. I wouldn't forget something like that...but I couldn't ask you to..."

"Are you crazy? If you buried something here, we're going to find it. I haven't had this much excitement in a while. Let me get some shovels." She unlocked the garage and disappeared inside.

"I don't know how to thank you..."

"Here," she said, handing him the shovel. "Don't thank me, you're digging, too. Show me where to start."

"Yes, ma'am." He grasped the shovel in both his hands, and pushed into the dirt at the back right corner of the building.

"Please, enough of this 'ma'am' business. Call me Alana. You're making me feel old."

"Okay, Alana it is." He smiled, pushing the shovel into the soil again. His arms strained, and sweat trickled down his brow, rolling down his neck.

"I haven't had this much exercise in...I can't remember how long," he panted.

"Oh! I forgot you were feeling sick! Here," she reached for his shovel, "I'll do the rest."

"No way. I'm fine." He evaded her reaching hand and pushed the shovel down, turning the scoop onto the quickly growing mound they had created. "Maybe someone found it before you moved here."

"I guess that's possible, but..." *Thud.* "Wait! Did you hear that?"

Bob dropped to his knees and began digging with his bare hands, dirt jammed under his fingernails; he nearly fell into the hole himself. When the box was clear on all four sides, he reached for the shovel again to push it up. Grasping the box in both his hands, he sat back on his heels, his breath coming in heaves.

"Oh, I can't wait to see what's inside it! You are going to open it, aren't you?"

"I...don't think so. I'm sorry. I appreciate all you've done for me today. But I can't open it now. It's just a bunch of pictures and memories, and I think I need to do this alone." He rose to leave.

"Oh. Well, yes. I understand." Her mouth turned down in a pout, contradicting her words.

"Thank you for everything. You've taken good care of the house, and for that, I thank you." He thrust his hand out for a quick shake and began walking around the house to the front, heading toward the car.

"Wait, you never told me your name!" she yelled.

"It was nice to meet you, Alana. Tell your husband thank you, too. I am forever in your debt." Bob called over his shoulder, never missing a stride.

He got in the car, placing the soil-covered box on the passenger seat, clay dirt littering the floor in clumps. Twisting the wires together, the ignition sparked and roared to life. Pushing his foot down on the gas pedal, he drove off in the direction of Brockton, MA.

Forget about changing the license plate. I'll just have to take my chances.

Chapter 63

Underwater Habitat

Christian collapsed, lying on his back on the floor. His breath came in heaving bursts, and he squeezed his eyes shut as he concentrated on the air that was even now re-entering his lungs. He wheezed and sputtered as he drank in the air like an alcoholic finding a long-lost stash of liquor. Beautiful, life-saving oxygen.

Another minute and it would have been too late. For the second time today.

But I did survive. Unless this is heaven. Or hell...

As his chest began to calm to a steady rise and fall, he opened his eyes and scanned the long, narrow space, a door at each end, finally landing on the man.

His captor—and savior—was shedding his dive gear; hanging it on a row of hooks on the wall next to others just like it. He leaned the flippers against the wall, next to others of various sizes, and hung his mask in a row of similar masks. Glancing in Christian's direction, the stranger moved to a sealed doorway and turned the metal wheel, leaning into it to use his body's weight as leverage, toned muscles flexing. The metallic echo filled the small space as the wheel squeaked with each rotation like nails on a chalkboard. Christian cringed.

The door swung inward, and the man reached out to grasp the petite hand stretched toward him, gripping his around the wrist, and he stepped through the oval doorway.

"Got 'im. No problem." He bragged as he joined the girl on the other side.

"Good work, Jayden. The woman?" She inquired.

One negative headshake was his response.

Looking back over his shoulder, he said, "Coming?"

Christian grunted, pushing himself to a sitting position, reveling in the ease with which he could now breathe. After a minute passed, he stood, though there was a wobble in his step as he moved forward. His arm darted out to lean for just a moment on the wall, and then he too accepted the small-but-steady hand as he stepped through the doorway into the room beyond.

"Where am I?" He asked as his eyes widened. This under-the-sea world was a surprise. As barren as the decompression chamber had been, this room was decorated with care. Paintings encased in glass lined the wall of this room, and furniture was scattered to give a homey appearance in this stark environment. A popular children's picture book lay on the glass table, and building blocks were stacked in the formation of a tiny bridge next to it.

"Let's get you settled, and I'll be happy to answer all your questions. If you would follow me?" she answered in a singsong voice as she began walking.

"I'd like to speak with whoever's in charge." Christian mumbled as he followed.

What choice do I have but to follow?

The girl in front of him was slight in stature. Her head came to his shoulder-height, putting her at about five feet, and her platinum blond ponytail bounced as she walked.

I'm following a child. How old can she be? Eighteen at the most. It's like 'The Twilight Zone' down here.

"Where are we? I'd like to speak to your parents," he demanded as he stopped walking.

She looked back at him. "All your questions will be answered. I promise. I have something to show you first. Trust me." She smiled and winked, and then continued through more oval doorways and down still more long, narrow corridors, confident that he would follow.

Trust her? Trust her? How can I trust her?

"I promise, you'll like my surprise," she assured.

He grunted in response.

"Here we are." Her lilting voice was soothing to the ears as she opened a metal doorway, gesturing for him to enter.

"What is this? Am I a prisoner?"

Laughter burst forth like a love song, starting slowly and building to crescendo. Eyes twinkling, she replied, "A prisoner? What a silly thing to say. You're no prisoner. You're our guest. Come." She gestured again.

Christian looked back at her once, and then lifted his foot over the doorway to enter the small room. There was a figure lying on a bed, covered to the shoulders with a thin blanket...

His indrawn breath preceded his dash to the bedside as one word escaped in a breath.

"Sofiana? My God, Sofiana!"

She's alive!

Her eyes fluttered open, and her groggy voice whispered, "Christian?"

The girl stepped back, saying, "I'll give you two time to catch up," as she closed the door.

The sound of the lock turning filled the small room.

Chapter 64

Apartment Complex, Barnstable, Massachusetts

Grayson sat forward on the small couch, elbows on his knees as he spoke, "May I see it?"

Crash, who had been intently listening to the conversation, stood and walked over to sit directly in front of him.

"Hi Crash. So, this thing healed you, and now you're pretty smart, huh?" Grayson asked.

"Yip. Yip." Crash leaned in as Grayson's hand closed around the small medallion.

"It's identical to Maggie Lee's trinket." His brows slanted downward as he whispered, "What are these things?"

"Yip." Crash licked Grayson's forearm, and his tail wiggled. The dog looked up at him, tilting his head.

"Great. Maybe you know what it is, but you can't tell us, can you, boy?" Gray sighed.

"Woof. Huff-huff-huff." The dog's head shook back and forth in a negative movement.

"No, you don't know what it is? Or no, you can't tell us?" The dog stared at him.

Grayson looked up at Jace. "This is incredible. He does have an intelligent look in his eyes, and seems to understand everything we say. Unlike other dogs..."

Three pairs of eyes landed on Rufus, who was even now licking his male-parts, one leg up in the air, drool hanging from both jowls, snorting sounds filling the small space.

"Definitely unlike Rufus," Gray laughed.

At the sound of his name, Rufus snorted even louder and continued his licking.

"Yep. Not like a typical dog."

Tandie, who had not spoken a word since entering the apartment, stood and began pacing. "This is crazy. How can any of this be true?" She walked back and forth, back and forth, hands in her pockets, then out, then in again.

"I don't understand how this small round object could have the kind of power you're implying," she mumbled as she made a lap around the room. "And yet, now that I think about it, Crash did do some incredible things when he was at my place..."

"What kinds of things?" Grayson prompted.

"Well—he watched TV. All the time. I just thought he was attracted to the flashing lights..."

"Anything else?"

She blew out a breath. "I guess—I think he used the bathroom, and flushed the toilet when he was done. And—I was reading the ingredients from a recipe out loud, and he—well, he brought me all the ingredients. I thought it was strange, but convinced myself it was a coincidence. And—he did bring me a potted flower instead of *flour*..." She knelt down in front of Crash. "I didn't understand what was happening, Crashy-Crash. I'm sorry."

Crash bounced up, placing his paws on her shoulders, and licked her from chin to temple before laying his head on her shoulder in a canine hug. Tears filled her eyes.

Jace looked at Grayson and asked, "So, this thing heals people. And dogs. So...Crash is, like, immortal now?"

"I don't know the answer to that question. What I do know is that it doesn't seem to work on everybody. We did a sort of a test, and it didn't heal me. I'm guessing Maggie's trinket only works on her. And if that's true, then Crash's only works on him."

"But why? And where did these things come from?" Jace asked.

Grayson shrugged. "I wish I knew. But someone is after them. One man has already been murdered, and I've been threatened. I was on my way to pick up Mike and Maggie Lee so we can go somewhere safe when I stopped at the market. We're going into hiding for the time being. I think you and Crash should come with us."

Jace looked at the floor, stuttering, "I—I don't know you. I mean, don't take this the wrong way, but how do I know *you're* not the one that's after these things?"

"Good point, Jace. Smart thinking. I don't know what I can do to convince you. Come and meet Maggie Lee, and you'll have no doubt. Once we get to the Johnson's house, you can decide if you want to stick with us, or go off on your own."

"I don't know..."

Grayson took his phone out of his pocket. "Hold on." He succinctly tapped the phone with his thumbs, then sat and waited. The silence in the room was broken only by the sound of Rufus snoring in the corner.

A minute passed, and his phone chirped. "Got it. Perfect." He held his phone out to Jace. "Maggie Lee sent this picture just now."

Jace looked at the screen, and he drew in a breath. Tandie hurried over to look over his shoulder. "Looks the same, alright. Okay. We're in," she declared.

Jace's eyes flew to hers. "We?"

"Of course, we. You didn't think I was gonna let you go without me, did you?" she asked.

Jace shook his head. "But, this could be dangerous. I think its best if..."

"What? You don't want me to come?" she burst out.

"It's not that..."

"Well, then what is it?"

"You could get hurt..."

"Ha! So could you. Or Crash...well, maybe not Crash. But you could. No way are you going without me. If Crash goes, I go too. I'm his Mama after all." Her eyes moved back and forth between Grayson and Jace. "Well? What are we waiting for? Let's go." Nodding toward Grayson, she added, "We'll take our own car and follow you."

Both men watched her and Crash walk out the front door, and were powerless to do anything but get up and follow.

"C'mon, Rufus." Grayson called as he walked through the door. "Let's go meet the Johnsons."

Chapter 65

Brockton, Massachusetts

Bob surveyed the area while circling the block. For the hundredth time, his eyes darted to the small piece of paper with the address scribbled in his own sloppy handwriting. After one more trip around the block, he swung up to the curb and threw the gearshift into park.

He took one deep breath, and unfolded himself from the stolen vehicle. Stretching his legs, he shaded his eyes from the brilliant colors of sunset and set off at a quick pace toward the house.

He stopped in place when the front door opened before he had a chance to knock.

A woman who appeared to be in her early thirties stood staring at him through the screen, her eyes going wide.

"Oh. I was expecting...Can I help you?"

"I'm looking for Maggie Lee Johnson. Is she your Mom?"

"Um. Why are you looking for M-Maggie?"

"I have something I think she'll want to see. Is she here?" Bob craned his neck to see over her shoulder into the house.

A man appeared next to the woman, and glared through the screen at him. The click of the lock could be heard as he pulled her away from the door to stand behind him.

"We're not interested in whatever you're selling." The red wooden door moved inward as he moved to pull it shut.

"Wait! I really need to see Maggie Lee Johnson. I'm not selling anything. I promise. It's about what she found on the beach..."

"If you're a reporter, we have no comment."

"I'm not. A reporter, that is. I'm a retired police officer. Please. I need to speak to Maggie Lee. I mean her no harm. I found something, too. A long time ago. It's a lot like the thing she found. I wanted to...I guess I wanted to compare notes, so to speak."

The woman stepped forward, placing a hand on the man's arm.

"It's okay, Mike. I believe him."

The man, Mike, stepped slightly to the side, but a scowl marred his handsome features and he did not move to unlock the screen door.

"You tell us what you found first," Mike demanded.

"Okay. May I come in? I don't like to talk about it on the porch."

"No," Mike snapped through the screen.

Bob frowned as he reached into his pocket. "I'd really like to show it to Maggie Lee if she's here."

"I'm Maggie Lee." The woman gently squeezed Mike's forearm and stepped closer to the door.

"You're—Of course. I should have known. Well, that answers that. We definitely have the same type of thing in our possession. I saw you on TV, and forgive me for saying so, but you look a little different than you did then."

"Yes." Her eyes were drawn to the silver trinket he held in his hand. "Mike, let him in."

Mike's eyes darted to hers, and after a moment he nodded. The click of the lock followed, and the door swung open.

"Thank you. We have a lot to talk about, I imagine," Bob murmured as he stepped into the cozy house, placing his good luck charm safely back into his front pocket.

"I'm sure we do. But we have friends coming. On their way now, actually. That's who I was expecting when I heard you on the porch. They should be here any minute. I'd prefer if we wait to talk to them so we don't have to go through it all again when they get here."

"Sure, sure. No problem. Are you sure you can trust them? These friends?" Bob asked.

"Absolutely! Well—we know we can trust Grayson. The others, we've never met," she said.

"You can't be too careful. You could be in danger. Especially since you went public with your find. Everyone knows you have it," Bob added.

"Yes. That is a decision I regret. And yes, I think we're all in danger." She stared out the window for a second, before continuing, "Would you like something to drink? Water? Tea? A beer?"

Bob nodded. "Yes, ma'am. I sure would love to have a beer. I haven't had one in—let's just say a very long time."

As Maggie Lee moved toward the kitchen, Bob clutched a hand over his pocket. "It's warm. No—hot. It doesn't usually do that unless it's..."

He looked up at Maggie, who had stopped in her tracks. She was also clutching her pocket. Their eyes met.

"What's happening?"

"I don't know. Let's find out." Bob pulled his good luck charm out of his pocket, and it pulsated red in his palm as he held it out.

His eyes followed her hand as it reached into her pocket, and pulled out her trinket. It glowed the same crimson hue, and throbbed in time with Bob's charm.

"Is this good or bad?" Maggie Lee asked, pupils dilated as she took a step closer to him.

With each step, the pulsing grew more frantic, and the incandescence became brighter.

"What the..."

Chapter 66

Underwater Habitat

Sofie eased up in bed, clutching at her midsection. Throwing her feet over the side of the bed, she stood on shaking legs.

Christian reached out to steady her, and then crushed her to his chest in a bear hug.

"We thought you were dead, Sofie. I didn't think I'd ever see you again." A single tear ran out of the corner of his eye, and she smiled at him, reaching up to wipe the teardrop away.

Suddenly, she became aware of his body pressed up against the length of her, and felt his hand cup the back of her neck just before he crushed his mouth to hers. She inhaled quickly, backing up a step, but her heart picked up its rhythm and in the next instant she found herself leaning into the kiss. It was nice to be held. To be wanted. She hadn't had someone kiss her like this since Grayson...

The comparison was like vinegar to sugar. This kiss was gentle—and safe. Nothing like the fire that had flared between she and Grayson every time they'd touched. Gray had been lava bubbling up from her very center; Christian was a spark of a small candle flame flickering in the wind.

Grayson.

Her eyes flew open and she placed a steady hand on his chest. Easing back, breath stuttering, she broke contact. She didn't want to kiss one man while thinking of another.

This isn't fair to Christian. He wants more than I do. I should never have let him…

"I'm sorry. Are you hurt? Of course you're hurt. What happened? How did you get away from Baby?"

She sank back down to the side of the bed and rubbed her hands over her face; glad he'd been the one to change the subject.

"I—don't remember. I think—I must have passed out. She was swimming with me in her mouth. I could feel her teeth on my stomach and on my back, but she didn't bite down…" She unconsciously reached for her midsection as she continued, "I thought I was dead, too. I must have passed out. I don't know why, or if, she let me go."

"This whole thing is strange. I've never heard of something like this happening. Have you?"

She shook her head. "No. Where are we?"

"I was hoping you'd know. We're in some kind of underwater research facility, or habitat, or something. It's completely hidden by the reef. I think we're prisoners."

Her eyes widened. "Prisoners? But, why? Where's Yaz? Is she with you?"

Christian's eyes dropped to the floor. "No. She's not with me. She was, but…"

"But, what? Is she still on the boat? If I know Yaz, she'll show up any minute to get us out of here, wherever we are." She smiled.

"No, Sofie. She won't," his voice broke.

Sofie searched his eyes and saw it then. Anguish. Flat, blue eyes filled with despair. The gasp tore out of her.

"No." The single word left bile in her throat, and she took a quick step back.

"I'm sorry, Sofie. She's gone." He reached a hand out toward her.

"No! I won't believe that!" she cried, swatting his hand away.

"I saw it with my own eyes. She was shot, multiple times, and left in the water to die. There was nothing I could do. They were shooting at me, too."

"I don't believe it! Wait. You thought I was dead, right? Maybe you just thought she died, but she's alive out there, and she needs us. We have to..." She gestured toward the porthole window.

"No. The difference is I *saw* her die, Sofiana. She's not coming back."

"So, you're saying you saved yourself and left her there to die?" she shot back, pacing rapid circles around the small room.

"Yes. That's exactly what happened. Men commandeered our boat with automatic weapons, and one of them hit her in the face. They took your research, and she wasn't having it. You know how fiercely protective she could be. I'm sorry. I can't tell you how sorry I am. I'll never forgive myself for listening to her. She told me to go, knowing what would happen, and I did. She sacrificed herself. Her last words to me were 'Tell my girl I love her'."

She flew at him, pummeling his chest with her

fists. "No, you're lying! How could you? How could you just leave her there?" He caught her wrists and let her cry, tears streaming and snot running. When she was spent, her breath sputtered out, and she sank onto the bed. "I need to know. Tell me everything. Don't leave anything out."

He sighed as he sank down next to her on the bed, and began talking.

The knock at the door startled her. She moved to stand as Christian walked to the door. The creaking sound of metallic gears filled the room just before the door swung open and a ponytailed head poked in.

"Hi! I'm not interrupting, am I? Have you had enough time to catch up?"

"Yes. We have some questions for you. Least of which is: Where are we? And how did I get here?" Sofie asked.

The young girl nodded. "And I'm happy to answer, but I have some news that I think you'll want to hear, first. Sad news. I like to warn people so they know what's coming."

"Sad news?"

"Yes. I think it's better if I tell you quickly. We found the body of an African American woman with gray-tinged dreadlocks. She'd been shot with an automatic weapon. We brought her here. I think you knew her?"

"Yes. Her name is...was...Yasmin." Sofie's voice cracked on the name. "Can I see her?"

"Of course you can. We just need a bit of time to make her more...presentable. We're getting her ready for you right now. Trust me."

"Who are you? And who's in charge here?" Christian took a step toward her, and his voice rose louder with each word.

"I'm Coraline. You can call me Coral. I'm in charge. At least until my Dad returns. If he ever does. He left, and I've been running things ever since. I'll let you know when you can visit with your friend for the final time."

With that, she flounced from the room.

Sofie's eyes found Christian's, and his scowl echoed her own.

"She's creepy. What the hell?" he hissed.

"I can't worry about that right now." She walked to the porthole, and stared out, unseeing. "I can't believe she's gone."

Chapter 67

G rayson met Jace and Tandie in front of the house and nodded his head toward it.

"This is it. Let me go first. I'll do the introductions," he led the way up the walkway as he spoke, the dogs trotting companionably along behind.

As he reached a hand out toward the doorknob, his body lurched as the silence was broken by Crash's sudden howling. Looking back over his shoulder, his eyes widened and he froze, arm straight out in front of him. The undulating sound grew in volume, and he saw Tandie, hands over her ears, hunch forward.

"Uh, Jace? What's happening to the dog tag?" Grayson asked.

"What do you mean...?" Jace turned, then dropped to his knees in front of Crash. "This is what happened when he was hurt. It glowed, and it was warm. That's the only time." He ran his hands over Crash's body, and inspected the wound site. "He...seems okay. Well, physically, anyway." He looked Crash in the eyes as the howling continued. "It's okay, dude."

Rufus barked in his nasal tenor, adding to the cacophony, eyes never leaving the other dog's collar. Crash moved into action, running full-tilt into the closed door, throwing his body against it. His front paws scratched forcefully, claws leaving visible marks on the door.

"Open the door. He's not going to stop until we open the door," Jace said.

Grayson grasped the knob and turned. As the door swung inward, he watched as Crash immediately disappeared into the house.

"Um. What the...?" The red glow coming from inside the house nearly blinded them as the pulsing grew in intensity, and Grayson stood in the doorway looking in at the scene before him, two humans and a dog standing facing each other in a trance-like state.

Jace brushed past him, followed closely by Tandie, as they entered the living room ahead of him.

As Gray cautiously stepped through the threshold, his eyes landed on the stranger who stood facing Maggie Lee, and his body flew into action. Instinct took over.

"Who the hell are you?" the words burst out of him as he grabbed the man by the shirtfront and shook, nearly picking him off his feet. When the connection was broken he let go.

The outsider stumbled backward, tripped over Rufus, and fell on his backside on the floor, still rubbing his jaw. The pulsing in the room ceased, the resulting silence in direct contrast to the commotion of only a second ago.

"Well, why'd you do that? Miss Maggie Lee and I were making some progress here, and now you ruined it."

"You didn't answer my question. Who the hell

are you, and why are you here?"

The man pulled himself up, leaning heavily on the piano table, and gingerly moved his jaw back and forth. He took one step toward Grayson, and offered his outstretched hand. "I'm Bob."

"Mike?" Grayson turned, squinting at his friend.

"Sorry, Gray. I should have warned you he was here. He arrived just a few minutes before you, and I was distracted by...I don't know what that was." He shook his head. "He has a trinket exactly like Maggie's. It's identical. And the trinkets reacted to each other..."

"I call it my good luck charm." Bob continued holding his hand out in front of him. Grayson slowly grasped the other man's hand in one quick shake.

"Sorry about that. We've had some dangerous people following us lately, so you can understand my trepidation at seeing a stranger here," Gray apologized.

He turned and gestured toward the others. "This is Jace, Tandie, and Crash. Oh, and this is my dog, Rufus. Guys, this is Maggie Lee and Mike. And Bob. Now that we've all been introduced, I think Bob has some explaining to do. Let's start with: Why are you here?"

His head turned toward Jace as he spoke for the first time since entering the house. "And why did my dog's medallion glow when we got here?"

"Yeah, we need some answers. Now."

All eyes settled on Bob.

Chapter 68.

Underwater Habitat

Yaz was dead. It was true. She'd seen it with her own eyes, or she never would have believed it. She turned to leave her beloved friend on the stark metal table. It didn't seem right, leaving her there.

I need to get her out of here. Bury her properly. Take her home to her sister in Jamaica.

"Sof, we need to find out what this place is." Christian interrupted her thoughts.

"I can't think about that right now. I need to be alone," she whispered as she drifted down the corridor.

Still wearing her tie-die sundress, Sofiana smiled through her tears. She'd always worn sundresses. Everywhere. Even on the boat. Her heart constricted in her chest.

She'd reached for her hand, and it had been so cold. *So* cold. So unlike Yaz, who always had warm, soothing hands.

I can't believe she's gone. I have to call Mom and Dad...

Upon returning to her room, she leaned back against the metal door for support. Her limbs had no strength left in them.

Sofiana swiped the torrent of tears from her swollen cheeks, but no matter how many times she did, still more spilled over to replace the ones she'd wiped away. Her breath hitched, and she fell onto the bed in a ball as the racking sobs shook her entire body. Each movement caused a pulling sensation around her abdomen, but she was actually glad for the pain.

Memories bombarded her mind. Memories of Yaz. She'd only been five when they'd met. A spoiled child, she hadn't welcomed this new interloper into her life.

"But Yasmin, I want to go diving like Mommy and Daddy!" Her lower lip jutted out.

"Call me Yaz. My mother called me Yasmin, and only when she scolded me." She'd winked before continuing, "There'll be time enough for diving, princess Sofiana of the sea. But not today."

Sofie pouted and kicked at the deck. "It's not fair. You went this morning."

"You're sure right 'bout that, little girl. Not much in this life's fair, you'll soon see. And I'm old enough to scuba. You're not."

"But..."

"You can beg and plead until the ocean dries up, but the answer will still be the same. Five-year-old girls can't dive. It's just the way it is."

"But I want to! My friend Rebecca went scuba diving..."

"Now, girl, don't you go telling me lies. I can see through all that to the truth, and you just end up lookin' silly."

Sofie's face flamed, and she leaned over the side.

"How long will they be down there?"

"As long as it takes, girl. Patience is a virtue, you know."

"I don't want to be pay-shent. I want to dive."

"Okay, girl. You want to dive now? Here you go."

Sofie's heart tripped, as she was suddenly airborne, body flying over the side of the small boat and into the open sea. Her legs started flailing before she hit the water.

Treading water, she brushed the hair out of her eyes and sputtered, looking up to scowl at Yaz, just before there was a giant splash next to her and then Yasmin was in the water with her. She splashed water in Sofie's face and whooped out a laugh.

"Well, you wanted to dive. We're diving."

Sofiana swept her arm through the water to return fire, and swam around the other side of the boat. Yaz made a grab at her leg, pulling her back, and she blew bubbles in the water as she giggled.

Thirty minutes later when they returned to the boat, the two collapsed side by side on the deck, struck by fits of laughter. Yaz's gold-colored sundress reflected the sunlight in bursts, spread out around her like a ball gown.

"You went swimming in a dress." She giggled.

"I always wear a dress. It's important to look your best. Dresses make me happy."

Sofiana couldn't help but notice how pretty she was, all wet, with a crown of ebony dreads encircling her head like a halo. Maybe this lady wasn't so bad after all.

"Yaz..."

"Yes, girlie?"

"That was fun. Thanks."

"Thanks for what? You don't think I had fun? Are you thinkin' I should thank you for the fun, too?"

"I guess so. Yes. Yes, I think you should." She held her hand in front of her mouth to hide the peals of laughter.

"Well then, thank you princess Sofiana of the sea. I had fun, too." She winked.

That day had been the beginning.

Sofiana fell into a fitful sleep.

Her head was pounding. Swollen eyes opened a slit, and she lifted a hand to rub small circles at her temple. Rolling to her side, pain consumed her the moment she remembered.

Yaz. Yaz is gone. Mom and Dad. I need to tell them.

Resolved to do just that, she threw her legs over the side of the bed and winced when her bare feet hit the cold tiles. Her eyes landed on Christian in a corner chair, the cabin filled with the sound of his small snores.

When she stood, he jerked upward, eyes blinking.

He cleared his throat. "Sofie. You're up." She watched his shirt lift as he raised his arms above his head, revealing the flat, toned stomach underneath. Her eyes darted away as she saw him notice.

"Yes. I need a shower, and then I want to find that girl, Coral, and figure out how to get out of here. I need to call Mom and Dad."

"I don't know if it's as simple as that, Sofie. I told you, this place is strange. I wonder if they'll let us leave?" he said.

"Why wouldn't they? It wouldn't make any sense

to detain us. If we don't check in soon, OCEANS ALIVE will be searching for us. These people have no reason to keep us here. I just need to talk to Coral."

"I hope you're right. Go. Get your shower, and then we'll find her together."

"Give me ten minutes." She disappeared into the tiny bathroom.

Chapter 69

Brockton, Massachusetts

J ace leaned a shoulder against the wall, standing just
slightly separate from the group as Bob held both
hands up in a show of surrender. He felt some of
the tension leave his neck when Tandie moved to stand
closer to him. His eyes traveled the room, taking in the
group.

Who are these people?

They stood in three separate units. He and
Tandie on one side. Mike, Maggie Lee, and Grayson on
the other. And Bob, in the middle, alone.

"I'm on your side, guys. I am not the enemy. I
do have some of the answers you seek, but I'm afraid
you're going to be disappointed because I'm just as in
the dark about most of this as you are. I promise, I'm
just like the rest of you."

Jace's eyes flew to Grayson's as the older man
spoke, "I'm not so sure about that. Start talking. Where
did you get that, what do you call it? Good luck charm?
And how did you find us?"

"Those are easy questions. I found the charm on
the beach when I was twenty-five. I've had it ever since.
It's healed me more times than I can count. As for find-

ing you, that was the easy part. I saw Maggie Lee inter-viewed on T.V." He nodded his head in Maggie's direc-tion.

Maggie took a step forward. "All of that makes perfect sense." Her eyes perused the group before she continued. "I don't know about the rest of you, but I can tell you that I for one trust this man. And the dog." She smiled down at Crash, who leaned his body up against her leg as he looked up at her, listening to every word. "I feel somehow...connected to these two now. I don't know what just happened. But they are a part of me. We are the same."

Mike stepped forward, growling, "I don't like this, Mag. I don't like this at all. These people are stran-gers. We don't know anything about them. What do you mean they're a part of you?"

"I can't explain it. But they feel like family. We can trust them."

Jace cleared his throat and stood up straight, his voice a near-whisper, "I don't know about any of that, but Crash seems to agree."

"This is ridiculous..." Mike burst out, turning to face Maggie Lee. "Babe, that thing is brain-washing you or something. Please, let's go with Gray. The three of us will go into hiding just like we planned. The rest of them can find their own way."

Maggie reached both hands up to cup Mike's face and leaned in to kiss his lips. "Do you trust me?"

"Of course I trust you. It's them I don't trust." Mike gestured to the others.

"If you trust me, you can trust them. We have to stay together. I don't know why. It's just a feeling, but I know it to be true," Maggie said, emphasizing her words with a brisk nod.

Jace looked away as husband and wife stared into each other's eyes. His Mom and stepfather had never looked at each other that way, and he felt like an intruder spying on this personal moment.

After a minute, Mike nodded. "Okay. Okay. If you say we can trust them, we'll trust them. But we need to get out of here."

His eyes were drawn to Bob as he spoke, "I agree. You all can trust me. I'm a retired police detective. We do need to get out of here. If I could find you this easily, then they can too."

"Who? Who are 'they'? And why are they even looking for us?" Mike demanded.

"I promise, I'll explain everything I can when we get somewhere safe. Have you checked your cars for bugs?" Bob asked.

"Bugs? Uh, no. We didn't think of that." Grayson mumbled. "Shit. That would explain a lot."

Bob walked toward the front door. "Let's take care of that now. How many cars will we need to take?"

Jace cleared his throat. "We'll take my car. Tandie, Crash, and I."

Grayson chimed in, "And I'll drive Mike and Maggie Lee. And Rufus."

"Okay, we'll take two cars. I'll ride with one of you." Bob raised his eyebrows, eyes roaming the room.

"The Camaro doesn't have room for anyone else. Unless you want Rufus in your lap."

"It's settled, then. I'll ride with the young-uns." Bob pointed at Jace.

Jace's eyes flew to Tandie's. She spoke for the first time since entering the living room, "I call shotgun!"

She smiled, her eyes glowing into his.

He felt Tandie's hand in his, and when she squeezed, he returned the pressure. His head jerked at Bob's next words. "I'll have to pull my car into your garage to hide it. I stole it, and they'll be searching for it."

Great. We're taking the retired-police-officer-turned-criminal in our car.

Chapter 70

Underwater Habitat

Sofie led the way, with Christian following closely behind. They weaved through narrow hallways, past cold, barren, military-style walls, in search of...someone. Preferably Coral, but anyone would do.

The sound of youthful voices filtered down the hall, and Sofiana came to an abrupt stop, Christian nearly plowing into her back.

"There are children here?" Sofie cocked her head to the side. "But, why?"

"That's the first I've heard them...though I did see children's toys in the room when I first arrived here. I'd forgotten about that." His eyes looked toward the sound. "I wonder whose kids they are? And why they're here? A field trip, maybe?"

"Let's go get some answers." Sofie marched down the hallway toward the sounds.

Rounding the bend, she again halted.

Three small heads turned to face them as they came into view. They sat around a child-sized circular table in blue plastic chairs, a Lego creation-in-the-making in the center, a multitude of brightly colored scattered pieces in an array of blocky shapes surrounding it.

"Hi," a small voice interrupted the silence that had befallen the room.

Sofie cleared her throat. "Hi."

"I'm Tia. I'm six, and I'm the oldest, so I'm in charge. You're the woman brought here by Cary-One, right? What's your name?"

"Cary-One? I don't know anyone by that name. I'm Sofiana. You can call me Sofie." She gestured. "This is Christian. Are your parents here?"

"This is Genna and Hurley. Coral told us about you." Brown eyes peeked around from behind the smaller girl, Genna.

"But are your parents here?" asked Sofie.

Tia shook her head. "No. We have Coral."

Sofiana's heart picked up its pace. "Are you visiting this place temporarily?"

"We live here," Tia answered nonchalantly.

"But..." In mid-sentence, Sofie lurched and turned as a windchime voice spoke from directly behind her.

"Alright, you three. Time to go wash up for lunch. You can continue your building after you eat." Coral pulled out Hurley's chair, and ushered the three into the next room, shutting the door behind them. She turned, a smile spreading slowly.

"So, you've met the kiddos. What do you think? They're wonderful, aren't they?" Coral smiled.

"Yes, I'm sure they are, but where are their parents, and why are they here? What's going on down here?" Sofiana demanded.

"I'm happy to answer all of your questions, if you'll just follow me." Coral turned and strode into the hallway.

Sofie's eyes swung around to meet Christian's, brows furrowed in thought, before turning to follow.

What choice do we have? What the hell is going on around here?

They turned into a laboratory-type room, beakers and microscopes lined up along a black rectangular table. The large porthole style window the only evidence that this science lab was underwater.

"Hurry, it's almost time. You're going to want to see this," their host gestured, indicating the window, and moved to stand in front of it.

"See what?" Sofie asked as she moved next to Coral. They were surrounded by reef, almost as if they were a part of the reef itself. Despite her misgivings, her biologist's mind sprang to life. "So, this is a research facility? Why doesn't anyone know about this place?" Her brows raised and rounded eyes took in the view. "This is the perfect observation spot!"

"Oh, yes! You're right about that, Sofiana. Can I call you Sofiana? I knew you'd understand. I've been following your career forever. I love your work! Have you had a chance to test the new tracking device you've been working on?"

"Yes, we just tagged a male great white, we're calling him Romeo. And then I tried to tag Baby, she's another great white I've been trying to track, but I can't remember if I got the tag on her or not." Sofie paused, cocking her head. "Wait. How did you know I'm working on a tracker?"

"I know everything about you. Oh, yes. Baby. So that's what you call her. We have a different name for her. We call her Cary-One. I named her when I was about

Tia's age. I shortened the scientific name—Carcharodon Carcharias—into an easier nickname because I couldn't pronounce it. I know a lot of people do that. That's why I've started going by Coral instead of Coraline. I like the idea of a nickname. Cary-One and I have known each other for a very long time."

Considering you look about seventeen, I doubt it's really been all that long.

"So, you mean you..." her voice trailed off as she spotted a man in scuba gear just outside the porthole. "Who is that?"

Coral nearly bounced in an attempt to harness her excitement. "That's Jayden. Watch. Trust me, you're gonna want to see this."

Sofie was powerless to look away. The man in the water had a long pole, with what appeared to be some kind of bait on the end. In his other hand, he held a sign with a large black circle pictured on a white background. Bits of flesh and blood seeped into the water, creating a murky cloud next to the man.

"Any second now...there!" She pointed off to the side just as a silver blur approached the bait. The huge great white shark wasted no time in snatching the bait, swallowing it in a flash after two chomps. As it swam by, the anchor-shaped scar stood out along its underside.

"It's Baby! She's here!" She put her hand up against the wall next to the window, and leaned in until her forehead was resting against the cool glass.

"Yes. That's her. Keep watching."

The shark disappeared from sight, as the man refilled his bait pole. Again, Baby came and grabbed the bait.

"We feed her once a day. Small amounts, so she'll keep coming back. Sharks don't have to eat everyday, you know. But with her, it's like clockwork. She returns at the same time every day. After feeding her for a while, I came up with the idea of doing some tests in homage to Pavlov and his dogs. She's very smart."

"Tests? What kind of tests?" Sofie asked without taking her eyes from the window.

"Well, we've taught her to retrieve. Sort of like a pet dog. Or so I've heard. I've never owned a dog," Coral said.

"A pet dog?" Sofie drew in a breath so fast it ended in a coughing spree.

Coral nodded. "Yes. Keep watching, please."

Sofie looked at her with wide eyes. "Oh, you don't have to worry about that. You've got my attention. Completely." The cool glass cooled her cheek as she continued to press against it.

"Here we go!" Coral pointed again.

The shark came back around, but this time made no move for the pole. She seemed to be waiting for something as she swam in lazy circles around the man. He held up a sign, this one with a large triangle pictured, and then shot something out of some kind of barrel launcher, and the shark took off after it and disappeared.

"Where did she...here she comes!"

Baby swam back into view, tail undulating in a flurry of movement propelling her easily through the water. Baby opened her mouth, and something floated out toward the man. He reached a hand out and caught it. Turning back to hold a ball the size of a volleyball up facing the window for his audience to see.

"I don't believe it! Did she just retrieve that ball?" Sofie's voice rose an octave.

"Yes. She retrieves all manner of things. As a matter of fact, she retrieved you, Sofiana. You are the first person she has retrieved, and we didn't know how she would react. But here you are, safe and sound. It all worked out perfectly," A cheery smile lit her youthful face as she spoke.

For the first time since Baby had made her appearance, Sofie looked away from the window, searching Coral's face. Her heart rate picked up, and goose bumps spread on her arms.

"Me? Wait, what are you saying? You *sent* her to retrieve me? Why would you do that? She might have just as easily killed me."

"Well, yes. We knew the risks. But we had to get you away from there. Trust me. She was our only chance at saving you. We thought it was worth the gamble."

Christian turned from the window, speaking for the first time. "Trust you? What could be worse than being carried around by a twenty-five-foot long great white shark like a rag doll?"

"Oh, believe me, there is something worse. And you wouldn't want to come face to face with it." A shadow passed over Coral's crystalline eyes.

Her usual smile and bubbly demeanor were gone, replaced by a quick flash of cold calculation just before she took a deep breath and replaced her smile, though this time it didn't quite reach her eyes.

Chapter 71

*On the Road, Driving Through Delaware
Water Gap Recreation Area*

Maggie Lee held her hand over her nose and groaned.

"That smell. Whew!"

"Sorry. Rufus, man, couldn't you wait until we were out of the car, at least?" Grayson shook his head in the dog's direction.

Maggie reached for the button control that adjusted the backseat windows, and pushed until it was all the way down. Her hair blew into her eyes, and she reached up to swipe it back while waving the other hand in front of her nose.

Grayson continued, "I think I'll find a place to pull over. He probably needs a break. We've been driving for five hours. We could probably all use the break." He glanced in the rearview mirror. "The boy's keeping up."

"Sign says rest stop, one mile." Mike pointed.

"What do you think, Rufus? Can you hold on that long?" Rufus closed his eyes and began snoring. "I still can't believe Bob found two bugs on each of our cars. No wonder Gold knew every move we made. I feel stupid."

"Well, at least they're gone now. That's what's important," Mike responded.

"Yeah, but we still have a stolen vehicle hidden in our garage. What will happen if it's found? They'll think we stole it. I don't like this." Maggie twisted the hem of her shirt in her hands.

"We can worry about that later. Right now, all that matters is we're safe, and together," said Gray.

"Agreed. We'll take one day at a time. It's all gonna work out, babe." Mike winked at Maggie when he looked back over his shoulder from the passenger seat. "Grayson, when are you going to tell us where we're going?"

"When we get there. The place is secure, I'm sure of it. There's no paper trail to lead anyone to me, and I've been there before. It's in the middle of nowhere. I spent a week there a few years back with...a friend." Grayson turned his head to stare out at the passing trees.

"A friend? You mean a woman? Oh, tell us everything!" Maggie clapped her hands.

"There's nothing to tell. We were together, and now we're not. End of story."

"At least tell me her name. Please? I need a distraction," Maggie pleaded.

Grayson took a deep breath and slowly let it out. "You're not gonna let this go, are you? Fine. Her name was Sofiana."

"Oh, such a pretty name. Why did you break-up with her?"

"I didn't."

Maggie's eyes widened. "Oh, no! I'm sorry. Did she...die?"

"No. She left me. Simple as that. She's a marine biologist, and she's very dedicated to her work. I got in the way. Okay, maybe I did start pressuring her to spend more time with me, but...shit. It doesn't matter now."

Maggie Lee and Mike exchanged matching incredulous expressions. "Who would dump *you*? Well, it's not such a pretty name after all. I don't think I like this Sofiana at all. I really don't."

"You should know that while Gold was following me and I thought it might be the end, I called her and left a message. I told her to meet us there. I know it was stupid, and I'm sure she won't come, but....I don't even know why I did it. I haven't talked to her in years..."

Maggie smiled. "Grayson. I think it speaks volumes that she's the one you thought of at the end. You love her, don't you?"

"Love? I don't know about that. I told you, I haven't seen her in years. It was just a knee-jerk reaction to talk to someone before I died. Don't read too much into it."

Mike interrupted, "But then this place you're taking us is not as secure as we thought. Not if you told someone where we're going. Maybe we should find another place to go."

"No. She may be lots of things, but we can trust her. I'm sure of it. She couldn't have changed that much. Ah, here's the rest stop." He eased off the road and pulled into a space at the far end of the lot. Jace followed, pulling into the adjacent space.

Crash bounded out of the car and greeted Rufus with a nudge. Rufus, who remained lying on the backseat even though the door was wide open, lazily lifted his head. Crash reached up, stretching on his hind legs, grasped the other dog's collar in his mouth, and pulled. Rufus pulled backward. It was no match. Rufus had the advantage of weight and muscle. And Rufus didn't do anything until he was ready.

Crash ran around the Camaro, grasped the long, narrow door handle in his mouth, and pulled. When the door opened, he nimbly leapt up into the car behind Rufus, and pushed.

Rufus' head whipped around as he fell out of the car, just barely catching himself on his stubby front legs before face planting on the asphalt. Crash looked down from his lofty position, and made a *huff-huff-huffing* sound.

"Crash-kins, you be nice!" Tandie scolded.

Crash hung his head, looking up at her from under his lashes.

The kissy faces she made in his direction took the sting out of her words, and she softened, "Oh, come here, baby. You know Mama can't stay mad at you for long."

When she bent down, he lavished her face with kisses. He turned and, using his teeth once again, pulled the far door closed, then jumped out and pushed the second door shut before trotting off to a small patch of grass.

Grayson shook his head. "Sometimes he seems like your average dog, and then he does something that makes you wonder..."

All eyes followed the two dogs as they relieved themselves.

"Right now, he seems like any other dog," Mike shook his head.

Bob stepped forward as he spoke, "You should

have seen him in the car. The young-uns had some kind of crazy music playing, and I mentioned changing the station. That dog leaned up between the seats and pushed the buttons with his nose until he found something better. Then, I swear he looked at me and winked. It's the craziest thing. I've never seen anything like it."

"You're saying he understood..." Mike interceded.

"Yes, that's exactly what I'm saying. At least that's what it seemed like to me," Bob replied.

"Yes. We saw it, too." Tandie looked at Jace, and he nodded.

Maggie Lee interjected, "What does it mean? If he's smart, what does that tell us?" She looked at Jace. "Was he always this smart?"

He shook his head. "No. Just since his accident."

"Tell them about my name," prompted Tandie, placing her hand on Jace's arm.

He took a breath. "I was talking out loud about not knowing her name." He tipped his head in Tandie's direction. "Crash spelled out the letters of her name on the floor."

"What? You're saying the dog can spell?" Mike's eyes went round.

"I guess so." Jace looked at his feet.

"Wait, how did he spell her name? With a pen?" Grayson asked.

"No." Jace shook his head. "He put things—toilet paper rolls, my inhaler, just random objects—on the floor to make the letters."

"This is incredible!" Maggie smiled.

"Weird, that's what it is. Dogs can't read and write." Mike frowned.

"Let's do a test to see how smart he is." Grayson turned toward his car, and began rummaging through the glove compartment.

"You love to do tests, Grayson. Maybe *you* should be a teacher." Maggie chuckled.

"Wait. Not here. We need to get moving. Let's save the test for later, when we're sure we're safe," Mike interjected.

"Agreed. We're only about 2-3 hours away from our destination. I think it can wait that long." Grayson stood, nodding his head. "Let's get moving."

"Wait! I'm going to run to the ladies room first. Be right back," Maggie called back over her shoulder as she hurried toward the small building.

"Wait for me!" Tandie yelled as she jogged to catch up.

Mike waited until the women were out of earshot and spoke to the group, "I will do anything to keep her safe. Anything. I thought I lost her. I won't lose her again. If I think this is going south, I'll get her out of there."

"Understood. I think we all agree. If it comes down to it, every man for himself," Bob crossed his arms over his chest.

"Good. I just wanted to be clear about my priorities." Mike turned and got into he Camaro, slamming the door behind him.

Chapter 72

Underwater Habitat: Mercury Reef

"Come, let's get a bite to eat. I have a proposition for you. Both of you." Coraline began walking.

"A proposition?" Sofie cocked her head as she followed Coral to what must be the dining room. They sat at a table, three plates already filled with food.

"We'd like you to stay here. Join our research team here at Mercury Reef. You'd be a valuable asset to the group." Coral sat at the table, but didn't touch her food.

"Your offer is tempting. Very tempting, in fact. The kind of work you're doing down here is...record-breaking. I'd love to dig deeper and..." her voice trailed off. "But I can't just stay. I have responsibilities to OCEANS ALIVE, as well as my colleagues. Does anyone know about this place?"

"No. It's top-secret. Our research is ground-breaking, and it needs to remain anonymous."

"But, why? You could get all the funding you need if you just..." Sofie pushed.

Coral cocked her head. "We don't need funding. That's not a problem for us."

Sofiana's mouth dropped open. "Not a problem. Funding is always a problem in our field."

"Not for us." Coral shrugged. "We've been around for a very long time, and we do well enough for ourselves. What we need is someone to join our team. As I said before, I've followed your work closely and I like what I see. We'd love to put your expertise to work for us."

"I'm flattered." Sofie paused, a sigh whistling through her lips. "I can't. At least, not right now. I'm fascinated by what you're doing down here. I have to admit; your offer is more than tempting. But I can't. At least not right now. I've lost my friend. She was more than a friend. She's family. I have to take her home. Lay her to rest in her land, with what's left of her family. She deserves that. I can't stay."

"I understand. I'm disappointed, but I understand. Maybe you'll come back, after."

"Maybe I will. So, I'm free to go?" Sofie asked.

"Of course you are, Sofiana. You're our guest. I only need your promise that you'll keep our facility a secret, and tell no one. It's important we stay a clandestine operation, if you know what I mean. And you're welcome to come back, anytime. Here's my card, with my personal phone number. Call if you change your minds." She pushed two cards across the table. "Both of you. I'll arrange for your safe transport to Jamaica. That's where you're going, right?"

"Yes. How did you know?" Sofie's eyes widened.

Coral smiled, but didn't answer. She stood. "Finish your meal, and I'll let you know when it's time to go." She looked at Christian. "I assume it will be transport for two?"

"Yes. I'll go with Sofiana. What about the children? Why are they here?" Christian asked.

"Maybe someday when you return I'll explain everything. But that's a story for another time." Coral inclined her head.

Sofie's troubled eyes met Christian's, but neither voiced what they were thinking.

"One more thing, Coral. Do you have a phone down here? I need to contact my parents and let them know about...Yaz."

"Oh! I almost forgot! We retrieved your personal items from the people who took them. I'll fetch them for you right away. I believe your phone is there. You won't have service until you're above water and closer to land. You'll have to use our line to make your call."

"Who are those people? The ones that boarded our boat, and killed Yaz?" Christian inquired.

"Oh, they've been trying to find us for years. We always make sure that doesn't happen. We're a lot smarter than they are, don't worry. We make sure to stay one step ahead. We saved you, didn't we?" Coral winked. "I'll have your things brought to you right away."

She flounced out of the room, ponytail bouncing side to side with each step.

Sofie frowned at Christian, whispering, "Always more questions, but never an answer." She stared at her hands, folded on the table. "Let's take Yaz home."

Chapter 73

Pocono Mountains, Pennsylvania

J ace squinted at the sun glinting through the forest trees and sat up, leaning his body closer to the steering wheel.

"That's the...driveway?" he whispered, maneuvering the car down the sloping dirt incline between two towering hemlock trees.

The car bumped along the unpaved road as he followed the Camaro.

Bob craned his neck, looking out the front window between the front seats. "It's a wonder Grayson's car doesn't get stuck out here. How far do you think we're going?"

After several minutes of bouncing along, Tandie moaned, "I need to pee. I hope we get there soon, or I'm gonna need to squat behind a tree somewhere."

Bob gripped the back of the front seat with two hands and leaned forward.

"You're going to need new shocks after this..."

"Wait, there's some kind of house up ahead..." Jace pointed.

"Cozy. I hope it has running water. I could use a shower. And a flushing toilet." Tandie opened her window, "Smells like Christmas."

Scattered blue spruce trees of various sizes stood proudly here and there, and a riot of colorful wildflowers grew knee-high, swaying in the breeze in a kind of natural dance.

As they neared the small cabin, Tandie exclaimed, "Oh! It's so cozy! I think we're all going to be very happy here. I can sense these things, you know."

Jace surveyed the area as Grayson pulled the Camaro behind the small cabin. The cottage was one structure attached in two sections, the first covered by once-white siding; the other, obviously an addition added in later years, oatmeal-colored paint chipping off the wood in places. Raised on cylindrical cement stilts, the entire building was off the ground about a foot. Soft, green moss grew thick, covering the cement and the ground around them. Rocks surrounded the base in piles, and a pipe jutted out from underneath to rest on a small concrete platform. A small wooden deck with rotting wood at the edge led to the front door. He turned to Tandie, and raised his eyebrows as he pointed at the pipe.

"Yes!" She pumped her fist in the air. He laughed.

I hope these pipes are still in working condition, for her sake, he thought.

He raised his eyes to continue his survey. The painted avocado shutters and matching front door were in need of a fresh coat of paint, and a multitude of weeds grew wild around the perimeter in abandon. Looking further up, he could see that moss almost completely covered the roof, as well. His perusal was interrupted by one quick *woof* from Crash. He turned in time to see his dog take off.

"Crash!" Jace raced after him, navigating trees, roots, and dips in the ground. The sound of running water greeted him, and he jerked to a halt at the edge of a creek. Crash stood in the water, letting it flow around him up to his shoulders, and looked at Jace with a canine grin. He tilted his head.

Woof-woof.

"Uh, no, I'm not coming in there. C'mon, Dude. Get out of the water." Jace put his hands on his hips.

In answer, Crash turned and walked toward a tiny waterfall, the result of piled smooth, round, river rocks. He stuck his face completely underwater, and came up with a fish in his mouth. The fish wiggled, and Crash dropped it and leaped backward, then began chasing it around, water splashing around him as he pounced.

Jace turned at Tandie's voice, "Hey, look! Steps! I think I'm in love with this place!" Without hesitation, she kicked off her shoes and walked down the stairs fashioned with flat stones disappearing into the creek. Crash abandoned the fish he'd been hunting to join her, bounding through the water, and when he reached her side he shook his entire body, starting at his head and ending with happy tremors at the tip of his tail. Tandie screeched and held her arms out in front of her as water sprayed her entire body. Jace barked out a laugh when she giggled, splashing water in the dog's face. The two ran around the creek like children frolicking on their first day of summer vacation.

Tandie gestured, "C'mon in, Jace!"

"No." Just to be safe, he took a backward step.

He felt a presence next to him just before Grayson spoke, "He seems like any other dog right now, doesn't he?"

"Yes."

"Are you alright with us testing his intelligence later? He's your dog, so it's your choice. I promise we won't do anything to upset him."

Jace looked down at his shoes, and then nodded. "As long as Crash is okay with it, I am too."

This guy's not so bad. He didn't have to ask...

Just then, dog and girl emerged from the creek, both dripping water. As they approached, both men stepped back.

Tandie and Crash looked at each other then began running toward the duo. Tandie launched herself toward Jace, wrapping her arms around him in a bear hug, his arms automatically reaching around to hug her back. Crash launched himself at Grayson, leaping up giving Gray no choice but to catch him. Rufus joined the scene, barking up at Crash in his master's arms.

"Don't be jealous, Ruf, I'm soaking wet." A reluctant laugh burst out and his shoulders shook as Grayson placed Crash on the ground.

Jace looked away from the duo and down at Tandie. The laugh died from his eyes, replaced by something more intense. He felt his body's instant reaction, and all that mattered at that moment was the two of them. Neither moved to take a step back, they just stood there, staring into each other's eyes for what seemed like an eternity. He slowly lowered his head, and she met him halfway. The kiss was sweet and exploratory, though an undeniable longing burned through the tenderness.

Grayson cleared his throat, "Uh-hem. Come on, Crash. I think they need some privacy."

They broke apart, eyes smoldering, but kept their arms around each other. Tandie broke the silence; "I don't think we're a divorced mom and dad anymore." She wrapped her arms more firmly around him, and laid her head on his chest. He held on tight, resting his chin on top of her head.

"No, not divorced. Tandie?"

She answered without lifting her head, "Hmm?"

"Thanks for coming," Jace whispered.

He could feel her answering smile against his chest. "Are you kidding? I wouldn't have missed this for the world."

She stepped back and winked. "Now, I really have to pee. Let's check out the inside of this place." She reached out, and he took her hand. Together, they walked toward the cabin.

∞∞∞

Grayson stuck his hand under the deck, groping around blindly. "Got it! I haven't been here in a few years, I was hoping the key was still here." He held up the small rectangular box.

The door squeaked on its hinges as it swung inward. A familiar musty smell filled his nostrils as he stepped into the kitchen area, and his eyes were drawn to the stove. A memory swept over him so fast he was dizzy with it. He could see her as clearly as if she were here now.

Sofie standing at the stove, spatula in hand, singing off-key to a heavy-metal song that blared out of the small under-the-counter radio. Eggs sizzled in the pan, and her wearing only a blue tank top and plain white underwear. And fuzzy slippers.

When she spotted him standing in the doorway watching her, she put the spatula down and in three long strides came to him, reaching up to bring his mouth down to hers. She wrapped herself around him, and he sank in, drowning in the moment, the place, the woman.

They walked together, lips locked in a desperate kiss headed toward the bedroom. They fell onto the bed in a tangle of limbs.

Suddenly, she was gone, and his arms felt empty. Cold without her.

"The eggs!" She jogged toward the kitchen; calling over her shoulder, "Don't move!"

"I couldn't if I wanted to," Grayson choked out. He almost lost it when she returned and her tank top hit the floor. She hooked her thumbs in the top band of her panties, and...

"Grayson. Grayson! Can we come in, too? I have to pee, remember?" Tandie pushed past him into the kitchen and looked around. "I love it here! It needs a good cleaning, but...it's so cute! Now, point me in the direction of the bathroom." She bounced further inside.

Gray took a deep breath. His heart was racing and his breathing erratic. Even her memory had that kind of effect on him. He shook his head, and followed Tandie.

"Wait, I'll have to flip the breaker to turn on the water. Fingers crossed..."

He flipped the switch, and called out, "Maggie Lee? Turn on the water in the kitchen sink, please."

"No problem. And...we have water, people! Best news all day," Maggie clapped.

"I found it!" Tandie called out, just before a door slammed.

"So, Gray, whose place is this, anyway?" Mike wanted to know.

"It belongs to my aunt's neighbor's son. We became good friends, and he hardly uses the place. There's not much chance anyone would trace this place to me. They only use it during hunting season, and I've been told I'm always welcome. I've been here before."

"Sounds perfect." Bob mumbled, a contemplative look crossing his face. "If someone wanted to really dig they probably could find you, eventually. But I think we're safe. For now."

"How long do you think we'll need to stay here?" Maggie Lee questioned. "And how will we even know when it's safe to go home?"

"Who knows? Maybe we can find a way to contact Gold without letting him know where we are. Despite sparing my life, I still don't trust him. But he may have his uses." Gray shrugged. "Why don't we make the most of it while we're here? Let's figure out what we need to do to make this place livable. I brought some supplies, but we'll need to do another shopping run to stock the place."

"Okay, we'll take inventory, and make a list of things we'll need. Jace and I will be in charge of shopping. I'm really good at it." Tandie winked at Jace, and he blushed.

Young love. Grayson sighed.

"Sounds like a good idea. And after that, we'll see just how smart Crash has become."

"First on the list...cleaning supplies." Maggie Lee wrinkled her nose at the trail of mouse-droppings that were scattered across the kitchen counter.

Chapter 74

Mercury Reef Underwater Habitat

Sofie wiped her wet face with the sleeve of her sweatshirt. To say breaking the news to her parents had been hard was a gross understatement. Through their combined tears, they made arrangements to meet in Jamaica, and her mother had volunteered to call Yasmin's sister to tell her the news and help plan the services. She gladly handed over that responsibility to her mother. Sofiana would make the final trip with the body of her best friend. They'd all be together within twenty-four hours.

I still can't believe she's gone.

Her breath hitched, and hiccups shook her body. She was drained in a way she'd never been before. This feeling was alien to her, and she looked around the room, not knowing what she should do next.

Eyes landing on the cell phone on the table, she reached for it. Her eyes focused on the little light indicating that she had a message.

Who cares? There's nobody I want to talk to right now. Except Yaz...

Pushing the menu button, she put the phone on the small end table, and strode to the bathroom.

A warm shower might...

She stopped in her tracks, eyes drawn to the phone. Turning, she sighed as she reached for the cell phone, and punched the voicemail button. A familiar voice filled the room, sending tingles up her arms.

"Sofiana. Sof. It's me, Grayson. I just...I-I don't know. I needed to talk to you. Something weird is happening, and I-I've been thinking about you lately. Thinking about us, and what went wrong...anyway, I just wanted to talk to you. Just talk. If I make it through this night, I'm going to the place we went to escape for Christmas. Do you remember where it is? That's where I'll be, with friends. Their names are Mike and Maggie Lee Johnson, from Brockton. Maggie found something that came from the ocean. You're gonna want to see it. It seems to have...power of some sort. If something happens to me, you can trust them. That's all I can say for now. Call me."

Sofie dropped the phone, then immediately retrieved it and replayed the message.

"If he makes it...something with power? What the hell is he talking about?"

Hitting the callback button, she got the message saying 'No Service'.

She listened one more time to Grayson's message, and then strode to the door with determination.

Chapter 75

Pocono Mountains, Pennsylvania

Grayson hooked up the old Nintendo gaming system to the ancient, boxy television in the living room.

No cable connection, but the games might still work.

He blew the dust off the top game on the pile, Super Mario Bros., opened the case, and inserted it into the console.

Somebody might need a distraction while we're here.

His eyes traveled the room. He ran a finger over the small kitchenette table, and it left a line in the dust. Next order of business, cleaning.

"Okay, everybody needs to pitch in. I found a broom and some dust rags. We may be here a while, so let's make this place livable. When the kids return, they'll bring more cleaning supplies, but we can get started on this now."

Maggie Lee jumped up, "Let's do this." She disappeared into the bedroom at the far end of the cabin, and emerged a minute later, arms loaded with bed sheets. "I'll shake these out and hang them outside to freshen them up until we can find a laundromat."

"Good idea. How many beds are there?" Bob

asked.

"There's one double bed and two twins in the back bedroom," Maggie answered.

"And two more twin beds in the small bedroom." Mike interjected.

"There used to be cots in the shed, I'll go see if they're still there. And there's always the sofa. I think it makes sense that Mike and Maggie Lee share the double, Tandie and Jace can take the twin beds in the small room, and Bob and I can sleep on the twins in the large room. If you two don't mind sharing the same room with us, that is." Grayson nodded toward Mike.

"Don't mind at all, Gray. Sounds like we don't even need the cots." Mike smiled. "Unless you snore. Then I'm kicking you out."

Grayson chuckled. "Okay, we'll explore the shed tomorrow. Let's take care of the inside today."

He turned to grab the broom, and stopped in his tracks. Turning to look back over his shoulder, he silently gestured for the others to look.

Crash had turned on the TV, and had the controller in his mouth. He placed it gently on the floor in front of him and pushed the button with his paw, using the controller to navigate his character on the screen. If his paws had been any bigger, he would have had trouble with the controller, but his medium-sized paws could work the buttons fairly easily. His electronic life ended quickly, but Crash pushed the button again and it restarted. This time, he got one screen further in the game before his player died. Again, he pushed the start button with his paw.

Grayson stood speechless. He glanced around the room. Bob stood frozen in place, a hand braced on the back of a wooden chair. Mike's mouth gaped open. The bed sheets were in a heap on the floor in front of Maggie Lee, and her hand shook as she raised it to her mouth.

"Is he...?" her voice quivered.

Grayson nodded. "Yes, I think he is."

He's playing a video game. Okay, he's not very good at it, but he's playing. This dog is even smarter than we thought.

∞∞∞

When Jace returned with Tandie, arms loaded with supplies, he noticed bed sheets gently swaying in the breeze on a line strung between two trees.

"They've been busy." Tandie said to him.

Several plastic grocery bags hung from their arms, and they placed their purchases on the picnic table outside.

Tandie walked to the door, shouting, "We're home!"

The sound of claws clicking on the wooden floors filled the silence, and Crash bounded out the door to greet them with wet kisses and happy little barks, balancing on his hind legs while pawing at them with his front.

Jace squatted down, giving Crash easier access to put his paws on his shoulders and lick his face. He buried his nose in the animal's fur for just a moment, breathing in the scent of dog, then pulled away. Though Crash's hair had taken on a musty, creek smell, Jace smiled. A stinky mutt didn't bother him at all. In fact, he kinda liked it.

"Miss me?" he asked the dog.

Yip.

"Find everything?" Grayson ambled out the door and leaned on the broom handle.

"I think so," Jace said.

"Question for you. Did you teach Crash how to play video games? You're a gamer right?" Gray asked.

Jace shook his head. "No. I mean, yes, I'm a gamer. But I didn't teach Crash to play. Why?"

"Because he spent the entire time you were gone figuring out how to play Super Mario Bros. He's getting better, too."

His eyes widened. "What?" Jace slowly stood, his head whipping to look at the dog.

Crash sat proudly, chest puffed out as his tail flew back and forth across the deck.

Yip. He seemed to smile as he barked.

"Wow! Crashy, you can play Mario? That's A-mazing! I want to see!" Tandie bent down and cupped Crash's face, scratching behind his ears. "You're such a smart boy! Mama loves her smart boy." She kissed his snout.

Jace began walking toward the door. "I want to see this, too. I mean, he watches me all the time, but I never..."

Standing in front of the TV, hands on his hips, Jace looked on as Crash started the game. His heart started pounding, and his gamer's brain took over.

"Jump! Good, now run...aww! So close!" He moved to sit next to Crash on the floor. "I can teach you how to..."

"Jace? You two can have a blast bonding over Mario later. Let's try to figure out just how smart he is. I think it's time for that test," Tandie's words jerked him out of the 'gaming zone.'

"Oh. Yeah. Okay." Jace reluctantly stood, dragging his palms over his pants. "Crash, is it okay if we ask you some questions?" The dog looked back and forth between the screen and Jace, finally answering with a reluctant *yip*.

Grayson stepped forward. "Good. I think he already barks once for 'yes'. Is that right, Crash? Do you bark one time when you mean 'yes'?"

Yip.

"Good. Good. Now, let's figure out how he can communicate 'No' to us. Anyone have any ideas?"

Yip.

"You have an idea, Crash?"

Yip.

"Okay, show us 'No'."

Crash whipped his head side to side in a negative headshake.

"Ha! That works. Why didn't we think of that?" Grayson chuckled.

Tandie reached into one of the grocery bags, and took out a puzzle. "We got the kind that had knobs on each piece. We thought he'd be able to pick them up with his mouth."

Holding the puzzle out for Crash to look at, she dumped the pieces on the floor, and stood back.

"Can you put the puzzle back together, Crash-kins?"

He tilted his head, staring at the pieces. Using his paw to push them around, he picked up the first piece in his mouth, and gently placed it in the corner on the wooden base. It was a slow process, but everyone stood quietly watching. Barely breathing. He repeated the process until the 20-piece puzzle was finished.

Yip. Huff-huff-huff.

Tandie clapped her hands, "I told you we should get the 100-piece!" Her laughter filled the room, causing Crash's tail to whip back and forth. He stood, then bowed with his bottom up, elbows down on the floor.

"Okay, so we got this. Because, you know, he spelled Tandie's name before. We thought this would be easier." Jace pulled something else from the bag.

In his hand he held an electronic children's alphabet game. Each letter was printed on a 2-inch by 2-inch square, and when the button was pushed, an electronic voice exclaimed the letter.

He placed it on the floor, and said, "Crash. These are all the letters. You can spell words to tell us... things. Want to try?"

Yip.

He sniffed the game, then looked up at each person in the room. He placed his paw on a letter. The enthusiastic voice blared the letter.

F!

"I'll write down each letter!" Tandie grabbed the notebook and pen from the bag and wrote F.

G! L! R! F! A! B! C!

"F-G-L-R-F-A-B-C? Fglrfabc. I don't think that spells anything."

Crash whipped his head back and forth. *Huff-huff-huff.*

Z! Z! Z! Y! S! W! W! A! B! C!

"Z-Z-Z-Y-S-W-W-A-B-C? Wait. Maybe he doesn't

know how to spell. I mean, he's only been smart for a short time..."

"But he spelled Tandie's name on the floor, remember?"

T!A!N!D!I!E!

The cheery voice rang out as Crash hit the buttons with his paw.

Tandie clapped her hands. "He was copying it! I have my name painted on the mirror in the entryway of my apartment. I pointed to it when he came over the first time and I told him my name. Even spelled it for him. Okay, yes I know I was talking to a dog, but that's beside the point. Turns out I was right to talk to him, because he's the smartest dog in the world! Anyway, he saw the letters, and knew what they spelled. He just needs someone to teach him! Is that right, Crashy? Should I teach you how to read?"

Crash leaped up, *Yip.*

Yip.

He ran in a circle and sat down in front of Tandie, raising his paw and placing it on her leg, tail whipping across the floor.

Yip.

"This is gonna be lit!" Tandie sat down on the floor, legs in a pretzel, and Crash jumped into her lap. "Mama will teach you all about the letters. Letters have sounds. Like /t/ /t/ T. You put letters together to make words, and words together to make sentences."

Crash looked up at her, a look of unnatural intelligence radiating from his brown eyes. He tilted his head as if to say: *tell me more.*

"This is so..." Gray shook his head. "I can't think of a word that exists to describe this. Before you teach

him how to read, I have a few more questions for him."
He stepped forward.

"Crash, do you know what this is?" He reached
for the object on the dog's collar.

Crash waited a beat to answer. He looked up at
Maggie, and then turned his head to look at Bob. His
shook his head hesitantly back and forth, indicating
'no'.

Maggie stepped forward. "I can tell you, the answer is no. It's just a feeling that comes from deep down
inside of me. Whatever these things are, they connect
the three of us, somehow. We are a part of each other,
and I sense there are more like us...out there. Sometimes I have an urge to go and find them."

Crash jumped up, eyes staring intently at Maggie
Lee. *Yip.*

Mike stepped forward and put a hand on her arm,
"What are you talking about, Maggie? Why didn't you
tell me this before?"

"Because I can't explain it. Don't worry, babe.
I'm not going anywhere. It's just an intuition, that's all.
I feel like I'm a part of something, I don't know, bigger
than this. Bigger than all of us. It's like, I'm still me...but
I'm different somehow, too. Do you feel it, Bob?"

He inclined his head. "Yes. I do. We're connected."

Yip. Yip. Yip.

Chapter 76

Airspace Over Pennsylvania

Sofiana watched the puffy, white clouds as the airliner cut through them. Her shoulders slumped, and her red-rimmed eyes burned. She reached up to rub them with the palms of her hands, and sighed. This was her third flight in two days, and she was both mentally and physically exhausted, though sleep still eluded her.

She turned away from the window to glance at the man sitting next to her. Christian had insisted on coming with her. She had not had strength left in her body to fight with him. He'd been nothing but kind and helpful since they'd left the underwater fortress, and though every fiber of her being wanted nothing more than to be alone right now, she didn't know how to get rid of him. She cringed.

I must be the most ungrateful woman in the world. He's been a rock these past few days, and I just want him to go.

Her shoulders raised in another drawn-out sigh.

It's my fault. I let him believe there may be a chance for us with that one kiss.

She didn't have the strength to worry about that

right now. Staring back at the clouds, she thought of her parents. After playing Grayson's message for them, they had readily agreed that she should go find him. Even though it meant that she would miss the services for Yaz.

A lone tear tracked down her cheek, and she swiped it away.

Just because I won't be there, doesn't mean I loved her any less.

Even knowing that, the guilt was almost unbearable. Her breath hitched as she swiped at two more tears. Once the crying began, it was impossible to stop the deluge.

She pushed her way out of her seat, barely making it to the bathroom before the sobbing began. Collapsing onto the toilet in the shoebox that passed as a bathroom, her head fell into her hands and her body shook with each heaving breath she took.

Oh, Yaz.

Her sister had informed them of the cancer that had invaded Yasmin's body.

Why didn't she tell me? She didn't have to suffer alone.

A low moan escaped her.

I can't bear this.

What can I do?

A small voice echoed in her head: *Find Grayson.*

Please let him be okay.

I need him to be okay. I can't lose him, too.

She steeled her shoulders, holding on to that thought with everything left inside her.

I'm coming.

Grayson.

She wiped her face and returned to her seat, shoulders set with a new resolve as the captain spoke over the loudspeaker.

"Everyone please return to your seats and fasten your seatbelts. We are preparing for landing, and we're circling the runway. I'll have you on the ground in about ten minutes. Welcome to Mount Pocono, and thanks for flying with us."

Chapter 77

Pocono Mountains, Pennsylvania

Mike stared out over the rushing water of the creek with unseeing eyes. Ferns stood proudly lining the bank, and birds could be heard chirping in the trees surrounding him. The tranquil scene—a backdrop to the melodic sound of moving water—should have soothed him, but nothing could do that right now.

He was worried about his wife.

Shoving his hands deep into the front pockets of his jeans, he paced back and forth in the darkening skies of twilight. Tripping over a smooth rock, he kicked it into the water.

The feeling of dread washed over him once again. It hadn't really left him since his wife's earlier declaration.

Connected? Part of something bigger? The urge to find the others?

He shook his head. None of this made any sense.

And all because of that stupid trinket. The urge to destroy the thing was nearly irresistible. A dull ache in his jaw alerted him that he'd been grinding his teeth as he paced, and his jaw slackened.

What can I do? How can I protect her from a feeling coming from within?

All I want is for Maggie to be safe. I'll do anything to protect her. If only I could convince her that we should leave. Just the two of us. Maybe Grayson, too.

He hung his head, kicking the dirt.

She'll never agree. I know her too well.

Or at least...I used to.

He turned at the sound of footsteps.

"Hi, babe. Watcha' doing?" She reached for his hand and squeezed.

Anxiety lined his face. "I'm worried about you."

"I can see that." She reached up to smooth out the wrinkles on his forehead, then cupped his stubbly cheek. "Don't be. I'm fine. I feel better than ever. You have no need to worry."

"I'm worried about what you said earlier."

"Don't. That's why I didn't tell you before. I didn't want you to worry. I love you more than anything else in this world. You and me, right? Now and forever. I know what you're thinking. I'd never leave you. You know that, right?"

"I thought I did. But lately..."

"Don't even finish that thought. I love you. Please stop worrying. There's nothing to worry about."

"Ha." He held up his closed fist, raising one finger at a time as he spoke, "One, you look like you're thirty. Two, we've got a dog in there learning to read. And three, there's this stranger you feel 'connected' to. You're right, what's to worry about?"

"Nothing. There's nothing to worry about. I have some news." She stepped back, head tilted back, a smile curving her lips. "It's good news. A miracle, really.

You're not going to believe it. I...sensed it, and I didn't dare believe it was true, but..."

"What, Maggie Lee? I can't take the suspense, and I sure could use some good news right about now. What is it?"

"Our dream is coming true. The one thing we thought we could never have. Maybe you should sit down for this." A giggle escaped, and she reached a hand up to stifle the sound. "No, I can't wait any longer to tell you. I'm pregnant. We're going to be parents. I asked Tandie to bring back a pregnancy test, and I just took it, and it came back positive. See?" She held the stick out for him. "It's a miracle." A giggle escaped. "Babe, we're having a baby. We must've conceived when my body got...younger. After my trinket healed me. It healed more than my head injury." She launched herself into his arms, and he held on tight, a frown marring his handsome face.

"We seem to be having a lot of miracles lately." His arms tightened around her, and he lay his head on top of hers, closing his eyes. "I can't believe it. We're fifty-five, and we're going to be parents? That's...incredible."

"I'm so excited. Let's go share our happy news with the others." She reached for his hand, pulling him toward the cabin.

From her position sitting on the wooden floor, Tandie bounced up in one fluid motion to embrace Mike and Maggie Lee. Crash ran around them in circles, then ran to his new toy and began frantically pawing at the letters.

H! A! P! P! Y! H! A! P! P! Y! H! A! P! P! Y!

Tandie hooted out a laugh. "I just taught him emotion words! Ha! Good boy, Crashy!"

He jumped up and gently lay a paw on Maggie's mid-section.

"Yes, Crash. We are happy." A tear tracked down her smooth cheek, and she couldn't seem to stop smiling as she scratched the dog behind the ears.

Grayson walked forward, hand outstretched. "Congratulations, you two. Wow. A baby." He pumped Mike's hand, and then hugged Maggie Lee.

Jace nodded toward the newly expectant parents, mumbling, "Congratulations."

Tandie grinned, and grabbed his hand. "Try to contain your excitement, Jace. You're embarrassing them."

He looked into her eyes, gave a quick yank, and pulled her against him. His lips connected with hers in a quick kiss.

"Oh." Tandie smiled up at him, leaned up on her tiptoes, and kissed him again.

"We have to celebrate this news. Let's have a campfire," Grayson exclaimed.

Tandie broke away from Jace, adding, "Great idea! We'll celebrate with s'mores. We picked up the

supplies when we went shopping. Let's go gather fire-
wood."

When she brushed past Bob, he turned and
walked into the bedroom, closing the door without
saying a word.

Chapter 78

Pocono Mountains, Pennsylvania

Grayson carefully balanced logs and sticks into a teepee-like structure in the fire-ring, and set fire to the kindling underneath. Within seconds, smoke began rising, and he leaned down to gently blow on it. The flames grew and danced as the wood caught fire, and he sat back on his haunches to observe, occasionally leaning down to blow again.

When he was satisfied that the fire would flourish, he sat back on an overturned log, and reached his hands toward the fire with a grin. "I haven't done this in years. I love sitting by a fire."

Jace whispered, "I've never done this."

"What? Never had a campfire? Well, then I'm glad I can introduce you to the fine art of fire-building." He winked at Jace. "It's easy, all you need is patience. Well, and persistence. If you don't tend the fire properly, it won't burn for you anymore, the flame will go out. Sort of like a woman." He slapped his leg and chuckled.

Jace laughed, then turned somber. He looked down at the fire and spoke quietly, "My family never... I mean...we didn't do things...together. Very much.

Thank you for..." he paused, blinking rapidly. "This."

Grayson watched the red climb up the younger man's cheeks. He reached over and placed a hand on his back.

"We're all a family now, right? I'm glad you're here."

Jace gulped. "Th-thank you. Me too."

Bob ambled down and leaned on a tree, just a bit back from the group.

"Everything alright, Bob?" Grayson asked.

"Yes. I'm sorry. I was just looking at some old pictures of my wife, and I'm missing her. I'm glad we're all here, too, so I'm not alone anymore."

Grayson walked over, lowering his voice, "That's what we were just saying. Come sit by the fire. Do you want to tell us about her?"

"I..." Bob's voice trailed off.

He was interrupted by the sound of a motor followed by a flash of headlights, and everyone stared toward the rumbling of the approaching engine. Out of the near dark emerged a white sedan, bumping along the grassy path toward the cabin and into the light shining from the porch light.

In a beat, the atmosphere around the fire shifted. Everyone jumped to their feet, groping for makeshift weapons. Mike grabbed a log from the pile and held it like a baseball bat, Jace pushed Tandie behind him, though she stood holding the marshmallow she'd been roasting in front of her like a sword, and the hair on Crash's back raised as low growls broke free. He placed himself in front of the group as the driver's side door opened, and a woman stepped out.

"Grayson?" a familiar voice called, causing goose

bumps to spread up his arms. It was a voice he'd dreamt of since they'd parted. Was he dreaming now? Gray didn't know if he could handle it if he was mistaken. His feet remained rooted in the grass, the fear of finding out she wasn't real keeping him still. If she was an illusion, he didn't want to do anything that would make her disappear.

Grayson's breath hitched, "Sofiana?"

Rufus, who had been sleeping by the fire, jumped to his feet and bunny-hopped on his stumpy legs to the woman. When he reached her, he threw himself onto his back, belly up, low mewling sounds escaping as his stub of a tail whipped back and forth.

Grayson took one step forward as Sofie squatted next to his dog. Her silky hair fell forward, covering her face. His fingers tingled as he remember what it was like to run them through that soft mane. He listened to her voice as she spoke to Rufus, and his heart skipped. This was, without a doubt, the very same voice that haunted his dreams.

"Rufus! Hi, boy. I've missed you. Come here, you." She scratched his belly, and then looked up, meeting Gray's eyes across the yard.

Just then, the passenger door opened, and a man stepped out. As if he'd been slapped, Grayson took an involuntary step backward just as Maggie Lee came to stand next to him. She placed a hand on his arm. "Are you okay, Grayson?"

He couldn't answer. His eyes were glued on Sofie's. He didn't have the power to look away as Sofie's eyes traveled up and down over Maggie. He saw the moment the softness left her eyes. He could read her thoughts before she spoke. Just as she'd arrived with another man, she assumed he was here with Maggie Lee. Grayson's heart constricted, and he suddenly found it hard to breathe. After all this time and she arrives with a boyfriend. Too late. It really was too late for them after all.

"I...got your message," she said.

Grayson shoved his hands into his pockets. "Who is this?" He nodded his head toward the man with her.

"This is Christian. He's a friend," Sofie answered.

"A friend. Good." He took one step forward, then halted. "Friend? Or boyfriend?"

"Christian's a friend, Gray." She cocked her head. "A colleague."

Grayson nodded, breath returning to his lungs for what seemed like the first time since she'd arrived. "This is Maggie Lee. She's a friend, too."

Then he was marching toward her with a look of determination, eyes smoldering into hers, calling back over his shoulder, "We're gonna need some privacy. We have a lot to discuss."

She gasped and dragged her heels when he clutched her hand and pulled her toward the cabin.

"Gray...?" She squeaked, but her body didn't resist as she followed along, his grip loose but firm. As soon as their skin made contact, it was like they'd never been apart. An excited tingle coursed from their clasped hands upward, and though they both knew she could easily pull free if she wanted to, her hand remained in his. He felt her fingers tighten on his own and a smile lit his face. Sofiana didn't do anything she didn't want to do, so he counted this as a victory.

He'd planned on having a long talk, nothing

more, but the air became thick with desire the moment they were alone. When they reached the bedroom, he kicked the door closed, and gently spun her around to face him. His eyes burned into hers until her knees went weak, and her lips parted.

His words were like a caress. "I've dreamed of this moment. And now you're here."

Staring into the heat of his eyes, she lifted her hand to his cheek, answering: "Yes, I'm here. And I have, too. Dreamed of this, I mean. We have a lot to talk about, Gray. I need to ... "

Flames practically leapt from his body to hers. "That's all that matters. We'll talk later. Come here. Let's live the dream. I need you."

He took one step, closing the remaining distance between them. They came together in mutual frantic need, lips communicating a desire that would never be satisfied. This had always been the one area they could agree upon. Heat pulsed between them like a living thing, both ready and willing to jump into the heart of the flame, neither possessing the strength, nor the will to turn away.

You're really here, and you're mine. I'm not letting you leave me again. He didn't utter the words, instead kept them bottled inside. For now.

Words later. Heat now. I can't get enough of the heat.

His hands fisted in her hair and he ignored everything, giving himself over to his senses. She smelled of Dove soap, felt like silk, and tasted of woman. Just like he remembered. His woman.

That was the last coherent thought he had before losing himself in her.

∞∞∞∞

Sofiana could feel the erratic beat of Grayson's heart under her cheek. In the aftermath, she lay stretched out on the bed, half next to him, half on top of him. She propped her head on her hand and looked at him from under her lashes.

"Hi." Satiated color bloomed on her cheeks.

Her head bounced when his chest shook in a chuckle. "Hi."

"So…you're okay?"

"Did I not feel okay to you?" He smiled, pausing to push back an errant piece of hair that fell into her eyes. The smile dropped from her eyes, though they remained focused completely on his.

"Gray. There's so much I need to say to you. Most of all, I'm sorry. I was wrong to walk away from you. I've never stopped loving you. I tried to convince myself I did, but it never rang true. I haven't…been with anyone else since you. It's always been you. I don't know why I couldn't see that before. I see it so clearly now. When I thought you were in danger…" her words hitched, and she couldn't seem to continue.

Grayson hugged her close. "You're right. You shouldn't have walked away. I tried to hate you for it. I tried to get back at you in many ways. I haven't been celibate. But I can tell you, everyone pales in comparison to you. I love you, Sofiana Marigold. Even though you have a crazy middle name."

She leaned up to kiss him, then pulled back.

"Your message. You sounded like you were in danger..."

"Come on. You have a lot to catch up on. And the others are probably wondering, too." He pushed himself up.

"Oh! What must your friends think of me?" She leaped off the bed and began picking up scattered pieces of clothing off the floor. As she dressed, she looked back over her shoulder and smiled at him.

His eyes followed her every move. "I really do love you, Sof. Don't ever leave me again."

Her eyes met his, and held. "Never. I tried living my life without you in it, and I don't like it."

He stood. Reaching for her, Grayson held on. Reluctantly, he stepped back. "Let's go. I'll introduce you to everyone, and we can all fill you in together. Some strange things have been happening. You're not going to believe it."

Chapter 79

Pocono Mountains, Pennsylvania

S ofie felt the heat rise up her face as Grayson introduced her to everyone. She shook each of their
hands, hoping they all believed the two of them
had just returned from a heart-to-heart talk and nothing more. A knowing grin from the woman called Maggie told her they all knew exactly what she and Gray
had really been doing. If possible, her cheeks turned a
deeper shade of red.

Someone had kept the fire going and the flames
danced, reaching toward the sky. Sofiana stood next to
Grayson, fingers linked, by the fire ring. She couldn't
bear to break the contact with him now that they'd
found their way back to each other. She glanced up at
him, and he winked. Her answering smile was involuntary, and spread into a grin. She turned toward the
others.

"Hi. I'm happy to meet all of you. May I ask what
brought all of you together? I'm not sure I know what's
going on. Grayson left a message for me, and in it he im-
plied he might not survive. I was…separated from my
phone for a while, and I got on a plane as soon as I listened to it." Her eyes shot to Gray's, and she spoke only

to him, "You scared me to death."

He squeezed her hand. "*I* was scared to death. I didn't think I would live much longer after I called you. I was sure it was the end. But if it brought you back to me, I'm glad for it. All of it."

"Why did you think you might die, Gray?" Sofie asked.

"A man was following me. He admitted he was there to kill me."

Her eyebrows shot up. "*What?* Why? Who would want to kill you?"

Gray squeezed her fingers again. Bringing their joined hands to his lips, he kissed the back of hers and she felt the slight jump in her pulse. She tore her gaze away as he spoke. "I think it's best that we start at the beginning. I'll let Mike and Maggie Lee tell their story, then I'll fill in my blanks, and then Jace, Tandie, and Crash. Bob's story is a little different, so we'll let him finish it."

Just then, the sound of someone clearing his throat interrupted the silence.

Sofie gasped. "Oh! Everyone, this is Christian. He's my friend and colleague," she blurted.

"Nice of you to remember me." Christian sat stiffly, arms crossed.

Sofie's hands flew to her cheeks, "I'm so sorry, Christian! I didn't...plan for the way that went."

A bitter laugh escaped. "Obviously. Maybe I should just go. You clearly don't need me here."

"Wait. Let's hear their story. I'm sorry. Truly." Sofiana's cheeks turned crimson.

"Don't really have a choice, do I?" He refused to make eye contact.

Grayson rose, extending a hand. "I'm Grayson. Sof and I had some unfinished business to discuss. Sorry for that."

"Christian." He nodded, eyeing Gray with a frown, reached out for one quick shake, then flopped back onto the rickety folding lawn chair.

Sofiana and Grayson exchanged a look. He raised a brow at her questioningly. Her already heated cheeks flamed hotter.

Maggie Lee stood up, extending her hand. "I'm Maggie Lee, and this is my husband, Mike." She gestured to him, and continued, "It all started when I found this trinket on the beach." She reached into her pocket.

Mike interrupted, "Don't forget to tell her how old you are, Mag."

Sofiana tilted her head.

"I'm fifty-five. Same as Mike. We've been married for 28—almost 29— years and I just found out that I'm expecting our first child." The smile spread, lighting up her entire face at once.

"Wait, did you say you're fifty-five?" Sofie's eyes rounded.

Maggie nodded. "Yes."

Mike pulled out his phone, scrolled, and held it out for her to see. "This is what Maggie Lee looked like at the beginning of the summer."

Sofiana leaned forward, studying the photo, her mouth forming an 'oh'.

"How is that even possible?" she whispered.

"Because of this."

Sofie's eyes were drawn to the trinket in Maggie Lee's hand. "I've seen one of those!" She leaned forward, elbows on her knees. "I've been tracking a great white shark for months, and I got close enough to get some shots of this thing lodged in its mouth." She pulled out her phone, scrolling through pictures. Using her fingers to enlarge the screen, she held it out.

Tandie broke the silence in the room. "Cool! Did you say you track great white sharks? Wow! That's like, the coolest job on the face of the planet."

Sofiana couldn't stop the smile from spreading over her face. "Yes, it is. I'll take you out sometime."

"Really? OMG! That would be..."

"Uh, guys? You're getting a little off topic," Grayson interrupted, "You found one of these in the mouth of a shark? Tell us." He looked around the room. "You know, I think we were all meant to find each other. It can't be a coincidence." He smirked. "Ha! That sounds like something Yaz might say! How is the old lady, anyway?"

Sofie's eyes immediately filled. She shook her head at Gray, a tear escaping to roll over her cheekbone.

Gray drew in a sharp breath. "What? Yaz?"

Sofie gave a slight nod. "She's gone, Gray. I can't believe it either—and it's all part of this. Let's catch each other up."

The silence was broken by Sofie's whisper, "This is just incredible. We now have four of these things between us. I wonder how many more of them are out there?"

Gray nodded. "Good question, but a better one might be: What the hell are these things?"

"And where do they come from?" she added.

Bob cleared his throat, and began speaking for the first time, "I can fill in some of the blanks. I haven't been completely honest with all of you."

"What do you mean? Bob?" Maggie Lee implored, rising to her feet.

"Wait. I'll be right back. I'll show you." Bob disappeared into the cabin and returned carrying a dirty metal box in his hands. He placed it on the ground near the light of the fire, and opened the lid.

The group leaned forward to peer inside.

"Pictures?" Maggie Lee's brow furrowed.

"Yes. These pictures only have meaning to me. They tell the story of my life. I'll start at the beginning of all of this. My life before I found my good luck charm was typical. I was twenty-five when I found it, and nothing has been the same since." Bob held up a black and white photo of a woman. "This is Victoria. She was my wife."

"Wait, I thought you said your wife's name was Julie," Maggie interrupted, sitting forward.

Bob inclined his head. "Yes. Julie was my second wife."

"Oh. I guess that's not that uncommon. Did you get a divorce?" Maggie asked.

"No. Victoria died. She was killed," Bob's eyes filled and he turned away.

Maggie placed a hand on his arm. "Oh my gosh! By who?"

"That's not important. She was my wife when I

found the charm. I was working as a prison guard at the time, and after I found this," he held up his good luck charm and continued, "things were never the same between us." He got lost in the picture for a time, and then visibly snapped himself back to the present. "This thing has been both a blessing and a curse. When I realized what it could do, I became obsessed with it. I was gone for long periods of time. All I cared about was harnessing the power of this thing. Studying it, learning how to yield it. I was unfaithful, I told myself it was all for the good of the cause. I sacrificed my marriage. I lost my son, Adam. I have regrets. So many regrets." He stared out the window, his eyes clouded over. "I was born in 1807."

At his words, a ripple of protest murmured through the group.

Maggie Lee gasped. "That's impossible! That would make you...213 years old!"

Bob shrugged. "Nothing's impossible. Haven't you learned that yet?" He answered wistfully.

"Tell us. Everything." Grayson growled.

Chapter 80

Pocono Mountains, Pennsylvania

B ob leaned forward, internally debating how much to tell the group.

They won't understand all of it. They'll never see it from my point of view.

He shifted so he was sitting with legs tucked underneath him on the moss-covered ground, metal box in his lap.

"You have to understand, I did everything I did to preserve this." He patted his pocket. "I have to live with all of my decisions. Looking back, I can see now that I was obsessed, and I let that obsession take over my life. I'm not asking for your forgiveness. I hardly forgive myself. I'm just asking you to listen."

"Bob, we're on your side. Please, tell us what you know. We need to know everything." Maggie Lee looked around the room. Crash wriggled forward, placing himself closer to Maggie and Bob. They formed a triangle on the soft earth with everyone else on the outskirts looking in.

"I don't know everything. But I'll tell you what I do know." His eyes clouded once more, and he began talking. "I was young and arrogant. I thought I was invincible. After I discovered the power of the charm, I took a lot of unnecessary risks." He shook his head. "You see, I don't know for sure, but I believe I am the first person to ever yield one of these. It spoke to me. To *me*. After I found it, I yearned for the sea. I left Victoria, and went in search of the origin. Nothing mattered to me except finding out what this thing was, and where it came from. I learned everything there was to know about the ocean, and became a proficient sea captain. I searched for a year with no luck." His voice trailed off.

"Go on. We're here for you, Bob." He felt the weight of Maggie's hand on his forearm, and his body jerked back to the present.

He continued, "We didn't have scuba diving like we do now, it was all in the beginning stages of development. Breathing underwater was only possible by breathing surface air through a hose, and even that was still being tested. I was living on my boat at the time, and one night as I drifted along in the waters near Cape Cod, something—for lack of a better word—called to me. I can't really explain it, but I was woken from a sound sleep and I knew that I had to explore the waters below me. It didn't matter that it was dark, or that I was likely plunging to my death. Something compelled me to jump overboard and swim toward the ocean floor. Like a magnetic force, I was powerless to stop..."

"Wait, you had no gear, and you just jumped into the water, in the middle of the night?" Sofiana leaned forward, elbows on her knees, eyes intently focused on Bob.

"Yes. As I said, my thoughts weren't my own. Some unseen force was controlling me...so I descended through the frigid waters, drawn ever downward. My lungs began to burn, but I was powerless to turn back. As my body propelled down of its own accord, my lungs gave out. The burning consumed my chest, lungs filling with seawater, body convulsing, and I felt myself dying. Suddenly, the ocean floor began to glow a luminescent red, and the water became warm. Almost hot. I could feel my good luck charm in the pocket of my pants heating up, and I was once again called from below. There, at the bottom of the ocean, was a mercury-like silver mass that fanned out, covering the seabed. It was low-lying, uneven and rutted, protruding up out of the sand. All at once it no longer mattered that I was underwater with no air. I placed both hands on top of it, and it...spoke to me. Communicated on a primitive level. In that moment, I knew that I could never leave that place. It was a part of me. Or rather, I was a part of it." He paused, and then continued.

"Blueprints formed in my head, and when I resurfaced, I got busy building an underwater fortress. A place I could live and remain as close to this...entity...as possible. Others arrived, a select few who were drawn to the same place just as I was. We all pitched in with the construction. The place was built well before its time. It was before underwater habitats even seemed possible. It's formed with the metal material, if that's what it is, from that mass. We called the place Mercury Reef because the metal had the iridescence of mercury in a thermometer. The name stuck, even though we know it's...some other kind of metal. I don't know if it's still there now. I haven't been there in many years."

"It's still there." Sofiana leaned even closer, adding, "I've been there." She looked at Christian. "We've been there."

Bob's head whipped around. "You've been there? How is that possible?"

"I'll explain it all after you're finished with your part of it." She looked at Grayson. "It's where Yaz was killed."

Christian spoke for the first time, "I think I saw it. The mass. It was covered with horseshoe crabs. Swarms of them." He looked at Sofiana and continued, "With all that was going on, I forgot to tell you about it."

Bob nodded, and continued, "Yes. They are drawn to it, just as I was. I don't know if they've been a part of it since the beginning, or if they discovered it there on the bottom of the sea like I did. A horseshoe crab's blue blood has natural healing properties. Humans have been bleeding them for years to tap into their unique 'power'. We believed these arachnid-like creatures might be alien beings sent here from another world along with the mass. For what reason? I have no idea. We never found conclusive evidence either way. But they play a role, somehow. We just aren't sure how."

"We?" Grayson's brows raised.

"Yes. There's more. I met a woman. Abigail. She had a good luck charm of her own. I didn't love her, but we were together so much it was inevitable that we..." his words trialed off. "We had a daughter together. I don't even know if my daughter is alive today. Because she was conceived by two who yielded this power, she was...special. Others, people connected to the mass just like me, lived there with us. Two men."

The faraway look washed over his face again. "Abigail and I, along with our daughter and the others, dedicated our life to the entity. Studied it, experimented, lived for it. Years passed, and I grew bored. I wanted more. A normal life. I yearned for the life I left behind. Visiting Victoria every five years or so and leaving again no longer sufficed. I'd loved her once, and I missed her. As I said, I never loved Abigail. She was only convenient. So I left. My daughter was only thirteen at the time, but still she refused to come with me. She'd always been a precocious child. Wise beyond her years. She knew what she wanted, just as I knew what I needed to do. My only solace was that she wasn't alone. The others were still there to dote on her every whim." His eyes clouded. "I traveled a bit, then tried to return to Victoria for good, pick up where we left off. When that didn't work out, I resolved to leave all of that behind and begin again. Eventually I met Julie, and we fell in love. We married, and had two children together. My sons, Kyle and Kevin. We had a good life. A normal life." He opened his palm and stared at the good luck charm. "But I never could seem to part with this thing. I became a police officer, and the charm brought me back from near-death more times than I can count. I could take risks others couldn't, because with this thing I was invincible." He paused. "When Julie got sick, I tried to heal her with the charm, but for some reason it only works for me. I wanted to die, too. What good is having the power to heal if you can't save those you love? I knew it would never be possible to be happy as long as I had this with me. It felt as if it had betrayed me in some way." He closed his hand around the charm. "I packed it away, hoping that would make it possible for my time on earth to end. And the longer I was apart from it, the more...normal I became. After all those years, my body became susceptible to disease once again. I developed dementia and rheumatoid arthritis. I've been living in an assisted living community for the past eight years, until recently when I was reunited with my good luck charm. It healed the dementia, along with the arthritis, and here I am."

"Wow. That's quite a story, Bob. I'm wondering why you waited 'til now to share it with us." Grayson looked at him through slitted eyes.

Bob broke eye-contact. "I didn't think you would believe me."

Maggie Lee stood. "He's telling us now, Grayson. That's what matters."

Grayson humphed. "So, we still don't really know what the thing is, only what it's capable of and where it is. Let's let Sofiana and Christian fill in the blanks of their story, and see if we can put any more pieces together."

Sofie stood, lifting her shirt to expose her midsection. "I got these puncture wounds when I was carried in the mouth of a great white shark to safety. The people in the underwater lab that Bob told us about are conducting research, and experimenting with training this particular shark. It's the same shark that has one of those," she pointed at Bob's charm, "in its mouth."

Bob's eyes went round, "They are training the sharks? That's new."

"Yes. They sent her to retrieve me. To save me from something...worse. Do you know what that might be?"

"Yes, I think I do. It's what killed Abigail." He crossed his legs again. "This mass in the water, it has made the waters surrounding it powerful. It gives off an echo of its healing properties to the things that live there. Oh, it's not like having one of these. Doesn't hold the power that my charm holds, but promotes faster healing and we think longer life. That area surrounding the entity is a fountain of youth, of sorts. So, it stands to reason that some things we previously thought extinct are still lurking down there. Even without the power of this thing no one really knows the true extent of what's living beneath the waves in the deepest regions of the ocean. But back to your question. We called that particular creature Buzz. Its scientific name is Helicoprion, but because of the circular tooth whorl in its lower jaw, it has the look of a buzz saw. Abigail was out exploring one day, and the thing came out of nowhere and sliced her in half. Even her charm couldn't repair the damage it did to her. It turns out, charm-bearers are not immortal after all." He looked at Sofie. "If the great white saved you from Buzz, you should be thankful."

"You're saying that Helicoprions still exist? I have to get back there to study... This is groundbreaking! Do you realize what this means to the field of marine biology?"

Jace cleared his throat, and Bob turned to face him. The boy held up a picture on his phone, and mumbled, "I looked up a Helicoprion. *This* is the thing that's still alive down there?"

"Yes. That's what Buzz is. And there's plenty more things alive down there that would shock the local community. The world, for that matter. That's why it has to remain a secret. Chaos would prevail if anyone learned about all of this."

Grayson leaned forward to take a look. "Holy shit! Sofie, you were in the water with that thing?"

She stood, hands gesturing. "I never saw it. But

something did ram into me when I was diving a few weeks ago. I wonder if..." She paused, searching out Bob's face, "Wait, what about the children? Why are they there?"

Bob's brow furrowed. "Children? What children?"

"There were three children, all very young. The oldest one, Tia, was six years old and introduced us to Genna and Hurley. When I asked them if their parents were with them, she said no, they were with Coral. Do you know why they would have children down there?"

Bob stood slowly, his hands wringing. "Coral? Coraline? She's there? Now?"

Sofie nodded. "Yes, she seems to be in charge down there, although she's just a teenager herself. Do you know her?"

He answered while rummaging through the pictures in the box, finally holding one up for the group to see. It was a black and white photo of a girl with a ponytail.

"Oh, Coraline is no teenager. She's my daughter," Bob whispered.

Chapter 81

Pocono Mountains, Pennsylvania

Grayson wrapped his arms around Sofie, and she snuggled against him. They had decided to sleep on the cots in the shed for some privacy, despite Mike and Maggie Lee's insistence that they sleep in the double bed.

"I'm glad Christian left. I don't like the way he looks at you." He held on tighter.

She sighed. "I feel awful. He's a good guy, Gray. I hurt him, and I'll never forgive myself for it. He was there for me during a really difficult time. But yes, If I'm being honest, I can admit that I'm glad he's gone, too. It was becoming awkward having him here glaring at us all day. And now we can focus on figuring all of this out."

Grayson ran his hand up and down over her back. "None of it seems real. It's all so far-fetched. Almost crazy. How can any of this be true?"

She traced his bicep, and he looked down into her concerned face as she answered, "I don't know. I'm a scientist. Science tells me there must be a logical reason to explain all of this, but I can't see it. This is beyond my knowledge base."

"I'd be happy to hear it if you come up with an answer to explain this mess."

"Yeah, me too. All I do know is that I want to find the people who hurt Yaz. They can't be allowed to get away with this," her voice quivered.

"I'm so sorry, Sof. I know how much you loved her. I loved her, too. If there's any way to find the guy who shot her, we'll do it. Together. When all this is over, we'll go to Jamaica and have our own tribute to her." His hand rubbed circles on her back.

"Mmm-hmm. Together." She snuggled closer.

"I think Bob is holding something back. I get the feeling he knows more than he's telling us."

"What more could there be? It seems as if he's been pretty honest about all of this. We have to trust each other if we're going to survive this."

He blew out a breath. "I know. You're right. But something just seems 'off' about that guy. I just can't put my finger on it…"

"Maybe it's just because he was born in a different century, but alright, we'll keep an eye on him. Even though Maggie Lee and Crash seem to trust him completely, and they're connected to him somehow."

"That proves nothing because Maggie Lee trusts everyone. And Crash is a dog. There are still so many unanswered questions. Like, who is Gold? Does he work for this Coral, or is he with the people who shot Yaz? And who are *they*, by the way? Or are they all one and the same?"

"Shh." She placed her finger on his lips. "I wish I could think of a way to take your mind off things. Just for tonight."

His chuckle carried out into the cool mountain breeze. "You have no idea how much I've missed you,

Sof."

∞∞∞

From a securely camouflaged spot just behind the bushes lining the shed, the two inside had no idea their conversation had an audience. When the intruder was sure that Grayson and Sofiana were occupied, the eavesdropper slunk through thickly growing wild rhododendron bushes, careful to tread lightly while heading toward the cabin. Even the bulldog, snoring loudly just inside the door of the shed, did not detect the unknown presence as he chased a cat in his dreams, legs flailing in a dream-state running motion.

No one noticed the quieting of the crickets as a person shimmied underneath the cabin's raised structure, undetected by all except the groundhog who scurried away into the darkness.

Chapter 82

Pocono Mountains, Pennsylvania

Sofiana got up early to use the bathroom and cursed under her breath. The toilet wouldn't flush. Upon further inspection, she discovered that there was no running water in the cabin.

"Well, I guess it'll be a light breakfast," she mumbled as she grabbed a bucket and headed toward the creek to fill it. She returned and dumped the creek water into the toilet to activate flushing.

She bumped into Tandie, eyes slitted as she headed toward the bathroom. "Toilet won't flush. We've lost running water. You'll have to use creek water to flush."

"Ugg," Tandie grumbled as she staggered forward. "That sucks."

"Yes. It does. I'll go wake Gray and see if he knows how to fix it."

"Umm-hmm." The bathroom door closed.

"Not a morning person, I see." She smiled as she headed toward the shed, bucket in hand. As she approached, Rufus stuck his head out, his front legs dangling off the edge. The movement of his stubby tail and entire back end wiggling elicited a groan from Grayson.

Sofie reached out to stroke the soft fur of bull-dog's head, and his face relaxed into a canine smile, happy snorts making his lips quiver.

"Oh, Rufus, I've missed you." She leaned down to kiss his flat snout, eyes meeting Grayson's as he squinted up at her.

"Good morning sleepy-head." She leaned down to kiss his cheek. "Gotta get up. We have no running water in the cabin. Do you know how to fix it?"

"Hmmm. I'll come check on it. Just give me a minute. Or ten."

"No problem." She winked, laying a water bottle next to his head, then turned toward the creek. Returning to the cabin she handed the full bucket to Tandie, water sloshing over the edge.

"Dump this in the toilet and it will flush," she said, bending down to wipe the floor.

"Oh. Okay. Good idea." Tandie took the pail and turned toward the bathroom.

Sofiana opened the refrigerator and pulled out a bottled water. "Good thing you guys got water when you were out."

She took off the cap, filling the water dish on the floor. Both dogs immediately began lapping up the water.

She handed a bottle to Tandie when she returned. "Thanks. We didn't get water. Didn't think we needed it with running water and all. This must be from Grayson's stash of supplies he brought along. That guy thinks of everything."

Sofie smiled. "Yes. He does."

Jace stumbled into the kitchen area rubbing his eyes. He stifled a yawn, and caught the water bottle in mid-air as the girls filled him in on the water situation.

"Sucks," he replied.

Mike sauntered into the kitchen next. He poured bottled water into the coffee pot and waited for the water to heat. "Heard you talking. No water, huh?"

"Nope."

"I'll check it out after my coffee. Nobody talk to me until I've had my coffee," Mike mumbled to no one in particular.

Tandie smirked, rolling her eyes. "We know."

Jace grunted under his breath, "Good luck getting her to stay quiet."

"What exactly are you trying to say, Jace?" Tandie wanted to know. She reached out to tickle his ribcage and a child-like giggle burst out. "Okay, I won't talk, I'll just tickle." She wiggled her fingers in his ticklish spot.

He bent over in fits of laughter, clutching his midsection.

Maggie and Bob were the last to join the group. "What's so funny this early in the morning?"

"Yeah, I'm an old man, and I need my rest. Who can sleep with all this ruckus?" he grumbled, reaching for a mug and filling it with coffee.

Sofie looked up and met Grayson's smile as he entered the front door. He held the door open for the dogs, "Have to go outside, guys?"

Both dogs ran happily out the front door, noses immediately on the ground in a search of the perfect spot.

"So, what's for breakfast?" Gray asked.

"We haven't gotten past coffee." Sofie winked.

"Let's not make any dishes dirty. How about you

and I go pick up some bagels to bring back?" Sofie tilted her head. "Unless you can fix the water situation before that."

"How about we pick up bagels, and I check out the water when we're done eating?" Grayson said.

"Sounds like a plan."

The silence of the morning was shattered by a sudden braying that carried on the wind. Both dogs began barking frantically. The crowd in the kitchen rushed outside. Rufus and Crash were both sniffing under the house, paws covered in dirt as they madly clawed at the hole beginning to form there. Crash ran back to Jace, and gently took his hand in his mouth to pull him over for a closer look. Jace dropped down on his hands and knees and peered underneath.

"Uh, I don't see anything, Crash."

Crash barked once. *Yip.*

"Yes? Yes, you don't see anything either? Or yes, there is something down there?"

Crash whipped his head back and forth.

No.

"No? I'm sorry Crash, I'm not understanding you."

The dog began furiously sniffing the ground as if on the trail of a scent. Head down, tail straight up, he zigzagged across the yard and disappeared into the thick rhododendron bushes growing wildly behind the shed.

Sofie followed Crash. "What do you think it means?"

"No idea." Grayson stayed close.

The ground around her seemed to rise up, and she blinked to clear her vision. There were two of everything she looked at.

"G-Gray? I-I'm diz-z-zy," her words slurred as if in slow motion. She fell to her knees, hands shaking as she rubbed her eyes. She felt Grayson's hands grasp her shoulders, her body falling sideways into his arms. The last thing she saw before the blackness descended over her consciousness was Tandie falling to the ground a few feet away.

Chapter 83

Pocono Mountains, Pennsylvania

It felt like there were bricks on his eyelids. Grayson pried them open, squinting into the darkness. His tongue was glued to the roof of his mouth, and it took several tries to get it unstuck. The slightest movement made pain shoot through his brain, and he slammed his eyes shut and pushed his head backward into the cushion of moss underneath his throbbing skull.

Off to his left he heard Rufus whimper and forced his eyes open again, squinting through the blackness. It was nighttime. The moon was almost directly above, creating just enough light to make out vague outlines. He struggled to a sitting position, trying to probe the darkness in search of...what? He belly-crawled to his dog, laying his hand on the bulldog's ribcage. Rufus' wet sandpaper tongue licked his arm, and he breathed a sigh of relief.

Think. What's the last thing I remember?
Sofiana! She fell...

Despite his body's sluggishness, he rose precariously to his feet, hands braced on his shaking knees.

"Sof? Where are you, Sof?" he croaked.

His head whipped around when he heard a groan, and it was like a white-hot poker stabbed deep into his cerebellum.

A male voice called out, "Grayson? What happened?"

Jace was standing on wobbly legs a few feet away, hand on his forehead. "Did we…drink too much? I think I'm hung-over." He called out in a weak voice, "Crash! Where are you, dude?" The exertion had him falling to his knees, and his body lurched forward convulsing in dry heaves on the ground.

"I don't remember drinking anything except water. Where is everyone? Sofiana!" Gray stumbled to the shed and reached for a flashlight. Shining it around the perimeter of the yard, he stopped when it landed on a body.

"Mike?"

His feet felt like lead. He moved as fast as his legs would allow, zig-zagging in the direction of his friend, head pounding with the exertion. Dropping to his knees next to him, he placed a hand on Mike's chest and took a deep breath when he detected a slight up and down motion.

His head jerked at Jace's yell, "Tandie's over here! She's okay!"

"Good. I've got Mike. Where's everybody else?" Grayson aimed the flashlight around in a circle. "Who's missing? Sofie. Maggie Lee. And Bob."

"And Crash." Jace interjected. "Come, Crash!" he called weakly. "Crash!"

His heart constricted in his chest. "Where *are* they? Last I remember it was morning. And we didn't have water. The dogs. They were barking…and Sofie fell. I must have passed out, too. How about you two?"

"I remember Tandie falling, and then I got dizzy and I guess I fainted. That must have been hours ago since it's nighttime now."

Grayson ran his hands through his tangled mass of hair, panic tightening his chest. He tried not to give into the clawing fear that gripped him. "What the hell is going on?" He cupped his hands to his mouth calling, "Sofiana! Where are you?"

Mike sat up on the moss, rubbing his temples. "Maggie? Mag?" His breathing became ragged, and his dilated eyes wild in the flashlight's glow. Struggling to stand, his voice cracked, "Maybe the girls and Bob are inside. Let's check the cabin. She has to be here. She has to. Maggie Lee!" Despite his words, his voice trembled.

"Good idea. Except I don't think they would have left all of us outside in the dirt if they're here. But you're right, we have to search the area to make sure they're gone. Then we need to figure out where they are so we can bring them home." He jerked the flashlight around them in a wide circle, frantically searching. "They're okay. I know they're okay. They have to be." His voice broke on the last word, but he rounded his shoulders and marched toward the cabin.

The four of them sat around the living room. Despair threatened to take them, but Grayson refused to give in to the dread that filled their hearts. They'd searched everywhere in and around the cabin, alternating between tears, cursing, and desperate accusations, and now sat staring at each other at a loss for what to do next. Gray scanned the small group. Mike had the look of a soldier returning from battle, haunted eyes speaking a million words while never uttering a sound. He held a towel packed with ice to the purple bruise on his forehead, caused by the fall onto a tree root when he passed out. Tandie's face was as pale as the white painted wall behind her, and her hand shook when she reached up to brush back her hair. Jace's cowlick stood on end, his red-rimmed eyes giving him a post-apocalyptic zombie-like appearance.

Rufus lay in the corner snoring.

That's the only thing that seems normal about all of this.

"What should we do? We have to do something." Mike's wild eyes gave away his panic.

"Where could they be? If we knew where they are…" Gray's heart pounded, fear ripped through his body making him numb.

"They were taken by someone. Do you think it was the guy who tried to kill you? The one who was following us? Gold?" Mike asked.

"It could be. It's been approximately 12 hours, so the trail is long gone. How will we find them if we don't know where to look? I don't know what to do." Gray's voice quivered as he spoke. "We were drugged. That much is clear. It had to be the water." He stood and ran out of the cabin, shimmying his upper body underneath. A few squeaky metallic rotations could be heard as he turned the lever on the water pipe, and then he crawled back out and raced to the kitchen. When he turned the faucet, water came gushing out.

"Okay, someone turned off our water supply, and loaded our fridge with bottled water that had been tampered with," Grayson added.

Tandie spoke for the first time, "Ugg. So someone was inside the cabin while we were all sleeping? That's just creepy."

"Yes. But that means if they wanted to harm us they would've done it then. So it stands to reason that Sofiana, Maggie, Bob, and Crash are all okay." Grayson paced the small kitchen.

"I pray you're right, Grayson. But why were they taken?" Mike wrung his hands.

Grayson tilted his head, thinking out lout, "That's a great question. Here's another one: What if it was one of us?"

"Excuse me? Who, exactly, are you accusing?" Mike squinted at him.

"No, I don't mean anyone here in this room. But Bob's another story. I haven't trusted him from the start, and I felt as if he was holding something back from his story last night. I'm a reporter, it's my job to study people. I said as much to Sofie yesterday. What if, after finding out his daughter is still alive, he called her and told her where we are? He could have easily shut off our water and drugged us. No one would be suspicious of him being here or going in the fridge.... Do you think they are at the underwater habitat he and Sofie talked about? And why was Sofie taken at all? The others all had a trinket/good luck charm/medallion. But she doesn't. She's not connected."

"Probably because she found one in that shark's mouth. That connects her. Or just because she knows about it. I don't know. As to where they are: The fact is they could be anywhere. I think the underwater habitat is as good a guess as any. But even if they *are* there, none of us here knows where it is. How will we ever find them? It's killing me to think about my Maggie scared somewhere. And in her condition." Mike's hands fisted at his sides. "I can't stand this. I'm not there for her when she needs me most."

"We can't go down that road right now, we have to think clearly." Grayson paced the small room. "I just found Sofie again, and I'm not going to lose her a second time. Don't worry; we're going to find them. Just think."

"That's kinda hard when your head wants to explode." Tandie interjected.

"Let's pack up. We'll head back toward the Cape and decide what to do when we get there. At least we'll be *doing* something." Grayson began grabbing random items.

Mike nodded, moving toward the bedroom as he spoke, "I agree. Let's get going."

Jace stepped forward, clearing his throat. "What if...could there, maybe, be a clue in Bob's box of pictures? A-About where that place is, I mean."

Grayson slapped him on the back. "Great idea, kid! That's a starting point, at least. Now, where would the old man hide the box?"

Tandie inhaled. "I saw him slide it under the bed!"

She ran ahead of Mike, falling down on her haunches to peek underneath. "It's here!"

"Okay. We don't have time to waste. Let's head out, and look through the box on the way. Everyone okay with that?" Grayson asked.

Mike was already out the door. "Yes. Let's go."

Chapter 84

Airspace Over the Atlantic Ocean

Maggie Lee peeked through her lashes, trying not to let on that she was awake. The warm, welcoming heat of her trinket could be felt through the fabric of her pants pocket, and she knew it was even now eradicating whatever drug had knocked her out. Muffled voices chattered around her, but she couldn't make any sense out of the words.

Pressure built inside her head as a *whir-whir-whirring* sound filled the small space, and she tried desperately to identify the familiar noise. A car engine?

No. More sporadic than that. Not a car...more like a... helicopter...

Slowly, she moved only her eyes to the person next to her. Her limp body was half-lying on top of him—or her—she couldn't tell which. She resisted her body's urge to sit up. Her eyes traveled up and she recognized long brown hair.

Sofiana.

At least they were together. How many others were with them? She turned her head slightly in search of Mike.

Where is he?

Sofie groaned under her, and she shifted her body slightly away, drawing the attention of one of the men in front. Blue eyes clashed with black as she met the eyes of the co-pilot. Her chin jutted out, causing a wave of pain to shoot up her neck.

Maggie's body felt as if it had been run over by a car. Again. She opened her mouth, mumbling, "Who are you, and where are we going?" Her voice was drowned out by the rotation of the helicopter blades, and she cleared her throat, repeating the phrase a second time.

"Who are you, and where are we going?"

The man casually turned his head, dismissing her.

Jerk.

She inched into a sitting position, fighting her body's current resistance to movement. Scanning the small copter, she found that she and Sofie were the only ones in the back seat.

Maybe the others are safe. Could they have only taken the two of us?

She placed a hand on Sofie's arm, giving a gentle squeeze. The other woman did not stir. Reaching into her pocket, she pulled out her trinket. It was glowing a warm red color, and she placed the trinket into Sofie's limp hand, closing it with her own.

Maybe it can help her heal like it does for me. It didn't work for Grayson, but maybe another woman...

Several minutes passed, and the red glow faded to silver.

Nothing. I don't understand why this thing only works for me.

Storing the trinket safely back in her pocket, she

lay her head back and closed her eyes.

Where is Mike? What if he's hurt somewhere, and he needs me?

She placed her hand over her still-flat stomach, letting the baby calm her. Her lip curved at the corner.

I'm supposed to take care of you, not the other way around, kid.

She inhaled and grabbed for the seatbelt when the helicopter jolted, and then began its descent. Apparently they had reached their destination.

Suddenly awake, Sofie gripped her hand, her squinty eyes searching the confined space of the chopper. She raised a hand to her temple, rubbing in a circular motion, eyes shooting silent questions in her direction.

Maggie Lee shrugged, and gave her hand a squeeze.

I wish I knew.

"Stick together," she mouthed.

The copter landed smoothly in the middle of the ocean. It swayed up and down on the rippling waves as if attached to an invisible rubber band. Reaching up to remove his headset, the pilot turned around, for the first time acknowledging his passengers. She could see her own reflection in his mirrored sunglasses.

"Hello, ladies. Welcome to paradise," he drawled.

"Who the hell are you, and why are we here?" Maggie squared her shoulders, her eyes boring holes into him.

"Patience, my dear Maggie Lee. I'm on your side. You'll find out all the answers you seek in just a bit. I'll leave all that to the woman in charge. Let's get you ready to go meet her, shall we?"

"How do you know my name? And where are our men?" Maggie demanded.

"I've been helping you. I told you, I'm on your side. No one has been hurt. They just took a little nap."

Maggie Lee closed her eyes, reaching out to give Sofie's hand a squeeze.

Oh thank God! Mike is safe. And the others.

She flinched as he leaned forward, reaching behind their seat. He tossed each of them a backpack.

"Helping me?" Her eyes narrowed, "Wait. Are you...Gold?"

He inclined his head, and then turned away from her to face her companion. "I trust you can help Maggie Lee get suited up, Sofiana?"

At her stiff nod, he turned around to speak to the other man.

Maggie's round eyes found Sofie's, and she raised a brow.

"It's portable scuba gear. Apparently, we're going down," Sofiana whispered.

"I've never been scuba diving before! I-I'm not going." Maggie shook her head.

She followed Sofie's eyes as her friend looked out across the endless expanse of water. "I don't think you have much choice. Just do what I do, and stay with me."

"D-do you think this is where that...creature is?

The one Bob told us about?"

Sofie broke eye contact before replying, "No. No, I'm sure that creature is nowhere near here. All you need to do is concentrate on your breathing, and follow me. Trust me. You'll be fine."

Chapter 85

Heading Toward Cape Cod, Massachusetts

Eighty-five miles per hour.

Grayson forced himself to ease up on the gas pedal. His heart rate was erratic, and he felt sweat beading on his forehead.

Can't get pulled over. We have to find Sof. And the others.

He set the cruise control to five miles above the speed limit, and checked the rearview mirror. They'd been driving for a little over an hour.

Seems safe right now.

"Anything?" he questioned.

Tandie, knees together, balancing the box in her lap, perused the stack of pictures. "Not yet. Just a bunch of old pictures. Here's that girl, Coraline. There are a lot of shots of her. You know, Bob's daughter? And then there are some of other people we don't know. This one says 'Victoria' on the back. That was his first wife, right? And wait, he wrote something under her name. It's hard to read. I think it says *I'm so sorry*—but it's smudged. I guess he was sorry for leaving her and having an affair." She snorted, eyes rolling.

Mike huffed. "Who cares? How are old pictures

going to help us? I don't see how this is going to lead us to them. We have to think of another plan, just in case. I can't stand this. Maggie needs me."

Jace spoke in his quiet voice, "How about Christian? I mean, he left, but he's been to the underwater place. He could lead us there. If he were still with us, I mean."

Grayson expelled a long breath. "I don't know how to contact him. Can you look up his name online? See what you come up with. I doubt we'll find his cell number listed, but maybe we can get an address for where to find him when we reach Cape Cod. That's a good starting point. Everybody keep brainstorming so we have a few options when we arrive. Sofiana and Christian work for an organization called OCEANS ALIVE. Look up how to contact them, too. Maybe they have records of where they were exploring when they last checked in. Coordinates, or something. I don't know."

"What will we do with that information? Does anyone here have experience on the water?" Tandie asked, looking around the car.

Gray shook his head. Tension crawled up his neck. "Not really. Sof took me out on the boat a few times, but she always handled the nautical part of it. I was a passenger. It's ironic. None of us has a clue, and the two people who could have helped us aren't here."

"At least Maggie Lee is with your Sofiana. If they're on the ocean, she can help her. She'll help her, right?" Mike met his eyes in the mirror.

"Yes. Sofie's the best in her field. She'll keep Maggie Lee safe. Don't worry."

"I *am* worried. Maggie needs me," Mike's voice

broke.

"We're all worried. And you're right, they do need us, but they're strong and independent, and we have to trust them to take care of themselves until we get there. We can't help them if we don't keep it together."

Tandie held a picture in the air. "Hey, here's a picture of...well, it's another picture of Coraline. Could this be the underwater place we're going?"

Gray took his eyes off the road to glance at the picture. "Yes, but I don't see how that helps us."

"Well, in the background, there's a maritime map on the wall behind the girl. It looks like an area is circled. I mean, if we could zoom on that picture, it might tell us where they're located, right?"

"Yes, but how can we zoom on a black and white picture? Does anyone have a magnifying glass?" Mike asked.

Jace interrupted, "Take a picture of the picture, and then zoom on that. I mean, it might be too blurry, but it's worth a try."

Tandie laughed and blew him a kiss. "Good thinking, Jace!" She handed the picture to him. He carefully balanced it on his lap and aimed his phone.

"I think it's too dark in here. I can't get a good shot. Can we pull over for just a minute?" Jace's voice was laced with excitement.

"I hate to lose time, but..." Grayson eased over to the side of the road, flipping on the four-way blinkers. "Hurry up."

Jace and Tandie jumped out of the car and sat on the side of the road. The day was overcast, perfect lighting.

At least the weather is on our side.

When the two returned to the car, Jace said, "Go. We got it."

"You mean you can read it?" Grayson asked.

"Not yet. But we took lots of pictures from different angles, and now I'll play with zooming in. I can do that while you're driving."

"Good. Let's keep moving." Mike pointed to the road.

Chapter 86

Deep in the Ocean, Somewhere Off the Coast of Chatham, Massachusetts

S ofiana felt at home completely submerged, a mouthpiece her only link to life-sustaining oxygen. Her new friend Maggie Lee did not. Eyes like gumballs, her chest heaved as she gulped air at a frantic pace despite all of her instructions before the descent.

If she doesn't calm down, she's going to hyperventilate.

She placed a steadying hand on her arm, and using hand gestures motioned for slower breathing as they'd practiced in their brief training session.

Breathe in. Breathe out. Breathe in. Breathe out.

Maggie's wild eyes bored into hers, but some of the panic receded as she placed her hand over her abdomen. Slowly and purposefully, she began to gain control of her breathing. Sofie nodded, then pointed and began scissor-kicking downward. Awkwardly, her companion followed.

Looking back over her shoulder every few feet, she led the way down, scanning the area for signs of life. The co-pilot, Jayden, was her guide, just as she was Maggie's. She recognized him as the man who had been training Baby the day she'd stood at the porthole window. And apparently, the pilot was the man called Gold she'd heard so much about from Grayson.

Have to keep an eye on that one.

For some reason, he had not come with them, but had remained above water. When she'd asked if he was coming, he'd mumbled something about "waiting for the others."

What others? Does he mean Grayson, Mike, and the others? Or someone else?

She wished Gold had come along, just so she could see what he was up to.

The sea was calm today. Teeming with activity, she observed various forms of sea life swarming around her. Harmless jellies floated serenely by. Grouper glided below as if in slow motion, their size skewed by distance. They would be much larger than they appeared from above as they got closer, she knew. A pod of Atlantic Herring darted below them, silver scales sparkling in the rays of sun breaking through the surface of the water. Her eyes followed the sunbeams to the surface and caught movement from above.

A boat! It stopped directly above them, water churning. *Maybe we could signal for help...*

She lifted a hand upward. A tug on her leg brought her back, and she looked down into Jayden's eyes. He gave a negative shake, and gestured. Through his facemask, the worry etched on his face was plain to see, and she tilted her head. Concern about the boat, or about something down here?

Glancing up one more time, she turned to continue her descent.

It must be the 'others' Gold had been waiting for.

Checking on Maggie Lee, she nodded and continued following. A minute passed, and she looked around. The waters were suddenly *too* serene. Where had all the sea life gone? Just minutes ago, in every direction, something darted or moved. Now, it seemed as if the ocean around them was devoid of life. A dangerous assumption. The absolute stillness set off an internal alarm louder than a gunshot.

Her eyes warily scanned the area.

Something is near. An apex predator.

I hope its Baby...

Heart pounding, she remained on full alert as they continued their downward trek. As they neared the ocean floor, she stayed closer to Maggie than was usual with a diving partner. The murkiness hindered her vision beyond ten feet, so if anything was out there, she wouldn't know it until it was almost on them. Meeting Maggie Lee's eyes, she gave the thumbs up signal, and forced a smile. For a first-time diver, she was doing better than expected.

Thinking back a few weeks, she remembered when she was rammed by...something.

It was the day she'd finally found Baby again. Yaz had yelled at her for going down alone. Yaz. It all seemed so long ago.

I can't think about her right now. Concentrate!

A shiver ran up her spine as she realized it had probably been the creature that day. The one Bob called Buzz. The not-extinct Helicoprion. Why hadn't it harmed her then?

Continuing to move along the ocean floor, her eyes widened when Mercury Reef came into view. She had been unconscious the first time she'd come here, and distraught when she'd left with Yaz's body. Now, her scientist's mind took in every detail. It was rectangular in shape, those circular porthole windows evenly spaced along the outside, eight of them in view. The reef grew all around it, providing sufficient cover from the casual eye. If she wasn't right in front of it, she would have missed it too, even though she'd been looking for it. Barnacles and anemones clung to it like a second skin, but the silver that shone in between the growth was shiny, mimicking the shimmer of polished tableware. She held up her hand, but no reflection showed on the surface.

Her inspection was abruptly interrupted by Jayden shouting into his mouthpiece, creating a flurry of rising bubbles and a zombie-like moaning sound that had her jerking around to see what caused it.

The beast eased by with a slow swish of his tail, in no hurry. No burst of speed. No signs of attack. Just a creature, lazily swimming around in its habitat.

Holy cow! A real-live Helicoprion. Buzz. He's beautiful!

Its massive, sleek body was at least twenty-eight feet long, and it stopped to make eye contact with Jayden before disappearing around the side of the building. Jayden went into immediate action, swimming underneath the structure to open the door to the decompression chamber, frantically spinning the wheel.

Sofie pushed Maggie Lee behind her toward the habitat, and stared after the creature. It was different than she had expected. There were so many theories about the placement of the tooth whorl on this species scientists had long thought extinct. Here, right in front of her, was living proof of its existence.

Since the whorl was the only fossil ever found to prove this shark's existence, scientists had all manner of ideas where it had been placed. Some had even speculated that it may have been attached to the fin or tail until a CT scan performed by scientists proved that theory wrong. A small smirk turned up the corners of her mouth. She now knew with certainty that the whorl was housed inside Buzz's mouth. Though invisible while the mouth was closed, she had observed the shark lazily open and close its mouth as it swam, and she'd seen that the whorl was indeed attached to the lower jaw. A notch in the upper jaw allowed its mouth to close completely, housing its deadly swirl of teeth hidden from view. She kicked once in the direction it had disappeared, but then remembered that Maggie Lee was depending on her...and the baby growing inside her, too.

She turned away, just as the beast came back into view, long pointed snout heading straight toward them, swimming just a bit faster this time. A 6-foot juvenile great white streaked past to her right, and in awe she witnessed a live Helicoprion feeding for the first time in known history. Well, at least it was her first time. The staff at Mercury Reef may have witnessed this event hundreds of time, she admitted. But no one else knew about it in the field of marine biology, she was sure.

The beast opened its mouth, and the vertical tooth whorl closed on its prey, slicing it cleanly in half. Red clouds of blood barely had time to dilute in the sea when it caught the remains of the small shark, swallowing it whole. Looking backward, it once again turned its head, this time making eye contact with her.

Turning back around, it moved off into the murk as Maggie tugged her arm.

Oh! I forgot Maggie Lee! What was I thinking? She must be scared to death!

She allowed herself to be pulled through the oval door, craning her neck to squint into the gloom once before disappearing inside.

As soon as she was free from equipment, she blurted, "That was awesome! I've never seen anything like it. It ate that juvenile white, and that baby shark was bigger than we are! I need to document this. Take pictures..." Her eyes practically glowed, and the smile lit her face.

Jayden frowned. "That shark could just as easily have bitten you in half. He's done it before. We've lost good people. He plays us, every time. Just when you think he's harmless, he attacks. He waits until our guard is down. We're all lucky to be in here, breathing air, Dr. Stone. I understand your excitement, but when you see Buzz, you need to get inside as quickly as possible."

"You know as well as I do that if he'd wanted to eat us he could have, and there wouldn't be a thing we could do about it. Tell me something. Is Buzz smart? Does it have a piece of that metal, or whatever it is, somewhere on its body? Like Baby—I mean Cary-One? We know a dog that has one, and he's super intelligent. And you train Baby, so I think that's true of her as well. What about the Helicoprion? Buzz?"

"Let's get you inside and we'll talk to Coral about all of that. There's a lot you still don't know. But we're about to change all of that." Jayden gestured toward the doorway.

"Okay. Let's go. I have a lot of questions. The first of which is: why was I kidnapped and brought here against my will?" Sofie demanded.

When silence was her only answer she dismissed him, turning to help Maggie Lee, making eye contact with her. "You did so good out there. I'm proud of you. You held up. Mike will be proud, too. We'll tell him as soon as we see him."

At the mention of Mike's name, Maggie's eyes filled with tears. She nodded.

"Thanks. For everything. I couldn't have done that without you." Maggie Lee turned her head and glared at Jayden, and continued in her best teacher voice, "Now, I want some answers. If you won't answer our questions, then take us to this Coral. You've broken more laws than I can count, and I want to know if my husband is okay."

Coral flounced into the room, ponytail bobbing. "Sofiana! Welcome back! I didn't think we'd meet again so soon after your last visit." A genuine smile lit her face.

"Don't act like I came here voluntarily. You told me I was free to go the last time I was here. Why am I back?" she hissed through clenched teeth.

"Yes, I did say that. And I meant it when I said it. But things have changed since then, and I wanted to keep you safe. This was the only way I could do that."

"Keep me safe? By kidnapping me?" Sofie tilted her head, staring down her captor.

"Yes. There is much I have to tell you. I'm going to answer all of your questions now. You're very important to the future of this place." Coral smiled again.

"Important, how? If you want me on your side, this was the wrong way to achieve that goal. I don't understand any of this," Sofie hissed.

"I know you don't, and I'm sorry for that. But you will. You're about to be our biggest fan. I hear you've already met Buzz?" Coral cocked her head, her eyes sparkling.

"Yes. A Helicoprion. A species thought to be long extinct. What's going on down here?" Sofie asked.

Coral splayed her hands in front of her. "Oh, Buzz isn't ours. He's with the others."

Sofiana nodded. "Gold mentioned he was waiting for 'the others'. Who are they?"

"I'll get to that. I told you, I'll answer all of your questions."

"Okay, so let's hear it." Sofie put her hands on her hips.

Coraline dismissed Sofiana, turned to Maggie and held out her hand. "You must be Maggie Lee! I'm Coraline. You can call me by my nickname, Coral. My dad never liked the nickname, but I think nicknames are so much fun!"

Maggie ignored the outstretched hand, placing her own hands on her hips. "Yes, we met your father. Why are we here?"

Coral clapped, her ponytail swinging. "I know! He's on his way now, and I can't wait to see him! It's been more years than I can count since I saw him last!"

Maggie Lee pursed her lips. "I want answers."

"Yes, yes, of course you do. I promise, as soon as my father arrives I'll fill all of you in at once. He's going to be so proud of the progress we've made in his absence. Make yourselves comfortable. They're coming right now. We only have to make sure Buzz is out of the area before Dad and the dog arrive."

Sofiana gasped. "The dog? Crash? But how will you get him down here?"

"Oh, that's why you came separately. We had to locate special canine diving equipment. I can't wait to meet Crash!" Coral practically bounced with excitement.

"Well, I can't wait to get some answers. Tell us one thing now. Is my husband okay? Are our friends okay? Gold said they were, but I don't know if I trust him." Maggie's eyes bored into Coral's.

"Yes. Our man drugged them, that's all. They'll all wake up with a headache, just like you did. We only hurt people if it's absolutely necessary. We're not monsters." Coral winked.

Chapter 87

Atlantic Ocean, On the Surface, Above Mercury Reef

G old held up his hand in greeting to the captain of the small vessel as it neared the helicopter. The sun's rays glinted off his sunglasses, reflecting a distorted image of the rolling waves and the approaching boat giving them a cartoonish appearance.

"Are they down there?" the other man shouted over the sound of the idling engine. The wind blew his blond hair sideways causing it to stand on end.

"Yes. Dr. Stone and Maggie Lee Johnson are on the way now. Jayden is guiding them, and you know Coraline never leaves her sanctuary for long. Bob and the dog will arrive shortly. You need to go. They can't see me talking to you, or they'll know I've switched sides. Go. I'll handle it. It's all going down tomorrow."

"I hope you can handle it, Gold. Or you'll have me to deal with."

Tilting his head to look over the rim of his glasses, he growled, "Don't threaten me. You know I don't respond well to threats. Now, get the hell out of here before I decide that I'm done with both of you."

The man, L-shaped scar a pale beacon on the backdrop of tanned skin, hesitated for a fraction of a minute, then nodded, satisfied. His smile lacked its usual neighborly charm. "See you down there, then. To-morrow. It all ends tomorrow." The water around the boat churned as he departed.

Gold inhaled the salty air on a long sigh as the boat retreated. He squeezed the muscle on the side of his neck and closed his eyes, tilting his head toward the sun's rays. The warmth seeped into his skin, spreading from his hairline down to his chin, and the wrinkles on his brow relaxed as they seldom did these days.

I hope this does end tomorrow. I need this to end.

His eyes flew open at the sound of the second copter's approach. Again, Gold raised his hand in greeting, hair flattened as the helicopter's blades slowed. The metal bird was expertly maneuvered by the pilot onto the undulating waves as if he'd done this hundreds of times.

When the blades came to rest, silently frozen in place, the door on the second chopper slid back, and Bob stepped down onto the float, raising his hand to shade his eyes. Crash stood behind him, leaning half-way out with his feet barely hanging onto the seat. On the other side, the pilot disembarked.

Gold nodded. "Eric."

"Gold."

"Are you heading down?" Eric asked.

"No, I don't think it'd be a good idea to leave two choppers out here, do you? Unless you were thinking of flying both out yourself?" Gold retorted.

Eric snorted. "Don't be a smart-ass. I was asking a simple question. I'm dropping these two off here, and then I'm heading back to land where I belong." Eric chuckled. "And anyway, you know as well as I do that she doesn't let me come down. Tell Coral I said 'hey', will you? I'm always happy to fly for a pretty little lady. Well that, and the pay's good."

Gold crossed his arms over his chest. "I'm not into delivering messages. That's not in my job description."

"What, exactly, is your job description, Gold? I'm dying to know what's going on down there." Eric pointed.

"Don't worry about it. Some things are best left to your imagination."

Eric snorted. "Yeah. Okay, man. Whatever you say."

Gold turned away, "Let's get this done."

"Fine." Eric reached up to pull one small and one large backpack from inside. "Here's your diving equipment, and this is the special order for the dog. Suit up. I'm not supposed to leave until you're down."

Bob unzipped the bag, taking pieces out. "Uh, it's been a long time since I've done this, and I've never gone down with a dog before."

"You'll figure it out." Gold nodded, eyes sharp.

Climbing back up, Bob disappeared into the helicopter. "C'mon, Crash. Let's get suited up." Twenty minutes later, he emerged in scuba gear. Standing on the float, he reached down to slide his feet into the flippers, then fell backward into the water. He looked up.

"Okay, Crash. Jump in," Bob called.

The dog hesitated just a beat, and then jumped into the water with a splash, paddling with all four legs to stay afloat. He looked like a canine astronaut, head inside a round glass dome. Bob grabbed for the dog's harness, and attached a tether to the dog. They were connected now, for better or worse.

Bob guffawed, "Good dog. Follow me." He bit down on his mouthpiece, gave a salute to Gold, and disappeared under the water in a flurry of bubbles, grasping the rope that linked them and giving it a tug.

Though it had been years since he had done this, Bob remembered everything about this place. It was a homecoming. Away too long. He could feel his heart rate pick up as he pushed forward. The feel of the water surrounding his body was comforting. A tight smile bloomed around his mouthpiece. He bit down in excitement.

Soon, I'll be reunited with my daughter. I can't wait to see how she's changed.

Next to him, four paws circling as if riding an invisible bike, Crash was holding his own. The dog kept up with his pace as he descended into the cavernous space below. When he slowed, Bob towed him along by the tether.

Aware of the inherent danger, he scanned the open waters surrounding him, and continued moving.

As they approached the halfway mark, he spun 180 degrees when he detected movement from above. Something big. On the surface.

His eyes widened. Something had fallen into the water from above. As he watched, the surface became tinted with a black, swirling color, turning the sea surrounding the—thing—cloudy and dark. He stopped breathing for just a few beats. When he realized what he was doing, he gulped air and continued down at a faster pace stopping every few feet to look up.

A body? Who is it? Gold? Eric? Or someone else?

His legs burned as they kicked in rapid bursts, the dog still keeping pace though he had to paddle double-time to keep up. He seemed to understand the need to get to their destination as quickly as possible.

Boom!

The two flinched as one, looking above. The muffled noise was followed by...rain? No, rain stops just below the surface as it merges with the saltwater. It doesn't continue downward as this was doing. Bob tilted his head as the tiny objects approached.

Bits of metal debris rained down past him, and realization dawned. Though it wasn't directly above him, he instinctively recoiled.

The helicopter.

Eyes wild, he gestured to Crash and they both picked up speed. He guessed that larger pieces of metal would soon follow, and he didn't want to be there to witness it.

Man and dog continued swimming at a frantic pace.

Not much farther...

Chapter 88

Mercury Reef Underwater Habitat

*T*ap-tap-tap-tap. Tap-tap-tap-tap. Tap-tap-tap-tap.

Sofie's fingers drummed the table. With eyes focused on the ceiling, she huffed. Pushing herself up, she reached the porthole in two long strides, placed a hand on smooth coolness of the wall. She leaned forward, glaring out at the surrounding sea. The ocean she loved so much suddenly seemed confining, entrapping her in the mysterious beauty of its depths. For the first time, she longed for land. And she ached for Grayson.

"I need to *do* something," she hissed through her teeth.

Her back stiffened at the touch of a hand on her back. Realizing it was only Maggie Lee, she relaxed degree by degree.

Maggie crooned in a motherly voice, "Shh. It's okay. Everything's going to be okay. We're gonna get out of this, and be with our men again. And I'm going to be a Mama. Maybe you will, too."

A hysterical laugh escaped her lips. "A Mama? I can't think about that right now. What are we going to do? We have to get out of here."

"We will. We'll get out of here. I can feel it." Once again, Maggie gently lay her hand on her abdomen, a slight smile curving her lips. "We have to believe. Both of us. It's going to be okay."

"Oh, I do believe it. Grayson and I just reconnected. I'm not going to let some crazy blond with a ponytail keep us apart. I just hate waiting."

Slamming her palm against the wall, her eyes gazed out over the endless expanse of sea floor. In her peripheral vision, she spied movement and turned her head in response.

A gray blur darted away before she got a good look. Leaning her cheek against the glass, she tilted her head to the right as far as she could to try to see what it was. Her breath steamed the glass blurring her vision, and still she watched, unblinking. She felt Maggie behind her as she waited, too.

"Was that Buzz?" Maggie Lee whispered.

"No, I don't think so. I wasn't big enough."

Maggie drew in a quick breath. "What...?"

"It looks like...Crash! Look, its Crash, and that must be Bob! Coral said they were on the way. That's incredible! I've heard about these things, but I've never seen a dog using scuba equipment."

Man and dog kicked through the water, Bob stopping to look upward every few feet. He pulled the rope that attached them and gestured to the dog, who kept up amazingly well for a canine swimming underwater. Crash's hair floated straight out around him, like a fuzzy aura surrounding him, dancing on the current as he moved.

"Bob seems stressed about something." Sofie once again pushed her face against the glass.

Her body convulsed when the white shark swam into view, heading right for the dog. She pounded on the thick window, screaming, "Shark! There's a shark! Bob! Crash! Shark!" Maggie Lee's voice joined her own.

Her eyes filled with the sting of tears and her hand flew to her mouth as the shark approached. The juvenile white swam in lazy circles around the dog. Bob placed himself as close to Crash as he could. His arm flung around the dog's midsection, and he kept moving. When the shark came at them, Bob placed himself between dog and shark. The shark opened its mouth and bit down on Bob's shoulder, then backed off and began circling again. A mist of blood seeped into the water.

"It was an exploratory nibble. Hopefully, it didn't like its first taste," Sofie whispered.

The shark swam out of view, and the duo swam on. Eyes wide, she heard Maggie Lee's cry as the shark darted at them from behind. "Shark! Shark! Behind you!"

The six-foot juvie's eyes rolled back in its head, mouth a gaping hole, tail propelling it straight toward Crash. The dog turned and lowered its head just as the beast attacked, and its teeth slid off the front of his bulbous glass mask.

Sofie let out a breath. "Go! Swim-swim-swim!"

Just then a giant piece of metal came barreling from above, landing only feet from the underwater habitat. The great white darted away with a swish of its tail. Sand swirled all around, blocking their vision, and the two women faced each other.

"Oh no! Where are they?" Squinting through the cloudy water, Maggie hugged her middle.

Sofiana was already at the door. Grasping the

wheel handle, she heaved and pulled.

"We're locked in."

"What if…?" Tears filled Maggie's eyes.

With a quick head-shake, Sofie grasped Maggie's arm. "No. They're okay. They made it."

Sofie returned to stare out the window. The sand was beginning to settle, and she could make out the shape of the hunk of metal on the sea floor. "Is that…a helicopter blade?".

Maggie stood next to her, peering through the glass."Yes, I think it is. But what happened to the helicopter, then?"

"And was anyone on it when it exploded?"

Chapter 89

Mercury Reef Underwater Habitat

Hours passed. The grinding of metal that preceded the opening of the door had Sofiana jumping to her feet in one quick move. In three long strides she stood inside the boundaries of Coraline's personal space, Maggie Lee right on her heels. She towered over the smaller woman, her eyes squinting down at her.

Hands gesturing in front of her, she demanded, "Where are Bob and Crash? Are they alright?"

"I take it you saw them through the window? Yes, yes. Don't worry, they're fine. Well, maybe a few bumps and bruises and...nibbles...but as you know their earth-rocks give them special healing capabilities."

"Really? They're really okay?" Sofie sighed, shoulders slumping.

A laugh escaped Maggie's lips. "Earth-rocks? Ha! You call them earth-rocks? Sounds like something a kid would make up."

Coraline smiled. "There is truth to that. I was little more than a child when I named them. And you call yours a trinket. You can call it anything you want, it doesn't matter anyway."

Maggie Lee cocked her head. "Do you have one? An earth-rock?"

She tilted her head. "Yes and no. Yes, I have one. But I don't need it. Not the way you do."

"What's that supposed to mean?"

Click-clack, click-clack, click-clack, click-clack.

Nails tapped on the metal floor, echoing down the hall. Sofie's head swiveled toward the door, just before Crash bounded into the room. He ran straight for Maggie Lee, body wiggling as he pounced, placing his front paws on her midsection.

"Crash! You're okay!" Squatting, Maggie lifted her chin to accept his frantic kisses. "Did that shark hurt you?"

His head swung in a side-to-side arc, tail wiggling back and forth.

"What about Bob?" Sofie urged.

Coraline answered, "My father is in the sick room, being tended to. The shark did some damage to his shoulder, but he's been hurt worse than this before. He'll be fine after his earth-rock hastens the healing process. He should be joining us shortly. I want him coherent when we're reunited for the first time."

She spun around at the sound of a voice behind her.

"Coraline."

"Father! You're healing faster these days. I've been waiting for your return for more days than I can count."

"I've thought about you. Missed you. Come here." Bob's arms engulfed Coraline.

Sofie stood back and witnessed the reunion. Her eyes narrowed.

Guess we know whose side Bob is on.

She turned and locked eyes with Maggie Lee, then Crash.

Yip.

Turning, she walked to the porthole, staring out into the living waters. The sand had settled, and she could clearly make out the shape of a helicopter blade jutting up out of the sea floor. She spun around, the cold emanating off the window sending a chill up her back as she leaned back, arms crossed in front of her.

"Hey, Bob. Um, I hate to interrupt this party, but I for one would like to have some answers. Coraline told us she would fill us in once you got here. Now you're here. Let's get started."

"Yes. There are some things I want answered as well." He stepped back, and reached around to give his daughter's ponytail a gentle tug. "Still partial to ponytails, I see."

She giggled. "Of course, they're efficient. And people tend to underestimate a girl with a ponytail. It gets the job done."

"Smart, as always. You look exactly the same. You still look like a seventeen-year-old girl. Last time I came for a visit, you were, what, like twenty-five?"

She nodded. "You don't look the same, Dad. You look old. You look sixty-something. O-l-d."

Bob chuckled. "Not as old as I did just a few weeks ago. Then, I looked eighty-something. I was separated from my rock. But I'm not now. And I'm feeling stronger every day. Especially since I got here."

She winked, her smile radiating from her face. With one more impulsive hug, she turned toward the table, gesturing for the others to sit. "Let's all sit down.

We have a lot to talk about."

Sofie paced the room. "I don't want to sit."

Coral took the seat at the head of the rectangular metal table, and gave a nod, gesturing toward the seat next to her.

Sofie blew out a breath. "Fine." She fell into the chair, elbows on the table. "Start talking." Maggie Lee sat in the chair directly to her left, and Crash jumped into a chair next to her. He sat tall, and stared down his nose at Coral.

"Please hear me out, Sofiana. I know you're upset about how you were brought here, but you have no idea how important your approval is to me. You're my idol. No one knows more about the sea than you. I've followed your career for ages." She turned to address the group, "I was born here. This is my home. I can count the times I've left this place on one hand. I'm happy here. I feel connected to it. Whenever I do leave, I am always drawn back. Like a magnetic force. It's where I belong." She sighed, staring into Bob's eyes. "So do you. I'm so glad you're back." Eyes filling, she continued, "Anyway, I come from two parents bonded with Earth-rocks, and we think because of that, I have special... abilities."

"I want to know what these Earth-rocks are." Sofie demanded, "Where do they come from? Outer space? Is it some kind of alien metal? Are extra-terrestrials taking over our planet? E.T. phone home, or something like that?" She threw her hands up, gesturing wildly to emphasize her words. "Wait, does that make *you* an alien? I've never believed in any of that, but I'm willing to have an open mind with all I've seen in the past weeks. I feel like I'm in a movie, or a video game or something."

Coral's bell-chiming laughter sent shivers up Sofie's back. The girl's ponytail danced side to side as she shook her head, as if the curls were on a spring. "No. That's what we thought at first, too, right Dad?" She smiled at Bob. "We've been studying The Core Site for years. At first we thought the same as you. Maybe it was an alien metal dropped from the sky, taking up residence on Earth, hidden in the ocean depths. We considered that it was growing roots down into the mantle, reaching for the very heart of Earth. But no, we don't think that anymore."

"So, what *do* you think, then?" Maggie interjected.

"Well, we are almost certain that it comes *from* the earth's core. Various tests have indicated that the core, both inner and outer, has a high iron content. As you know, we humans have iron as a mineral present in our blood. We think the rocks choose to bond with people of high blood iron levels. Like attracting like."

Maggie Lee interrupted, "So, that could be why the rocks don't work on everyone?" She spoke directly to Sofie. "We did a test. Grayson cut his finger, and my trinket didn't heal him. It wouldn't work on you in the helicopter on the way here, either."

"Ha! That's right, Maggie Lee! I forgot how smart you are. You are a school teacher, after all." Coral looked around the table. "Also, we think once it bonds with a person, it won't bond with anyone else. We've never seen one Earth-rock work on two different people. We're still researching that bond. That's why when your Earth-rock was taken from you, Maggie Lee, we helped you get it back. We do know that when it comes into first contact with a person—or animal—that it forms a bond with, it injects some of its substance into them, altering their DNA just slightly. We've been studying the substance for years without being able to identify it. It's unlike anything we've ever seen. In your case, Maggie, it has given you healing powers. In Crash's case, or in Cary-One's, it has altered their brains to make them more intelligent along with the power to heal."

Maggie Lee leaned forward. "Wait, I didn't feel any kind of injection when I found it on the beach. I think you must be mistaken."

"Oh, you wouldn't feel it. The 'needle' is microscopic, and can't be seen by the naked eye. You can imagine that there would be little to no pain on contact."

"Wait a minute. This is crazy. You want us to believe all of this just because you're telling us? Sorry, but you lost my trust when you kidnapped us. And what makes you think it's coming from the core? I'm still more inclined to believe the alien theory." Sofiana rolled her eyes. "I can't believe those words just came out of my mouth."

"From what we've been able to observe, it seems the earth's core has a slow leak. It may be a hole the size of a pinprick, but a hole is there. We call that area The Core Site. The Core Site is growing. Very slowly, only centimeters each year, but growing in diameter nonetheless. We have no idea how long its been leaking, but we've been here studying it over a hundred years, and we have meticulous notes on all of our research here."

Sofie stood up and paced to the window, then back. "I want to see all of your research. If the earth's core is truly leaking, that can't be good for the future of our planet. If there's a leak, and the earth's core cools... it could be the end of earth. It would mess with the magnetic and electrical energy that we tap into, and I don't even think your healing powers could cure what would happen to life on earth in that event."

Coral inclined her head. "You may have access to all of our notes. Anything you want, no secrets. But I should warn you it goes deeper than the scientific research."

Sofie sat back, crossing her arms. "What the hell does that mean?"

"Well, we think the earth's core is alive, to a certain extent. Aware. I know, I know, it sounds crazy when you say it out loud. Just hear me out. Not the same as you and me. Not even the same as animals." She nodded toward Crash and smiled when he made a huffing sound. "A much more primitive sort of awareness, if that makes any sense. Sort of like in botany. Plant life is aware of what it needs to stay living, like how a flower leans toward the sun's rays for survival. We think the earth's core may be a living organism...in the same sense as, in simple terms, a tree is alive. It will do what it takes to survive."

Maggie Lee cleared her throat. "None of this makes sense."

Coral shrugged. "I understand how this might be hard to believe. I've had years of research and observation to go on. But this is all new to you, so I understand your hesitancy."

"Okay, go on. Let's all assume you're right. The Earth itself has an awareness. So what?" Sofiana gestured for her to continue.

"Well, it also has healing properties that it passes

on to other living things. I haven't aged much since reaching maturity because I stay close to The Core Site. Maybe it wants to aid life on earth by improving it. Animals that stay near it are surprisingly resilient, even without bonding with an Earth-rock. And then there are the horseshoe crabs. They stay close to it, too. Flock to it. Their blood and healing properties are physically different from ours. People have harvested the blood of horseshoe crabs for over 50 years to use parts of their blood to detect bacteria. Their blood is high in copper, which causes the blue color versus the red in our blood. Its clotting abilities are remarkable, and its antibacterial properties are astounding. They heal at a much faster rate than humans. Within hours instead of days. We believe the reason for that is their bond to The Core Site. So, the real question—one that we haven't been able to answer with any certainty— is which event occurred first? We know that the horse-shoe crabs have been around since the beginning. A very long time. Did the horseshoe crab's blood evolve from proximity to The Core Site, or did they have the ability all along and are simply drawn to the power emanating from inside the earth? Has there always been a leak in the core, or did it develop over time? We have no way of knowing for sure how they are connected. But we've also detected high sulfur levels at The Core Site, and where there is sulfur, it is almost certain there will be copper. It could be where the horseshoe crab's copper-based hemocyanin in their blood comes from. Our blood is iron-based hemoglobin. Iron and copper. Two substances found in and around The Core Site."

The utter stillness that followed filled every corner of the room. The air was thick with the blare of pure silence. The second hand on the wall clock made several rotations in the quiet space. *Tick-tick-tick-tick.* A stomach rumbled. Someone sniffled. The dog panted, then quickly closed his mouth to stop the sound waves that rolled off his tongue. He slowly shook his head side to side, and a high-pitched whine escaped.

"I agree with Crash. This is all very unbelievable." Maggie lay her hand on the dog's side, and his tongue darted out in a quick lick.

Sofiana cleared her throat. "I want to see the research, and I want to visit The Core Site. As soon as possible."

Maggie placed a hand on her arm, "Don't get distracted by all of this. We still need to get out of here."

"Oh, I'm afraid that isn't possible, at least right now." Coral interrupted. "We are under attack, so you'll need to stay here, at least until we know it's safe for you to leave."

"Attack? By who? I don't see any attack. And what about my husband? Our friends? Can you give us assurances that they will be safe?"

Coral shook her head. "I'm afraid not. I can't know what's going on out there. But I can keep all of you safe down here. Sofie, a friend of yours is already here. Safe."

"A friend?" She frowned.

"Yes, I'll go get the research, and send him down." Coraline bounced out of the room leaving them alone, an aura of jubilation surrounding her like a cheerful cloak.

Sofiana spoke first, "Well, here we are. Just the four of us. Like a reunion of sorts. Here's what I need to know from you, Bob. Did you know all of this? The

Earth's core, iron and the law of attraction, the whole she-bang? Did you know this when we were all at the cabin?"

Bob's eyes darted down to the shiny metal surface of the stark table, breaking eye contact before he answered in a barely audible whisper, "Yes."

Sofie slammed her hands down on the table with a reverberating *thwack* causing the surface to vibrate. Though her palms stung, she leaned forward, just inches from his face, and ground out between gritted teeth, "Grayson was right. We never should have trusted you. You could have told us, but chose to lie instead. I won't forget that."

Maggie frowned. "Bob, why? Why didn't you tell us all of it?"

He slumped in his chair, "I didn't think you'd believe me. I'd just told you my age. My story. And that's all unbelievable enough. I didn't lie. I just left the rest out of my story. Everything else I told you was true. I swear it."

"Really? Didn't we ask you what these things are?" Maggie Lee patted her pocket, cupping the trinket through the cloth. "You said you didn't know. That's lying in my book."

"You're right. And I'm sorry. I didn't give you all the information that I could have. I see now that I was wrong. If I could go back and change it, I would. But would you have done anything differently if you knew all of it then?" He shook his head. "It doesn't matter now."

Yip. Yip-yip-yip.

Crash leaped off the silver chair in one fluid move, and sat next to Maggie Lee, head held high.

Maggie place a hand on the dog's back. "I agree, Crash. It does matter. We can't make the mistake of trusting him again."

"I've told you I'm sorry. You know the whole story now. I'll leave you since my presence seems to upset you. But you *can* trust me. Remember, the three of us are connected. We're connected to everyone who has bonded. I've lived through a lot. The younger version of me? Him, you couldn't trust. He did things I'm ashamed of. The older me? The one that's standing in front of you now? I promise you can trust him. Me." He pushed up from the table and turned toward the door.

Sofie stopped him. "Wait. What about the children. Your daughter didn't say anything about the children she has down here."

"I don't know anything about children, and I haven't seen any kids around here yet. That's the part of the story that I truly don't know. The only child that was down here while I was here was Coraline, I swear it. But I'll go find out. I won't be far if any of you need me."

When he reached the doorway, another man blocked his way.

"Christian?" Sofie ran toward the door and grabbed him in a bear hug, not even noticing that he did not return her embrace. "Christian? How are you here? Did they kidnap you, too? I thought you were safe because you left before all of this happened."

"No, I wasn't kidnapped," his voice was devoid of emotion.

"Then why are you here?" Sofie asked.

"After I left, I contacted Coraline. She gave us her card, remember? You didn't have a need for me anymore, now that your boyfriend is back. You cast me aside. So, I'm working here now."

"Did you know what they planned to do? The kidnapping, I mean?" Sofie's words came out slowly, her eyes sharpening.

"As a matter of fact, I did. Actually, I'm the one who shut off the water to the cabin and planted the drugged water bottles. Coraline assured me no one would be hurt, so I agreed. And she was telling the truth. Everyone's fine."

Sofie took a step backward, hands dropping to her sides. "I can't believe you would do that to me."

"Do what to you, Sofiana? I nearly died for you. I've followed you everywhere, taking orders, waiting. Waiting for you to notice me in the same way I notice you. But, you know what? You played me for a fool. I realized when I saw you with Grayson that it was never going to happen for us. I'm free of you. I make my own choices now. I'm done being a follower."

"What if someone back at the cabin had been hurt? What if one of us would have overdosed? That would have been on you," she spat.

"Yeah, I guess I'll have to live with that. But no one did overdose, so no worries. Oh, and I work for Coral now."

Maggie stepped forward, her hand fluttering to her chest. "Christian, I can't believe you did this."

"Well, I don't really know you, anyway, so I guess I can live with that, too. Coral's doing the kind of research I've always dreamed of doing." His eyes cut to Sofiana. "Much more important than your tracker, *Dr.* Stone. It's groundbreaking. And I'm going to be part of it. I'll be bigger than you someday."

Sofiana sank into the nearest chair. "I'm truly

sorry about...everything. I never meant to hurt you, and I should never have kissed you. That's on me. The rest is on you. I hope you'll be happy in your new position. And guess what? You're still a follower. The only thing that's changed is who you're following." She turned away then back again, eyes narrowed. "What do you know about the children? Have you learned anything more about them? Or the people she thinks are attacking?"

"You'll have to get that information from Coraline herself. Have a pleasant stay here. Maybe I'll bump into you again before you leave."

"Do you have any idea when we'll be allowed to do that?" she demanded.

Shrugging, Christian turned and strutted from the room.

Chapter 90

Mercury Reef Underwater Habitat

B ob hurried down the narrow hallway. Memories flooded his brain, and he stopped to place a steadying hand on the wall. Breathing heavily, his heart was torn.

I can't believe I'm back in this place. When I left the last time, I swore I'd never come back.

Even now, he could feel the magnetic pull of The Core Site. He was the first. First to form the bond with the core. His blood sang a joyous song of reunion even as his mind rejected the attraction. He'd never asked for this. This reunion was tearing him in two.

Still, it was so good to see his daughter again, to know that she had not only survived but had flourished here. At least he had that before he died.

If I stay here, will I ever die?

That had been the reason he'd left in the first place. Near-immortality was not as desirable as it seemed. The agony of suffering through watching all the people you care about die, while still going on. What was the point?

For many years, he'd done terrible things in the name of research. Unforgivable, even. He'd committed more atrocities than he could count, and he was weary. Weary of it all.

And his daughter was the same. Leaving her had been the hardest decision of his life, but he'd been desperate to return to a normal life. She'd been young to be left on her own, he'd known it, but she had always been smarter than a typical child. *And she wasn't alone. She had Gold and Jayden to look after her, even after her mother died.*

Memories of his first life flooded his brain.

Victoria.

I left her for all of this. Her and our unborn child.

She'd been pregnant when he'd left after that last visit home before returning home that one final time, and he'd known it. But still he was drawn back to the siren call deep in the depths of the sea. There was no excuse. No excuse on Earth could exonerate him from all of his wrongdoings. Unforgivable, terrible acts he couldn't take back.

He closed his eyes, and in his mind she appeared. A vision of Victoria, as plainly as if she were standing right in front of him. He'd been the only one to ever call her beautiful. Maybe a better word to describe her would have been handsome. Her tall stature and square face, hair pulled severely back in a bun. But she'd been loyal to only him; loved only him, and still he'd left her over and over again.

He thought of the last time he went to see her. Flashed back to the horrible scene as his head shook side to side in denial, a tear leaking out of the corner of his eye even as he relived it as he had done many times in his dreams.

"Victoria, I'm home. I'm staying this time. I'm sorry

I ever left. I'm going to make it up to you. You and Adam."

"Get out. Get out!" Victoria screamed, spittle flying from her lips. "I don't want to see you anymore. You think it's acceptable to show up every five years just to leave again? Not anymore. That's not the way a marriage is supposed to work. There was a time I wanted nothing more than to see you come back to me. But I'm empty now. I have nothing left. Just leave. I don't want you here."

Stepping forward, he grabbed her arm. "I will not leave. This is my house. You'll learn to forgive me, and we'll be fine. I said I'm sorry. I promise I won't leave again."

"No. I don't want you here. You think you can be gone for years and then just return as if nothing ever happened? Get out!"

Bob's temple throbbed. "I'm not leaving. We have a son together. I want to get to know him. Adam needs a father."

She collapsed on the floor, body convulsing in hysterical laughter even as fat tears streaked down her cheeks.

"Why are you laughing? Have you lost your mind?"

"I might as well lose my mind. I've lost everything else. Why do you care now, when you never have before?"

"What do you mean, you've lost everything? Where's Adam?"

He bounded up the stairs, searching each room, calling his son's name. His words echoed back at him, mocking him. When he turned at the top of the stairs, she was right behind him. Grabbing her forearms, he shook her.

"Where's my son? Where's Adam?"

Her laughter sent chills from the base of his spine up to his frontal lobe. He heard white noise as the pounding in his temples began.

"I asked you a question. Where is Adam?"

"He's gone. They took him, and it's all your fault. They said they wanted your son. They took him and he's dead, all because of you."

Rage burned in his eyes and he shook her harder. When he let go, she stumbled backward, arms grasping at nothing but air. Thumping down the stairs, her head bounced off the railing once, twice, until her body landed in a twisted heap at the bottom, twitching. Her leg twisted to the side at an unnatural angle, blood pooled behind her head. He didn't know how he reached the bottom of the steps as he squatted next to his wife and felt her carotid artery for a pulse with two fingers. Nothing. Even the twitching ceased and she lay unmoving. Throwing back his head, he howled to the empty room, his pain echoing off the walls.

No Adam. No Victoria. He had nothing.

He stood as if in a trance.

The rest came back in flashes that burst in front of his eyes like a strobe.

Calling for help. His wife's death, determined an accident. It was common knowledge she'd been distraught since her son went missing. She either fell, or threw herself down the stairs to end her own suffering. Most believed the latter.

In the days that followed, he gathered all the pictures and memories he had of his time with Victoria, as well as his time at Mercury Reef, and buried them in the yard.

Time to start a new chapter in his life.

Chapter 91

Mercury Reef Underwater Habitat

"Look, the door's open. Guess that means we're free to go." Sofiana stepped through the doorway, gesturing to Maggie Lee and Crash. "Follow me."

The three padded through the hallway uninterrupted. Sofie lowered her voice, "The children were this way the last time I was here."

Crash's claws echoed as he prowled along behind. Despite the alerting sound, no one materialized to lock them up.

"This place seems deserted," Maggie whispered.

"Last time I was here, it was the same. I have no idea how big Coral's crew is. The only people I know of are Coral, Jayden, the children. And Gold."

"Don't forget Christian, and Bob. I'm not sure which side he's on." The creases in Maggie's forehead deepened.

"We have to assume he'll side with his daughter if it comes to that. We can't trust him."

Maggie Lee sighed. "I know. It just makes me sad." At Crash's whimper, she reached down and patted his head. "At least we have each other."

"Here it is. This was the playroom where I met Tia and the other children." Sofie reached for the circular handle. The grinding sound made her cringe, but she turned the wheel until the door opened inward.

Sticking her head inside, she called, "Hello?"

The sound of hushed voices filled her ears as she stepped into the room. "Hello? Tia? Hurley? Genna? It's me, Sofie. We met the last time I was here. It's okay to come out."

Tia stepped out from behind the couch, followed closely by the other two. "Hi, Sofie. You're back. Coral said bad people are coming. Are the bad people here?"

"No. Just me, and I have some friends for you to meet. None of us is bad, I promise." She placed her hand over her heart with a smile, then gestured to indicate the two behind her. "This is Maggie Lee. She's a school teacher. And this is Crash."

"Aww! A puppy? I've always wanted a puppy!" The children flocked around the dog. Crash raised a paw and placed it on Tia's arm, his canine grin evidenced what he thought of the attention. His tongue darted out to lick Genna's nose, and her giggle burst out like chimes on the wind. Hurley stood an arm's length away, but a shy smile lit his face. Crash leaned forward and nudged his arm. Hurley raised his hand, and Crash nuzzled it.

"Yes, and he's a very smart puppy. Smarter than most because he has an Earth-rock," Sofiana said.

"He's bonded with an Earth-rock?" Tia tilted her head.

Sofie nodded. "Yes, it healed him and it has given him intelligence beyond the normal canine abilities."

"Like Cary-one," answered Tia.

"Yes. Like Cary-one." Sofiana's lips turned up. She squatted next to the little boy. "Do you want to pet him, Hurley?"

He looked up from under his lashes, and as crimson climbed from his neck to his cheeks, his head jerked in a barely imperceptible nod.

"Come on, then. He's very friendly. He won't bite."

Crash looked at her and rolled his eyes, then focused all his attention on Hurley. He lay on his back in front of the boy, exposing his belly.

Yip.

Hurley stretched his arm toward the dog, and placed it on the animal's stomach. Crash wiggled his body back and forth, and a laugh escaped the boy before he could hold it back. He experimented with wiggling his fingers, and when the movement brought forth a near-purring sound from Crash, the child moved a step closer.

"Pup-py." He whispered, eyes focused solely on the dog. "Cwash."

Tia whispered, "Wow, Hurley likes the puppy. He's very shy, and hardly ever talks to anyone."

"Do you mind if we ask you some questions, Tia?" Sofie lay her hand gently on the girl's arm.

Tia's eyes found Genna's before she looked back at Sofiana. "Yes. Coral wouldn't like it, but I guess it's okay. She hardly lets us do anything," she pouted.

"Great, let's start with your parents. Where are they?" Sofie asked.

Once again, the girls made quiet eye contact.

Tia sat down on the floor, and Genna sat next to her. They joined hands.

"We're not supposed to tell anyone. But we like you. And you have a puppy. So I guess it's okay."

Tia did the talking, while Genna listened intently, nodding her head occasionally.

"Coral's my mom. I mean, she doesn't like me to call her that, but she told me she carried me inside her so I know what that means. It means she's my mom. Genna and Hurley were brought here when they were babies. That means Coral's not really their mom, right? I think they must have had parents once, but they don't know them."

Genna's gentle voice added, "Sometimes, I dream. Not of bad things, it's a good dream. There's music and chocolate eyes. I love chocolate. And a song about sunshine…"

Maggie Lee inhaled, her hand raised to her burning cheek. "How long have you been here?"

Tia's brows drew together. "What do you mean? This is my home. I'm always home."

Genna whispered, "Coral told us about the scary people. We don't want to leave. If we do, the bad guys will get us."

Tia nodded. "The Core Site wouldn't talk to us if we left. Coral said so."

"The Core Site…talks to you? How does it talk to you?" Sofiana asked.

"Up here." Genna placed her pointer finger on her temple.

"In your head? Does it talk to you like I'm talking to you right now? With words?"

Tia laughed. "No." Genna's giggle joined in. "Why did you come here, Sofie?"

"Coral kidnapped us and brought us here. That's

not really fair, is it? We'd like to leave."

"No, but Coral says not everything is fair. We have to do what's best for us. It must be best for us for you to be here." Tia smiled. "I like you, Sofie, so I'm glad you're here."

"Thanks, I like you, too. But it's not okay to harm others to do what's best for you, right?"

"Oh, no! Did Coral hurt you?" Tia frowned.

"Well, no. Not really. But..." Sofie sighed.

"Oh, good." Tia's smile bloomed, as if she were the adult teaching a misinformed child.

Sofiana's shoulders raised on a deep sigh. *This isn't getting us anywhere.*

"Does each of you have an Earth-rock?" She tried a different route.

"Yep. Inside."

"Inside what?" Sofie asked.

Tia lifted her shirt and pointed to her midsection. "Inside me."

"So it's not an Earth-rock? You're saying since you're connected to The Core Site and it talks to you, you don't need one?"

Tia's giggles echoed off the walls. "No. You're silly, Sofie. I have an Earth-rock inside me. Coral put it there to keep us safe."

Maggie Lee took an involuntary step backward, arms held protectively in front of her midsection. "She means they implanted it into her body."

"What?" Sofie stood, hands trembling. Crash jumped to his feet and whined.

She felt Maggie's hand on her arm and allowed herself to be dragged to the far corner of the room, listening to her friend's hushed voice, "I think they took the other two from their families, brought them here, and implanted them with trinket-rock-things. What *is* this place? We have to get out of here. I'm getting a bad vibe all of a sudden. My baby's not safe here. And neither are we."

Chapter 92

Mercury Reef Underwater Habitat

B ob veered left at the end of the main hallway, as familiar with this place as if he'd never left. He knew where to find her. Or at least, he used to. He approached her bedroom door and saw that it was cracked, so he grasped the handle without announcing himself and strode into the room.

"Father!" Coraline had been leaning over a desk and quickly jumped in front of it, folding her arms across her chest. "I wasn't expecting you in here. Let's go to the lab and I'll share my research with you. Wait 'til you see all the progress we've made since you left." She beamed her innocent smile.

"What's that your hiding, Coraline?"

"Hiding? I'm not hiding anything. There's nothing to see here. If you'll come with me to the lab, I'll show you everything."

"Okay. I want to see the research. But show me what's on the desk behind you first."

"No. It's none of your concern. Just personal stuff. You remember the way to the lab, right?" she asked while taking a step forward.

"Coraline," Bob's voice rose.

She sighed. "Can't I have some privacy in my own room? I'm 184-years-old. I really don't think I need my Daddy's permission..."

"Coraline," he said, pushing past.

"Fine! But I can explain..."

His shoulders raised with his quick intake of breath, "What is this? Why do you have this?" Between his thumb and forefinger he held a picture.

"Well, you had to know I'd want to know what you were up to. Make sure you were safe and everything," she mumbled.

"We agreed when I left after my last visit there would be no communication."

"Yes, we did. And I didn't communicate, did I? I kept my word. I just watched you." Coraline frowned.

"This isn't a picture of me."

She shook her head. "No. But it's your family. Your new family."

"This is my daughter-in-law, Bianca. Kevin's wife. Why would you only have a picture of her? And this far along in her pregnancy...it must be a recent shot."

"Yes. I wanted to know all of your family. Even if they can never know me, they're my family, too."

Bob placed the picture in his pocket. He sighed. "I guess I can understand that. I'm sorry you've been alone."

"I know you are. I don't forget that it was my choice to stay here. I could have come with you. You wanted me to. Begged me each time you came for one of your short visits. I just couldn't leave. I still can't."

He sighed, hanging his head. "I know. Just as I couldn't keep coming back. Come. Show me your work."

They walked hand-in-hand from the room.

∞∞∞

Maggie Lee tore from the room, chest heaving. Her eyes burned radiant blue like the heart of a flame, and she clenched her fists at her sides.

The words spilled from her lips, "Coral! Where are you? Coral!"

Sofie ran to catch up. "Maggie Lee. Wait! We should stick together. Splitting up is a bad idea."

"I don't care. I want answers. Now." She began marching down the hall, calling out, "Coral!"

She heard Sofiana's curse, followed by footsteps behind her. Maggie didn't care. She was on a mission. For the children.

This place is creepy, even if I do feel oddly at home...

Ignoring the incoherent whispers pushing into her brain, she shoved everything aside except standing up for the children, her baby, and all the innocents.

Her sneakers squeaked on the smooth polished floor, and she marched on, shouting every few feet. "Coral!"

They came to a bend in the hallway, and a door just around the corner stood slightly ajar. Maggie Lee yanked it open and burst into the room, letting her rage carry her like a canoe whisked away by the swirling rush of whitewater rapids.

Coral and Bob both froze in place in front of the computer screen, heads turning in unison toward the movement at the door.

Maggie was struck by the family resemblance she hadn't noticed before. Not so much in appearance, but in mannerism. The cock of their heads, the slighty raised brows, a hand on a hip. Then a picture of the kids down the hall halted her thoughts, the rage bubbling up again. "What is going on here? What are you doing with the children?"

Bob nodded, standing a little straighter. "Yes, Coraline. That's what I was coming to ask, and then I got sidetracked. I'm curious. We've never had children here before. Well, except you. Why are there children here? Who are they?"

Coral remained silent, chewing on her bottom lip.

Maggie paced, hands gesturing as she ranted, "I'll tell you what I think. We just talked to the kids down the hall. One of them is your granddaughter, Bob. Her name's Tia. She's beautiful, and said that Coral is her mother, though she doesn't want to be called that." Maggie sneered in her direction. "Tia told us the other two children were brought here. That they once had families, but they don't remember. And even worse than that," She fumed, taking a step closer to Coral, "Your daughter did surgery on them to implant Earth-rocks inside their bodies. *Inside* them. How do you justify performing unnecessary surgery on innocent children? They're babies!"

She stood back, arms crossed, and listened to father and daughter speak as if they were alone in the room.

Bob cleared his throat. "Is this true, Coraline?"

"Yes. I have a daughter. She is special, like me. We

426

both come from you. And both of us were born to two parents bonded with an Earth-rock. The rocks inside of their bodies are more powerful than we ever thought possible. Healing occurs at a much greater rate. I'm not sure Tia needs one with her genes, but you can't be too careful. Better safe than sorry, right? I wasn't taking any chances with her."

"What about the other two? Where did you get them?"

She huffed. "Dad, you know how important the research is. The children are well taken care of here. They have plenty of food, lots of toys, and they are privileged to live near The Core Site. They'll grow until prime maturity age at the same rate as us, and live longer lives than anyone else on Earth. Like us. They'll be nearly immortal."

"But at what cost? Did you take them from their families, Coraline?" Bob's voice was little more than a whisper.

Coral nodded emphatically. "Yes, and they are better off for it. I did them a favor. They are the chosen ones. Both are from parents that have made the bond."

Bob slowly pulled the picture of Bianca out of his pocket.

"And Bianca? You were planning to take her baby, too?"

Her eyes practically glowed as she stared at her father. "Yes. I was planning to bless the child with this life. The infant is from your bloodline, just like me. Like Tia. We are the strongest. And stronger still together."

Bob seemed to deflate like a leaky balloon right in front of them. "Oh, Coraline, what have you done? I can't let you take my son's baby and bring it here. This is what I was trying to escape all those years ago. It's not what I want for my family. I see now that I never truly got away. I can't run from it anymore. I was fooling myself." His flat eyes stared into his daughter's. "You'll not steal any more babies. I don't care who they were born to."

"Look at the research, Dad. If you'll just look at all of our research, you'll see. I did it all to help them. They'll have a better life than they would have. Like me."

"No, you did it to help yourself." Bob slouched and drifted down into the hall. "And it's all my fault. This has to end." He called back over his shoulder, "Maggie Lee? Will you take me to meet my granddaughter?"

"Absolutely." She pegged Coral with her fiery cobalt eyes before stomping from the room.

Leading the way, Bob and Sofiana behind her, Maggie gulped air in deep breaths.

Get control of yourself. The children can't see you like this.

Crash stuck his head out of the door as if sensing their approach, and it helped. She placed a hand on his head, gently rubbing. He leaned his body against her leg. The throbbing in her temples receded just a bit. "Are the kids okay?"

Yip.

"Okay. Bob didn't know about the children." She paused to look into Bob's eyes. "I believe him."

The dog leaned forward, nuzzling Bob's hand. On contact, Bob took one jagged breath, and stepped through the door.

Maggie Lee was right behind him. "Tia? I'd like

you to meet Bob. He's Coral's father. Your grandfather." She sat down to witness this momentous meeting.

Tia stepped forward until she was standing directly in front of him, her head tilted. "Hi."

Tears filled his eyes. "Hi."

"Can I call you grandfather? Or do you want me to call you Bob?"

"Uh, I don't mind if you call me grandfather." Color filled his cheeks.

"Good. Welcome, Grandfather. This is Genna, and this is Hurley. Hurley doesn't talk much. I'm the oldest, so I'm in charge," Tia smiled shyly.

"Wow. That's a big responsibility. I'm proud of you for taking charge of your friends," Bob said.

"Oh, we're not just friends. We're all the same." Her smile grew.

"Connected. I understand. And now you're all connected to us, too. We're all carriers, just like you."

Tia nodded. "That's good."

"Yes. Yes, I think it is. Like a family," said Bob.

She reached for his hand, turning. "Do you want to build with us? We're using magnet tiles. I'm building a school building."

"Um, sure. I'd love to build with you." Bob sat on the floor near the blocks. "Have you ever seen a school?"

Tia shook her head. "No, we have school here. I've never left home. We're always home."

"Well, maybe I'll take you on a trip sometime. Would you like that?" he asked.

Her eyes widened. "Yes! I want to see trees. I saw pictures and they seem really big. Is it true the leaves turn pretty colors? Oh. But...do you think it will be alright with Coral?"

His mouth thinned. "I'll talk to her. I'm sure it'll be alright. I'm her father, after all."

"I want to go." Tia tipped her head back, looking up at him with an expression more serious than any six-year-old should carry. "Know what?"

"What?" Bob asked.

"I think I like having a grandfather. It's nice."

"You know what?" he answered.

"What, Grandfather?"

"I think I like having a granddaughter, too."

He held out his hand, and she gently placed her tiny hand inside of his, silk against sandpaper. Closing his hand around hers he smiled into her endless indigo eyes, so like his own.

Once again, Maggie Lee was struck by the undeniable family resemblance.

Chapter 93

Mercury Reef Underwater Habitat

"**W**ell, isn't this a touching picture?" Gold stood in the doorway. "Welcome back, Bob."

"Gold. It's been a long time." Bob jerked, and got slowly to his feet. "Did you know about the children? That they were taken from their families?"

"Yes. Coral's orders. I did the dirty work, as usual. Part of the reason I'm not happy here any longer. I've grown weary of immortality. It's not worth it anymore. I had my Earth-rock removed. I'm just like all the other humans now. But that's not why I'm here. There's someone you should meet." He stepped back, gesturing behind him.

Another man stepped forward. The same one Gold had secretly talked to on the boat, just yesterday. The very same man who had stolen Sofie's research off her vessel when she'd been taken by the shark, the L-shaped scar an unmistakable identifier.

"Hello, Bob." The group focused on a man of medium height, clean-cut blonde hair, and laser-beam blue eyes who stood blocking the doorway. Bob's wide eyes cut downward to the gun the stranger was pointing at his chest. His mouth dropped open with a sharp intake of breath, and he stepped back.

Sofie raised her hands. "Who are you?"

He tipped his head in Bob's direction. "Ask him who I am."

"I-I don't know you. How did you get in here?" Bob stammered.

"Oh, I have friends everywhere. Not all of yours are loyal. And you do know me. Or at least, you should."

"Gold led you here? Does Coraline know?" Bob asked, eyes flicking to Gold.

The man shook his head. "Not yet, no. But her time down here is over. I'm taking this place over, and you're going to help me, old man."

Bob held his hands out in front of him. "How do you know about this place? I don't understand."

"Do I really have to spell it out for you?" the man shook his head. "Tsk-tsk-tsk. You'd think a father would recognize his own son."

"Son? My sons don't know anything about any of this, and I'd like to keep it that way. What are you after, telling these lies?"

The other man snorted. "Lies? No. I've done my share of lying, but I'm not lying now. Would you like to know my name?"

"I don't..."

"I guess I've changed a bit since I was four. My name is Adam, *Dad*. Nice to see you after all this time. I've been waiting for this moment for far too long. Remember when you came for a visit when I was about four-years-old? I was so excited when Mom told me you were coming. I didn't sleep all night knowing I was finally gonna meet my Dad. You stayed two days, and then you left without a word. I thought I wasn't good enough to make you want to stay."

Bob's face lost all color. "No. Adam? How can it be? Victoria said you'd been taken, that you were dead..."

"We'll get to my mother in a minute. I have questions about that, too. But yes, I am your son. My full name is Adam Robert Green. Your dear, sweet daughter Coraline, my adoring stepsister, the result of your affair with another woman, had me taken from my home. Kidnapped. Taken away from everything I loved. I was a child." He paused, shaking his head side to side. "I grew up in this place. A prisoner, hidden beneath the sea." He tilted his head. "I wondered if she ever told you. I can see by your face she didn't. She was still a child herself, but always had someone to do her bidding." He gestured toward Gold. "It doesn't matter now. None of it matters. This place is mine. The Core Site is mine. I'm going to harness its power, and use it for the good of mankind. More than you or my darling sister ever did. You chose to keep it secret and use it to benefit only yourselves. At least I'm willing to sell the power to the highest bidder. I've already negotiated with the government. As you can guess, they're very interested. All that's left to do is divulge this location. I have a small group loyal to me, but I have some unfinished business before I bring in more of the others." He paused. "Now, I'm going to ask you a question, and I need your honest answer. Did my mother really fall down the stairs, or did you kill her?"

"Adam, I had no idea. No idea about any of this. I thought you were dead. Please, you have to believe me. I would never have..."

"I asked you a question, *Dad*."

"Adam, please..."

"Three, two..."

"It was an accident! She was kicking me out. S-She told me you'd been taken, that you were dead. We were at the t-top of the stairs." A lone tear ran a jagged path over his cheek. "I grabbed her arms, she stumbled backward...it was an accident, I swear..."

The gun flashed like a strobe, three quick bursts of light through a silencer. Blood seeped through his fingers forming a triangle on his chest as Bob made a gurgling sound, falling to the floor. "I'm...so...sorry... Adam," he wheezed.

Tia ran to his side, "Grandfather!" She placed her hands over his, tears spilling onto them in rivulets. Crash lay next to Bob on the other side, a growl daring Adam to approach. Genna and Hurley huddled in the corner, crying. Maggie Lee wrapped her arms around them, shielding them with her body.

"Well, that's one down." Adam rummaged through his father's pocket even as he watched him gasp for air, his fingers now clutching the good luck charm. "You're not gonna use this to survive this time, Dad." He snatched it away, winked down at his father, then looked up at the others, throwing the rock in the air and catching it one-handed. "Okay, first order of business. We're removing the stones. No worries, I'm a trained physician. Who wants to go first? Shall I start with the youngest?"

"Please, let us leave. We have nothing to do with what Coral's doing down here. She kidnapped us, just like she did you and these children, too. We'll take the children with us. They don't need to be here for whatever you have planned." Maggie Lee pleaded.

Adam's head was shaking before she finished. "No. The children stay. They're not...normal."

"Yes. Yes they are. Please. They're innocent, just like you were when you were brought here. They're here only because of their parents, just like you were. Let us take them. Free them as you once wanted to be freed," Maggie Lee begged. "I wish I could go back and save *that* little boy."

He squeezed his eyes closed, hand raised, hitting the butt of the gun against his forehead several times. A red mark remained on his brow when he moved his arm away. His breathing was ragged as he visibly struggled to regain control. "We have to remove the stones first. No one leaves with an Earth-rock. After that, I don't care what you do with the children. But Coraline? She stays."

Her youthful voice traveled from the hall as she approached. "Of course I stay. This is my home, silly. I don't want to leave. Hello, Adam. You shot Dad? You know he'll heal, right?"

"Coraline. So good to see you again," Adam's words dripped with sarcasm, a sneer distorted his face.

"I wish I could say the same about you, brother. You were much nicer when we were younger." She smiled fondly, the kind of grin any sister would reserve for her only brother.

"Nicer? You mean when I cried myself to sleep every night because I missed my mother, my friends? Back when you locked me in my room, and kept me prisoner down here? When you implanted one of those...things...inside me?"

"Yes. I did all that. For *you*," Coral hissed.

"Can't you see that? You're still alive, aren't you? You wouldn't be without it, you know. You should be thanking me."

Adam's laughter echoed. "Thank you? It's not a blessing, living this long. You cursed me the moment you brought me here. I would rather have lived one normal life and died peaceably, than to live this prolonged life of anguish." He paced, his words shaking with barely contained anger. "There's something I need to know. Why?" He stopped, facing Coraline. "Why did you take me? You never did tell me."

She shrugged. "It's simple, really. There are two reasons. One was the research. The work we're doing at the Core Site is—and has always been—my priority. The other reason? I suppose I brought you here because father had decided to leave and not come back. Though I respected his decision, I needed a piece of him here. And maybe a small part of me didn't want you to have him if I couldn't. I was only a child, as you said. So, before he left, I sent Gold to come and get you. I knew our father was going to do some traveling first before he came home to you and your mother, so that gave us the time we needed. It was easy." She splayed her hands, shrugging again. "I really have no regrets. You helped us learn so much about the initial bond. You were our first implant. Join me. We can run this place together. We *are* siblings, after all. We don't have to be on opposite sides, you know."

"For the research? Always back to that. My life sacrificed for research, and some jealous little girl's whim." Adam's face went a shade of red that was nearly purple. "I'm through talking. I came here to do something, and I intend to do it."

"Oh? And what's that, may I ask?" Her smile exuded innocence.

He squeezed the trigger. Four shots fired in quick succession. Coral gasped, looking down at herself. The small room seemed to shake as if alive in the aftermath of the gunshots. The magnet-tile building collapsed, folding into itself in a loud clatter on the floor. The silence that followed was somehow worse than screaming would have been.

Coral clutched her hands to her chest as blood seeped through, the smile slowly fading from her eyes.

"You...shot me." She smiled, her teeth smeared red. "But I can't die, re-mem-ber?" Her lilting voice gurgled, and blood ran a line from the side of her mouth. She fell to her hands and knees, staring into the crimson puddle growing under her.

Adam nodded. "I know, but I need you incapacitated for a while. I have other plans or you."

"Stop it!" Tia ran forward, her little fists pummeling Adam's legs. "Stop it! That's my family!" She grabbed his gun arm and bit down, drawing blood. Next to her, Crash bit down on Adam's leg at the same time.

"Ouch!" He shoved Tia, aiming the gun at her when she fell backward. His leg swung forward sending Crash across the room. "Do that again, and you're next. Both of you." Tia pulled her knees to her chest, sobs quivering through the length of her small body. Crash whimpered, crawling painfully to her side.

Maggie Lee stepped in front of the weapon. "Leave her alone. She's just a child."

"Fine. How about I talk to you, instead? You have something I want. Hand over your Earth-rock."

"My...why? What do you need it for? It only

works for me."

"Just hand it over, and no one else needs to get hurt," Adam held out his hand, palm up.

"But w-what will happen to my baby if I don't have it anymore?" Her hand splayed across her abdomen. "Will I get old again before the child grows to term? Let me keep it, just until after the baby is born. Then you can have it. I give you my word," Maggie Lee pleaded.

Adam shook his head. "Sorry. No one is leaving here with one of my rocks."

"But..."

"Maggie, just give him what he wants. I'm sure the baby will be fine." Sofie whispered.

"Smart lady, and pretty too. Thank you, Dr. Stone." Adam winked in her direction before turning back to Maggie Lee. "The baby should be fine. Usually anything healed by the stone is permanently healed, which means you should start aging at a normal rate again without it. Don't worry, you'll still look like you're thirty-years-old and live a longer life for it."

Tremors raced through her arms and up her body as she dug into her pocket, then held out her shaking hand with her trinket in the center of her palm. He snatched it from her, and a coldness gripped her as soon as it was gone.

"Thanks. Now, the dog." Sofie unclasped the dog's collar, removing the medallion. Crash mewled, but allowed it. She placed it in Adam's outstretched hand.

A smile spread across his face, though his eyes did not crinkle. In his palm he held three Earth-rocks. A triad of power.

"Now, for the others. Who wants to go first?" He

raised an eyebrow at the children.

Gold interjected, "He knows what he's doing. He removed my rock, and I'm still standing. Believe it or not, he really is a doctor." He nodded his head in Adam's direction.

"And then you'll let us leave?" Maggie Lee asked Adam.

"Yes. I left a boat anchored a little ways from here. You can go, with the children. All you have to do is make it to the boat and you can leave. I won't be needing it. As soon as I reveal the location of this place it will be swarming with military. I'll even give Buzz the signal to let you go. Though the creature has been a bit ornery of late. Growing too smart for his own good, that one. That's what happens when you make wild animals intelligent. Eventually they start to think for themselves."

The low rumble echoed in Crash's chest, and he sat up straighter and bared his teeth. Sofiana stood by his side, her hand resting on his back.

Maggie stooped down holding out her hands toward Hurley. "Come on. Don't worry. I'll be with you the whole time. I promise, I'll be right outside the door," she crooned. When she picked him up, he held onto her biceps and turned his face into her chest.

"The infirmary is this way, follow me." Adam sauntered through the door then turned back, sticking his head inside the room. "Oh, nobody leave this room. If you try, my man will shoot you."

Gold frowned in his direction, but spread his legs and crossed his arms over his chest.

Adam began whistling as he walked down the hall.

Chapter 94

Mercury Reef Underwater Habitat

Tia leaned over her grandfather, staring intently at his wounds. She placed her open palms on top of the hole right over his heart, and closed her eyes. Several moments passed, and she moved her hands to the next wound, and repeated it again with the third. He remained lying in a pool of his own blood, pale and unmoving.

She turned, repeating the process with Coral. Then she sat back on her haunches and looked up.

"They're gonna be okay." Her breathing was ragged. "If he was smart, he would have removed my stone first. I'm the strongest."

A laugh broke through Gold's façade, and he nodded his head at her.

"True," he whispered.

"Mr. Gold? Why are you doing this? I thought you liked me." She tilted her head, a pout marring her face.

He nodded slightly and gave one quick wink. Tia's brows raised.

Within minutes, Maggie returned with Hurley, gently laying him on the chair. He groaned and turned on his side in the fetal position, little body racked with tremors. Her pale face and black eye circles belied the smile on her face as she moved to stand in front of Genna.

"Come. I'll be with you, right outside the door, and I'll be waiting for you as soon as the procedure is over." She held out her hand, and Genna hesitantly reached for it. "Once your Earth-rocks are removed, I'll take you someplace safe."

Tia rushed to Hurley's side the moment they were gone.

"Hurley, let me see your boo-boo." He shook his head 'no' and didn't move.

"Please. I can help you," she pleaded.

Hurley turned to look at her, and as if in slow motion turned his body. She lifted his shirt. "Ha! Good job, Hurl!" She turned to the others. "It's already healed. Nothing but a tiny scar."

"But I saw him. H-he cut me," he breathed, voice shaking.

Sofie took a step forward, "Wait, you were awake for the procedure?"

At the boy's tortured nod, a deafening silence shrouded the room.

"I'll go with Tia. You stay with them." Gold nodded in the direction of Genna and Hurely, volunteering to take Tia for her procedure so Maggie Lee could sit with the other two.

"It's okay, Maggie. I'll go with them," Sofie said.

Tia walked in front of Gold, head held high. He turned, talking so low only Sofie could hear, "Take the others and go. Coral will never let Tia leave, but you can save the other two. Go. I'll help. I have a plan." He turned to escort the girl to the infirmary.

Sofie froze. "No. We're taking Tia, too. He said he would let us leave, on his boat. All of us."

He turned back. "You don't really think he's gonna let you go, do you? There's no boat."

"We can't leave Tia behind," Sofie argued.

Maggie interrupted, "What's going on?"

"Gold says there's no boat and we should take the two kids and leave, I said we're not leaving Tia behind."

"No way. We're all getting out, or nobody's getting out," Maggie Lee agreed.

"What's everyone whispering about?" Coraline groaned.

Bob and Coral sat, backs against the wall. For the first time, Coral's ponytail hung loosely, tendrils escaping to frame her face with unkempt curls. She looked both innocent and vulnerable. Blood left a streak weaving through one blond spiral, and a scarlet smudge slashed across her cheek marring her porcelain skin. Her blue eyes squinted, appearing to glow with emotion.

Minutes ticked by. Gold returned, shaking his head, and muttered under his breath to Sofie, "You lost your chance." He paced to the wall and back, then whispered, "I'll buy you some time. It's up to you to get them out of here."

"Deal." Sofiana nodded, staring into his eyes. "Thanks."

Tia chirped as if she hadn't just returned from invasive surgery. She sat between her mother and grandfather, clasping each of their hands in her own.

Adam waltzed into the room, an air of confidence surrounding him.

He looked at Coral. "Ah, you're awake. Healing faster than you used to, I see. Now, I need you to show me all of the research you have. I want to be up-to-date before I take over."

Coral's head lifted a notch. "I'm not showing you anything."

"Oh, you'll show me everything, big sister."

Sofiana stepped forward. "We're free to go? You did say once you had all the Earth-rocks we could go to the boat, right?"

He looked at her intently before answering, and then flicked his hand in her direction. He laughed. "No. No one leaves. I only said that so you'd cooperate. I wanted my rocks."

"But I let you perform those surgeries so we could leave..." Maggie Lee stammered.

"You didn't *let* me do anything. *I* let *you* live. Sorry. I've learned how to get what I want from the best." He jerked his head in Bob and Coral's direction.

Christian barged into the room. "What's all the noise down here...?" His eyes widened when they landed on Adam. He pointed his finger, "You. You're the one who shot Yaz."

"What? He shot Yaz?" Sofie shrieked. She took two menacing steps toward him, blood in her eyes.

Adam took one step backward, hands up as if she pointed a gun at him. "I didn't want to kill her. She attacked me. I guess you could say it was an accident. All I wanted was your research notes."

"I'm gonna kill you." Sofiana stalked toward him, hands fisted at her sides.

Adam's laugh bounced off the wall of the small room. "I can't die, remember?"

That stopped her in her tracks long enough for Gold to intervene, grabbing her arm. "Now! Go!" he yelled at her, and charged into Adam with his head and shoulders down. Crash leaped into the fray, ripping the gun out of Adam's hand with his mouth, canine teeth sinking into the skin at his wrist, drawing blood. He turned and dropped the weapon at Sofie's feet. She bent to pick it up, looking for Adam, but her eyes found her old friend.

Christian slunk into a corner, eyes wide, body cowering.

"Christian, come with us." She held out her free hand. He didn't even look at her.

Maggie Lee grabbed Genna's hand, picked up Hurley, and screamed to Sofiana, "Get Tia! We have to go! Come on, Crash!"

Sofie once again aimed the gun toward the two rolling around on the floor in deadly combat and hesitated, waging her own inner battle. She couldn't get a clean shot, and Gold had helped them. She didn't want to risk hitting him instead. But she didn't want Adam to get away with murdering Yaz, either. Her body shook with the need for revenge, so much so that the fingernails of her clenched fist dug into her palm leaving crescent moon dents, and her gun hand shook violently. She wanted to cry and scream at the same time. It was all so unfair. He should pay.

But Adam won't die, anyway.

Her head jerked down when Tia grasped her fisted hand. She took a deep breath, and closed her hand around the girl's. Their eyes met, and it took everything she had to force her feet into action. With great effort, she shoved the gun into her waistband and moved away from Yaz's killer, each step taking her away from vengeance.

"Christian, come with us!" she called again over her shoulder as they turned to go.

He shook his head, cowering further into the corner.

Coral stood, blocking the doorway. "You're not leaving." Gold and Adam rolled around the floor, knocking the table sideways, chairs scattering across the room, crashing like thunder. Gold's gun skidded across the floor.

Crash bared his teeth, hair on his back standing rigid, taking a menacing step toward Coraline. She backed up.

Tia looked at Coral, and spoke quietly. Her intense eyes narrowed as she formed the words. "Yes. We are, *Mother*. We are leaving. Don't try to stop us. I don't want to hurt you." Coral took another step backward. "You could come with us." She held out her hand.

"I'm not leaving, Tia. And you're not, either. The research..."

"I don't care about the research anymore. I'm leaving. You can come with us, or get out of the way. Move." The rumble in Crash's chest grew in volume, and he took another step toward Coraline.

Coral backed up against the wall, sliding down with a *thump* into a sitting position.

She looked down at the floor. A long, weary sigh

hissed through her still blood-stained lips. "You'll be back. It calls to you. Don't worry. I'll welcome you back when you do."

She turned her head away.

Across the room, Gold picked up a glass enclosed picture frame displaying a child's crayon drawing of a tree that had fallen off the wall in the scuffle, and smashed the corner of it into Adam's throat as he straddled the other man. Blood gurgled out of his mouth on a surge of crimson that ran down in a jagged line across his cheek and splattered onto the glass frame like crimson rain. Adam reached out, desperately searching for the gun that was just out of range. When Gold shifted, Adam stretched just enough, grasping the butt of the weapon. Bringing it up, he fired. A small red circle appeared on Gold's forehead as he collapsed on top of the frame, his limp body pushing the glass further into the other man's throat.

Another gunshot fired from across the room, and Adam looked at his chest. "Y-You shot me, Dad?" he rasped through his mangled throat.

"I had to stop you. At least temporarily." He turned to Coral. "Forgive me. I have to stop both of you. What you're doing is wrong. These people are innocent. You'll both heal. I hope you can forgive me when you do." His finger squeezed the trigger a second time, and blood blossomed on his daughter's chest. "I have to make things right. Finally."

The others were already gone, and he ran toward the decompression chamber.

Chapter 95

Waters Surrounding Mercury
Reef Underwater Habitat

*B*reathe in, breathe out. Just have to get as far away from here as possible and then I'll figure something out. There has to be a boat, even though he said there wasn't. How did he get here if there isn't a boat? Unless someone dropped him off...

Focus on one thing at a time. Breathe in, breathe out.

Sofiana held Tia's hand and stopped to look over her shoulder through the oval of her facemask, squinting through the swirling bubbles. Crash was tethered to a hook on her wetsuit. Maggie Lee followed with Genna and Hurley. And Bob took the rear.

Eyes alert, she scanned the surrounding waters, searching for movement. Turning back again, she gestured.

Hurry.

She veered to the left, kicking and moving as fast as the group could keep up. Lazy bubbles rose up in a whirling pattern, contradicting the urgency of the moment as they floated gaily to the surface. The children were doing remarkably well given the circumstances.

She smiled around her mouthpiece, even as her

eyes filled with unshed tears. *Wish I could tell Yaz that even children younger than five can scuba...I'd give anything to hear her laugh right now.*

She bit down on the rubber, grinding it between her teeth until her jaw hurt. In her peripheral vision, a faint red glow could be seen emanating from the ocean floor up ahead. She blinked and looked again. Definitely glowing.

The Core Site.

She turned to swim the other way, gesturing to follow, moving on. Tia tugged on her sleeve, pointing and murmuring, her mumbled words lost in her regulator. She looked back over her shoulder, and shook her head when she saw the group was not following, but was instead advancing toward the glow.

No. Stay away from it! She wanted to shout.

Treading water, she floated. She had no choice but to follow.

Have to stay together.

Crash's four legs kicked frantically, his tether taut as he strained toward the light. As she closed the distance, the glow seemed to pulse underneath them, and the bottom writhed and moved below. Her eyes widened.

The horseshoe crabs.

Moving on, the mass seemed to grow as they neared. Bob, Maggie Lee, Crash, Tia, Hurley, and Genna formed a line as they descended, and after unhooking the tether that attached her and the dog, she stayed a little back from the group. They were a unit, bonded in a way she could not be, making her the outside observer.

Suddenly the horseshoe crabs parted, exposing

the width of the mass that stretched for what seemed like a half-mile, low on the ocean floor. It was low and rutted the silvery vermilion veins shining through it, rising from deep within the very center of the Earth itself. It seemed to pulse below them like a heartbeat, bringing the sea to life as it tinted the water in flashes of scarlet. Earth-rocks lay scattered across the surface in piles, emitting rhythmic pulses that coincided with the ocean floor beneath them.

As if mesmerized, five humans and one canine reached out with their palms—and paws—outstretched until they connected with the Earth's core, pushing the rocks aside to better connect with the source. Hair standing on end, their silhouettes blurred into one. Sofie observed the scene unfolding in front of her as if in a dream-state.

What the ...

She inhaled sharply when something slammed into her from behind.

As had happened on that not so long ago day when she'd been reunited with Baby, something hit her, sending her body spinning feet over head through the water. Disoriented, she opened her eyes, desperately fighting to regain her bearings. Pushing the pain aside, body sailing through the water she collided with the group in front of her in a tangle of limbs, instantly breaking their contact with The Core Site.

Snapped out of their trance-like state, they formed a unit around Sofie, and she looked out from the inside of the circle of friends surrounding her. Protecting her. She shoved her way through so she was part of the line, giving her head a negative shake when Bob tried to push her behind again.

They may be connected to The Core Site, but I'm the best swimmer.

Buzz swam lazily into view, mouth opening and closing as if chewing, flashing the tooth whorl in an nearly playful manner. For endless minutes, it continued its languid trek, circling the group. The beast made eye contact with Sofiana as it glided by.

Incredible!

She sucked in oxygen when the creature suddenly changed direction, swimming directly toward them. Screaming into her mouthpiece, she warned the others. The shark spun its body 180 degrees, slapping its huge tail into the group, and then swam away.

The hit effectively separated them, and they were flung back unceremoniously in multiple directions, loose stones scattering in every direction. Struggling to reconnect, in a flurry of kicking legs and frantic arms, they pushed through the water until the group reunited as one. Maggie Lee, last to join the group, turned to draw Genna closer and lost sight of Hurley for just a second.

Sofie's eyes bulged watching Hurley drift off to the side as if in slow motion, and she started kicking in his direction just when a juvenile great white appeared heading straight toward him. She ignored the burning of her muscles and kicked harder. The shark opened its mouth, pointed serrated teeth framing the gaping maw as its eyes rolled back signaling its intent to attack.

I'm not going to make it in time!

A huge gray blur shot out of the murk, nudging the small great white with its huge, scarred snout. Sofie drew in a sharp breath just as she reached Hurley.

Her relief was quickly flooded with questions as she grasped his small arm.

Baby! This must be one of her pups!

As she looked on, the larger shark herded her offspring. Could it have been pushing the young fish away? Possibly teaching it to fight its natural instinct? Does that mean these enhanced sharks have the ability to feel compassion? What about other sea-life living close to The Core Site?

Is the juvenile shark smart, too?

Another thought burst through her fascination.

Where is Buzz?

Her eyes scanned the waters. The giant Helicoprion seemed to have vanished.

Pulling Hurley along, she re-attached the dog's tether with the other, grabbed Tia's hand, and began swimming toward the surface, frantically waving her arms for everyone to follow.

Staying as close to each other as possible, they began their ascent, back to back in a circle, constantly scanning the surrounding waters. Working together.

Stopping to allow their lungs to decompress, wide eyes continued to dart back and forth in the water. Sofie looked toward the surface and stopped breathing for a beat.

So close to the surface. So close! We can do this. One thing at a time...

Her heart pounded in her chest. Fighting the urge to kick toward the surface immediately, she held everyone stationary. She wanted all of them to make it safely to the boat, and going up too fast could be nearly as deadly as encountering a shark thought long extinct.

Oh, please let there be a boat! I don't know what we'll

do if there isn't...

One thing at a time.

Her eyes scanned the surface, and she could not see a boat within view.

Just keep moving. Can't give up.

Silently calculating the time they'd been down as well as their current depth, she estimated how long they needed to wait before moving on. She waited. Glanced at her watch.

Should be good to go.

Touching her hand to Maggie's sleeve, she nodded and pointed up. Her friend inclined her head. Keeping the children close, they kicked upward.

A scream escaped into the water when Buzz reappeared as if an apparition, swimming above them, gliding like an airplane overhead, blocking the sun. The sudden darkness was like an omen, and Sofie growled into her mouthpiece. Above, the beast cut off their path to air, and freedom. And it knew exactly what it was doing. They froze. Wide, wild eyes meeting Maggie's, Sofie was at a loss for what to do. Over the next minutes, the pattern repeated time and again. Each time they made a move in an upward direction, Buzz circled around, blocking their way.

She began moving the group horizontally; inclining just slightly with each slow, steady kick. It didn't take long for Buzz to catch on and begin agitatedly darting back and forth above, his mouth chomping frantically up and down, up and down as if to say: *This is what you'll get if you keep coming.* He darted to the side, circled the group in one quick motion, and then returned to his post above them.

Sofie remembered Bob talking about Coral's

mother, Abigail. How this creature had sliced her in half in one bite. A shiver ran the length of her body, eyes darting to the surface. The short distance seemed an impossible dream, always just out of reach even though it has been right there all along. They could run out of oxygen and drown just feet from the surface. Wouldn't that be the ultimate irony? So close, but yet so far. Impossible dream.

In this state of furious panic, her mind took a whimsical bend. Funny thing, dreams. She'd always thought if you just stretch yourself a little farther, push yourself a little harder, every dream is within reach with resolve and hard work. She'd turned her nose up at people who seemed to her too weak to chase after their dreams. To her way of thinking, there was always a way. But somehow, in this moment right before death —and she was nearly certain of their impending doom —she thought she understood. Like a lightbulb flickering to life after flipping the power switch. Everything is not always within reach for everyone at every time. Her own life had been relatively easy. She had the constant support of her parents, and because of them a clear career path, as well as a respected family name that opened the right doors for her in her chosen field. The Stones didn't have a ton of money; enough to meet their needs and a little more, but with student loans available—though she was still paying them— she had been able to achieve her goal in record time. Oh, she'd worked hard to get where she was, but she suddenly realized that wasn't always enough for everyone in every situation. Ironic, that this epiphany would come now as she awaited probable death. Sometimes, it was hard to put yourself in someone else's shoes when your own life experiences were so different from another's. She looked longingly up at the sunlight filtering through the moving water—a beacon of flashing yellows and blues. This revelation hardly mattered now, as they hung midway between an underwater war and the precious air above. Not to mention the long-thought-dead sea creature threatening them. Safety so close, but yet so far.

Forcefully shaking herself out of her reverie, she straightened her back. She refused to give in to the dark despair that was even now taking root in her body. Blinking back the tears that threatened to fall behind her mask, she stiffened her back, taking deep, purposeful pulls of oxygen. Right now, her only dream was to get everyone out of this alive.

Breathe in, breath out.

Stretch, Sof. Think. How can I get us to safety? Think. Think!

She froze, and the others mimicked. Silently communicating with Maggie and Bob, they formed a triangle, pushing the children into the center. She tried to push Crash along with them, but he shook his glass-encased head awkwardly back and forth. *No.*

Through Sofiana's plastic mask and his glass helmet, their eyes met, his radiating more intelligence than any canine breed known to man. Crash now possessed an acute awareness unnatural to his species, and an empathetic nature some humans struggled to achieve. In him, a dog's usual happy-go-lucky, loyal-to-the-end attitude was multiplied exponentially. Reading all of this in his eyes, she knew he would neither change his mind nor back down. She closed her eyes, for a moment laying her mask against his glass bubble, then nodded slowly. A tear trickled slowly from the corner of one eye as she turned, positioning herself next to the dog. Back to back the group ascended, flippers barely moving in their slow upward climb.

At least the children are safe. For now. That's all we can do. Protect them as long as we can. Focus on the children.

A tiny thought whispered through her brain: *But what happens to them when we're all gone?*

Sofie shook her head, knowing the answer even as she denied it. *No. It won't happen. I won't allow it to...*

Suddenly, out of the murk, Buzz darted toward her. Sofie closed her eyes, bracing herself for the deadly jaws to close around her neck or midsection, slicing into flesh and bone. A moment seemed an eternity as she waited for the death-blow. When the impact did not come, she opened her eyes wide, and shrieked into her mouthpiece.

"Nooo!" The muffled sound carried through the water as Bob swam toward Buzz. When he got close enough, he veered to the side and when the beast turned its powerful body, Bob wrapped his arms around its thick pectoral fin. Linking his fingers, he held on as the beast bucked, its writhing body an impossible mount. Yet somehow, Bob held on. The Helicoprion desperately tried to rid itself of its passenger like a wild horse with an unwanted rider. Though it failed its first attempts, it persisted. The two disappeared. The farther away they swam, the less Sofie, Maggie Lee, Crash, and the children could see as their underwater vision failed them. Finally, in one last explosion of bubbles, Buzz and his passenger were gone. The spectators, watching from above, squinted into the murky waters, breathless with both anticipation and despair. Time ceased to exist as they waited and watched.

All at once the two returned, man and beast whizzing by like a bullet flying from a muzzle. In a flash, they darted past the onlookers. Sofie had time to glance into the wild eyes of the Helicoprion as it sped furiously by. Its gigantic body rolled and rolled, like an alligator in a death-spin. In the last loop around, Bob lost his grip. As if in slow motion he drifted sideways, evidence of his disorientation in his sluggish-but-jerky motions. The seconds slinked by as if on a time delay, and the group watching held their breath. They were powerless to help, reduced to mere observers in this silent battle.

When Bob regained his bearings, he swam down, drawing the shark away. It was moving in fast, and Sofiana knew—there was no time for denial and regrets, they would grieve later if they somehow managed to survive this—how this would inevitably end. She pushed the children upward kicking with all her strength toward the fresh air above.

Bob sacrificed himself. I have to save the children so it wasn't for nothing.

Glancing down one more time, she blocked the view from Tia and the others as the Helicoprion caught up to Bob. With one quick and powerful bite and a jerk of its head, it ended the man who had started this whole chain of events. In a heartbeat's time, gone. Sofie's breath hitched as the water clouded with blood. So much blood. But she couldn't think about that now. *The children.*

The beast circled around, opening it mouth wider than seemed possible, swallowing what was left of Bob in two gulps. Then, it turned back toward the small group hovering near the surface. Sofiana looked up.

Almost there. Don't look down.

Sunlight was streaking through the surface water, and it shone like a shooting star casting living highlights in Hurley's hair just before he broke the surface.

She turned.

Buzz, tail undulating in a flurry of motion, was almost upon them. They had seconds only.

No! Not the kids!

She reversed, kicking off toward the beast just as Bob had done.

At least I can stall the beast and maybe save the others. Like Bob.

Peripherally, she caught movement to the left. In a sudden flurry of motion Baby darted from the side, colliding with the larger beast, biting down on its underbelly and drawing blood. The impact stopped Buzz's momentum and the two spun off to the side. Another gray blur appeared, biting into the Helicoprion's dorsal fin. The juvenile white. Yet another young shark came from the other side, latching on with its jaws. Baby and her offspring, working together to save them. Or themselves. It didn't really matter which.

A hysterical laugh bubbled in her throat, threatening to rise and burst from her lips. She tamped it down, fearful that if she let it go she'd never stop the crazed laughter. Horrified that it might be the last thing she did before she died. The thought of losing her mind like a madwoman, hysterical giggles the last sound she made before she was taken as a shark's supper was unacceptable to her. Her mind screamed: *Stop it!* She brought a sudden visage of Grayson to mind. What would he say right now? She wondered. Probably something like: *You, die in your ocean? Now, that's crazy talk.*

Taking a long, calming breath, she reversed again and kicked upward, just as a flurry of activity on the surface churned the waters above.

Could it be?

Yes! Yes, it is!

A boat! Several boats?

Or am I hallucinating?

Her head swiveled to find the others. Did they see what she was seeing? But when she searched for them, they were nowhere to be found. Had they been eaten, too? Like poor Bob, who was sliced cleanly in half and then devoured only minutes ago as they all watched. When she'd looked away, had Buzz eaten all of them? Was the Helicoprion, even now, toying with her? Had it defeated Baby and her offspring only to come back, saving her for last? Sofiana swiveled around again, searching for her group.

And then she saw why they were gone. The others were already free of the water. In the boats above. She was almost positive they were real. She could see the hull, chipped white paint and covered by barnacles.

It can't be a hallucination if I can see details, right?

Her legs scissored closer and she dared not look below her.

Almost there. Just a little more...

Reach for your dream.

Her hand reached up out of the water just before her head broke the surface. At the same time, something large hit the water right next to her, the splash causing the water to writhe around her. Bubbles scurried this way and that, and when the water calmed she saw the beloved face in front of her and her heart pounded.

Grayson!

Is he real?

She reached for him as their heads emerged into the air above, and she tore the mouthpiece from her mouth, throwing her arms around him. He crushed her body to his, burying his face in her dripping hair, lips trailing kisses all over her face.

Dreams. Sometimes they shift and grow into something more real. And sometimes you just have to reach out and grab what's right in front of you.

"We have to get out. Out of the water. I'm so happy to see you," Sofie panted.

When they were safely on deck, they wrapped around each other. There was no other way to describe the way one of them seemed to meld into the other as if they were one entity.

"You came," she whispered. "You're real."

"Of course I did, and yes, I am. Just in time, it seems." His crooked smile melted her heart into a puddle in her chest. She looked across the deck and her eyes filled at the other reunions taking place along with hers. Mike and Maggie Lee, staring into each other's eyes, Tandie talking fast, as she and Jace showered hugs and kisses on Crash. Crash's body wiggling and dancing. She smiled.

My family.

Her traveling eyes landed on two more familiar faces.

Sofie's eyes widened. "Mom? Dad?"

"Sofiana Marigold! Thank God you're safe! We were so worried. When Grayson contacted us, we called OCEANS ALIVE right away. They helped us pinpoint your approximate location, but it was the coordinates on the picture that got us here."

"Coordinates? Picture?" Sofie frowned.

"Yes. We'll let Grayson fill you in." Her mother grasped her shoulders, tears flowing from the corners of her eyes. "I love you, Sofiana. You know that, right?"

"Of course I know that, Mom. I love you, too. And you, Dad." Sofie held on tight.

After they separated, she held out her hand to Grayson. "Okay, who are all of these people?" Her eyes looked to the sky, where local and national news helicopters hovered. "What's happening?"

"Well, when we couldn't contact Christian, I had no choice but to call your parents. They pulled some strings, threw their weight around and got us here. Then I did what I do best. Reporting. I told a story. I called just about every news station in the country and told them about a kidnapping and healing waters near the Cape. They all jumped at the story of a modern day 'Fountain of Youth.' Not that they believed me, but the idea intrigued them enough to investigate. I imagine this is going to be a very popular place for people to swim very soon."

Sofie laughed. "You're brilliant. I had no idea what we were going to do when we reached the surface. I have a few things to fill you in on. About Christian. And the children." Her eyes darted to the trio huddled together, an olive-green army blanket wrapped around them.

He nodded. "Yes. And then I want to get you

alone."

"Ditto." The smile spread from her lips to shine from her eyes.

"And then, we'll talk about the wedding. I think a fall wedding would be beautiful, don't you?" Gray asked.

Sofie leaned back to look into his eyes. "Wedding? Who's wedding?"

"Yours. And mine." Gray smiled, love shining from his eyes like rays of hope.

"Is this your way of asking me to marry you? This isn't really romantic, you know. I can think of lots of better ways..." His lips stopped her in mid-sentence. She sighed into his mouth, returning the kiss.

Gray pulled back, eyes searching hers. "Sofiana. Will you marry me? And if you say no, I'm throwing you back into the water with the sharks."

"Well, that would scare most women, but if you're trying to scare me, you've got the wrong lady." She laughed, shoulders shaking.

"Oh, no. I've got the right lady, alright." His eyes became intense as they stared into hers, unblinking. Waiting.

"Yes. Yes, Grayson. I would love to marry you. You're my dream. I wish I would have realized that sooner. I'm sorry, for everything. Now, where are we going to live? Are you okay living on a boat?"

"No way. I want a white picket fence. For Rufus, of course. We'll talk about it later." He pulled her against him, and sighed the contented sigh only a person in love can understand.

"Ha! We're going to have to talk about it sooner or later, buddy. But for right now, I'm happy just to sit here with you." She lay her head on his shoulder, his warmth seeping through. She snuggled closer when he tightened his arms around her.

"Me too. This is home." He lay his head on top of hers and closed his eyes.

Mike and Maggie Lee settled down beside them. "Did I just hear that we're going to be invited to a wedding?"

The two beamed. "Yes. In the fall."

"Congratulations, you two. I couldn't be happier for you." Mike reached a hand out to clasp Grayson's in a quick shake, and Maggie hugged them both. "And we'd like you both to stand as Godparents to our baby. If you would. I—we—wouldn't be here without you." Maggie Lee lovingly patted her midsection.

Tears filled Sofiana's eyes. "We'd be honored to be the baby's Godparents."

Maggie Lee placed her hand on Sofie's inclining her head to the three small figures huddled together under a shared blanket. "Right now, we have to help these children find their way home. Genna and Hurley have families that have been grieving for them. We need to find them. They need to go home."

Sofiana pushed away from Grayson, a frown lining her forehead. "That's our first mission. But, what about Tia? Where will she go?"

Chapter 96

Two Weeks Later, Brockton, Massachusetts,
The Johnson Residence

Maggie Lee Johnson watched from across the yard as Tia pushed the shovel into the loose soil, scooped the dirt, and dumped it onto a pile next to the hole she had dug. Grasping the bright yellow gerbera daisy by the roots, she pushed it deep into the ground, her dainty fingernails coming out caked with dirt. Ignoring the gloves that lay beside her, the girl preferred to feel the earth on her skin and the musty smell that accompanied it. A brown streak smudged her cheek. Using her bare hands to tamp it down, she reached for the watering can and poured water all around the base as she'd been taught. Such a fast learner. She reached for the shovel again.

"She still hardly talks," Maggie Lee whispered, chewing on her bottom lip. "I want to help her, but I can't do that if she won't talk to me."

"Have patience, Mag. She's been taken from everything she knows. She'll be okay. She just needs time, babe." Mike wrapped his arms around her, resting his chin on her hair. "Think about it. She's lived in an underwater bunker all her life. This is quite a transition for one little girl."

She sighed, laying her cheek on his chest. "I know. I do. I just feel so helpless."

"What we're doing is enough." He kissed her temple. "She loves the planting. It was a good idea to teach her. Maybe I'll build her a tree house, since she likes to be outside so much."

"Do you think she'll talk to everyone when they get here?" Maggie leaned back to look up at him.

Mike shrugged. "I don't know. We just have to give her the space she needs. She'll at least talk to Crash, if no one else."

"I can't wait to see everyone. These past two weeks have been a whirlwind. I miss them. All of them." She smiled. "They're family now."

"I'm sure they'll be happy to see us, too." He rubbed circles on her back.

"I wish we could see Hurley and Genna, too. But I'm so happy they've been reunited with their rightful families. The look on their parents faces when they saw them..." She sighed. "But we have to respect their wishes." Maggie Lee wiped a stray tear that dripped from her eye and sniffled.

"Remember, both families said we could visit after they settle in." Mike soothed.

She nodded. "We're going to take them up on that, as soon as possible. Maybe that would help Tia feel better."

Maggie stretched up and pecked Mike's cheek, then strolled over to the garden, pushing her hands into the back pockets of her cut-off jeans. "The flowers look beautiful, Tia. You're a natural botanist." Maggie's heart tripped when the girl spoke.

"Do you think there are Earth-rocks buried in the dirt?"

"I...don't know, kiddo. I guess there could be. Would you like that?" Maggie asked.

"Yes. I feel...lost. I miss The Core Site. We are connected to the Earth." Tia gestured to the soil below.

Maggie Lee gave a slight nod. "I felt it, too. Down there. It...communicated with us, somehow."

Continuing her task, Tia replied, "Yes. It wants our help."

"I don't know what we can do to help. I think we broke contact before it could tell us," Maggie added gently. "What do you think?"

"It gave us what we need. The Earth wants to survive, and The Core Site wants us to help it. That's why it made some of us special." Tia looked away, dismissing her. She reached for the shovel, eyes downcast.

Maggie chewed on her fingernail, lost in thought. She looked up when Grayson and Sofie arrived, Rufus plodding lazily behind.

"You're here!" Maggie rushed over, embracing both of them. "Congratulations on landing an agent for your book, Grayson. I'm so proud of you. I want the first copy signed when it comes out, okay?"

"You got it." He winked. Nose pointed in the air, he called, "Please tell me that's ribs I smell? Mike?"

"You bet it is. Only the best for my family." Mike beamed.

Gray turned to Sofiana. "Mike makes the best ribs in Massachusetts."

She laughed. "Can't wait to try them." Her eyes cut to Tia in the side yard. "Still not talking?"

"Not very much, though she did talk about

The Core Site just a moment ago. Something about the Earth wanting to survive. I felt it, too, when we touched the rock. It's almost like it wants us to be more resilient in the event that the leak at the core affects life on Earth. To ensure its own survival, it must also help us survive. Symbiosis."

Sofie stood, hands on hips. "Hmm. I wondered what was happening that day, when you all joined hands at the rock. I don't know about any of that, but Tia's had a sheltered life. It's going to take some time for her to adjust to just being a kid."

Maggie's lips turned up. "You're right. I think maybe she's beginning to be ready for that new life." She reached for her hand and gave it a quick squeeze. "I think dinner's just about ready. Let's go sit down."

They sat around the wrought iron picnic table, discussing mundane things as they waited for the others to arrive. Conversation came to an abrupt end at the sound of a familiar bark, and Crash, head held high, trotted into the yard followed by Jace and Tandie, hands clasped and swinging between them as they walked.

"Crash!" Tia ran to the dog and fell to her knees, dirt-caked hands outstretched. His tongue flicked repeatedly, raining kisses all over her face. Her giggle rang out. She returned to her gardening, chattering all the while with the dog by her side. They worked together. Crash dug the hole with his paws, and Tia pushed the roots into the soil.

"It's so good to hear her laugh." Maggie Lee sighed, leaning into Mike. She placed her hand over her abdomen, closing her eyes. She sat up straight, eyes wide. "I think I felt the baby move!"

"Wishful thinking, maybe?" Mike laughed.

"No way!" Tandie ran the last few steps, placing her hand on Maggie's mid-section. "Isn't it too soon for that, Maggie Lee? Oh, I can't wait for the baby to get here. Do you have any names picked out?"

"Not yet. We have time." The couple beamed.

"So, what's new with you two?" Maggie asked.

Tandie's hands gestured as she spoke. "Well, Jace has news. He's joined a gaming tournament."

"That's great news, Jace! I hope you win." Grayson slapped his back.

"Thanks." Jace looked at his sneakers, hiding the smile that bloomed on his pinkened cheeks.

Grayson asked the question everyone was wanting to. "How's Crash? Is he...still the same?"

Tandie beamed. "He's driving us crazy with magnetic letters and word cards. I work with him every day. The other day he spelled 'Cabin'. I think he wants to go back."

Maggie Lee smiled, her hands clasped in front of her as if she could barely contain her excitement at the prospect of a planned gathering. "That's a great idea! Let's schedule a group get-away next summer. Grayson, do you think we could go back?"

"Sure. I'll let my friend know this time." He paused. "Did you all hear about the military take-over at Mercury Reef?" Grayson asked.

Mike turned from the grill, a frown arched his lips. "No. What happened, Gray?"

"Well, the media was swarming the place, and then the military arrived. They're trying to cover the whole thing up. A little hard to do when the story had already been airing when they got there, but you know the military. They'll make it all disappear if they can."

"What do you supposed they'll do with the place?" Mike asked.

Grayson shrugged. "Use it for their own gain, I suppose. Create soldiers that can heal, maybe? Your guess is as good as mine. We're out of the loop, so we'll probably never know. I'm just glad to be away from that place."

Sofie stared at the clouds lazily rolling across the sky, a far-off look in her eyes. "I wonder if Baby and her pups survived? Or Buzz?"

"Guess we'll never know that, either. We'd never be able to get anywhere close to the place as locked-down as it is right now." Mike replied.

Maggie Lee slapped her hands on her thighs. "Hey, I wanted to tell all of you that I researched a little about Bob's sons, Kevin and Kyle. I wish we could tell them their Dad's story, but I don't see how that would help them. But I did hear that his son Kevin's wife, Bianca, had a healthy baby boy. They named him Robert."

"Thank goodness Coral didn't get her way. I wonder what happened to her?" Maggie's words were little more than a whisper.

Sofie, hands on her hips, retorted: "We may never know. I just hope she got what she deserves."

"Time for bed, Tia." Maggie Lee called as she bent to scrutinize the children's picture books on the shelf in the newly painted and decorated room for their almost-adopted daughter. When the adoption went through, she would officially be Tia Johnson. Tears burned behind Maggie's eyes, and she cleared her throat. "Do you want to pick the book tonight, or should I?"

She looked up from her perusal at the complete silence that greeted her.

"Tia?" She stood, poking her head out the door to look down the hallway. "Tia?" Her feet gained speed and her heart rate bounced in her chest.

Where is she?

Rounding the corner to the bathroom, she saw Tia squatting down in the corner, crooning, "It's okay, I'll help you. Come here."

Maggie leaned over the girl's shoulder. "What'cha got there?"

"A cricket. He's hurt."

Maggie saw that its back end was crushed as if someone had stepped on it, its crooked antennae twitching. She sighed. "Sometimes things die. It's the circle of life. Shall we flush him? It might be the most humane thing to do."

"No! He's fine." She cupped her hand around the insect protectively, held her hands up to her cheek, and closed her eyes. Thirty seconds ticked by in silence.

"There." She opened her hand, and the cricket, whole again, leaped onto the tile floor and out into the hallway. Maggie's mouth formed a silent 'Oh'.

"I thought you lost that ability when they removed your implant."

Tia giggled. "Nope."

Maggie frowned. "Just don't tell anyone except us, okay? Not everyone will understand. You wouldn't be safe."

"Okay." Tia skipped to her bedroom, sliding under the covers.

After the story was read and Tia tucked in for the night, Maggie wandered into her own bedroom. Heading first toward the bed she pivoted, changing direction at the last second. Gliding to the bureau, Maggie Lee slowly inched out the top drawer, trying to hide the scraping sound.

Mike rolled over, yawning. "Coming to bed, babe?"

"Yes. Be right there."

Pushing the clothing aside, she felt underneath for a wool sock pushed to the far corner of the drawer. Upending the sock, she watched as her new trinket dropped into her palm. She sighed. During her visit to The Core Site that day with the others, she had picked it up off the ocean floor and placed it safely in her pocket without even thinking. She hadn't told anyone she'd taken it. Not even Mike.

No one else needs to know. I'll keep it just until the baby's born. Just to be sure. Then I'll return it to the sea.

Epilogue

Military Base, Unknown Location

C oraline fought her restraints, the skin at her wrists burning like acid. Straps attached to silver chains pinned her arms and legs to the metal table, and her body writhed and strained to escape. Grunts echoed off the barren walls as she worked tirelessly toward her one goal: Freedom.

Her eyes traveled to a large glass window devoid of decoration separating this room from another, and she sucked in a breath when she registered what was lined up on tables in the room next door. Despair shook her to her very core. The trembling started in her hands and traveled through her limbs into her torso and up to her brain. Her teeth chattered.

Hundreds of horseshoe crabs lined the table at the far side of the room, their bodies angled up, strapped down with bony tails pointing toward the ceiling. Cerulean blood dripping into glass jars.

"No," she breathed.

She threw her head backward against the hard metal slab, and closed her eyes as pain shot through her occipital bone. The shriek that erupted from her center shook the small laboratory, and several jars fell off shelves, pointy shards scattering across the floor, indigo blood splattering.

"No."

Her head whipped to the side when a man approached. Her eyes flicked to his nametag. Martinez. "Ah, Coraline. Nice to meet you. I'm so in awe of your body's healing abilities." He lifted the vial attached to her arm by a tube, her blood falling by slow drips to fill it. His fingers flicked the glass, and then he pulled that bottle off and replaced it with a new one. "Fascinating. I almost expected your blood to be blue like theirs." He jerked his head toward the horseshoe crabs. "No matter. I want to conduct some experiments to discover just how fast your body can heal itself. If you don't mind?" He smiled.

"Get away from me! Don't! Don't touch me!" The scream tore out of her, making her throat raw. Her head thrashed, and a tear escaped from the corner of her eye, falling onto the metal table.

He reached out to hold her arm in place, and her body bowed in protest. The man standing in front of her, Martinez, looked across the room. Head cocked, his brow twitched. At his look, two men materialized. Military-issue boots squeaked on the linoleum floor as one stopped at her feet and the other stood by her side. They grasped her arms and legs, using the weight of their own bodies to hold her down.

Lying with her head back, eyes squeezed tight, her brain withdrew into itself searching for solace. Her body stopped straining, legs hung limp and arms relaxed by her sides. The torn skin around her wrists was even now re-knitting itself. As if through a tunnel, she heard the man laugh, a giddy sound that did not register through the cracks to her consciousness. But she was beyond him now. Safe. Back at the habitat. Home.

She barely felt the cold steel of the blade slicing into her forearm, and was completely numb when the man found more inventive ways to conduct his research.

Mercury Reef Underwater Habitat

They dove in groups of ten, the huge crane slowly lowering the stainless steel cage they had built to enclose the seepage from the Earth's core that had been forming in the ocean here for decades. Possibly centuries. Warned of the possible dangers of swimming with what lurked in these waters, they carried weapons as part of their diving supplies, though they hung loosely at their sides. They were part of a top-secret military band sent here by the U.S. government to lock down the area and discourage anyone from 'showing an interest' here. When they were done, only a small faction stayed behind.

Orders received in the dead of night directly from the president himself, "Watch each other's backs, and keep each other safe. The future of life on Earth depends on you. Make us proud. Good luck."

Christian watched the procedure from the window of the habitat, and kept observing as they departed. He was in charge of this place now.

With Coral and Bob gone, I don't have to answer to anyone. No one will ever play me for a fool again.

Lieutenant Hart strode into the room. "Suit up. We need you."

Christian stood tall, looking down his nose. "You have all those men out there, what do you need me for? I'm staying here to study this research."

The other man smirked. "That research is being confiscated as of now. You no longer have access to the records or anything pertaining to the studies that were conducted here. We need you to bring us up to date on the species in the area. That's the only reason you're still here."

Christian's face fell. "But...that's not fair! I was here first..."

Hart sneered. "Yeah. That strategy might've worked when you were ten, but not here. Suit up."

"Uh..."

Another man strode into the room, and Lt. Hart stood at attention, hand flying up in salute. "General."

Christian's head swung up. His eyes widened. "Adam?"

"That's General Green to you, civilian," Adam reprimanded, a gleam in his eyes.

"But...I don't understand..." Christian stammered.

"Leave us Lieutenant," Adam barked.

Hart saluted before marching out the door. "Yes, sir."

Adam's smile didn't reach his eyes. "I told you I

made a deal with the military. I just neglected to tell you that I *am* the military. Where do you think I've been all this time?"

Christian broke eye-contact. "I-I have no idea. So..."

Adam gave a curt nod. "Yes. That's right. I'm in charge of all of this. You work for me now."

"What happens if I want to leave?" Christian whined.

"Oh, Christian, that's not a choice for you right now. I need your help. I'm ordering you to help."

"But..."

"Suit up. We're going to The Core Site in ten minutes," Adam ordered.

Christian stared at the floor. "Yes. Sir."

Fifteen minutes later, Christian and Adam kicked toward the site, now enclosed in an iron cage. Adam unlocked the large metal gate, and it glided silently open. The two men swam inside, latching the door behind them. A faint glow emanated off the ocean floor, casting its ruby hue on the gate and onto their black wetsuits. Adam turned toward the sea floor. The small rocks, lying loosely on top of the mass, were piled there. He gestured, demonstrating what to do. Christian nodded, and they each began collecting rocks and placing them into pouches on their belts.

A colossal gray blur sped by the cage, jarring the men from their mission. Christian shouted into his mouthpiece, the mumbled sound traveling incoherently through the water. He grabbed onto the bars, his facemask pushed up against it.

Was that...?

He stumbled back when the beast sped back,

ramming straight into the cage, its pointed snout sticking through where he had been standing mere seconds before. If he hadn't moved quickly out of the way...

Buzz.

The Helicoprion backed off, gnashing its teeth, whorl chomping up and down, up and down. He could see bits of flesh and gore wedged between the teeth as its jaws convulsed. It began swimming lazy circles around the cage.

Suddenly, there were two beasts circling.

Baby. She's alive.

She slowed on her way past, her eyes boring into his before continuing her vigil.

Christian glanced at his oxygen gauge.

The two sharks seemed to be working together. Enemies united against a common foe.

Watching.

Waiting.

Biding their time.

From the Author:

Thank you so much for reading BENEATH THE WAVES! This is one of my favorite stories, filled with characters that spoke to me even before I got their stories down on paper. Even their names—something I typically struggle with—came to me as if whispered on the breeze. I can only hope they become as real for you while reading their tale as they were for me while writing it. From the very start, I've known this novel would be special and somehow significant to me and my writing.

During the research phase of the writing process, my husband and I took an impromtu trip (we changed the location of our anniversary trip—thank you babe!) to Cape Cod, Massachussets, so I could get a first-hand feel for the area. I chose this location in particular because of the large number of great white sharks living in the waters surrounding Cape Cod which is important to this story. (By the way, we fell in love with this area and have gone back to visit again since the first time.)

On our research trip, we decided to go on a whale-watching tour, just to get a feel for being on a boat in these waters. While cruising out to sea, I joked, "Wouldn't it be great if we saw a great white shark?" Both of us laughed, knowing the improbability of that ever happening in truth.

When the captain announced that he'd just gotten word of a dead whale up ahead, my eyes went wild. Was it possible? Could it be? I've always loved sharks, so I'm completely aware that when something dies in the ocean, apex predators—*sharks*—come to feed.

Our boat approached the carcass, and my heart skipped as we saw our first glimpse of a triangular fin sticking out of the water near the dead whale. While our wide eyes looked on, we witnessed two great white sharks and a blue shark feeding on the meat of a minke whale carcass.

The on-board marine biologist informed us just how rare this sighting was, and tears filled my eyes as a deluge of emotions got the better of me. A once-in-a-lifetime sighting was happening right in front of us. Words can't fully describe the gamut of feelings that coursed through my body in that tiny window of time.

Magic happened that day. Was it fate? Coincidence? Luck?

Whatever the cause, it cemented my notion that this book would always hold a special place in my heart. As I continued writing this novel in our hotel room in Hyannis, Cape Cod, I knew. I was meant to write this story.

On a side-note: I finished writing this manuscript at our cabin in the Pocono Mountains—the very same cabin that appears in the book.

I hope you enjoy it...and if you do, please consider leaving a review anywhere you're able. Reviews help in more ways than you know. Thanks in advance for your help!

Keep On Reading,

Kristen
www.KRISTENLJACKSON.com
Facebook: @kristenjacksonauthor
Twitter: @KLJacksonAuthor
Intstagram: @krisjack504
Find me on LinkedIn, Pinterest, and Tumblr, too!
Contact: kristenjacksonauthor@yahoo.com

This picture was taken by me on the Whale Watcher Cruise.

Books By Kristen L. Jackson

YA Contemporary Fantasy Novels published by Black Rose Writing:
Keeper of the Watch, Book One
Magic Harbor, Keeper of the Watch Series, Book Two

Prequel Novella published by Lightning Creek Publishing:
Dimension Keeper (Keeper of the Watch Series: The Prequel) ***Subscribe to www.KRISTENLJACKSON.com, and receive a link to download your **FREE eBook** today!***

Children's Picture Book published by Schiffer Publishing:
Jocelyn's Box of Socks

Sci-Fi Fantasy Novel by Lightning Creek Publishing:
Beneath the Waves